AT MIDNIGHT IN VENICE

Charles Dickens Investigations
Book Five

J C Briggs

Also in the Charles Dickens Investigations Series

The Murder of Patience Brooke

Death at Hungerford Stairs

Murder By Ghostlight

The Quickening and the Dead

AT MIDNIGHT IN VENICE

Published by Sapere Books.

20 Windermere Drive, Leeds, England, LS17 7UZ,
United Kingdom

saperebooks.com

Copyright © J C Briggs, 2019
J C Briggs has asserted her right to be identified as the author of this work.
All rights reserved.

No part of this publication may be reproduced, stored in any retrieval system, or transmitted, in any form, or by any means, electronic, mechanical, photocopying, recording, or otherwise, without the prior written permission of the publishers.
This book is a work of fiction. Names, characters, businesses, organisations, places and events, other than those clearly in the public domain, are either the product of the author's imagination, or are used fictitiously.
Any resemblances to actual persons, living or dead, events or locales are purely coincidental.

ISBN: 978-1-913028-81-7

Love, in the universal opinion of wise men, is nothing but madness …
what clearer sign of lunacy than to lose yourself pining for another?
Orlando Furioso, Ludovico Ariosto of Ferrara (1516)

Our life is twofold: Sleep hath its own world,
A boundary between the things misnamed
Death and existence: Sleep hath its own world,
And a wild realm of wild reality…
'The Dream', Lord Byron

PART I: PICTURES FROM ITALY, 1844

Sunday 10th November 1844
Ferrara

To John Forster

At sunset when I was walking alone, I arrived upon a little scene which seemed perfectly familiar to me, and yet I had never been in this place, in this life.

In the blood red light, there was a mournful sheet of water, just stirred by the wind, upon its margin a few trees. In the foreground, a group of silent peasant girls were leaning over the parapet of a little bridge, and looking down into the water; in the distance sounded a deep bell; the shade of approaching night on everything. If I had been murdered there, in some former life, I could not have seemed to remember the place more thoroughly, or with a more emphatic chilling of the blood.

What an unreal and spectral place is this Ferrara — a city of the dead. Pestilence might have ravaged the streets. In one part there is a prodigious castle, with a moat about it, a sullen city in itself. You remember Byron's poem, 'Parisina' — of Parisina Malatesta who fell in love with her stepson, Ugo? I saw the very black dungeons of this castle where legend says they were imprisoned and then beheaded on the orders of the cruel Marquis, her husband. Byron tells that Parisina went mad. Perhaps she did and was locked away in some dread vault like Mr Poe's Madeline Usher. Whatever the truth, their names have outlived their agony for they are written in smoke on the ceiling of Ugo's cell. I saw them.

The red light stained the outside castle walls as they have, many a time, been stained within, in old days; but for any sign of life they gave, the castle and the city might have been avoided by all human creatures from the moment when the axe went down on the last of those two lovers…

Tuesday, 12th November. On a Canal in Venice.

That same monk — the one he had imagined earlier in the prison cell under the Doge's Palace. A monk, dark-robed and hooded, ghastly in the day and the free bright air, but in the midnight of that murky prison, Hope's extinguisher, and Murder's herald. He had had his foot upon the spot where, at the same dread hour, the shriven prisoner was strangled.

That had been a dream conjured by the awful stone cell within its guilty door deep below the water, a dream half lit by the winking torch he carried. But this?

In a phantom street, the houses rising on both sides from the water, Dickens's black boat glided soundlessly past open doors, decayed and rotten from long steeping in the wet, past figures coming through a gloomy archway, into shadows and the deep silence that follows the cracked tocsin that sounds midnight.

A lamp flickering at a corner. Laughter. The sound of music. A sudden light spilling from a casement. Then a wild cry. That same monk — a fleeting glimpse of a face turned to him as the hood fell back. A glimpse of white bone and eye socket.

A girl's face, too. An open mouth and a necklace with a cross at its end being drawn tight about a slender white neck.

The black boat slid under a bridge so low and close that it seemed ready to fall down and crush him. A corner turned. The monk and his victim gone — fled as the dream in the morning. And the water. Only the black water creeping noiseless and watchful, winding round and round in the city's many folds, like an old serpent. The water knew.

Tuesday, 12th November1844,
Hotel Danieli, Venice

To John Forster

I never saw the thing before that I should be afraid to describe. But I saw it here this very night in Venice — a curious and unsettling thing among the many strangenesses I have encountered in my travels about this country of ancient ghostly castles, gloomy catacombs, and leaning towers where long-untrodden steps moulder to dust.

I wrote to you the other day of that brown-hooded monk I dreamed in that old dungeon under the Doge's palace. I fancied I saw him again, his hood fallen away to reveal the skull beneath and his hands pulling at a necklace about the neck of a girl — a necklace hung with a jewelled cross which caught the light from a half-open casement. Then my gondola glided under a low bridge. The figures were blotted out instantly. When I looked back the vision was gone…

The next morning, Charles Dickens stood at his window at the Hotel Danieli to look across the shining lagoon to the dreamy brightness of the island of St Giorgio Maggiore. There, perhaps? He watched the red and orange sails of a fishing boat, and further away the topi used by the sardellanti, and he saw the great ships sailing with stately indolence to far-off lands. Nearer, there were groups of sailors working at cargoes, bales and casks, merchandise of many kinds. Looking down, he saw that his gondolier, Francisco, was waiting. Free, he thought, free to go anywhere. Across to the Lido to walk on the sand, or to Murano to look at the glass makers. Out of doors, surely, on this bracing day.

Yet, in the dark place where his sleep had been disturbed by fragments of dreams in which he was lost in sinister alleys, trapped in impossibly dark cells, or drowning in soundless water, there was the sense of something unfinished. That dream of drowning had woken him. He had slept again, this time drifting along serpentine waters in a gondola in which there was no boatman. His first sight of the blue morning had dispelled the dream, but he had not forgotten what he had seen before the bridge had swallowed him under its black arch.

How long had it taken him to glide from the scene of the crime — if indeed, there had been a crime — to his hotel? It hadn't seemed long, but then time in Venice was not like time anywhere else. In some little courtyard with its well, its cracked doorways, its faded green shutters, and its silence, you felt that time had stood still. Even when there were people, the old women in their black dresses gossiping in their impenetrable dialect might have been there since the days of Othello — perhaps they had chattered about the black general and the beautiful young wife whom he had married in secret. He had seen Desdemona lean down through a latticed blind to pluck a flower.

And you sometimes saw a masked figure in a swirling cloak who might have stepped from a Renaissance painting, and there were faces from the pictures he had seen. There the speaking silent face of a girl with the face of the very one who stared out from Tintoretto's 'Assembly of the Blessed', and that bearded young man, he had seen his likeness in Titian's 'Assumption of the Virgin'. Old Shylock, too, surely he had seen him passing to and fro upon a bridge. There might be rags, or fustian breeches, or drab dresses, but the faces were the same as those he had seen in portraits where velvets purred, silks sighed, and satins rustled like fallen leaves.

He thought of the monk and the maiden. Had that been a dream, or had he stepped out of Time? If Time's curtain had parted in that spellbound night, then he, Charles Dickens, had seen the past alive for a few moments and had felt that same chill feeling he had experienced in Ferrara by that melancholy water at sunset where he had remembered something that could never have been.

He had heard the chimes at midnight. At the Danieli, he had looked at his watch. It had been quarter past the hour. He wanted to see that open window. He wanted to know who had held that torch which had illuminated the monk's ghastly face. He could walk, but where? He remembered Francisco taking him under the Bridge of Sighs, and he remembered thinking of the prisoners who crossed it and for whom the doors were closed on life and hope. The blind prisoners in perpetual darkness. After that, it had been a dream.

Francisco was smiling hopefully. Dickens descended into the gondola.

'Where we were, Francisco, last night, I should like to see it all in daylight.'

'*Certo*, as it pleases the *signore*.'

Francisco wove his way through the painted poles, giving the cry '*Premi*' to tell a fellow boatman to pass on the right and '*Stali*' to another who must pass on the left. He turned to glide under the Bridge of Sighs again. Occasionally, he called out a greeting to another gondolier or to a man guiding a barge loaded with vegetables from Chioggia, or glassware from Murano.

A black-draped gondola passed them, a drum beating a solemn tattoo. After it the funeral barge went by on its way to St Michele, the island of the dead, its bier hung with black. Francisco crossed himself and Dickens bowed his head. When he looked up, he saw his bridge, the wrought iron one. He remembered it for there were few bridges topped with iron. He called to Francisco to stop and they glided to the steps at the top of which Dickens stood to look at the palazzo.

He looked up to where he thought a window had been open so that the light spilled out, but the windows were boarded up. In fact, the place was nearly a ruin. Yet the building he had seen was on a corner. He remembered the little canal going down the side where a water gate might be. Ah, he remembered the lamp on the corner of the building. It had been lit, he was certain. Dickens's memory was exact. He could remember faces vividly; he could recall the texture of hair, the colour of eyes, a wart on a nose. He closed his eyes and saw again the monk's face of white bone and the glint of jewels round the white neck. He opened his eyes. It had happened here, he was sure, but it could not have. No one lived in that crumbling palace.

He crossed the bridge to see if there were a window that might have opened. At the end of the bridge, he saw that the lamp he had thought alight was broken, and there was no possibility that a casement had been thrown open to let out the torchlight. He saw how the ochre plaster had peeled off in great flakes. The lower windows were darkened with rusty bands of iron.

Perhaps it was the wrong place. He and Francisco could go on. There might be somewhere else. He was about to turn back across the bridge when he saw that what he had taken for a bundle of rags in a doorway near the entrance to the little canal seemed to stir. An arm emerged from the bundle and then a head. Dickens stared at a bearded face and a pair of sleepy brown eyes.

'*Scusi*, *signor*,' Dickens began.

The eyes laughed and the mouth yawned. 'The English, so polite,' a wry voice said. The accent was Italian, but the words were in English. 'Permit me to rise.' He stood up and offered a bow. The ragged sacking fell away and Dickens saw that he had once been well-dressed. His suit was an old one, much rubbed about the knees and elbows, and he wore some kind of black opera cloak, patched in places and torn at the hem. His shoes were the remnants of evening pumps, very scuffed, and far too flimsy for the winter.

Dickens bowed back. 'The palazzo,' he said, pointing, 'no one lives there?'

'You want to buy it?' the man laughed.

'No, I thought I saw a light — last night.'

'Someone like me, perhaps, lodging there. I prefer the open air.'

'Could be. I thought I heard music and laughter.'

'I doubt it, *signor*, even if someone lodges, I do not think they play music in the night.'

'No, I suppose not. It's just that I thought I saw…' Dickens did not know how to go on. It was too fantastical. No one would believe such a thing.

The ragged man waited, his warm eyes amused. '*Una bella signorina!* You fall in love, and now you pursue your dream. Venice, she does that. There are beautiful women at every window, but not here, I think.'

Dickens laughed. He rather wished that he had seen a beautiful woman; that he had fallen in love. 'Alas, no, but there was a monk —'

'*Monaco*? Not impossible.'

'He was with a young woman.'

The dark eyes gleamed. 'Again, not impossible. A father confessor, perhaps?'

'He had his hands at her neck — there were jewels. I thought — I thought he was murdering her.' There, he had said it, and it did sound ridiculous. He looked at the man.

'Not impossible,' he smiled at Dickens, 'that is Venice for you. Beauty and wickedness are bedfellows here. Perhaps he was placing the jewels round her beautiful neck — it was beautiful?'

'I suppose it was — I don't remember that, but he looked wicked. A hideous face in the light from that window —'

'The window which is boarded up. I think not, *signor*, a dream, a masquerade, a carnival.'

'I know. It is very easy to imagine anything in the enchanted night. A dream, I daresay, so many dreams I have had here. I thought I saw Desdemona leaning from a window — a vision, of course.'

'You wish to see inside the palazzo? I know the way in. I can show you if…'

'Might I pay you for your trouble?' Dickens asked, not wanting to offend, but knowing that here was a man in need. At least he could see if there were any signs that someone had been in the palazzo. Doubtful, of course, but a ruined house, a lovely woman and a devilish monk? One might make a story out of that.

The man bowed. 'As you see I am a fallen man. The casino — ruined. You are not a gambler, *signor*, I think.'

'Not in that sense. I have too many responsibilities.'

'But you are here alone, dreaming of a beautiful woman.'

'Not exactly. I came to see and what I have seen is beyond all my expectations. Venice is a wonder of the world.'

'Unless you are a fallen man. Then Venice is a cruel mistress. And she loves her wealth as much now in her days of oppression.'

'The Austrians?'

'Our cold masters — their cruelty is ice. At least the cruelty of Venice has passion. Now, *Signor* —?'

'Dickens.'

'From London?'

'Yes, and may I know your name, sir?'

'Aurelio Paladini, sometime courier and guide to rich tourists, now a beggar, but I will be your guide in the palazzo. We see if your beauty resides within.'

'There was no beauty at the window— only the light spilling out.'

'You have the *gondoliere*?'

'Yes, Francisco, he is waiting at the steps.'

Aurelio Paladini gave a piercing whistle and Francisco stood to see his customer with a ragged fellow who looked as if he hadn't a lira to his name. He frowned, recognising the man who slept in the doorway. He knew him of old.

'He knows you?' asked Dickens.

'We are not friends. I sometimes assume the role of *gazzero* — I use my hook to draw the gondola up to the steps. One can earn a couple of centessimi that way from the passengers, more from the tourists, but, let us say, I am unofficial. *Gazzeri* are employed by the state. Francisco does not like me.'

Dickens signalled to Francisco to wait and he and Aurelio crossed the bridge where Aurelio spoke in the Venetian dialect. From what Dickens could gather, Aurelio was telling him that the Signor wanted to see the palazzo and that they would go down the little canal to the water gate.

Francisco looked doubtful. 'If the *signor* pleases.'

Not exactly, thought Dickens, wondering if it was a good idea after all, but there was something engaging about Aurelio Paladini, and he certainly needed the money. He and Aurelio went down into the gondola.

'We go another way,' Francisco said.

After a few twist and turns, the gondola entered the narrow canal at the other end and arrived at the water gate. One gate had rotted away giving them room to slide into the tunnel and come to rest by a narrow ledge. It was dark as ink and reeked of dank water and decay. Dickens thought again of those cells beneath the Doge's palace in which the prisoners stood waist deep in water. He heard a sickening plop as of something dropped into the silent water and imagined rats. What a fool he was.

Francisco lit his gondolier's lamp and Aurelio took it. He climbed out onto the ledge and helped Dickens up beside him. Francisco sat back in his boat to wait. He was used to the eccentricities of his customers — the English men, especially. They often wanted to see things which were out of the way, but a rotting ruin where no one lived? Still, he would be paid whatever his customer chose to do, and Aurelio Paladini, too. He didn't grudge the man his tip on this occasion. He just didn't like him pretending to be a *gazzero*.

Aurelio pushed open the dilapidated door which led into a narrow passage where the walls ran with water and Francisco's oil lamp cast shadows and the light caught drops of green water. There were stone steps leading upwards to another door.

Dickens placed his feet in the hollows worn by those who had gone before him, and grasped the iron hand rail to stop himself slipping. The steps were green with algae in parts and treacherous. Already he felt that nobody had been here for years — centuries, perhaps. He looked up to see Aurelio's cloak swirl as he turned to look down. He experienced again that sense as if he had stepped back in time. Count Aurelio Paladini returning from the carnival, and who was he? Signor Dickens, in love with the count's beautiful sister whom he had seen leaning from a casement one enchanted night.

He heard the creak of wood and went gingerly up to the top. Another door led into a large chamber with a marble staircase and a marble floor strewn with straw and old bits of furniture. They went up the marble staircase and into what was once the great salon. Here there were cracked gilt chairs from which horsehair stuffing poked out of mouldering velvet, a drunken old sofa listing on its two remaining legs, a fallen statue with a cracked head. The glory that was Rome, thought Dickens, looking at the senatorial nose which had broken off, and the stone-blind eyes in which cracks seemed like tears.

The room had an aged smell of time and decay. The air was very cold, stifling in the stillness and profound silence. No one had been here. There had been no laughter, no music and no open casement. Aurelio was removing one of the boards from the windows so that a greenish light came in. It looked worse now, just a wreck of a place. Dickens looked up to see the crumbling frescoes on the ceiling. He could make out half a face, a hand with only three fingers, a bit of a once muscular arm — the artist's work decaying bit by bit. Someday there would be nothing left.

'*Ecco!*' Aurelio exclaimed, pointing.

There was a torch, burnt out of course. Someone had been here. Someone had seen the monk and the maiden. His heart beat faster. He looked at Aurelio who was picking up the torch.

'It is cold, Signor Dickens; there is nothing to say that someone was here last night.'

Dickens looked round the decaying chamber. It was odd, though — someone had been here at some time, but when he looked again, he could see that there were other torches in blackened sconces, one of which had slipped from its mooring. Perhaps the torch had simply fallen to the floor.

'I suppose not. I shall never know — a mystery. Whose was this palace?'

'There is a story,' began Aurelio, grinning, holding the torch.

There would be, and it would cost him. 'Tell all,' Dickens said. He could never resist a story.

'It concerns the Count — Count Mariano, whose family had great wealth and lived here. The count's wife betrayed him with her husband's friend, the Count Dellombra — a handsome man with the hair of deep black —'

Dickens couldn't help smiling. 'Dellombra — an odd name, though with his black hair, I suppose —'

'Strange, it is, but true, Signor Dickens —' Aurelio grinned again — 'True as any story told by candlelight at dusk, and stranger yet — if you permit?'

Dickens nodded. He did want to know the fate of the dark count.

Aurelio continued. 'The black Dellombra fell sick and died. Shortly after, the countess fell sick, and knowing that the shadow of death was upon her, she ask her maid to keep the vigil in the long night. The countess breathe her last, and the maid hear the footstep coming up the stairs and into the chamber up there.' Aurelio pointed upwards to where the peeling cherubs pointed too. 'Count Dellombra had come in the dark night for his beloved. He raise her up, and down the steps they go, the maid lighting the way to the lowest cellar. The count strike the torch from the maid's hand and all is shadow. Then they vanish. The maid tell her story, after which she, too, sicken and die. She haunt the palazzo now, seeking her mistress, no doubt. The place has been empty since.'

'Lighting her way with a torch?' Dickens grinned back at Aurelio.

'I do not say so, *signor*, but it is possible. Anything is possible in this haunted city.'

'And the count?'

'Suicide.'

'So many tales of love and death. I saw the castle at Ferrara.'

'I know it well.' Aurelio's dark eyes looked troubled suddenly then he smiled again, 'The story of Parisina Malatesta and her lover — these things do not happen in London?'

'I suppose they do, but not me — I am glad to say.'

They laughed together and shook hands. Dickens gave Aurelio his money — a generous sum. He forbore to tell him not to gamble it away, and refused his offer to find him *una bella signorina* — a real one this time. Francisco took him back to the Danieli. He would be leaving for Verona tomorrow.

Thursday November 14th 1844,
Verona

To John Forster

So, now, my dear Forster, you know all of my meeting with Signor Aurelio and my exploration of that ruined palace, and the story of the count and his lady, the chilling tale of the maid and her torch.

But here is a most horrible sequel to the story of my monk and the maiden in Venice. The next day I came to Verona and read in a newspaper of a poor girl dragged from the canal, strangled by her rosary. Speculation is that her beads caught on a piece of ironwork and wound themselves tight around her neck so that she could not free herself.

I know no more. Perhaps I saw her death at that dreamy midnight and the monk came in because I had dreamed him in that dark cell under the Doge's palace.

Now that is Venice for you — impossible — something past all writing of or speaking of — almost past all thinking of. A dream of beauty and wickedness for which my maiden and my monk are, perhaps, just a metaphor…

PART II: DEATH BY WATER, LONDON, 1850

1: Strange Meeting

Something swished above Charles Dickens's head. There was a grunting sound. And a face. A hanging face. A dead white face. The face of a devil — or what you thought the devil would look like if you met him in a dark alley. An upside-down face. A face in your face. A long arm, limp and dangling. And something black, hanging like a large ugly bird or huge bat. Dickens thought of vampires.

The whites of two upside-down eyes stared into his. Dead? Dickens stepped back. To walk into a dead man hanging, what a horror. The eyes blinked and opened. Alive. Humorous. And, by God, the upside down mouth was smiling. He could see strong white teeth. Very much alive, then.

'Help me down, would you? Caught my cloak on the window there.'

Dickens looked up. Sure enough the thick cloak was caught on a window latch.

'I'd be much obliged if you could hurry it up. Damned uncomfortable and I ought to be on my way sharpish.' A courteous, laughing voice — a little breathless, of course, in the circumstances.

'By all means.' Dickens grasped the man's armpits and held him steady while he pulled the cloak free. There was a tearing sound, then the man was on his feet, his back to Dickens. Astonishingly, he leapt in the air, did a somersault and landed behind Dickens, who turned to face him as he was sweeping up a plumed hat from the mud.

The window above flew open and a bottle dislodged Dickens's hat and shattered on the stone. Then there was the loud report of a gun, which knocked him off his feet.

Someone shouted, 'Gerrout of it, yer divil. I'll blow yer brains out next time.'

The sound of a police rattle followed, then running feet. The acrobat hauled Dickens to his feet and lugged him away round a corner into an alley so narrow that he was dragged along, tripping and stumbling over his own feet.

The alley twisted into another and another. It was as if they were going round in ever-decreasing circles. Dickens felt dizzy, but the acrobat whirled him on, holding his hand in a surprisingly strong grip. An obliging door opened and up they went, up narrow stairs, and into a little room where a young woman sat upside down, it seemed. The room was turning round him.

'Jianna, my love, meet Mr Charles Dickens.'

Dickens could hardly speak, so intent was he in getting his breath back, but he managed a crooked bow to the woman seated before him. He had an impression of a pale oval in the shadows, hair parted in the centre and two dark eyes looking at him gravely.

'Sit down, my dear sir. Brandy, I think.'

Dickens sat on a threadbare chaise longue to which the acrobat had pointed with the air of a man inviting him into his salon. The young man handed him the brandy in a cracked glass. Dickens drank it up and felt the world come into focus again. The white face was gone and in its place there was an ordinary human face, quite brown and glowing, with a pair of shining brown eyes and a tousle of chestnut hair.

'Much obliged — you have the advantage of me, sir.'

'The advantage is all yours, Mr Dickens. Your face is known to so many. How could I not know you, sir? The obligation is mine. You rescued me from my difficulty.'

'We are even, I think — your friend with the shot gun?'

'Ah, Mr Rarx — pawnbroker. I am his particular enemy. I have a habit of removing certain valuables and some things not so valuable for my true friends whose need is greater than his. A redistribution of wealth, you might call it.'

'Robin Hood?'

The acrobat laughed. 'They call me Magpie — a snapper-up of not unconsidered trifles.'

'Had you a particular trifle in mind?'

'I did — I do.' Magpie burrowed into the pocket of his dilapidated black velvet cloak. 'A watch — gold and very precious to the man whose rightful property it is. I felt that Mr Rarx had held it long enough.'

'I see that Mr Rarx might well have been somewhat discomposed. Will he send the police after you?'

'He does not know me — except in this.' Magpie picked up the mask he had thrown down. 'Disguise, sir. The black cloak, the white mask — you understand the soubriquet.'

Dickens nodded. What an extraordinary man — threadbare, shabby, yet clearly educated. There was something aristocratic about the arched brows and long nose — an Elizabethan in his ruffled shirt, the collar of which resembled a ruff, and that black and white striped waistcoat — Dickens had owned one just like it. Perhaps Magpie had picked it up at a second-hand clothes stall. And his companion in her dark velvet dress could have been a princess — in this light anyway. Had he stumbled into a fairy tale, or a play?

'You are an actor, perhaps?'

'Actor, acrobat, troubadour, conjuror, fortune-teller, truth-seeker, righter of wrongs — not unlike yourself, sir, in the last.'

'Or some of the others.'

Magpie grinned. 'A magician they say.'

'Truth-seeker today — or tonight,' Dickens clarified. 'I am looking for a young woman — two, in fact. I only know that the first might live in Hemlock Court.'

'Hemlock Court — not far from here. Just off Carey Street — who do you wish to find?' Magpie asked.

'A servant girl. Her name is Jemima Curd. She was employed in the household of — let us say — a man of some repute — and I wish to find her in connection with the disappearance of another young woman, employed in the same household, the daughter of a friend of mine who is, naturally, worried beyond endurance. It may be that she vanished with a young man.'

Magpie gave him a sly look. 'Ah.'

'I thought to try the servant girl — I wanted to find out if she knew of any relationship between the young lady and the young man. My friend knew nothing of any love affair.'

'I suppose a young lady living from home might not tell her father — or mother?'

'She has only her mother — I suppose she might not tell. But whatever the case, the girl is missing and her mother has asked me to try to find her.'

'I know Hemlock Court — do you wish me to show you?'

'It is far too late now — I shall find it tomorrow. Off Carey Street, you say?'

'Go down Shire Lane into Little Shire Lane from where the first right turn takes you into Hemlock Court.'

'I am much obliged, Mr —?'

'Magpie will suffice, Mr Dickens. Shall I take you from here into Drury Lane?'

'If you will — I confess, I do not know quite where I am now.'

Magpie was on his feet, wrapping himself in the black cloak. He left the mask where it was and put on a shapeless hat. Dickens bowed to Jianna. She was very beautiful, but there was a quality of remoteness about her. She was like a painting in her velvet gown, a painting of an unfathomable woman. She regarded him seriously, and in some way, without interest. He realised then she that she had not spoken a word.

2: Hemlock Court

Dickens knew Little Shire Lane, a tumble of wooden houses with projecting gables overhanging so that the lane became a tunnel, dark even in the morning. An infamous rookery of crooked houses linked by secret passages, trap doors and hidden panels which had once provided escape routes for vagabonds, thieves, sharpers, and the smashers, the counterfeiting gangs who had inhabited the Retreat, a rambling double house.

Hemlock Court, as poisonous as its name suggested, was reached by another narrow lane. The smell was of stale fish and blood from the slaughterhouses which proliferated in this dim corner of St Clement's, and of soot and coal from number nineteen, the premises of James Merrit, coal and wood merchant. A man in a leather apron lounged at the door. He did not know of Jemima Curd, but Mrs Gambol, the laundress two doors down might help.

He picked his way along the muddy court and knocked at number seventeen. Mrs Gambol — who looked as if she never would — or had — eyed him suspiciously. She carried a piece of hard soap which looked like a bit of a mantelpiece.

'Mrs Gambol?'

''Oo wants ter know?' The bit of mantelpiece came dangerously near.

'I am in search of a young lady called Jemima Curd.'

'Wot fer?'

'It is in connection with her former employer.'

'Lost 'er place, I'm told. Them Curds is no better for watchin'. Flitted, anyway, weeks back.'

'You don't know where?'

'In the night — they allus does that. Could be anywhere.' Mrs Gambol waved her soap vaguely.

Indeed, they could, thought Dickens, thinking of the muddle of dark courts and passages. 'Did you know Jemima Curd?'

'Little thing — pretty. Best of 'em, I serpose, but them Curds —'

Dickens interrupted before she expiated once more on the sins of the Curd family. 'As far as I know she was not dismissed for any wrongdoing, Mrs Gambol, only that she was no longer required by the family.'

'So, wot you want 'er fer?'

'I hope she may have some information about a missing person.'

'Perlice, are yer?'

'Private investigations.' Dickens put his hand in his pocket. 'I am authorised to pay for information — by my employer.'

Mrs Gambol's sharp eyes narrowed. ''Ow much?'

'Depends on what your information is. Three shillings, if it's useful. For example, the whereabouts of Jemima Curd, or the name of anyone who might tell me more about the family.'

'Awright.' Mrs Gambol turned in the doorway and shouted, 'Martha! Martha!'

A younger version of Mrs Gambol appeared with red arms fresh from the copper and a wide red face. 'Ma?'

'Tell this gent wot yer knows about Jemima Curd.'

The girl looked from her mother to Dickens.

'Go on, tell 'im — yer knows somethin', I daresay. I saw yer gossipin' when she came back. Wot she tell yer?'

'Sed the governess 'ad gone off wiv the Italian — that's why she lost 'er place — the young lady got sick an' woz sent away ter the country so Jemima wasn't needed no more. She woz goin' ter be a lady's maid for the young lady. Jemima sed there woz ructions. The 'ousekeeper sed she'd try ter get another place fer Jemima.'

'Do you know where?' Dickens asked.

'Dunno, sir. Jemima was ter go back ter see Mrs Pick an' she musta cos I ain't seen 'er since.'

'Did she go before her family went away?'

'No — they'd gone when she came back. Jemima dint know where they woz.'

'When did she come back here?'

'Dunno — coupla weeks ago, mebbe.'

'Where did she stay?'

'Mrs Link's down Ship Yard, little alley on the left there's two 'ouses. Mrs Link's is on the left.'

'Much obliged, Miss Martha and —' he looked at Mrs Gambol's open red hand — 'Mrs Gambol, here is your money. If you hear anything more about Jemima you can reach me at my office at Wellington Street. Ask for Mr Wills. I'll pay, of course.'

The thick hand closed over the three shillings. Mrs Gambol nodded.

Dickens turned back towards Little Shire Lane to the turning into Ship Yard.

Mrs Link told him the same story as Martha had. Her sympathy was all for Jemima Curd. A good girl, she said, who'd done well at the household of Sir Neptune Fane — shame, it was that she'd lost her place and her family.

'Bad lot, sir. Mother's a drunk, an' Mr Curd, a poor weak, shambling thing — never could keep a job. Picked rags, they did, for a few pence. Relied on poor Jemima for a few bob. She came when she could — you know what it's like when you're in service, sir. She'd treat them to a Sunday dinner, a little bit of mutton an' a few roast potatoes. She'd take it to the baker's for cookin'.'

'When did she come here?'

'Oh, a good few weeks ago then she went back to see this Mrs Pick, 'opin' fer a new place. I ain't seen 'er since. Took 'er box o' things so I thought she mighta got a new place.'

'Did she tell you anything about the Fane household — the tutor or governess, for example?' Mrs Link's sympathetic face prompted him to tell her more than he had told Mrs Gambol.

But she could tell him no more than Martha had. Jemima had said nothing about where the Italian or the governess had gone.

Dickens thanked her and gave her two shillings and asked her to send to Mr Wills at Wellington Street if she heard anything at all of Jemima or her family. He had more hope of Mrs Link than Mrs Gambol, though he thought Mrs Gambol might act if she thought there might be more money forthcoming.

And, as for his next step, he would have to speak to Sir Neptune Fane in whose house at Chelsea Jemima Curd had been employed. Charles Dickens could hardly question the housekeeper, Mrs Pick, without seeing Sir Neptune first. He knew of the man — a Member of Parliament and a powerful one, an ally of Disraeli in the Conservative party.

Home now, though. He ought to tell Anne Brown, his wife's maid, what progress he had made. She had asked him to help her find the elusive governess, Violet Pout. Violet was the daughter of Anne's old friend, Amelia Pout, who had married a prosperous grocer. Mrs Pout still ran the shops with her son. Violet had been sent to school and had done well enough to secure her position as companion to Miss Mariana Fane and governess to her younger siblings. And now, she was missing and Mrs Pout did not believe that her daughter would have eloped with a music master.

He thought about Violet Pout's pretty looks. He had met her with Anne and Mrs Pout, and had thought her rather confident of her own charms, not the least of which was her very pale blonde hair which shone under her little grey bonnet. She had been demure, but there was a knowing light in her pale blue eyes which he had seen as she looked at him. Something calculating there, he had thought, as she had looked down modestly when her mother spoke proudly of her appointment at the house of Sir Neptune Fane.

Mrs Pout had given the impression that such a post was certainly more to be envied than Anne's position as lady's maid in Charles Dickens's house. Sir Neptune, Mrs Pout had repeated, and Dickens had wondered how the cherished Violet would find the position of governess — that in-between role, not a servant exactly, but not a family member either. It could be a lonely existence.

He had thought of Ruth Pinch whom, in his *Martin Chuzzlewit,* he had placed in a wealthy brass and copper founder's house. He had hoped that Miss Mariana Fane would be a gentler, more amenable girl than the brass founder's Sophia, and Sir Neptune might be a more refined man than Ruth Pinch's employer. Though he suspected that Violet Pout could look after herself.

Anne Brown was not entirely at one with Mrs Pout over the matter of the tutor. Such things happened, she had observed. So they did, Dickens had thought, all too often. Why should she not fall in love with a no doubt handsome Italian music master? And run away with him. Such things happened, too. But Anne had begged him for her old friend's sake. He was fond of her. She had loyally accompanied them to America and to Italy, looking after Catherine, patiently enduring the long, uncomfortable journeys and the heat. He could not say no so had agreed to try to find Jemima Curd to find out what she might know about Violet and the tutor. Chelsea then — at least he could tell Anne he had tried.

3: Violet Dreaming

May 1850 at Wisteria Lodge, Chelsea

Violet Pout is indeed a very attractive young woman, tall and slender with very pale, shining fair hair and an appealing air of modesty. Her fair skin blushes easily and she has a habit of lowering her blue eyes when receiving a compliment — which is often. She had learned at school how to carry herself and how to behave like a lady. Lady Fane had been most impressed by her modest and reserved demeanour. Some young women were much too forward.

'She is undoubtedly a lady,' Lady Fane had said to her husband some weeks ago, 'and she is well-educated. She will be most suitable as a teacher for the younger ones and a companion for Mariana when it is appropriate.'

She stood, waiting nervously for his verdict. She could not always gauge his mood, but she must have the matter settled. It was too much for her to take charge of the children. She wanted only to go to her room.

He finished what he was writing and blotted the paper. To her relief, he smiled. 'If you are sure, my dear; her background is in trade is it not?' The question was asked in relation to the idea of Violet Pout's being a suitable companion for his elder daughter.

'I only mean that Mariana would like company sometimes — they could play the piano, do embroidery, sketch in the garden. I don't mean that they should be friends. Miss Pout might chaperone Mariana when I cannot — perhaps an afternoon call, some shopping…'

Lady Fane could not very often chaperone her daughter. Her delicate health prevented that, but she understood young women enough to know that Mariana would like to pay a visit or go to the shops sometimes.

'Well, I hope it is the right decision — this time.'

Lady Fane blushed, thinking of the previous governess, dismissed under suspicion of theft. Denied, of course. Lady Fane had felt it was her fault — her lack of judgement. 'If you'd prefer…'

'No, I shall bow to your judgement. But, we must have it clear, Mary, my dear, Miss Pout is to know her place. If she accompanies Mariana on a visit, it must be as her governess.'

He had picked up another piece of paper. Lady Fane had gone to lie down.

It will soon be time for breakfast. Violet Pout pins up her hair, pleased at its shine, rather displeased at the plainness of the style, but a governess is not expected to have ringlets and ribbons. She gazes back at her own blue eyes — as beautiful as her hair, she thinks, and she can open them very wide when she needs to. Blue eyes give an impression of innocence. She knows that. She opens those eyes which look back at her from the glass and puts a drop of belladonna in each. What she does not see is that their pale blue is a little hard, and that in repose, her mouth looks discontented, but she smiles at herself and is satisfied. The modest hair and demure grey dress will not be forever.

She is impressed by Wisteria Lodge — the footman, Pryor, had shown her in with such majesty that she had almost mistaken him for Sir Neptune. Of course, she knows that a governess's place is lowly enough, but there will be opportunities.

She has consulted 'The Ladies' Oracle', her book on fortune-telling in which you rest your pencil on a sign and choose a question to ask from a list. The sign your pencil indicates leads to another number which is the page where you will find the answer to your question: *"Will I find a lover?"* And the pleasing answer: *"Your bright eyes will win you one."*

Mother wants her married. She hoped that her daughter would meet distinguished people — they had speculated in the parlour above the grocer's shop. They had consulted 'The Ladies' Oracle':

"What kind of man am I destined to love?" "Amorous, gallant and able to converse with his eyes."

Mother had talked of bankers, lawyers, politicians. Literary men, artists, musicians, Violet had wondered. Mother had sniffed. Men who had connections; that was important, a man of good family, well-bred — and money, she had added.

And when the answers in the book were not what they wanted, when the answer told of a man losing his teeth and with greying hair, they read the cards, delighted when Violet turned up the Queen of Clubs. Clubs always portended happiness. Hearts were good — they foretold triumph. Spades, they shuddered at. Never good portents.

4: To Chelsea

In the afternoon, after he had finished his work for *Household Words* at the Wellington Street office, Dickens took a steamer to Cadogan Pier at Chelsea. Sir Neptune Fane lived at Wisteria Lodge in Upper Church Street. Not far from Cheyne Row where his friends, the Carlyles, lived. Now that was a thought. Did Thomas or Jane know the Fane family? Jane might know something, or her servant might. Servants talked. Jane's housemaid or cook might know Jemima Curd. He would call on her if he found out nothing useful.

It was cold on the river under a grim steel sky and a keen wind blowing, but he stood on the deck, gazing at the passing traffic, steamers going in the opposite direction, the wherries, the luff-boats, and a lone skiff. The steamer passed under Westminster Bridge, past the Houses of Parliament, then the great Penitentiary at Millbank into Lambeth Reach, then Vauxhall Bridge and into Chelsea Reach.

He supposed that eventually he would have to persuade Anne that if Violet could not be found then Violet's mother would have to report the matter to the police. He knew that his friend, Superintendent Sam Jones, would tell him that it should be reported to the police at Chelsea. But he also knew that Mrs Pout would be very reluctant to have the police involved.

From Cadogan pier he went along Cheyne Walk towards Battersea Bridge and the right turn by Chelsea Old Church. Wisteria Lodge was one of several large detached houses at the top of Upper Church Street, the gardens of which backed onto Chelsea Park. The carriage drive led to an imposing brick house, built at the beginning of the century, Dickens guessed.

It spoke of wealth and had what he thought was a satisfied air of comfort, though the wisteria which gave it its name was leafless as yet. It was about the same size as his own house in Devonshire Terrace — perhaps that, too, had a look of complacency. Perhaps all large, comfortable houses had it, knowing they would outlive their occupants. But what secrets, he wondered, were to be found behind those windows and that smart black door with its heavy knocker? Every house, every room, every heart had it secrets, including his own. Dangerous things, secrets, they had a habit of being told.

In a window to the right of the colonnaded porch there was an impression of firelight flickering. He saw that there was a bell beside the door. He took off his top hat and smoothed his hair and put on his hat again. He felt nervous as if he were some importunate poor relative from whom the silver spoons would be hidden. It was the nature of his errand, he supposed. What, really, was he to say to Sir Neptune? He feared that his enquiries might suggest that he thought Sir Neptune knew more about the governess and the tutor than he had told Mrs Pout. He thought about Anne Brown's worried face. He rang and waited.

A liveried and powdered footman opened the door and looked down from a great height at the visitor.

'Mr Charles Dickens to see Sir Neptune, if he might spare me some time.' Dickens offered his card.

The footman's haughty demeanour changed in an instant. 'Mr Dickens. Oh, come in, I am sure Sir Neptune will see you. My word, I am. We all read your books, sir, and Lady Fane and Miss — er — well, all of us.'

Dickens stepped into a large hall out of which a marble staircase ascended in icy magnificence from the black and white chequered floor. A great gas-lit lamp descended on a golden chain from the high ceiling. There was a gilded mirror above an ebony console table upon which there were two rather sepulchral urns. The footman took his hat and gloves and placed them on the table and then with the card on a silver salver, he made his stately way up the stairs.

Dickens looked at himself in the mirror, straightened his collar, and smoothed his hair again. There you are in the looking glass. He grinned at himself. *And who are you, sir?* his reflection asked. That's a secret. He heard voices, arranged his face into an expression of becoming seriousness and turned to see the footman returning, followed by Sir Neptune Fane, almost as tall as his footman — footmen were engaged for their height — though not quite as exquisitely dressed. His dark hair shone in the light. He came down, smiling. He was a very handsome man, and familiar somehow — Dickens must have seen him at some event or other.

'Mr Dickens, this is an unexpected honour. I am very glad to see you.' He offered a well-manicured hand which Dickens took. It was a firm handshake, the hand of a man sure of his place in the world. Dickens saw that his eyes were warm brown and very genial.

'I am much obliged, Sir Neptune. I have come to speak to you on a matter of some delicacy.'

The brown eyes did not falter. They did not show any surprise, either. A man of supreme self-control, Dickens thought. Sir Neptune looked straight at him, raising a dark eyebrow. 'Then you must come into the library. There is a fire. Pryor, organise some tea, if you will.'

Dickens followed Sir Neptune into the library which was everything one might expect: a mahogany table scattered with books and papers, glass fronted bookcases containing formidable leather-bound tomes — the library of an important and busy man. Meant to impress. It suggested authority, but Sir Neptune's expression was still genial as he motioned Dickens to a comfortable armchair by the fire.

'A glass of sherry, perhaps, my dear sir, while we wait for the tea?'

Dickens assented and they sat opposite each other, glasses in hand.

'Now, Mr Dickens, what on earth is this delicate matter?'

'I am in the way of an emissary from Mrs Pout.' Was it the flickering fire or was there just the ghost of a shadow across the genial face?

'This is about Miss Violet Pout. May I ask what is your interest?'

'Mrs Dickens's personal maid, Miss Brown, is Violet Pout's godmother and, of course, a close friend of Mrs Pout. Mrs Pout is much distressed by her daughter's absence. They thought you might see me.'

'But I have spoken to Mrs Pout. I am very sorry for her. I told her what I know — that Miss Pout and our music tutor, Mr Sabatini, disappeared on the same day. I am afraid that I believe that there must have been —'

The door opened. A lady stood there. A thin, rather tremulous looking lady who hovered at the door.

'Oh, I beg your pardon, Sir Neptune, I wondered…' She made to retreat.

Dickens stood as did Sir Neptune, who said, 'Ah, my dear, come in and meet Mr Charles Dickens.'

Dickens bowed as Lady Fane came towards him. She looked anxious. She would have been pretty and delicate as a girl, but she had faded, he thought, a dried flower of a woman, insignificant beside her handsome, vigorous husband. Under her lace cap, he could see that her hair had faded, too — it had once been golden, he surmised. He felt rather sorry for her.

She said how glad she was to meet him, praised his books, so enjoyed *David Copperfield* — 'That poor child,' she said, 'such hardship in the bottle factory and poor little...' she blushed. He wondered if she was going to say Little Em'ly, the girl who had been seduced by Steerforth. Perhaps she thought of her erstwhile music tutor. She stood uncertainly after he had thanked her, and looked at her husband as a servant might look at her master of whose temper she was never sure.

'Well, my dear, sit with us. We are waiting for tea.'

A silent maid glided in with the tea and glided out again. A well-oiled household — except for the recent affair. Lady Fane arranged the cups, which tinkled slightly as if her hands trembled. Dickens felt a tension in the air and darted a glance at Sir Neptune. He looked irritated — because of wife's nervousness or because he did not want her there? However, he received his cup with an amiable smile at his wife. Dickens took his cup. Lady Fane picked up a cup and saucer and put it down again. She looked at her husband.

Sir Neptune addressed her. 'Mary, my dear, Mr Dickens has come about Miss Pout.' He looked at Dickens. 'My wife's maid, Miss Brown, is the close friend of Mrs Pout, who is most anxious about —'

'Oh, has she not returned home? We thought — that is — I thought that Miss Pout would be sure to...' Lady Fane's fingers worked under their lace mittens.

Sir Neptune picked up her unfinished sentence. 'Apparently not, my dear, and I have told him what I told Mrs Pout, that we have no idea where she has gone.'

That seemed final, thought Dickens, but he resolved go on — he did not want to go back to Anne with exactly the same information that Mrs Pout had received. Lady Fane must have some opinion that was not just her husband's.

'Lady Fane, I realise that the matter is a delicate one, but I do wonder if you believe that Miss Pout has gone away with Mr Sabatini?'

The red stained her pale cheeks again, deeper and ugly somehow. One hand gripped the other. Her mouth opened and closed and he heard her take little, shaky breaths. He wondered if she might faint and cursed himself for misjudging the situation. Too eager. He should have been more careful. She looked at him and there was definitely alarm in her eyes. He did not dare look at Sir Neptune, but as he expected, Sir Neptune took the matter in hand.

'It is very delicate, Mr Dickens, and, of course, we are upset. We placed our trust in our governess and music teacher. We are very disappointed. Before my wife came in, I was about to tell you that we can think of no other explanation for their disappearance than the obvious one. I am very sorry for Mrs Pout, but I do not know what I can do.'

'I do see that, Sir Neptune, and I am much obliged for your time. I do not suppose that your elder daughter —' Now, he felt it. A tremor in the air — something like a telegraph message sent along an invisible wire between Sir Neptune and his wife. The daughter did know something. He waited, feeling his heart beating faster.

Sir Neptune turned his frank gaze upon Dickens. 'I think not, Mr Dickens. Our daughter, Mariana, is visiting relatives in the country. You can imagine that we are most anxious to shield her from any unpleasantness. She is young — a mere seventeen years. I do not know what gossip she may have heard from the servants —' Had Jemima Curd gossiped, Dickens wondered, and been dismissed? Sir Neptune went smoothly on — 'but that both the governess to her younger brother and sister and her own music master have departed simultaneously has naturally upset her — has upset us all.' He looked at his wife, giving her the cue to speak.

The hands worked again. Lady Fane looked at her husband, not at Dickens. 'It has — most distressing, a young girl like Mariana to suffer so —'

'Not suffer, my dear Mary, I will not go as far as that. The healthy country air will do her good. Mariana is young — she will recover from this upset, with her lively cousins, long walks, and some parties, I daresay. Now, Mr Dickens, I am sorry that we cannot be of more help.' He stood up and went to ring a bell at the fireside.

It was a dismissal, courteously and smoothly done, but the tone said 'enough'.

Dickens rose. *In for a penny*, he thought. He looked at Lady Fane. 'I wonder if you have information about Mr Sabatini. Where his family might be?' They must know. They would hardly employ a strolling vagabond with a hurdy-gurdy.

Lady Fane's eyes went to her husband, who answered, 'Of course, of course. Sabatini lived with his mother. She is Irish. His father was an Italian painter of some repute, I am told.' Sir Neptune sounded as if he did not quite believe it. 'He is dead now. They live in Osnaburgh Terrace — number seven.'

Sir Neptune escorted Dickens to the door where the footman waited. The library door did not close. Sir Neptune would be listening. Dickens could not therefore speak to the footman. He wanted to ask about Jemima Curd; he had realised that it would have been impossible to ask Sir Neptune or his wife. What business was it of his that they had dismissed a servant? In any case, the footman would not be willing to answer, he was sure. The man had his job to think of.

Dickens went out of the front door, merely bidding the footman a courteous farewell. He walked swiftly down the drive and onto Upper Church Street again. What now?

Had Jemima Curd shared the speculation about Violet Pout and Rolando Sabatini with her seventeen-year-old mistress? Had Mariana told her mother, and had that resulted in Jemima's dismissal? Had she found her rackety family again? It was a pity that she could not be discovered. He dared not seek out Mrs Pick who had promised to try to find a position for Jemima. Sir Neptune had made it clear that he could do nothing.

He thought about Lady Fane. What a bundle of nerves she was, and that use of the word 'suffer' which Sir Neptune had rather quickly dismissed, why was that important? He said Mariana had been upset — no doubt she had been. Any sheltered young girl would be. Lady Fane's word was "suffer". There was a difference, he thought. Sir Neptune obviously thought so. It implied, perhaps, a closeness between Mariana and Violet and then a betrayal of that friendship.

Mrs Pout had not been able to talk to the young lady. Mariana Fane did know something and had been packed off to the country. Not that his speculations helped. He certainly would not be able to talk to her even if he knew where she was. So, two people who had information were not to be found. Sir Neptune's servants were off-limits — and the footman, he had stumbled over the word 'Miss'. What did he know? Well, he could ask at the Carlyle house. And then he would have to go to see Rolando Sabatini's mother. Perhaps she knew something.

5: At Mrs Carlyle's

Dickens walked down to Cheyne Row and stopped at the tall narrow house. He went up the steps and gave a double knock. No one came, but there was a light upstairs. He knocked again and heard hurried footsteps. A harassed looking Mrs Carlyle opened the door.

'Charles Dickens!'

'The same. No servant?'

Mrs Carlyle's troubles with her servants were the stuff of legend — a series of comic interludes, unless you were the recipient of half-plucked fowls, stale fish, burnt soup, or a drunken cook, insensible on the kitchen floor. No wonder Thomas Carlyle suffered agonies of dyspepsia.

'Deaf,' said Jane as she led him up the stairs, 'it came upon her of a sudden and she says she'll die of grief listening for bells and never hearing them.'

They sat down in the parlour. Nero, the little white dog, came to put a friendly paw on Dickens's knee and looked at him with longing black eyes. Jane loved her little dog — more than any human, he sometimes thought.

'He wants a sugar lump.' She took some sugar from her pocket and Nero went to claim it. 'What breeze blows you to our windswept Chelsea on a winter's evening? Thomas is away on a visit and says he will be back by six o'clock, which means half-past, I daresay. Now, tea is an impossibility, I should think — there will be much ado in the lower regions over a fowl to be plucked. If I order tea I shall have to go down and I cannot face the fowl — or Fanny for that matter.'

'No, indeed, I have taken tea. I will tell you where in a moment. I came with a view to speaking to your servant.'

'I wish you joy. She is a nervous, helpless creature inclined to burst into tears at the sight of a winding sheet at the candle — fancies that a bit of dripping wax is an omen of death. She'll die on the spot if you speak to her. You'd better tell me about it.'

'It's a long story, Mrs Carlyle. I have just come from your neighbours at Wisteria Lodge.'

'Ah, the handsome sea god, Sir Neptune, with a little scrap of seaweed clinging to him like — I was going to say a barnacle, but I realise my metaphor is somewhat mixed.'

Dickens laughed. How like Jane Carlyle — the husband and wife skewered with deadly accuracy by that sharp tongue.

'Exactly my impression.'

'I didn't know you knew them.'

'I don't, or didn't. It is about the missing governess and the music tutor.'

'Oh, I heard about that. Disappeared on the same moonlit night so rumour painted by many tongues has it. I rather doubt the moon.'

'What have you heard?'

'Just that, really. It was not even a nine days' wonder. Sir Neptune has made no comment. One would not expect Lady Fane to talk — she hardly goes about. I heard the rumour from a gaggle of gossips I took tea with. What has it to do with you?'

Dickens told her about Jemima Curd, Anne Brown and Mrs Pout. 'So, I felt I ought to try to find out something. I tried to find Jemima Curd, but she's vanished, too. I rather wanted to question this Mrs Pick, who was going to find Jemima Curd a new place, but I could hardly question Sir Neptune's servants without seeing him.'

'What did you make of them?'

'Hard to say — but he could not help me. He rather took the view that Violet Pout and Rolando Sabatini have eloped together, and it was not his concern. I could not speak to the daughter, who is away in the country. She's the one who would know about a love affair, I suppose. I detected some alarm in Lady Fane when I asked about her daughter. Do you know anything about Miss Mariana Fane?'

'Only that she is in the country. It's understandable. They would want to protect her.'

'Yes, Lady Fane seemed to think she had suffered, though Sir Neptune was quick to say that she would recover her spirits very quickly. Lady Fane struck me as rather a nervous type — under his thumb, I thought.'

'Yes, she is — both, that is. I have met them a few times. Solicitous in company, plenty of "my dears", but I tend to think on how many devoted husbands are apt, from mere habit, to get devoted to other people's wives.'

'And has he?'

'I have not heard so, but then he'd be careful. He's a rising man. Lady Fane isn't much to look at and she don't say much — next door to a fool, I think. She had the money — daughter of a wealthy banker. He's the son of an Irish clergyman family — well-connected but without means. He's done well — looks and charm, Mr Dickens, go a long way these days. I need hardly say that Mr Carlyle finds him shallow.'

Dickens smiled at her. 'You need not — all shine and no depth.'

'I, of course, go wherever I am invited, however much I dislike the people who ask me.'

'You do not like Sir Neptune?'

'I am inclined to agree with Thomas, though Sir Neptune is very civil to an old thing like me. Now, don't say anything, Charles Dickens. I am nearly fifty, and you know what a brimstone creature I am.'

Dickens grinned at her. He thought her very pleasing to look at, dark-haired and slender with large dark eyes shining with intelligence. Giuseppe Mazzini liked her and she liked him, and when she stroked Nero he saw such a tender, soft look in her eyes. But it was very true, one had to be wary. His compliment remained unsaid.

'So, you thought my servant might know something of Jemima Curd, or about the governess?' Jane Carlyle asked.

'I thought you might know the Fanes and that there might be some acquaintance between the servants.'

'Well, we shall have to go downstairs, and farewell to the old adage that a thorough lady is one who has not entered her kitchen for seven years. I am always in mine so what that makes me, I cannot say. Perhaps a gentleman is always a gentleman wherever he may be.'

'And a lady, a lady, even in her kitchen.'

They went down, Jane making as much noise as she could on the stairs. Dickens made a clattering, too, but still the girl started as they entered the kitchen. Dickens feared for Thomas Carlyle's supper, more or less plucked now. There were a great many feathers in the air.

Jane ignored the fowl and the feathers. 'Fanny, dear,' she began.

Fanny's eyes filled. She was a short, dumpy girl but with a pretty face, a clear complexion and the look of a startled hare.

Jane became brisk and spoke loudly. 'Mr Dickens wishes to ask you some questions about Jemima Curd, Miss Fanes's maid.'

'Oh, she ain't there no more cos of Miss Mariana bein' sent to the country after the — er — governess left.'

Dickens realised that briskness was the most efficacious manner of dealing with Fanny. Her tears seem to have dried. 'Did Jemima tell you anything about the governess and the music tutor?'

'Said it couldn't be true. Music teacher was more with Miss Mariana. Jemima said Miss Mariana was sweet on 'im. I saw 'im — 'e was 'andsome. Jemima thought Miss Pout 'ad 'er own sweetheart.'

Dickens did not comment. 'You don't know where Jemima is, I suppose.'

'Dunno — up an' went all of a sudden. Gone 'ome I serpose.'

That was no more than he knew. Still the suggestions about the tutor's and Violet's separate love affairs were worth pondering. He thanked Fanny, told her she had been most helpful, and gave her a florin. Jane took advantage of the girl's pleasure to tell her to try to get on with the fowl and that she would come down later to assist.

'Well, Charles, perhaps Miss Fane's languishing after the tutor was the reason they sent her away. Perhaps the music tutor was playing her false. It might explain Lady Fane's talk of Miss Fane's suffering.'

'And Sir Neptune's quick refuting of it. Long walks in the country, eh? What kind of girl is Miss Fane?'

'Very pretty — a young version of her mother, I imagine. Shy, I thought, not that I paid much attention. Insipid as the white of an egg. Hardly interesting at all — to me at any rate.'

She wouldn't be, thought Dickens. 'But to Rolando Sabatini, perhaps?'

'Quite. So, you need to find Miss Jemima Curd, or to find another servant to talk to. I doubt the housekeeper would tell you anything — more than her job's worth to gossip. I daren't set Fanny on it — she's not clever enough to dissemble. I can only ask in a few days if she has heard anything from Wisteria Lodge. That's the best I can do.'

'And I am much obliged, Jane. Let me know if you hear anything. My kindest regards to Mr Carlyle — when he comes.'

Jane showed him out. She did not hold out much hope of finding out anything more, but she was intrigued. A little detective work. Perhaps she could call on Lady Fane — when Sir Neptune wasn't there.

6: At Osnaburgh Terrace

Osnaburgh Terrace, well, well. Dickens had not been there since 1844, though it was a mere step from Devonshire Terrace. He had rented number nine for a few months before he had gone to Italy, from May to June, he remembered — the Osnaburgh encampment he had called it. And what was interesting was that Robert Smirke, the artist, had lived at number three and St. George Pierce, the still life painter, had been his neighbour at number ten. Perhaps it was not surprising that Mrs Sabatini, whose husband had been a painter, lived there, too.

Smirke was dead, he knew that. He had died in 1845 at the great age of ninety-two. It was hard to imagine — he would be ninety-two in — great heavens, in 1904! Now that was unimaginable. The twentieth century. What an extraordinary thought. He didn't suppose he would live until then. Though his grandmother, Elizabeth Dickens, had lived until she was eighty — a formidable old woman who had given him a silver watch. He would die at his desk, he thought. Better to die, doing.

But St. George Pierce was still living — he could visit there, see if he knew anything of the Sabatini family. Bound to. The father had been an artist. However, first he would visit the widow at number seven. He passed number nine and came to a house in darkness. Perhaps Mrs Sabatini had gone away, too. He looked down into the area steps. In a lighted window of what must be the kitchen he could see a woman kneading bread. Probably not Mrs Sabatini. A servant?

He went down the steps and knocked at the area door. It was opened by a white-haired woman who looked at him suspiciously.

'I wonder if I might speak with Mrs Sabatini?'

The white-haired lady gazed at him with eyes like hard jet beads. 'No here.' She waved her floury hand at him. Its message was 'Go away.'

That was definite. She sounded Italian, and she was shutting the door. He tried again. '*Scusi signora, solo* Mr Dickens, Charles Dickens —' she didn't close the door, but the little black eyes remained hostile — '*prego, ecco mia carta per* Signora Sabatini.'

The woman took the card without another word and the door closed. He heard the key in the lock. Perhaps she thought he was selling something. He went back up the steps and stood by the railings. He could see her through the window examining the card, turning it over. Would she throw it in that cheerful kitchen fire? But no, she put in the pocket of her apron and disappeared from view. Mrs Sabatini might get it.

He stood on the pavement. Was it too late to go to see St. George Pierce? He glanced up at the curtained window on the right side of the porch. He was sure that there was the briefest glimpse of light. Someone had twitched the curtain, he was certain, but it was gone now. A memory came to him of Italy, of Venice — that time when he had thought he had seen a light from a ruined palazzo. He had been wrong then. Probably was now.

He turned away and walked past number nine to number ten. Pierce was an artist — he wouldn't mind a late call, surely. He knocked. A rather lovely girl answered the door. Lily, it must be, Pierce's daughter. She knew him at once.

'Mr Dickens — how astonishing! I saw you the other night at the theatre. You were with Mr Maclise. There was such a crush that I had not the chance to speak to you. And now you are here. Are you come to see Father? I can take you up.'

She led him upstairs to Pierce's studio where the painter was contemplating a rather beautiful composition on his easel.

'That's a beauty,' said Dickens.

'Well, well, Charles Dickens! How long is it?'

'Too long, I am ashamed to say.' He looked again at the painting. 'My word it is lovely.'

'"Nature and Art", I call it. It's a commission for a wealthy brewer.' It was a picture brimming with colour — reds and pinks, Dickens's favourites, in roses and jewels, blood-warm rubies, and pearls silvered where the light from a casement caught them, and a rich crimson carafe, chased with more silver, and deep purple grapes, so polished and bursting with juice that you could taste them.

'The colours are wonderful and the whole thing resembling and refining upon nature — those rubies taking on and deepening the colour of the roses, and I feel as if I leaned nearer I should smell them.'

'You'd smell varnish, I'm afraid, but I appreciate your comments, Mr Dickens. However, I take it you did not come just to look at my pictures.'

'Alas, no — I do have an ulterior motive. I came about your neighbour, Mrs Sabatini. It's a long tale which concerns several missing persons, one of whom, in particular, I am an under an obligation to try to find.'

'Well, while you are telling, perhaps you will take some wine. This,' St. George Pierce said, holding up the beautiful red glass jug chased with silver, 'is an Italian wine, given, coincidentally, by my neighbour, Mrs Sabatini.'

Dickens took a glass. 'With beaded bubbles winking at the brim.'

St. George Pierce smiled. 'Did you visit Keats's grave when you were in Rome?'

'I did, and very moving it was. That inscription about his name being "writ in water" struck me most powerfully. If only he had known.'

'Well, yours will not be writ in water — we know that already.'

'Nor yours, indeed,' Dickens answered, gesturing at the picture, 'this is the very flask, I see. Reminds me of Venice.'

'Where Agosto Sabatini came from, though Mrs Sabatini is Irish; what did you want her for?'

Dickens recited his tale, ending with the query about whether the lady had gone away.

'Not that I know of. I haven't seen Rolando at all. You say he is supposed to have eloped with this Miss Pout?'

'That is what I have been told by Sir Neptune Fane. I had a lead to a Jemima Curd, a servant of Sir Neptune's, but she has vanished and the young lady, Miss Mariana Fane, who might have known something, has been sent to the country.'

A barrel-organ started in the street. Pierce went to close the window. 'I was getting rid of the smell of varnish.'

'He was rather good, the musician — better than average. Professional, I daresay.'

'Fallen on hard times,' Pierce said. 'Lily will give him something, though, that means he will be back. He's Italian.'

'He would be. There are so many thousands living in London that I despair of finding Rolando Sabatini. He could be playing a barrel-organ in a street somewhere.'

'And the young lady?' Pierce asked.

'I honestly don't know. Her mother has enquired of family, school friends, everyone she could think of. I don't know that

I can do more, but I should like to learn something about Rolando and his family.'

'Agosto Sabatini, the father, came to London in 1820 as little more than a boy, I think. He was taken up by the poet Ugo Foscolo. Some family connection, I believe. Sabatini attended the Royal Academy Schools. I think Foscolo paid. Sabatini did well. He made a decent living — portraits mostly and taught Italian as well as painting.'

'And Mrs Sabatini?' Dickens asked.

'A very beautiful woman. A love story, I believe. Her father was quite a comfortably off man, some kind of lawyer in Ireland. She met Sabatini over here — how, I don't know, but her father gave her the house on her marriage; however, she hasn't a great deal of money, not enough to keep the boy without a profession. Hence the music teaching.'

'Can you believe the story of the elopement?'

'Depends on the girl, I suppose. Rolando is very devoted to his mother, especially after Agosto Sabatini's death which happened five years ago when the boy was sixteen or so. I wouldn't have thought he would risk hurting his mother. In any case, why would they elope? They could have resigned their positions, returned to their respective homes, and continued a respectable courtship.'

Dickens thought about Violet Pout. Pierce's words were quite sensible. He thought about the respectable house at number seven, the reasonably successful father, the beautiful mother, whose father had been a lawyer. Why should Violet Pout wish to conceal that? Mrs Pout, surely, would be pleased enough, though she might have set her hopes higher. He remembered that refrain "Sir Neptune". Unless Mrs Carlyle's maid's words were true, that Violet Pout had her own sweetheart.

'You are quite right,' he said to St. George Pierce, 'why would they conceal their relationship? It is hardly so surprising a situation.'

'It certainly is not — Mrs Sabatini fell in love with her drawing teacher, married and lived happily ever after. I doubt she would have objected to her son doing the same thing.'

'I am much obliged to you, my dear Pierce, for the information, though, if anything, matters are more obscure than they were before I stepped across your threshold. I can only wait and see —'

'If anything turns up, as your Mr Micawber would say.'

Dickens laughed. 'And, if not, then I must turn my attention to coals, I suppose. At this point I cannot share the sanguinary imaginings of Wilkins Micawber.'

Dickens rose to go. St. George Pierce stopped him with a motion of his hand. 'I've remembered something. Rolando Sabatini told me that Miss Fane was sitting for her portrait.'

'By whom?'

'I don't know. It would have been when he was here last — some months ago. There were a good many people so I suppose we must have been interrupted. It was just a passing comment. I think we were looking at the picture there.' He pointed to the portrait of a young woman on the wall: Lily, the artist's daughter. 'Someone he knew, perhaps?'

'I will have to ask Mrs Sabatini — if I get to see her. I left my card.'

'I am sure she will want to see you. Who would not?'

'Unless she has something to hide.'

'I really doubt that, Mr Dickens. I know enough of her — an honest woman, who will be most anxious about her son if he is missing. He may be away with her.'

'Of course, I never thought of that — too busy conjuring sinister plots. I should have asked the lady in the kitchen.'

'She would not have told you, the Signora Minelli — very protective of her lady, and of Rolando. She has been with them for years.'

'The dragon at the gate — she wasn't very welcoming. Oh well, I shall have to possess my soul in patience and hope that the Signora Sabatini is unable to resist me.'

Dickens walked away into Albany Street and turned up to Park Square, past the Diorama. Before he had ever been, he had seen pictures from Italy there. As a very young man he had paid his shilling to see the Basilica of St. Paul near Rome; he had seen the inside of St. Peter's, all lit up with tapers; he had even witnessed the village of Alagni in Piedmont crushed by a terrifying avalanche; he had shivered at the shimmering iciness of Mont Blanc; he had been dazzled by the waters of Lake Maggiore rippling under the effects of the clever play of light through hidden windows and skylights, light which was altered by the use of binds and shutters manipulated by lines and pulleys — not that he had known all that. He had been lost in wonder.

He had gone again only a few years ago to see the interior of St. Mark's in Venice. The novelty had worn off — perhaps because he knew how it all worked, perhaps because he had seen it in life, but still the spectacle had brought back vivid memories of that time in Venice. You forgot the science of it, seeing the outline of the familiar cupolas and columns in twilight shadow. Within you marvelled at the way the twilight dissolved as tapers lit up and the shadows became worshippers at a succession of altars, and all the while organ music played then the morning light dimmed the tapers and the figures faded. The cloud-capped towers, the solemn temples melted into thin air. He might have been back there and would be stepping out of the church to find Francisco, the gondolier.

Venice, he thought now, where Agosto Sabatini, Rolando's father had come from, and where, for all he knew, Rolando had returned — with Violet Pout, maybe? Or, perhaps not. What of a possible other lover? He could only hope that Mrs Sabatini would contact him. At least he could tell Anne Brown that something might come of that.

7: Dry Bones

'In a water tank?'

Sergeant Rogers nodded. Superintendent Sam Jones raised an eloquent eyebrow and indicated that the sergeant should sit and tell his tale. 'Brief as you can,' he said, knowing Rogers's tendency to embellishment — something acquired since his promotion to sergeant. He seemed to think that a lengthy account carried more weight.

'At the back of an empty house in Alfred Place — number five in the South Crescent. Stemp and Feak was — were —' Rogers was aiming at improvement in every way — 'on their beat when they sees a labourin' man lookin' up an' down the street. He waves them over and says they've found bones in a water tank — human bones because they've seen a skull. Stemp and Feak go to look. There's another cove standin' by the tank with a spade. There was no water in it and these two had been clearing out the silt. Feak came back to Bow Street to report it.'

'How long has the house been empty?'

'Five years, so they said. It's being fitted up for new tenants.'

'What have you done so far?'

'Stemp's guarding the bones and I sent Feak to the agent's to find out who owns the house and who lived in it five years ago, and who's taking it over. We got the agent's name from the foreman. He's still there. I told him to wait.'

'Good — the bones'll have to go to the mortuary. I've an idea. I'll go to see Doctor Symonds at King's College Hospital. I've worked with him before. I'll get him to look at them. What are your thoughts?'

'Well, the workmen had taken the cover off. The tank's lead, o' course, and stands on bricks. An' I'm thinkin' if someone wanted to hide, a kiddie, say, they couldn't have slid it back in place — a kiddie could have got trapped, but a man, well, a man could have shoved it off, I daresay.'

'Someone trapped in there? That's a horrible thought.'

'Or a body, sir, dumped?'

'Could be. Let's see what Doctor Symonds has to say. Anything else I should know?' Jones knew his sergeant very well — Rogers would have a titbit saved to the end.

'Stemp recognised one of the labourers —'

'And?'

'Peely Peel,' Rogers grinned.

'So Stemp gave him a long hard stare?'

'He did an' he says that Peely looked shifty, but then he always does, and he knows Stemp. Made him nervous, p'raps. Anyhow, Stemp wonders what Peely's inched. He was first in the tank.'

'Stemp was thinking of valuables?'

'He was — a watch, or coins like on that body that was taken out of the river at Waterloo Bridge.'

Jones remembered the skeleton of a man discovered at the bridge. There had been a purse of sovereigns with him. 'Oh, yes, and he'd been missing for years.'

'Stemp asked them if they'd found anything else. Course, Peely was indignant — doin' an honest day's work an' all that. He wasn't in the tank when Feak and Stemp got there.'

'Turned respectable, has he?'

Peely was a frequent guest at Bow Street police station — pick-pocket, filcher of gold watches, jewellery, silk-snatcher, anything small and easily sold on.

'I doubt it — seein' what he might get from the house, I shouldn't wonder. Think of it, sir, all locked up for five years. Untouched, says the foreman who was doin' up the inside. Peely and his mate had been puttin' all sorts o' stuff into crates. An' Peely's a known associate of our favourite fence, Fikey Chubb.'

Jones laughed. 'So, he is. Dear old Fikey — not seen him for a while. Well, tell Stemp to keep his eyes on Peely until I bring Doctor Symonds.'

Jones went to find Doctor Symonds. King's College Hospital was not far from Bow Street, just across Drury Lane in Portugal Street. *Murder*, thought Jones, *you had to wonder about a skeleton found in a water cistern.* No doubt Doctor Symonds would be able to tell them something about the bones.

Doctor Symonds was in the mortuary. He offered to bring the bones to the hospital where he could examine them. Two mortuary attendants accompanied them.

'Of course,' said Jones as they walked into Drury Lane and up to Broad Street, 'the five years may not be relevant. The house has been unoccupied for five years so it could be less — someone dumped an inconvenient dead body in an unused cistern.'

'Unlikely more than five years. If the body was put there when the house was occupied, the water would be contaminated. They'd know about that soon enough.'

'What can you tell from a skeleton of five years?'

'Approximate age, sex, of course, and if there are any broken bones that might tell us if the person jumped in — though that seems very unlikely if there was a cover on. Broken or fractured bones might tell me if the person had been injured. I had a case recently — a woman dragged from the river — the verdict was found drowned, but traces of indentation of the temporal bone suggested a blow to the head — not that we could know what made that blow.'

In the back garden of the house in South Crescent where Sergeant Rogers waited, Jones had a look in the tank. It was as Rogers had described. There was silt in the bottom — about a foot deep and he saw the skull and the bones which Peely had uncovered. The skull was small — a child's? Trapped as Rogers had speculated. Or a woman? The muddy silt had been turned over and Jones could see what might be the remnants of cloth.

'Bring everything you can,' he said to the mortuary attendant who climbed up the ladder and began to hand over the bones to Doctor Symonds and the other attendant.

Jones watched as Doctor Symonds carefully placed the skull into a cardboard box he had brought for the purpose. Various bones followed: the long bones of arms and legs, rib bones, the bones of a foot, a hand, and others too encrusted with mud for him to tell what they were. There did seem to be some pieces of cloth and what looked like bits of leather, possibly from a shoe. The man in the tank was doing a thorough search.

'Buttons, I think,' the man said to Doctor Symonds, handing him the little pieces. The doctor rubbed at them with a piece of cloth.

'Silver buttons.' He showed them to Jones. It was not possible to tell from where they had come. Might be a dress or a waistcoat, but silver suggested that the owner had been someone of some substance. Not a child then, thankfully. A child with silver buttons would have been missed.

Jones thought about the houses in South Crescent. There were seven substantial town houses, tall and narrow and rather elegant in their semi-circular arrangement. The inhabitants, he guessed, would be professional men, lawyers, doctors, merchants and so on. He needed to find out who the neighbours were and who of them had known the occupants of number five. In his office he had a copy of the *Royal Blue Book* — a most useful volume which would tell him the names of the neighbours. However, he wanted to wait for Feak to come back with his findings. Jones preferred to ask his questions from a position of some knowledge at least. He wanted to know who had lived in the house and he wanted to know more about the skeleton.

Doctor Symonds was sealing the box. He bade farewell to Jones and told him that he would let him know about the bones by tomorrow.

Now, thought Jones, *let's have a look at Peely and his mate.*

They were in the kitchen basement where Stemp was keeping his gimlet gaze upon them. Not that there was much about Peely that was worth gazing upon. Peely, full name, Robert Peel, was as unlike his tall, handsome politician namesake as a crow from a swan. Peely was a short, squat, thatch-haired man with a face the colour of old potato peelings and nose like a twisted root. A smell of decayed vegetables hung about him as if he had been brought forth from an old sack long forgotten by the green-grocer. He lounged against a kitchen cupboard, his hands in his pockets and gave Jones a leering grin.

'Wotcher, Mr Jones, long time no see.'

'Going straight, Mr Peel, I believe.'

'Got me nippers ter think of.'

That was a first, Jones thought. Peely's lad, about ten, was as much a thief as Peely — and cleverer. Even Stemp hadn't managed to make anything stick on him. Peely's wife and daughter had looked half-starved and beaten down when they had come to Bow Street in search of Peely. However, Jones made no comment. He merely asked if either of them had seen anything other than the bones.

Peely spoke first. 'Dint look, Mr Jones. Give me a shockin' turn. I was outta there like a flea off a dog's arse.'

'And you, Mr Hand?'

'No, I stood on the ladder when Peely shouted an' saw a bleedin' death's 'ead grinnin' at me. Then I goes ter find the bobby.'

So, Peely had been on his own in the tank while James Hand had fetched the police. He had certainly had the opportunity to filch something. Jones thought about the silver buttons. What else might have survived?

'Turn out your pockets, if you please.'

Peely was, naturally, indignant. ''Ere wot's the bleedin' game? Honest workin' men, we is. Yer sayin' we've inched somethin'?'

'Not at all, Mr Peel, I have my report to make. I need to be thorough.'

'More than yer job's worth, eh? Well, I ain't 'idin' nuffink.'

Peely emptied his pockets. There were a few pennies, a bit of string and a wooden button in one, and in the other a dirty heel of bread. The contents of James Hand's pockets were similarly unprepossessing. Of course, Peely would have had time to hide something valuable. They'd have to search.

'Thank you. Where do I find you both? You'll be needed for the inquest.'

James Hand gave his address readily. Peely looked uncertain for the first time.

'Where, Mr Peel?'

'Between lodgin's.'

'Where are your wife and children?'

'Wiv 'er ma, up in Camden — Bayham Street.'

So much for his nippers to think of. 'And you?' Jones insisted.

'At Fikey Chubb's. Got a crib there fer a few days.'

Jones indicated to Stemp that they were to go outside. *Let Peely sweat*, he thought.

'He'll 'ave 'idden somethin',' Stemp observed. 'I know it. Want me to 'ave a search?'

They looked round the garden. It would take an age and it would be dark soon. There were some outbuildings, plenty of shrubbery, flowerbeds, a little summer house with broken panes and a back door, which would lead to the mews, probably.

'I think we'll send him on his way — out of the front door and you can wait. He'll come back if there is anything and you can nab him then. I'll put a man in the alley. How long was James Hand away before he saw you and Feak?'

'Ten minutes or so, Peely said, though Hand didn't really know. Coulda bin longer and Peely 'ad plenty o' time to stow somethin'.'

Peely and James Hand were escorted out through the front door. Jones went to speak to the foreman in charge of the redecoration of the house. It seemed that all the furniture and goods had been removed over several days and were to be sold at auction. Mr Faithfull, the house agent, looked after all that.

While they waited for Feak to return, Jones went through the empty rooms. Stemp went back into the garden with his bull's eye lantern — might as well have a look, he said, unable to sit still.

There was nothing to tell who had lived there. Jones looked at the pale spaces on the wall where pictures had been; he went up the hollow-sounding stairs and hearing the echo of his tread felt the desolation of the lonely house where his own bull's eye lamp cast shadows in the falling twilight. He peered into empty bedrooms; in one a cracked mirror showed him a haunted looking man who seemed like a ghost in the shadows.

He went up to the top storey, where in one attic room there was still an iron bed frame with a rolled up mattress of ticking lay. There was a cracked bowl and jug on a marble stand. The room smelt of dust. It was very cold. *Servant's room*, he thought. I need to find out who the servants were. Could the skeleton be that of a servant girl? But then the silver buttons? Someone must know.

A sound below took him clattering down the flights of stairs to find Feak with an anxious-looking well-dressed man. Mr Faithfull, the house agent, he surmised.

'Mr Faithfull, sir,' said Feak. 'I asked him to come to talk to you.'

The House agent held out his hand. 'Francis Faithfull — my premises are at 33 Conduit Street. We are auctioneers and valuers as well as letting agents. Constable Feak has told me about the — er — bones. I thought you would want to know about the family.'

'Superintendent Jones from Bow Street. I should very much like to know about the house owners. You are auctioneers. I take you are selling the contents of the house.'

'We are.'

'Then I should like to examine the contents — the furniture and so on — after you have told me what you know of the family. It is getting very dark — and cold in here. Perhaps we could go to your offices?'

8: Can These Bones Speak?

Think of Christmas in the tremendous wastes of ice and snow that lie in the remotest region of the earth, in the interminable white deserts of the Polar Sea...

Dickens put down the paper. The article for *Household Words* was on the subject of the missing Franklin expedition. The ships *Erebus* and *Terror* had set out in May 1845. Nothing had been heard of Sir John Franklin since. He thought of that icy wasteland. Missing, perhaps buried deep under great mountains of snow, never to be found. He had written that perhaps somewhere at the end of 1850, Sir John and his fellows might keep Christmas. Heaven grant it so... There was hope, he had written. Not that he believed it.

Missing. Violet Pout and Rolando Sabatini, and Jemima Curd — all three might just as well be buried in that frozen wilderness for all he could find out. He had heard nothing from Mrs Carlyle in the last two days, and Mrs Sabatini seemed to have vanished, too.

He blotted his paper, took his hat and coat. He would walk over to Bow Street and have a word with Sam Jones — it would be good to talk to him, if Sam had time for a chop.

As he neared the police station, he saw Jones coming towards him. In a hurry, it seemed. No chop then.

'Bones,' said Jones, 'I'm off to see a Doctor Symonds about a skeleton. Come with me if you want and we can have our chop later.'

On their way, Jones told him about the discovery of the bones in the water tank. 'The house agent, Mr Faithfull, told me about the old lady, Mrs Wyatt, who had died there five years ago. The house has been shut up since then. It belongs to her brother, a clergyman who lives in St John's Wood. Now, of more interest at the moment, it seems that Mrs Wyatt had some sort of companion, a Miss Flora Lambert, a young woman of twenty years, but Mr Faithfull didn't know what became of her. What I saw of the bones suggested a female.'

'Murder?' asked Dickens.

'Could be — I do wonder how a body got in there. Anyway, let's go in and see if Doctor Symonds can tell us anything interesting.'

Doctor Symonds could. He had fitted the bones together to make a complete skeleton of an individual which lay on the mortuary slab. All that was left of a once living, breathing creature. Such a small collection of pieces. They seemed very pitiable to Dickens — a woman, or a child? Left to die in a water tank or disposed of as so much rubbish.

'A woman,' Doctor Symonds said, 'from the formation of the pelvis, which is larger from wing to wing than that of a man. As you can see, she was about five foot tall.'

'Some bones are broken,' Jones observed.

'Yes, the arm and the left leg, consistent, perhaps, with her having fallen or having been dropped into the tank — and one of the neck bones is fractured.'

Dickens interrupted. He had remembered something. 'I heard a story, years ago, about a young woman who had been engaged for fourteen years to a poor fellow who was fighting his way, very slowly, to the Bar. He was called at last, but he suffered a congestion of the brain. The young woman was taken to see him — he died at the moment she arrived and she, desperate with grief, threw herself from a window, and by a kind of miracle, plunged, head-foremost into a water tank.'

'She died?' asked Doctor Symonds.

'No, but her wits were gone. I was thinking about if this woman had gone into the tank when there was water in it. In my story, the young woman, Miss White, was unconscious, but otherwise unhurt.'

'You are thinking about the broken bones — our woman might have drowned if she could not get out, but she would not necessarily have broken any bones.'

'Unless she hit her head when she went in, thus fracturing the bones in the neck,' Jones put in.

'The skull shows no sign of damage, but a fall might well cause the fracture of the neck bones, though, as I said before, a body in a full water tank would very soon pollute the water.'

'Then she went in or was put in once the house was closed up, five years since. The agent didn't know if the tank was emptied then. I can't think that a woman would use a tank as a hiding place — a child might and be trapped, but a woman —'

'Could it be that she was dead when she was put in there?' Dickens was thinking of murder, of a body hidden in the water tank — concealed for five years, perhaps.

'It could be,' said Doctor Symonds. 'The broken neck could have a different cause.'

'How might that occur, if not from falling into the tank?' Jones asked.

Doctor Symonds looked at him. 'A severe and sudden twist to the neck may break the second cervical vertebra as here.'

'The hangman's fracture?'

'It is possible. There is evidence of tuberculosis of the neck vertebra, which would mean that there would be significant weakness in the neck, but, of course, it is not for me to speculate on the cause of death. Such a break in the vertebra might well be the result of a fall in a young woman who was suffering from tuberculosis of the bone. I can only tell you what I see.'

'Can you tell her age?'

'Approximately. These are the bones of a person between the age of sixteen and twenty-two. The posterior teeth — the *dentes sapientiae* —' Doctor Symonds pointed to the skull — 'are not protruded, but partly formed within the jaw.'

'Any sign of dental work?' Jones wondered if a dentist might be of help in the identification. Missing teeth might help.

'None — the teeth are in very good condition. However, there is one more thing about the skeleton which may help you to identify your victim. Look at the hands.'

Dickens and Jones obeyed and saw what they had not seen before. The left hand had only four digits. The little finger was missing.

'Could the finger bones still be in the tank?'

'They could — they are very small bones —'

'Could the woman have had a finger missing?'

'She could, Superintendent, but it's impossible to tell. However, look closely at the metacarpal of the little finger on the right hand. See how the bone is enlarged.'

'What can you tell from that?'

'Another sign that she had tuberculosis of the bone. There are other indications at the knee and elbow.'

'That might be helpful. Was there anything of interest in the other items?'

'We found the partial leather sole of a shoe — a woman's shoe and some pieces of wool, which are here. You will see that I have cleaned them and the pattern is a green and purple check — a woman's shawl, perhaps, and here is a bit of silk, discoloured, but once green. The silver buttons have no distinctive marks, but they are decorative. Again, a woman's, perhaps. I should also add that my findings show that the body has been in the tank for a good number of years — certainly as many as five.'

Leaving the hospital, Dickens stepped aside from a dog gnawing at a very large bone. Dickens thought about the proximity of the burial ground, where he had seen very often the gleaners who collected bones from old graves, sometimes dug up by dogs or brought to the surface by heavy rain. The state of the city's graveyards was a civic disgrace. The dog gave him a look of sly triumph.

Jones was already striding across Portugal Street. As always, he knew where he was going. Dickens caught up with him in Gate Street. The Ship Tavern was their destination.

'Cutlets?' Jones asked as the landlord, Daniel Stagg, approached.

Dickens thought of bones. Pie? Sausage? Cheese would be safe, he thought, but Jones was already discussing the steak and kidney pie with Mr Stagg, whose recommendations could be relied upon. Dickens and Jones were old friends of the landlord. Two glasses of pale ale came while they waited.

'I need to find out if that tank was emptied after Mrs Wyatt died. It occurred to me that it must have been empty and I had a horrible thought about an unconscious woman being trapped under that lid.'

'Dear Heaven, Sam, that's a horrible idea — worthy of Mr Poe. Someone would have heard something — she would have woken up and screamed her head off, surely.'

'That's true. And your very helpful story about poor Miss White made me think how unlikely it is that it was some sort of accident and —'

'The hangman's fracture — that's a grim thought.'

'It is, so I conclude that she was dead before she was put in the tank.'

'Murder, then?'

'Very possibly — probably. I need to find out about Miss Lambert — if she is missing — and the servants of the household. Mr Faithfull, the house agent, gave me the name of Mrs Wyatt's solicitor and her brother, the clergyman. Anguish.'

'Toothache?' Dickens asked, looking at Jones, whose hand was at his jaw.

'No, it's his name.'

'Whose name?'

'Mrs Wyatt's brother, the Reverend Henry Anguish.'

'Good heavens, that's a new one — born to suffering, I shouldn't wonder.'

'I hope I shall not add to his woes by bringing news that Miss Lambert was the woman in the tank. But I shall have to ask about a young woman who may have had tuberculosis.'

'Or a missing finger.'

'Hmm — that would simplify the matter. I doubt I could be so lucky. The Reverend Anguish lives in St. John's Wood — Hamilton Terrace.'

'When shall you go?'

'This afternoon, after I have been back to Bow Street. I am expecting news from Rogers, who is at the house agent's now, looking at the furniture and other things from South Crescent, which are waiting to be auctioned.'

'The Purloined Letter.'

'What?'

'Poe again — a story, the solution to which lies in the contents of a secret letter. I was thinking about a hidden letter — from the murderer. That'd be handy.'

Jones grinned. 'If there is a murderer; I just wanted to see what evidence there might be about the occupants of the house. Secret letters I leave to novelists.'

Dickens laughed. 'I suppose he'll find a laundry list or something — a recipe for the cook's steak and kidney pie.'

The pies and mashed potato had arrived and were, as always, very good, though Dickens found that bones would keep insinuating themselves. He pushed his plate aside.

'Were you coming to see me about anything in particular?' Jones asked. His plate was clean.

'Not really — I just wanted to tell you about a missing young woman — well, two, in fact, and a young man.'

'You've lost three!'

'Not exactly. I was asked to make enquiries about the daughter of a friend of Anne Brown, Catherine's maid, a girl called Violet Pout. She was governess for Sir Neptune Fane's children —'

'Fane? The Member of Parliament?'

'Yes — you've heard of him?'

'Not in a parliamentary way — there were some diamonds stolen about a year back and then they mysteriously turned up — all very hush, hush. That's why I know the name. Anyhow, tell me about this governess.'

'It seems she has run off with the music tutor. Not that the mother, Mrs Pout, believes that.'

'Do you?'

'I don't know enough about the young lady, really, and I know nothing about the young man except that someone told me that he loved his mother and would not want to hurt her. This person — an artist who lives near the mother — also commented very astutely, I thought, that two young people from entirely respectable families would have no reason to run away, so I am none the wiser.'

'And they've asked all the obvious people?'

'They have, I have. I went to Sir Neptune's. The couple disappeared at the same time and he believes they are together.'

'The mother hasn't been to the police at Chelsea?'

'No — the usual thing — Mrs Pout doesn't want a scandal.'

'How long have they been missing?'

'Three weeks or so — they went from Wisteria Lodge in the first week of November.'

'Hm — not so long — does she think her daughter is in danger of some kind? If so, then she shouldn't be worrying about a scandal. The young couple are of age?'

'Over twenty-one.'

'Then there isn't much you can do. As far as you know neither has committed a crime, no one is in danger, and it sounds as if they went away by mutual consent. The police won't be much interested. But you said two young women?'

'One Jemima Curd, maid to Miss Mariana Fane, who, incidentally, has gone to the country. Jemima Curd left some days after Miss Pout. I had a suspicion that she might have known something, and Mrs Carlyle's maid suggested that it was Miss Fane who had a tenderness for Mr Sabatini. I wondered if he had played her false with Miss Pout, but I can't do anything about Miss Fane. I'm stumped.'

'The maid — that strikes me as odd.'

'It seems that she wasn't wanted anymore, since Miss Fane had gone to the country.'

'Which suggests a rather long stay in the country. You'd think the maid would have gone with the mistress.'

'There was definite tension in Sir Neptune and his wife when I asked about Miss Fane. Sir Neptune talked about servants' gossip. I wondered if Jemima Curd had been dismissed for talking too much.'

'And now she can't be found.'

'I found out that her family was in pretty poor straits. They've done a flit from their lodgings, according to a neighbour. Jemima Curd was supposed to go back to see Mrs Pick, Sir Neptune's housekeeper, about a possible new place. She was lodging with a Mrs Link in Ship Yard and just didn't come back.'

'You need to talk to this Mrs Pick.'

'I know, but how? Sir Neptune Fane gave me the decided impression that the matter was closed as far as he was concerned.'

'Well, he wouldn't want to be involved in any scandal, either. It seems to me you have done all you can.'

Dickens looked downhearted. Jones knew that he liked to keep his promises, and that the sense of something unfinished would be like an itch that needed scratching, but he didn't think he could help.

'People go missing all the time.'

'So they do. That's the trouble with London, all sorts of people sucked down into the great whirlpool, gasping for breath, drowning in madness, malice — and mud.'

'Depressing, I know, and families like the Curds flit from lodging to lodging — perhaps Jemima has caught up with them. Young couples vanish to other towns. The police only get involved when there is a crime committed.'

'And as far as I know there hasn't been.'

'Then, it's fortress Wisteria you need to conquer.'

'We couldn't use the old trick — policeman concerned about household security, spate of robberies? A uniform, old 'un, will work its way with the women.'

'*We?* You mean *me*. I doubt it — too risky. If I sent Rogers, for example, I'd have to inform the Chelsea police. Sir Neptune would be bound to find out. If I didn't inform them then there'd be enquiries about a man masquerading as a policeman. Too complicated. Now, I need to be back at Bow Street — are you walking to Wellington Street?'

'I am. I might as well do something useful.'

9: The Raven is Hoarse

'Sir.'

Dickens and Jones turned as they were about to cross Drury Lane. Constable Stemp caught up with them. He was dressed in a labourer's garb of fustian breeches and an old jacket with a moth-eaten woollen scarf round his neck and a greasy looking cap on his head.

'Peely never came back, sir, so I've been on the 'unt fer 'im an' 'is lad. Saw the foreman at first light. I asked 'im again about the days Peely was workin' there an' 'e remembered a boy 'angin' about. Seemed to be thick with Peely so I guessed it was Micky Peel, an' the foreman's description made me sure. Peely's given the stuff to that lad, I'll bet.'

'So you've tracked him down?'

'I went to Fikey Chubb's first. 'E wasn't best pleased to see me.'

'Nor you him, I daresay,' said Jones.

Fikey Chubb, known fence and receiver of stolen goods who kept a shop as his front, was not fond of the police. He had been rough handled by Stemp very often and had spent time in the Bow Street cells, leaving behind him a whiff of sulphur and the distinctly unpleasant smell of sweat and onions. He never washed.

Stemp grinned. 'Stinkin' devil, 'e is, dancin' about like 'is feet was on fire, but 'e swore Peely ain't been there. I tried all 'is known haunts. No one's seen 'im so I went up to Bayham Street to see Mrs Peel, thinkin' the lad would be there. She doesn't want Peely back. Micky's with his father and Mrs Peel gave me an address down near Hemlock Court. I took myself there. No Peely, but the lad was in the street with some others, playin' about with stone marbles. 'E didn't know where Peely was, an' that was that, I thought, but the lads started throwin' their stones again and my eye caught a glint of gold as one of the marbles rolled to my feet. It wasn't a stone. It was this.'

Jones took a small glass object from Stemp. It was a button set in gold and the glass was dark red with little flecks of gold in it. 'Looks like a waistcoat button — see where the shank was.'

'I asked Micky where 'e got it. Course, 'e said 'e'd found it, but 'e looked a bit shifty so I gave 'im tuppence for it — said it was important evidence, and came away sharpish.'

'You're thinking it was stolen.'

'Musta bin — looks expensive to me.'

'It is,' said Dickens who had examined it. 'I don't think it's English. I think it's Murano glass — from Venice. I saw a great deal of it when I was there. These gold flecks are very characteristic and I'll bet the gold is real.'

'I suppose he might have found it,' Jones said. 'A waistcoat button is an easy thing to lose.'

'Especially after one of Daniel Stagg's steak pies.'

'There's somethin' else. Why I stopped you, sir. Rarx's pawnbroker's ain't far from Hemlock Court. I wondered — with Peely lodgin' hereabouts — whether 'e mighta pawned somethin'. 'E'd be in need of ready money if 'e ain't bin to Fikey's…'

'Sound thought, Stemp. So Rarx it will be. Coming?' Jones turned to Dickens, who looked slightly anxious, he thought. 'Know Rarx, do you? Fenced the family silver?'

Dickens laughed. 'No, I haven't. I know of Rarx,' he temporised, not wanting to admit to Sam that the man had shot at him with a blunderbuss and that he had escaped with a thief. He wasn't sure that the Robin Hood argument would carry weight with Sam. Rarx wouldn't recognise him, surely. 'Yes, I'll come.'

Rarx's shop was on the corner of a little court next door to a gin shop, a low, dirty-looking dusty shop with a piece of glass in the door, displaying three red balls on a blue ground on which some faded letters could be made out. It seemed that Mr Rarx advanced money on plate and jewels, though who had plate or jewels to pawn in this benighted wilderness, Dickens could not imagine, except for those who had stolen goods to offer.

There were no plate or jewels of any value in the window. In their place lay a few old china cups, several sets of chessmen, some battered silver watches, most with no hands or just one, two or three flutes, a prayer book — Dickens could quite understand that a man living hereabouts might abandon his prayers and take to gin — some mouldy looking pictures, blankets, sheets, hats, bonnets from what looked like the Napoleonic era, and a set of carpenter's tools — no doubt pledged by the widow and never redeemed — or the carpenter had resorted in despair to the gin shop.

There were certainly no gold watches such as the one Magpie had shown Dickens. He saw then that there was a side entrance, no doubt for those of the more respectable kind who did not want to be seen. Perhaps it was through the side door that gold watches were taken and through which the likes of Peely took their stolen goods.

Dickens looked up to the window above Rarx's shop, remembering the bottle smashed at his feet and the blunderbuss, and Magpie who lived somewhere in the alleys around, but Dickens could not have told where. The madcap dash from Rarx had been so confusing that he had no idea in which direction he had been whirled. He remembered that the gunshot had blown his hat off. Had he looked up? Had Rarx seen his face? Hardly. The narrow street had been lit only by a gas lamp.

A hideous cracked bell sounding like the cry of a raven heralded their entrance to the pawn shop where an ancient crone with hooded eyes and a nose the shape of a beak was looking over something gold. She looked like a vulture inspecting his dinner. She did not look up — her principle being that the longer the importunate customer waited, the more desperate he or she became. However, she started at the sound of Jones's voice.

'Mr Rarx, if you please,' barked Jones.

'Oh, Mr Jones, what a start yer gave me. What can I do for yer honour?' She smiled ingratiatingly, her loose mouth opening like a money bag to reveal a glint of gold teeth.

'I beg your pardon, Mrs Rarx —' Jones could be ingratiating where necessary — 'I should like to see Josiah — matter of business. Police business.'

Mrs Rarx continued to smile and rang a tarnished brass bell, which stood on the counter. She looked at Stemp, who was standing by the door. Dickens kept discreetly in the shadows. 'Close the door, dearie, will yer, an' turn the sign ter closed.'

Stemp obeyed. Mrs Rarx rang the bell vigorously again and they heard footsteps. A heavy curtain opened behind Mrs Rarx to reveal Josiah Rarx, whose hooded eyes proclaimed him as Mrs Rarx's son, having the same look of a carrion bird. Dickens expected him to caw. '*Rarx!*' he would cry. Perhaps it was he who had given the raven's cry, not the bell at all. He made no sound now.

'Stolen goods,' Jones said.

Rarx nodded and indicated a door to the side through which Dickens and Jones followed to find themselves in a narrow corridor from which various closed doors could be seen. No doubt the rooms in which private business was transacted by those who wanted — or needed — discretion.

Rarx opened one of the doors and Jones stepped in. Dickens remained at the door. Rarx's eyes had passed over him without interest, but it was better to remain in the shadows.

'Robert Peel, otherwise known as Peely, and his son, Micky — I have reason to believe that they may have brought stolen items here — a chain, watches, silver —' Jones had no idea what he was looking for or indeed if anything had been stolen, but Rarx was not to know that.

Something in his tone seemed to convince Rarx, who took some keys from his pocket and opened a drawer beneath the counter on which he placed a necklace and a ring.

'Lad brought these. Said Peely found 'em.'

'So, he did — on a corpse.' Not quite true, but it gave Jones the right to recover the property.

Rarx made no sign. He merely croaked, 'Take 'em.'

The raven is hoarse, thought Dickens.

Jones scooped up the jewels and they went out by the side door.

'Doesn't say much, does he?' observed Dickens.

'No, but there's depths. He's quite capable of knocking a man down or shooting at him. Peely may well pay for this. Rarx has no feelings except for his money. He not only looks like a vulture, he is one. Rich as Croesus, they say, and doesn't spend a penny. Same with that old witch, the mother.'

Dickens felt better about Magpie — Rarx deserved to lose some of his stock if Magpie were prepared to risk the blunderbuss. Dangerous, though, but then Magpie was clearly a man who enjoyed risk.

Stemp joined them and under the gas lamp they looked at the jewellery. The ring was gold with a little ruby set in it — a woman's ring. The necklace was made up of gold and red glass beads linked by a golden chain which was broken.

'It looks like a rosary,' Dickens said, looking at the jewelled chain glinting in Jones's hand. 'There's a cross on the end of it.' The cross was gold in colour, but tarnished.

'So there is. I wonder, was our victim Catholic?'

Dickens took it and looked more closely. 'Murano glass beads — like the waistcoat button. From Venice.'

'Well, my next stop is St John's Wood — I need to see the Reverend Anguish. He might recognise these and the button. Do you want to come?'

'Imagine the anguish of my soul if I do not — to miss the chance of seeing the man with that name!'

10: Anguish

Inside the cab which took them to St. John's Wood, Jones regarded an unusually silent Dickens.

'You're very quiet.'

'Could a person be strangled by a chain with those beads?'

'Possibly, but strangling doesn't break the bones. That would be caused by someone exerting force, say with an arm under the chin and a twisting of the neck as it happens in hanging — the weight of the body after the drop can lead to —'

'No more, Sam — hanging's a hideous business.'

'So, it is, but in the case of Flora Lambert, I suppose her neck being especially fragile might have been broken by the pressure of the chain. What's on your mind?'

'I was thinking of something I saw once when I was in Venice — something I thought I saw. I was never sure if it was real…'

'Venice does seem to keep cropping up — the glass beads, the button. What else?'

Dickens told him about what he had seen all those years ago and how a girl had been found drowned, thought to have been strangled by her own rosary.

'Good Lord, Charles, the things that happen to you.'

'I know — extraordinary, ain't it? I came home with a head full of dead lovers and ghosts. I thought it would make a good story, but somehow I never got round to it.'

'It wasn't murder, then?'

'I don't know — Venice was like a dream, especially in the darkness, all flickering lights and sudden gleams of water and so quiet it was eerie at times. Afterwards, seeing the boarded-up palace, I did think I'd imagined it, but then I read about the drowned girl and I wondered, but now I think about a chain wrapped round a slender neck and pulled tight.'

'I suppose it could happen — the strangling I mean, though it would be unusual. Rope, cord, handkerchiefs, stocks, even apron strings and stay laces — I've heard of all those as means of strangulation. The number of cases where some folk try to strangle themselves, and in the cells, too. It happened last year. A woman called Catherine Larry tried it with her shawl — horrible business.'

'Such desperation. Lor', Sam, it's the last thing I'd want to do.' It was a horror, Dickens thought. That sensation of choking, he knew himself at times of stress — sometimes he woke at night with what he described as a seizure of the throat. A terrifying sensation as if you couldn't breathe. 'Greenacre tried that, didn't he?'

James Greenacre, the Edgeware Road murderer, had tried to strangle himself in his cell after he had been found guilty of the murder of his betrothed. The hangman had finished the job. Grim thought.

'He did.' Jones was silent for a while. 'Now I think of it, there was a case when I was a constable — years ago — a prosperous lawyer strangled his wife with his gold Geneva watch chain. She was unfaithful, as I remember.'

'But, Venice, Sam — my missing tutor's father came from Venice according to St George Pierce — the man who told me the history and there's the rosary —'

'A bit of a leap, ain't it? I'm not sure how your missing musician can be connected to a death that occurred years ago.'

Dickens grinned at him. 'Yer niver knows, Samivel. Veels within veels.'

To which gnomic utterance, Samivel merely murmured, 'Mr Weller,' in reference to Mr Tony Weller, the original Sam Weller's coachman parent.

The wheels of their cab slowed and the cab stopped and they were deposited in St John's Wood Road. Hamilton terrace was just over the road. As they crossed, Jones started at the sound of a very loud harsh cry of a bird.

'Heavens, what on earth's that?'

'Rarx followed us? No, it's Landseer's menagerie.' The painter Edwin Landseer lived at number one St John's Wood Road. 'You'd be amazed at what he keeps in his garden. The painter, McIan, gave me an eagle once. I sent it to board with Landseer when I went to Italy and er — forgot — to get it back. I never liked the way it looked at me — or the children — measuring us for his dinner with a hungry eye.'

'I hope that's not it in the trees — looking to get its own back on you.'

Dickens laughed. 'No, he keeps it chained to its perch.'

'Poor thing,' said Jones, imagining the great bird crying for its freedom.

'He had a lion once.'

'Dear Lord, these artists.'

'It was dead — sent from the zoo. He wanted to paint it. Even Landseer shrank at the idea of a live one. I wonder if he knows anything about Agosto Sabatini, the music tutor's father. Dead now, but he was an artist and quite successful, it seems, as a portraitist.'

'You can ask, but in the meantime, here we are at the Reverend Anguish's house.'

Number five Hamilton Terrace was part of a terrace of tall, narrow house built in the 1830s — a gentleman's residence with an elegant white-pillared portico with steps up which Jones went to ring the bell.

An elderly maid of somewhat lugubrious visage answered the door. She looked worried when Jones announced that he was a policeman. Dickens saw that she wondered whether they should be let in or sent down the area steps. However, when Jones asked to see the Reverend Anguish, she said she would fetch the mistress, and they could wait in the hall. She went upstairs slowly.

After a few minutes, a tall, well-built woman with rather formidable shoulders appeared at the top of the stairs, dressed in severe black, relieved only by a white cap covering grey hair rolled in little curls like tight sausages. She regarded them with irritation.

'Not a word,' whispered Jones to Dickens.

The woman came slowly down. She looked at Jones with cold grey eyes, her steel brows knitted in a line across a broad forehead. His assistant was beneath her notice. 'I am Miss Anguish. My brother is very ill at the moment and cannot be disturbed. You may state your business, though what my brother can have to do with the police, I do not know.'

'I am sorry to disturb you, Miss Anguish. It is a matter of goods stolen from Mrs Wyatt's house in South Crescent.' Jones decided to tread carefully. It would not do to begin by mentioning the skeleton found in the water tank. He might not mention it at all in the circumstances.

'You had better come into the drawing room.'

They went into a room which ran the length of the house to the back where the windows looked out over some desolate looking trees. There was a piano in that part of the room and in the part in which they stood there were sofas and chairs and a fire burning. Dickens noticed a Bible on the chair by the fire.

A comfortable room, not luxurious, but homely, even a little shabby.

Miss Anguish motioned Jones to sit. Dickens remained near the door by a little table upon which he saw a desk portrait of a young woman — Flora Lambert? He looked at the face — a pale, rather long oval face with grey eyes and a thin mouth. Not exactly plain, but not exactly pretty, an ordinary face, though young, and rather touching for that. More so, he thought, if there were Flora Lambert's bones in that disused cistern.

'I wonder if you recognise these?' Jones was saying, as he took from his pocket the ring, the button and the rosary which Miss Anguish took in her large capable hands and examined through a pair of spectacles which she took up from a table. She frowned over the rosary beads.

'I have not seen these — er — beads before, or the button. But I know this ring. It was stolen you say?'

'Yes, a labourer working at Mrs Wyatt's former home is suspected of stealing these items which were recovered from a pawnbroker's. To whom does the ring belong?'

'It was Miss Lambert's, Flora's. She was companion to Mrs Wyatt. My brother gave the ring to Miss Lambert for her eighteenth birthday. I am surprised that she should leave it behind. She always wore it.'

'And the beads are not hers?'

'I hardly think so. My brother is a reverend gentleman of the Church of England.' Miss Anguish sounded most offended.

'Where is Miss Lambert now?'

'She is dead, Superintendent. She died of tuberculosis in a sanatorium not long after Mrs Wyatt, my sister-in-law — in 1845.'

So, not the body in the water tank, thought Jones, and yet the year was possibly the same and the swollen bone had suggested tuberculosis to Doctor Symonds — a curious coincidence? But how to proceed? He needed to know more.

'Did Miss Lambert leave South Crescent before Mrs Wyatt's death?'

Miss Anguish looked at Jones impatiently, 'No, it was a week or so after. Why do you wish to know? It looks as if she left the ring behind. It was stolen. Now you have recovered it. What else is there for you to know?'

Jones took the plunge. 'The skeleton of a young woman was found in the empty water tank at South Crescent and we believe that the labourer took the jewellery from that. There is a little finger missing from the left hand.'

'Miss Lambert possessed all her fingers — if not much else. It is impossible that it should be Flora Lambert. The doctor at the sanatorium sent a letter informing us of Miss Lambert's death.'

'Did you or your brother attend the funeral?'

'No, we did not.'

'Why was that?'

'Really, Superintendent Jones, I do not see what business it is of yours. Flora Lambert died very suddenly. My brother has not enjoyed good health for some time — he had a stroke just before the death of Mrs Wyatt and so when the news of Miss Lambert's death came, I was too much occupied with those things. The doctor wrote that he would see to the funeral and the burial. There was nothing I could do for Miss Lambert.'

Miss Anguish's lips closed in a firm line. Dickens wondered if she had not liked Flora Lambert. "Not much else" was rather reproving. Her tone had been very brisk and it was clear that she did not want to say more. Would Sam dare?

Sam Jones dared. He changed tack. 'Forgive me, Miss Anguish, but I must ask a few more questions. The discovery of the skeleton raises suspicions of foul play. There is evidence to suggest that which I may not divulge. You are the only person at the moment who can tell me anything about the household at South Crescent.'

'Very well.'

'I need to know if there was any female servant between the ages of sixteen and say twenty-two years who was employed at South Crescent.'

'Mrs Wyatt employed a cook and a personal maid. The cook, Mrs Peartree, had been with her for many years and was certainly older. She was left a sum of money by Mrs Wyatt and retired to a house in Camden where she set up home with Miss Peach, Mrs Wyatt's maid, again much beyond twenty-two years. They keep a lodging house — most respectable, I do not doubt.'

'There would be a laundress, I suppose, and, perhaps, servants from time to time who came South Crescent to do heavy work?'

'That is so, but I cannot tell you anything about them. Miss Lambert would have known. She ordered the household for Mrs Wyatt.'

Jones slipped in another question. 'What was her relationship to Mrs Wyatt?'

'Flora was an orphan, the daughter of a cousin of Mr Wyatt. He died many years ago, but Mrs Wyatt corresponded with members of his family. They were a poor lot, but Mrs Wyatt pitied the girl and took her in. She was sixteen at the time. She was useful, though hardly grateful for her good fortune. Mrs Wyatt was kind to her and my brother was fond of her pretty ways. Those she showed only to him. He is too good a man to suspect artfulness.'

Now, thought Dickens, noting the bitterness in her tone, here's the nub of it. Miss Anguish did not like Flora Lambert — indeed, it seemed that she did not trust her. She was ready to talk now — it was always the way. Even after five years, there was a spark of resentment which sprang into a blaze as if Jones had poked a slumbering fire.

'She was dissatisfied?' Jones asked.

'She was. I think she hoped for more than keeping house for an elderly lady, though she was as poor as a church mouse and would have had to earn her living somehow. She was not educated to be a governess, too gently born to be a mere servant. My brother and Mrs Wyatt intended to provide for her in the event of Mrs Wyatt's death. She might have married respectably then.'

Jones noted the word "Then". Did that imply that Flora Lambert was intending to marry without respectability? Or something else? Now that Miss Anguish's tongue had been loosened, he risked another question.

'Did Miss Lambert wish to marry someone not quite respectable?'

Miss Anguish looked very sour at that question. 'There was a young man — an artist of some kind, I believe, and foreign, so Temperance Peach thought. Flora had tried to persuade my brother that he should commission a painting — nonsense, I thought. My brother was hardly fit to have his portrait done. Miss Peach told me that he had been in the house — at night, drinking wine.' Her face took on a reddish tint. 'A lover — in the house. But Miss Peach and cook did not tell Mrs Wyatt. She was not strong enough to deal with that kind of thing.'

'They told you.'

'Naturally, it was their duty to do so — wine, forsooth. They had Mrs Wyatt to think of. It was my duty to speak to Miss Lambert. She denied it, of course, but I warned her that she was not to encourage any young men. Her duty was to care for Mrs Wyatt. I knew then that Mrs Wyatt would not live long. It seemed to me that Miss Lambert could wait.'

Duty, thought Dickens, unbending duty, which made no room for the promptings of a girl's heart. Pity Flora Lambert, poor as a church mouse, and spied on by the two servants.

'You did not know the name of the artist?'

'I have no idea. Whoever he was, he was patently unsuitable.'

Dickens longed to ask if the artist were Italian, but Sam had told him to keep quiet. He had seen that Charles Dickens might well be a further irritant to Miss Anguish.

'Would Miss Lambert have come to live here after Mrs Wyatt's death? She would have needed care as she was ill.'

'That was the arrangement — it was hardly suitable. I certainly do not need a companion. I really could not see how I was to look after a sick woman as well as my brother. I told my brother that she should go back to her relatives, but, of course, he is too kind. She was to come and I should have to bear it.'

'How ill was she?'

'She began to be ill about six months before Mrs Wyatt died. She had pain in her joints and in her left hand. Her doctor thought she was suffering from arthritis, but the physician from the sanatorium, Doctor Lucas, wrote in his letter that she had tuberculosis, though there had been none of the usual signs.'

'How was it that she went to the sanatorium?'

'I saw her after Mrs Wyatt's death. It was her duty to supervise the closing of the house, but she told me that she felt so unwell that arrangements had been made for her to go to a hydropathic clinic — Manor Park, in Malvern. I assumed that Doctor Adam sent her — he was her doctor here in London.'

'You didn't speak to Doctor Adam?'

'I had enough to do to settle Mrs Wyatt's affairs, and I was not well myself. I suffer, too, from pain in my joints — but I must bear it. That is my lot. Fortunately, I was able to rely on Mrs Peartree and Miss Peach to tidy up the house, and Mrs Wyatt's solicitor sorted out the papers and the will.'

'Did Miss Lambert benefit from Mrs Wyatt's will?'

'She was left an annuity which reverted to the estate on her death, and Mrs Wyatt left her three hundred pounds to be paid as a lump sum, but then the letter came from the hospital in Malvern. Rest and water treatments had been prescribed, but the disease was more advanced than had been realised. Every care had been given, the doctor said.' She rose from her seat. It was clear that they would learn nothing more. 'Now, Superintendent, I must get back to my brother. I have much to do and I have to say that, though I am grateful for the return of the ring, I fail to see what more assistance I can give you over the matter of a skeleton in a water tank.'

11: An Invitation

Number one Devonshire Terrace was a matter of a few minutes' walk down by Regent's Park and to Dickens's house they went after Miss Anguish's door closed smartly upon them.

'Let us think while we walk,' said Jones. 'This is a jigsaw in which there are missing pieces, but I wish to ponder the incomplete picture before we talk about it.'

Cups of tea and slices of cake came on a tray to Dickens's study. Jones ate his slowly, noting with amusement that Dickens wolfed his down and was, as always, eager to give his impressions.

'Excellent cake,' Jones observed, brushing the crumbs from his jacket.

'I should not have given you any had I known how long you would be about it. Thinking, were you?'

'I was. About tuberculosis of the bone and the coincidence of a skeleton with signs of that disease and a young woman suffering from the same disease — as I think it must have been, from the symptoms Doctor Symonds described — who dies suddenly at a sanatorium in Malvern —'

'Whose death is reported by letter and whose funeral is not attended by any relative.'

'As far as we know. I think my first call tomorrow must be on Miss Lambert's Doctor Adam to find out if he recommended her stay at Malvern.'

'If she were there at all. It all sounds a bit odd to me, and there were other things: her lover, an artist, a portrait painter and foreign, foreign, Sam.'

'Thought to be, Charles, by Miss Temperance Peach whom I must see.'

'Miss Fane was having her portrait painted by an unknown artist. Suppose — I merely suggest — bashfully, humbly, meekly —'

'I know what you suggest and suppose, and I can see how you suppose it, but for the moment, it is just supposition — and very thin, I may say, equally meekly and humbly, of course —'

'The very image of humility, Samivel, but do go on. I shall hear you with all meekness.'

Jones grinned. 'Until you can find out more from the Fane household, or from Mrs Sabatini who may or may not be in touch with you, I must follow the clear set of footprints which lead me to Doctor Adam and Miss Peach.'

'Miss Anguish has broad shoulders and large hands and —'

'Changed your mind, have you?'

'She didn't like Miss Lambert. She could be suspect.'

'Everyone's a suspect —'

'Even my Italian artist.'

'Very clever. If he exists and if he is Italian, or foreign, or anything at all. When you find him, you can bring him to me bound in chains. Will that do?'

'Five bob on it?'

'It would be a cruelty to do so.'

'Faith, Samivel, where's your faith in the Inimitable? Have we not stood shoulder to shoulder looking into the canon's mouth?'

'As to shoulders, no doubt Miss Anguish had the strength to do it, but dislike is not necessarily a motive for murder, and I should think she's a God-fearing woman.'

'Yes, I noted the Bible — repentance, perhaps?'

Jones laughed, 'Give over. We'll keep her in mind. Now, I must go. However, as you are so interested in artists, Italian, or otherwise, you might like to come with me to see Mrs Peartree and Miss Peach. If they're anything like as grim as Miss Anguish, your youthful charm might be needed to smooth my path.'

'Ah, them woz the days, old 'un, when I woz a brisk young blade, whose gradual decay, I observe with increasing melancholy.'

'You'll be a mere sprig to them. Come to Bow Street at eleven. I shall have seen Doctor Adam by then.'

Dickens sat in his library after Jones had gone. The fire burnt low and a chill crept into the room. He shivered, but made no move to stir the coals. He was thinking of Venice and a monk's cowl and a bone-white face. After all these years, it came back so vividly. That dead girl dragged from the canal with a rosary round her white neck. And a girl dead in a water tank where a rosary had been found and her neck broken.

Of course, it was impossible. Jones was right to be sceptical. He hadn't time to be chasing ghosts. Yet Dickens felt as though something vibrated in the air, that the events in which he was entangled were somehow connected. Some intuition, he thought, a feeling like that of one of Macbeth's witches: a pricking of the thumbs.

There was a knock at the door. *Something wicked this way comes.* He laughed to himself as it was only John, his manservant, whose anxious face peered round the door.

'Shall I make up the fire, sir? It's cold in here, and I've brought the letters.'

'No, John, thank you, I will do it.'

Dickens put on more coals and stirred up a warming blaze and looked at his letters. Well, here was a turn-up. A letter from Mrs Carlyle.

My dear Mr Dickens,

I have been avisiting and taking comforts to the ailing, and have seen Mrs Pick to whom I took some cranberry jelly — my own, I boast to say. Scottish cranberries, too. My excuse was that I had heard that Lady Fane was unwell and thought the jelly might do her some good.

It is astonishing what a forthright, eccentric old creature like me can accomplish. Mrs Pick was too surprised to do more than take the jelly, and, of course, too polite to wonder about my enquiries, on behalf of Fanny, about Jemima Curd. It was clearly news to Mrs Pick that Fanny and Jemima were such friends, but I assured her on that point. She did seem rather flustered about the matter. And, oddly, Mrs Pick said that she did not expect Jemima Curd to return. As far as she knew, Jemima Curd was with her family. That is a matter upon which you may speculate, I daresay.

Now, to a more significant matter: my justifiable pride in the ease with which I had scaled the walls of the fortress led me to enquire if I might see Lady Fane. Mrs Pick went to ask and I was ushered into the presence. In the drawing room by a very cheerful fire, I babbled about cranberry jelly, extolled the virtues of the wine of Constantia, produced a little bottle — what Thomas will say, I know not — advised a small restorative glass with a home-made biscuit and produced — not my own — a little packet of oatcakes sent from Scotland — and hoped that Lady Fane would soon feel better.

Lady Fane was quite bowled over — she would be, thought Dickens — *she confessed to feeling delicate and complained of breathlessness and headaches. I confided my own torment with the migraine, we exchanged various possible solutions, and ended firm friends, becoming quite confidential. Lady Fane became quite pale and fluttery again when I enquired about Miss Fane's health — as was natural in the circumstances — and I think I am right in sensing alarm — and fear. There is some secret in that house, I am certain. However, I changed the subject and I did not refer to Miss Pout or the tutor, not wanting to seem merely nosy.*

However, the end of this thrilling tale is that Mr Carlyle and I are invited to a reception at Wisteria Lodge tomorrow night. I trust that you may wish to escort me. I am, as you well know, such a retiring old soul that I could scarce go alone, and what a pleasant coincidence it will be that my gallant friend, Mr Dickens, is visiting Mr Carlyle who is too indisposed to attend. Naturally, I must hope that Lady Fane is not put out by the appearance of Mr Dickens. Sir Neptune's feelings he will no doubt keep to himself, and we may pursue our discreet enquiries…

Dickens laughed to himself at the word "our". Clearly Mrs Carlyle had taken to her investigations with zest. He wrote back immediately, expressing his regret that Mr Carlyle should be so indisposed as to miss the engagement and averring that nothing would give him greater pleasure than to accompany Mrs Carlyle to the reception.

And then he thought for a while longer. Jane Carlyle had written of Lady Fane's "alarm and fear", and had sensed that she should change the subject. Had Mariana Fane loved Rolando Sabatini and had he betrayed her by running away with Violet Pout? Sir Neptune would be furious if his daughter had been hurt. That might well account for the couple's disappearance. Was Lady Fane afraid of what Sir Neptune might do? But they would not want a scandal. Better that it should be hushed up and Miss Fane sent to the country. Perhaps he would find out more tomorrow night, or Jane Carlyle would. There might be gossip. Jane had sharp ears.

And he thought of Jemima Curd. It was odd that Jemima Curd had not returned to see Mrs Pick about a possible position — she would surely be in need of employment, but then her family might have needed her more if she had found them.

12: Sour Grapes

'Doctor Adam wasn't much help. He remembered Miss Lambert only vaguely. He consulted his records, told me he had prescribed laudanum for her aches and pains, and thought he may have suggested that she might try hydrotherapy at the sanatorium in Malvern. It was what he usually suggested. He heard about Mrs Wyatt's death and had assumed that Miss Lambert had moved away. He thought no more about her.'

Dickens raised his eyebrows. 'And that was it?'

'It was,' Jones said. 'I asked him if he had heard anything about her death from Miss Anguish or her brother and he said not. I've written to the Malvern sanatorium enquiring after Doctor Lucas and his patient, Miss Flora Lambert. In the meantime we'll go up to Camden to see what our ladies know. Rogers got the address from Mr Faithfull, the house agent — Little College Street.'

'I know it.'

'I want to know about that cistern and when they stopped using it, and if there were any other young women employed at South Crescent. I know there's the ring, but it could have been stolen from Miss Lambert.'

'And Miss Anguish did not recognise the beads. I suppose they could have belonged to someone else, but how did they come to be in that water tank?'

'No idea, but let's see what we can find out about Miss Lambert's young man.'

The cab took them up the Hampstead Road towards Camden. Dickens knew it all. Here where the railway bisected the road by Granby Road had been his old school, Wellington Academy, and beyond, across a few streets with their shabby terraces, gloomy little shops and lodging houses, was Bayham Street where he had lived when John Dickens had brought his family to London.

Then there was Johnson Street, the house his father had rented after his release from the Marshalsea debtors' prison, a narrow street of red brick houses, very dark at night for there was no gas light then in 1824, and from there he had walked to the blacking factory which had moved from Hungerford Stairs to Chandos Street off Covent Garden.

He knew Little College Street, too. It hadn't changed much, he thought, since the days when his family had lodged with Mrs Roylance at number twenty-seven — the same smoky, muddy, dingy street. What a nomadic life they had led. It was odd, he thought now, how this case seemed to be taking him over old ground. He had, in one sense, not moved very far. Devonshire Terrace was not so far away. But where was home? Not here, certainly, in this dreary terrace of houses.

They stood outside the house at the end, larger than the others. It was neat, true, and the steps were swept and the curtains clean, but he knew that inside it would be like Mrs Roylance's, likely to be dark, cramped and gloomy, and smelling of cabbage as if the ghosts of every cabbage that had ever boiled there wafted about the rooms in search of spectral diners.

Jones was about to knock on a peculiarly long-faced miserable knocker when the door opened and a girl stood before them, a maidservant, they assumed, with a long, narrow face not unlike the door knocker, though without the shine. She looked about fifteen, but she was neatly dressed, and clean, apart from a black smudge above her mouth like a moustache. She carried a hearth broom, wielded like a weapon.

'Single ladies only, 'ere, sir. We don't takes gentlemen. There's a lady — which she ain't — Miss Wozenham — at the end. Takes single gentlemen — which they ain't — if yer don't minds the damp and cares for gravy. Gentlemen sits up too late an' they drinks spirits an' smokes an' knocks at doors where they ain't wanted.' She glared at them as she recited this catechism, 'An' no dogs neither.'

Dickens glanced round to see if some slavering hound had pursued them and was panting to be admitted as a board lodger, but there was only a one-eared, peevish-looking cat which made for the door. The girl shook her broom at it. 'You ain't welcome, neither.' The cat fled. It must have been male, thought Dickens, or a lady back from some disgraceful liaison.

'I should like to see Mrs Peartree, if you would tell her that Superintendent Jones of Bow Street is here.'

The girl's eyes opened very wide. She gazed at Jones as if he were a being from another planet. Clearly this was not a house where policemen made morning calls.

'Mrs Peartree, if you please.'

She turned back into the house and a door opened. They heard a sharp voice. 'Make sure they wipe their feet.'

Dickens obediently used the boot scraper and Jones was placing his foot on that useful object when the girl came back to announce that Mrs Peartree and Miss Peach would see Superintendent Jones. She waited while Jones scraped both boots. Then they were shown into a parlour, a neat carpeted room with a large black horsehair sofa resembling some gloomy catafalque. A coffin would have fitted on it very neatly. Two upright chairs were placed at each end of a square table behind which the two women stood like a pair of undertaker's mutes. There was no smell of cabbage — just of carbolic, cleanliness, and godliness of the kind shrivelling to the soul.

Fruit did come into Dickens's mind as he looked at the two women who were waiting — but neither pears nor peaches. The bloom was long gone on the peach. Two pairs of sharp eyes like pale gooseberries or sour grapes stared at them. Keep your eyes peeled. They looked as though they did.

They must be sisters, Dickens thought, though Miss Anguish had not said so. They were both tall with large, flat faces, wore black dresses shaped around them like grave clothes, and looked as melancholy as Hamlet's aunts — if he had had such relations. He wondered if Mrs Peartree had been married. Cooks were often given the courtesy title of Mrs. He failed to imagine a Mr Peartree in this angular room. Men were not admitted, so the gaunt maid had said.

The taller woman announced herself as Miss Temperance Peach. Mrs Patience Peartree was the younger. Miss Peach nodded grimly as she rolled down her sleeves over two brawny arms — they could have hefted a ton of coal, never mind poor little Miss Lambert.

Jones wasted no time. He explained that he was investigating human bones found in the cistern at South Crescent. He wanted to know when the cistern had last been used.

'We had an indoor cistern installed well before Mrs Wyatt's death. The old cistern wasn't clean. The laundry — well, I can't tell you what it was like sometimes. It must be —'

Mrs Peartree finished her sister's sentence. 'Seven years ago, at least, Temperance. You remember what a muddle we were in — workmen an' their dirty boots an' whistlin' like a flock of birds. But, I suppose —' her gooseberry eyes looked sharp again — 'Bones, you say — in our old cistern?' She sounded affronted.

Miss Peach looked similarly outraged. 'Human bones! Someone put a body in there. We might all have been poisoned, but it can't have been when we were there. Think of the smell, Patience, we'd have noticed, surely. The wickedness of it.'

'Were there any other servants employed — any young women, for example?' Jones asked. 'The bones we found belong to a young woman between sixteen years and twenty-two.'

'Sometimes we'd have a charwoman — we had Mrs Fudge when the cistern was put in the kitchen, but she wasn't young — strong, though — a bit coarse, for our liking,' Miss Peach answered.

Mrs Peartree agreed with that, and continued, 'Her daughter, Polly — now she was a young thing. Strong, mind, and willin' about shiftin' the heavy things.'

'She married, though, and now I think of it, she went off to Australia. Mrs Fudge couldn't —'

They were never to know what Mrs Fudge couldn't for Jones interrupted, 'Any other young women you can think of?'

'Only Miss Lambert, Mrs Wyatt's companion — or was supposed to be,' Mrs Peartree replied.

'She died in a sanatorium in Malvern or somewhere,' added Miss Peach.

'Miss Anguish told us that. Miss Lambert's doctor, however, told me that he did not actually send her there. Can you remember the circumstances of her going?' Jones asked.

Mrs Peartree answered, 'She wasn't well — all kinds of aches and pains. After Mrs Wyatt died, she upped and went — left us to do all the work. Said she'd to go to a clinic or some such place. Miss Anguish wasn't pleased. She thought Miss Lambert should wait until the house was closed up. Oh, but no, she had to go at once.'

'Did someone take her to Malvern?'

'You're thinking about the young man, I daresay.' Miss Peach's peeled eyes glittered.

'Miss Anguish told me that there was some acquaintance — a foreign gentleman, she said. What can you tell me about him?'

'Supposed to be an artist. Italian, she said. I wouldn't care to say what he was. Not a person you'd want to know. Very quiet — up to no good, that's what I think.' Dickens glanced at Sam, but his face was studiedly neutral.

Miss Temperance Peach was in full flow, 'She went too far, did Miss Lambert. He was in the house — at night. Drinkin' wine in the drawing room, the pair of them. Givin' orders, indeed, for dinner. It's one thing giving orders, and quite another to take 'em. A person might order a dinner — t'ain't for certain she'll get it —' Miss Peach had the Danish family's failing — a tendency to soliloquise.

'Nor wine, neither,' Mrs Peartree supplied her tuppenceworth — well, half-pennyworth.

'We don't hold with strong drink —' Miss Peach sniffed and Dickens thought about the brandy and warm he had rashly taken at lunch. He almost stepped back, but Miss Peach had more to relate — 'an' Mrs Wyatt dyin' in her bed. Well, Miss Anguish told her a thing or two about that an' he didn't come again an' I checked the spoons an' Mrs Wyatt's jewellery box.'

At the mention of jewels, Jones drew out the rope of beads from his pocket. 'Do you recognise this?'

Miss Peach stared at it as if he had a live snake in his hand. 'No, I do not — nasty heathen thing, it looks to me. Catholic, is it? That Italian's?'

Jones put it back in his pocket and showed them the waistcoat button, but they shook their large heads. 'Do you know if Miss Lambert continued to see him?'

'Don't know what she did in her time off, but we know what she didn't do an' that was her job — poor Mrs Wyatt. If we hadn't been there, the Lord knows what the old soul would have done. Still, it was peaceful at the end, God rest her.'

'What was his name?'

'Tony, she called him, Tony, forsooth. Mr Tony is an artist, she said, as if he were royalty — such a song and dance about a beggarly foreigner.'

'Only Tony, no other name?'

'I don't remember. Patience?'

'No more do I.'

'So this Mr Tony did not come to take her to Malvern?' Jones persisted.

'No, she went off with her box in a cab, and then we shut up the house and moved here,' said Mrs Peartree. 'Mrs Wyatt left us well provided for, the dear good woman. We take only respectable folk here — single ladies only, no men, thank you very much — not of any kind.' She gave Dickens a look which suggested that if he thought to ask for sanctuary here, he would be given very short shrift. He wondered what kind he was.

Jones asked for the address of Mrs Fudge. Though indignant and complaining about all the prying and poking into respectable folks' business, Miss Peach complied.

With that, Dickens and Jones departed, escorted to the front door by Miss Peach as if she were their gaoler. As they crossed the street, Dickens glanced back to see Miss Peach supervising the girl in the sweeping of the steps. Ridding the premises of the contamination of their unworthy masculine selves, no doubt. He chuckled.

'Antonio,' he said, 'I'll wager Antonio. Five bob, eh, old 'un? Want to raise the stakes?'

Jones laughed. 'No, I do not. I'll admit you may be right. However, it's not much help without another name.'

'Ah, but I can ask amongst my artistic friends. Someone will know him. We know he's an artist —'

'Or, said he was. Still, you can ask and I'll be grateful for that even if it costs me five bob.'

'What now?'

'Bow Street. I should like to see if there is any news from that place in Malvern.'

A letter was waiting from the Manor Park Sanatorium. Jones opened it in his office while Dickens looked on, holding his breath.

Jones put down the letter.

'Well?' Dickens asked.

'There was no patient by the name of Flora Lambert, and there was no Doctor Lucas, not now, not ever.'

'It is she, then. Must be.'

'Flora Lambert left South Crescent in a cab with her box and was never seen again. Now we think that her bones were in that water tank which had not been used for a couple of years. So where did she go in that cab?'

'She went to Signor Tony, I'll bet,' said Dickens. 'She was in a hurry. What a life she must have led with those two black spectres and a possibly querulous old invalid —'

'Not to mention Miss Anguish listening to tales about her.'

'Quite, and I think about the lover, the mysterious Mr Tony — an artist, and probably handsome where she was rather plain. I saw a little desk portrait of her. She wasn't much to look at, and she'd be lonely — four years of servitude — and longing for something — some romance in her life.'

'You think that in her loneliness she might have been duped, seduced by a handsome foreigner?'

'She was no beauty, but she had expectations in the event of Mrs Wyatt's death. Money lends charm to the meagrest form.'

'So why did he kill her if he was interested in her money?' Jones asked.

'You're right, it doesn't make sense. She hadn't even received the legacies when she left so he could hardly expect to make off with her fortune.'

'So Mr Tony didn't kill her. The bones are not those of Miss Lambert and she is living a perfectly happy life with Mr Tony somewhere in —'

'But the money, surely she would have claimed it,' Dickens interrupted. 'No one could deny her whether or not she had eloped with an Italian artist.'

'True, therefore something surely would have been heard of her. And, moreover, our witnesses say that she left — with her box — so who brought her back to South Crescent and why, and was she dead when she was brought back?'

'Mr Tony killed her and, knowing of the tank, hid the body there.'

'That's the best I can think of that the moment,' Jones agreed. 'But what the motive could be, I cannot think.'

'Wot a mystery it is, as my coachman, Topping, is wont to remark. Wot a go is natur', he tells me, before fading out of the room, and leaving me none the wiser — which is where we are now.'

‘I have to say your philosophical coachman is no help at all. But I’ll tell you what — no second name, only Mr Tony. Why is that?’

‘He didn’t want to be identified if — when — did he plan to kill her? That brings us back to motive — lor, Sam, what a coil this is.’

‘We’ll leave motive for now. I’ll send Rogers to interview Mrs Fudge — see if we can find out more about Mr Tony. She may have seen him. Now, what about your missing Miss Pout?’

‘Plunging into the very vortex of society, I am, Mr Weller — a swarry, as the genteel folks say.’

‘And where is this vortex to be?’ Jones asked.

‘Ah, well, I am bidden to accompany Mrs Carlyle to a reception at Wisteria Lodge tomorrow evening.’

‘How d’you manage that?’

‘Mr Carlyle is unwell — indigestion at the thought of gluttons feeding, so Mrs Carlyle, knowing my sympathetic interest in the family, has asked me to escort her. She has hopes that we may hear something to our advantage. She has sharp ears, Mrs Carlyle. I may say that I do not expect Sir Neptune Fane to greet me as a long-lost friend, but curiosity drives me on. You never know, beans may be spilt. However, I must fade from your presence now I think of it for I must dress the part.’

‘And what part may that be?’

‘Humble literary man — and quiet as a cat watching the mousehole, fixing my charmed gaze upon on my victim.’

‘Some cat.’

‘Some mouse.’

13: The Goldfish Bowl

The long room glittered with diamonds and hundreds of branched candles, all these lights doubled in the gilded mirrors; there was the heady perfume of flowers, the sound of laughter and music. Servants flitted about offering champagne in crystal flutes on silver salvers. Sir Neptune, it seemed, or Lady Fane, perhaps, spared no expense for the fashionable crowd assembled here.

Lady Fane greeted Mrs Carlyle, who explained that Mr Dickens was escorting her as Mr Carlyle was indisposed. She hoped it was not a presumption, but she found such occasions a little intimidating, and Mr Dickens had been so good and so gallant to accede to her request. Dickens smiled as if he were merely a cipher, and concealed his amusement. Jane Carlyle intimidated by anything — there were those who found her sharp tongue more than a little cutting when she had a mind to it.

Lady Fane murmured polite nothings, but she did not seem at ease. He noted the same anxious fluttering of her hands that he had seen before. Her eyes darted nervously as she waved them on to join the crowd of fashionable guests.

Jane whispered that she would waft away and talk to her gossips. 'I see Lady Morgan — she knows what's what.'

'You'll not be too intimidated?' Dickens asked mischievously.

She tapped him with her fan, but her eyes were amused and off she went, an elegant figure in her dark red gown.

Dickens looked about him, recognising many of the faces — politicians, mostly of the Conservative persuasion, Sir

Neptune' party. He saw his friend, Lord Lytton, tall and red-haired, stooping over a dark-haired man. Ah, Mr Disraeli. There were Lord Walpole and Lord and Lady Barnet. A rising man, Sir Neptune, expected to take high office if the Conservative party were to win the next election, and given the disarray of the Whigs, that did not seem impossible. For himself, Dickens had liked Peel who had died in July, and it was the Peel faction who supported Lord John Russell's ministry against those in his own party who disliked Russell's educational and religious policies. Prime Minister Russell, he liked, too. He had dined with him on several occasions. Lord John approved the work of the Sanitary Commission which Dickens firmly supported — he was to be part of the deputation going to address Lord John in the New Year. Not, he thought, that the sanitary arrangements of the poor were much considered by Sir Neptune's well-dressed guests.

He saw the aptly named Sir Octavius Pouncey, the Honourable Member for Verbosity, bearing down on him. 'No surrender,' was his frequent cry as if this sceptred isle — another favourite of the patriot — were to be invaded instantly by Pictic hordes or another Armada. Dickens darted away to pay his attentions to Lady Pancras, ancient as the old church, deaf as a marble effigy and, if rumour were true, nothing saintly in her past. He smiled and gestured like a demented puppet to which antics she screamed, 'I am not deaf, Mr Disraeli.' He apologised without enlightening her, kissed her gloved hand, and faded into another group which included Joseph Paxton.

The talk was of the Great Exhibition to be held the next year and the building in Hyde Park. While Paxton answered questions about the design and building of the Crystal Palace, Dickens kept his eye on a gilded mirror in which he could see the reflection of Sir Neptune, who was at the centre of a group of admirers. He saw the Foreign Secretary, Lord Palmerston — a Whig, but always at the best houses, and still flirting at the age of sixty-six. He was talking to a rather beautiful woman with red hair and very pale skin, whose elegant white shoulders emerged from a sea-green dress.

Groups formed and reformed as if by some unseen command — all part of this clockwork household. This reception demonstrated how the curtains had closed on the sordid drama of the governess and the music tutor and had opened on a shining scene. In the mirror he watched the play as if it were a kind of dumb show, seeing the mouths opening and closing, and thought of bright gold and silver fish in shining glass bowls, gasping round and round their little world. The candlelight rippled like water. There a cod fish, eyes staring and face wetly pale; there a set of shark's teeth, and there six pennorth of sprats who might well be gobbled up if they did not take care.

'Mr Dickens.'

He turned and there was the beautiful copper-haired lady in her sea-green dress with aquamarines at her ears and throat and a wreath of green leaves decorating her hair — most striking and unusual. A mermaid, perhaps. He bowed.

'I have wanted to meet you, Mr Dickens, but I had not expected to see you again so soon.'

Dickens was used to people wanting to meet him, but the words "again" and "soon" were a puzzle. He would have remembered her. She was certainly very beautiful. 'I am afraid I do not —'

Her striking green-blue eyes glinted with amusement. 'I saw you at Osnaburgh Terrace.'

'At Mr St. George Pierce's?' Perhaps she had seen him coming out.

'At number seven.'

'You were there.'

'I am afraid I was spying on you.'

So there had been someone at that window. 'You are Mrs Sabatini?'

'No, Mr Dickens, I am Dolly Marchant, Mrs Sabatini's sister.'

'I wanted to talk to her about Mr Rolando Sabatini and Miss Pout — Miss Pout is the god-child of my wife's maid, Miss Anne Brown. Miss Pout's mother is most anxious about her daughter —'

'I will talk to you, but not here, I think. Come to my house — perhaps you would call — the day after tomorrow at seven o'clock. Florence Cottage in Grove Road, St. John's Wood, the first house beyond the Catholic Church.'

'I am much obliged, Mrs Marchant.'

Dolly Marchant turned to go, but her way was obstructed by Sir Neptune, who appeared quite suddenly. Had he been spying on them?

'Mr Dickens, a pleasure, of course, but I had not expected to receive you again so soon. You know Mrs Marchant?'

A curious echo of Mrs Marchant's words — perhaps Sir Neptune had been listening. His brown gaze was as frank as it had been before, but Dickens detected a slight edge to his voice. Now was it for him or for Mrs Marchant?

'I have only just had the honour of meeting Mr Dickens. I did not know you were acquainted with him,' Mrs Marchant said easily enough, but Dickens noted a glint of anger in her eyes, though her lovely mouth smiled.

'Mr Dickens came here to enquire about Miss Pout and Rolando — it seems that one of his — er — servants — is connected to Miss Pout.'

Sir Neptune turned to Dickens who nodded. The emphasis on "servant" made it a trifling matter and suggested a kind of bafflement that Dickens should be concerned with a servant's problem. Sir Neptune did not like him at all. 'Mr Dickens came to enquire on his servant's behalf. I told him that unfortunately we could not help. I gave him your sister's address. Perhaps Mrs Sabatini can assist?'

'Mrs Sabatini is not at home at present.' Dolly Marchant was curt to Sir Neptune, but something flashed between them like a spark of fire on glass. She turned to Dickens. 'I will certainly let you know, Mr Dickens, when she returns.'

'I am much obliged, Mrs Marchant, and to you, Sir Neptune. I thank you for your hospitality.'

Dickens moved away as someone tapped him on the shoulder — Doctor Humphrey Palmer and his wife in puce that matched her complexion exactly. He was glad to see them, though Palmer was an old windbag. However, he could smile and smile at the doctor's discourse while watching. He manoeuvred himself so that he could watch Sir Neptune and Mrs Marchant.

They were walking towards a pair of glass doors which led into a conservatory. He could see lights in there, seeming to reflect off glass. Sir Neptune had his hand on her back. It was a curiously intimate gesture. However, there was tension in her shoulders. She carried herself very straight. They did not speak.

Then they were gone, his view of them obscured by a tall woman in a garishly striped turban with a diamond fixed to a peacock feather. Madame Emerald, whoever she was, took his proffered hand and gazed at it as if she were reading his fortune. She seemed to be. He felt a slight shudder as she turned his hand in hers which felt scaly. She wore a ring in the shape of a snake's head in which two red eyes glinted. A bracelet of the same kind adorned a bony wrist. *Charlatan*, he thought. How on earth did she come here? A fairground entertainment for the guests, he supposed.

'Mr Dickens, you —' She looked at him then and he saw something in her dark eyes which made him wonder. What could she see?

'No future, Mr Dickens,' some wag called out and there was general laughter during which others put forward their hands and Dickens stepped away. What on earth was she going to say? *Some nonsense*, he thought, but there had been something fearful in those black eyes.

He looked towards the glass doors which were now closed. What was happening in there? There was something between Sir Neptune and Dolly Marchant, an odd mixture of hostility and intimacy. And, now he thought of it, Sir Neptune had referred to Rolando not Mr Sabatini as he had when Dickens had asked his questions. There must be some closeness. Yet Mrs Marchant had not referred to her invitation to Dickens to visit her. She had only said that she would contact him about Mrs Sabatini.

He thought about what Mrs Carlyle had said about devoted husbands. As far as he had seen, Sir Neptune had not been near his wife. But, no, there he was, most solicitously bending over Lady Fane who was seated near the glass doors with Mrs Carlyle. Sir Neptune was leading his wife towards another door. They went out and Dickens saw how Lady Fane leant upon her husband. Dolly Marchant was nowhere to be seen.

Mrs Carlyle came to him. 'She is ill. I think we should slip away. I will tell you all when we get home.'

Mrs Carlyle went to retrieve her cloak. The tall footman brought his hat and coat. He waited in the hall.

'Mr Dickens.'

Madame Emerald was beside him. 'Take care, sir. There is darkness coming.'

Before he could reply, Jane came and Madame Emerald went up the stairs.

'An odd creature,' Jane observed.

'You know her?'

'Of her — I have no patience with all these fads. Seances and fortune-telling — all nonsense, though she has her believers. The Queen herself takes an interest, it is said.'

'A crystal ball might be handy at the moment. I could do with seeing the future.'

'Well, cross my palm with silver and I'll tell you what I have learnt this evening.'

At Cheyne walk, Dickens and Mrs Carlyle took a glass of the famous wine of Constantia and a biscuit.

'You first,' said Dickens, raising his glass.

'Lady Fane is in a most fragile state. When I sat with her, I thought she might faint and suggested she might like to go into the conservatory where it might be cooler. She seemed very agitated, but then Sir Neptune came out of the conservatory and took her away. She looked frightened —'

'Of him?'

'I don't know, but something very odd happened. Someone had asked about Miss Fane, when might she be coming back to London, and it was then Lady Fane seemed almost to collapse and in the bustle of assisting her to a chair, I heard a whisper — that Miss Fane is ill — that she is at Hammersmith being cared for. Some kind of nervous collapse was mentioned.'

Dickens looked at her. 'Are you thinking what I'm thinking — Hammersmith?'

'Doctor Winslow's hospital?'

'It fits — that word "suffering", used by Lady Fane about her daughter and hastily contradicted by Sir Neptune; Lady Fane's fear; Miss Fane's sudden departure, and the insistence that she is down in the country; Lady Fane's inability to respond to a simple question — and — and — the sudden dismissal of Jemima Curd.'

'And, now I think of it, Mrs Pick was flustered when I told her that Jemima was a particular friend of Fanny's — Mrs Pick knows something.'

'She must. These all point to some illness in Miss Fane, and we know that in Hammersmith, Doctor Forbes Benignus Winslow has established a private mental asylum.'

'Some hysteria brought about by the disappearance of Rolando Sabatini and Miss Pout?'

'He betrayed her? Well, well, no wonder Sir Neptune was not pleased to see me. Not that it gets me much further forward except that it explains why Sir Neptune was so reluctant to say more than that he could not help me. Can't blame him, though — if it were my daughter…'

'What will you do?'

'I met someone else, a certain Mrs Marchant — the sister of Mrs Sabatini.'

'That is an intriguing connection.'

'It is, and more intriguing is Mrs Marchant's relationship with Sir Neptune — she was with him in the conservatory.'

Jane gave him an eloquent look. 'Where Lady Fane did not want to go.'

‘I sensed some hostility between Sir Neptune and Mrs Marchant and yet I had a sense of closeness, too. She has asked me to call on her the day after tomorrow.’

‘In the meantime, if I hear anything, I will let you know. In the circumstances, I can hardly put my nose into Wisteria Lodge again even to enquire about Lady Fane.’

‘No, I think not. I had the distinct impression that Sir Neptune was not pleased to find me talking to Mrs Marchant.’

‘I’ll send a note to you. Time may reveal something.’

‘And many unexpected lights may shine upon us — with luck. Now, I must give you goodnight, and my compliments to Mr Carlyle.’

It was of Jemima Curd that Dickens thought as he rode home in a cab. She must have known that her mistress was ill. Did she know about the mental asylum — if that were where Miss Fane was being cared for? If that were true, had Jemima Curd been paid to disappear? According to Jane Carlyle, Mrs Pick had not expected her. Perhaps her story to Martha Gambol and Mrs Link about going to see Mrs Pick was just a story and she had been paid enough to support her family and they had all gone to new lodgings.

14: Of Coals and Coffins

Mrs Fudge served tea, bread and butter, and information, for which Sergeant Rogers was thrice grateful. She had given up the laundry, she informed him, on account of a legacy. Not much, but enough to make her comfortable in her son's house. He was a coal merchant and had done well for himself by marrying the only daughter of James Merritt. Dead, Mr Merritt, but Simon Fudge kept the name for his wife's sake. In any case, it was a good business. 'Made sense, dint it, ter keep the old name?'

These things Rogers already knew from her former neighbour in Percy Street, not far from South Crescent where she had lived when she served Mrs Wyatt. However, the hot tea was welcome, as was the bread and butter for a man who had walked a mile or so from Bow Street to South Crescent and back again to Hemlock Court where Mrs Fudge was sitting in somewhat grimy state in the parlour. And Rogers was patient. His opportunity would come.

'Not but what there ain't plenty o' laundry. 'Tis the coal dust, see —' she wheezed — 'gets on the chest. The smuts is dreadful. Most of our laundry goes ter Mrs Gambol down the street,' she informed him with some complacency, 'but I does the lace and the delicates. She ain't much used ter the sorts o' things I did fer Mrs Wyatt.'

Rogers finished his tea. He had worked out his strategy. Mrs Fudge would relish a sensation and sensation would loosen her tongue about Miss Lambert. He leaned forwards. 'Now, Mrs Fudge, what I have to tell you is very confidential — a police matter, you see, an' it's about South Crescent. A body — well, bones to be exact — the bones of a young female, and our enquiries have led us to suppose it may be Miss Flora Lambert.'

The effect was as gratifying as he hoped. Mrs Fudge almost choked on her bread and butter. 'Miss Lambert? But she went off to 'orspital, or clinic — Miss Peach was right put out, an' Mrs Peartree. Me an' my daughter, Polly, wot's now in Australia an' doin' very well — not but wot I misses 'er, I can tell you, Sergeant — we 'elped with cleanin' an' closin' up the 'ouse after Mrs Wyatt passed. It can't be.'

'She never went to the clinic, Mrs Fudge — we found that out. Now, I was wonderin' if you know anythin' about a young man, a foreigner we've been told she was friendly with?'

'Seen Miss Peach, 'ave yer?' Her little eyes were sharp. She wouldn't have missed much. 'In such a takin', she woz, when Miss Lambert took 'im ter South Crescent — an' Mrs Peartree. Pair o' old cats — dint believe in any Mr Peartree, I can tell yer. That furriner drinkin' wine in the drawin' room. I 'eard Miss Peach tellin' Miss Anguish. Poor Miss Lambert, she led a bit of a dog's life with them three, an' 'e seemed a nice young man for all 'e woz a furriner.'

'Do you know where he came from?'

'Italian, she told me.'

'Who?'

'Miss Lambert — told me all about him one day. It woz my day for takin' the sheets off the beds an' there she woz in 'er room, cryin' 'er 'eart out. They offended 'im, she sed, an' 'e woz proud, see, poor but proud, an' 'e woz an artist, an 'e woz paintin' 'er picture — mind, I got the impression she woz payin' fer that, not that I sed anythin' — but she woz afraid 'e wouldn't come back. Lost 'im, she sed. Desperate, I thort she woz. I felt that sorry cos she woz poorly, too, pains in 'er 'and.

See, my Polly woz ter marry Fred Littimer an' 'e — well, I wasn't sure 'e woz ter be trusted — I knows wot girls feel, an' poor Miss Lambert wasn't no beauty, not like my Polly — pretty as a picture, she is — lovely hair, though Miss Lambert, reddish-blonde, it woz and very thick. My Polly's dark, though, just like —'

Rogers interrupted. 'You met him?'

'The Italian? Once in the street. Mr Tony, she called him. You think she went off wiv 'im, an 'e — well, 'e woz an' 'ansome young man. 'Adn't much ter say fer 'imself, though, just bowed ter me. Very perlite, I thort.'

'Can you describe him?'

She screwed up her eyes so that they almost disappeared. 'Tall, I thinks, an' dark 'air — on the long side, an' a beard, short. Dark eyes — looked away from yer. Odd fellah, now I thinks of it. Thin face — don't serpose 'e 'ad much food. She was a skinny little thing, too. Now, my Polly takes arter me — a fine figure, I woz, though I don't serpose yer'd think it. I've filled out since I woz doin' the laundry work.' She helped herself absently to yet another thick slice of bread and butter.

She certainly had, Rogers observed — a fat little woman wedged in her chair like an old feather mattress, but she looked at him with her shrewd eyes. 'Bones in the old cistern, eh? Yer really think Miss Lambert woz done in? By the furriner?'

'We don't know, Mrs Fudge, but we'd like to find him. You don't know where he lived?'

'Nah, she niver said. She went away soon arter an' I thort it woz all over wiv 'er bein' poorly. An' 'e so good-lookin'. Still, yer niver knows what folk might do. Why, my Aunt Caroline knew a woman 'oo knew Mr O'Connor wot woz killed by Mrs Manning — she woz a furriner — Mrs Manning, that is —

French or Swiss or somethin' o' that kind. Stands ter reason, don't it.'

Hearing that enigmatic conclusion, and deeming it not very helpful, even though it was true that Mrs Manning had been foreign, Sergeant Rogers made to depart. Mrs Fudge remained in her chair. At the door, he thought of something the Superintendent had told him concerning Mr Dickens and Hemlock Court.

'Do you know the Curd family?'

'Oh, yes, they used ter live in a room at Mrs Todgers down the way. Gone now. A bit since — they couldn't pay the rent. Went in the night, the Lord knows where — work'ouse, I'll wager.'

'And the daughter, Jemima?'

'In service at Chelsea. Best of 'em — pretty little thing an' looked it when she came back a time or two. Good food, see, and good air. Quite rosy-cheeked. Someone came askin' about 'er the other day, so Mrs Gambol said — private investigator — rum lookin' cove wiv starin' eyes. Looked right through yer, she said. My son saw 'im. Yer could talk ter Mrs Gambol or Simon.'

Rogers felt an urge to laugh. No need, he thought. He knew who the private investigator with the staring eyes was — not that he would repeat that unless to his wife, Mollie, but she'd be indignant. Very fond of Mr Dickens was Mollie.

'No-one hereabouts knows of the Curds?'

'Try Worships in Little Shire Street — the coffin-makers. Some relation works there. Anyway, name's Nolly Turner.'

Rogers made his way to Little Shire Street. The sound of hammering directed him to the workshop above which a sign bore the legend: *Worship and Churchyard, Carpenters and Coffin-*

makers. The hammering naturally brought to mind coffin nails — two coffins, one empty and one with its lid on, bearing a brass plaque with an inscription upon it, were propped up, one on each side of the door.

He called out and the hammering stopped. A cheerful young man — in spite of his calling — appeared at the open door with hammer in hand and nails in his mouth.

'Mr Turner?'

The young man eyed Rogers's uniform, nodded, and vanished inside to be replaced by another young man who did not look so cheerful — perhaps more affected by the trade, or, more likely, by a policeman asking for him. He gave Rogers a suspicious look.

'I'm looking for Mr and Mrs Curd, who lived in Hemlock Court. Are they relations of yours?'

The young man took the nails from his mouth and put them in the pocket of his leather apron. 'Moved on.'

'Do you know where?'

'Work'ouse — 'Olborn Union up Gray's Inn Street. Bound ter 'appen.'

'And Miss Jemima Curd?'

Nolly Turner's hard stare softened. 'Went fer a job.'

'Do you know where?'

'Up in Clerkenwell, she sed, goin' ter be a maid for some old friend. Excited, she woz, sed she'd tell me all about it when she was certain.'

'When did you see her last?'

'Few weeks ago, I thinks. Can't be sure — sed she'd get her parents an' the other kids out o' the work'ouse when she woz sure o' the job. Seemed excited — sed it was a good job. I woz glad. Jemima's a worker, but 'er parents ain't no use — Uncle George, 'e's as weak as water, an' 'is wife'll drink 'erself ter death one day. Can't do nothin' fer folks like that — work'ouse it's gotter be. Pity about them kids, though. Jemima tried ter —'

'She didn't give you her friend's name?'

'Nah, just sed it woz a chance. See, sir, some of us wants ter get on. Yer might think this ain't much, but there's chances in coffin-makin'. Folks gotter die. We did good business in the cholera.'

Well, that was one way of looking at it, thought Rogers, but when he thought of last year's outbreak, he could only think of the suffering of those he had seen, sick and gaunt with horrible white tongues, wrinkled skin, and terror in their sunken eyes. The blue death they called it. He had seen a man die in the street, his face contorted and horribly discoloured. He glanced involuntarily at the coffin with its lid.

'Pity about that'un. Customer sed it want needed — dunno why. Still, it makes a good show fer us. Brings in the customers.'

Sergeant Rogers went on his way, pondering upon this mystery. Buried alive, p'raps an' rescued — there were stories in the paper o' things like that an' then you heard of folk risin' from the dead. He wondered if you'd be welcome back. Not if they'd got their hands on all your worldly goods an' had to give 'em back.

He supposed it could happen. P'raps Mr Dickens would know. He knew a lot of peculiar things. Rum cove — Mrs Gambol had that bit right.

15: Time's Curtain Parted

At Bow Street, Constable Stemp handed a box to Superintendent Jones. 'Mr Faithfull's boy brought it. There's a note.'

So there was. Mr Faithfull had apparently discovered the contents of the box in an old chest from South Crescent which had been put, mistakenly, into an auction lot comprising some articles from another house. Mr Faithfull had recognised the chest which had been in the long-dead Mr Wyatt's study — a room never used. There was no key, but Mr Faithfull, mindful of the bones, had instructed one of his men to open it.

Not more bones, Jones hoped, but Mr Faithfull had usefully made a list of the contents in his neat hand. Jones opened the box and withdrew the items according to the list:

One rope of pearls — property of Mrs Wyatt
A leather-bound volume of sermons with a packet of ten sovereigns hidden in the spine — the book bearing the signature, George Henry Lambert Wyatt, 1784.
An emerald ring — property of Mrs Wyatt
A pair of diamond earrings
A water-colour sketch of a young woman

Jones gazed at the portrait. It wasn't signed. He looked up at Stemp. 'Go over to Wellington Street, will you, and ask Mr Dickens to step over. Tell him we've found something — don't tell him what.'

As Stemp went out, Sergeant Rogers arrived from Hemlock Court.

'These were sent from Faithfull's — found in a chest which had been put with the wrong auction lot. Stemp's gone for Mr Dickens.' Jones held up the picture. 'This might be Miss Flora Lambert. Mr Dickens saw a portrait of her at the Anguish house.'

'An' the other stuff?' Rogers asked.

'Mr Faithfull seems to know that some of the jewels belonged to Mrs Wyatt. The chest was locked and the key missing.'

'Miss Lambert hid them, you think — a sort of dowry, p'raps — if she was goin' away with Mr Tony?'

'That might well be the case. Find out anything from Mrs Fudge?'

'She saw Miss Lambert with Mr Tony — tall, dark hair, beard — not much help, I know. She thought he was an odd sort, but then he was foreign, she said as though that explained it. But she did say that Miss Lambert had been cryin' one day because Mr Tony was offended by the servants an' she thought he'd leave her. Desperate, Mrs Fudge said, desperate, she was.'

Jones looked at the coins and jewels on his desk. 'Was she now?'

'An' I found out somethin' else. I remembered that Mr Dickens'd been to Hemlock Court about that missin' girl, Jemima Curd, so I asked. It seems that a Mrs Gambol, Mrs Fudge's laundry woman, had been visited by a private investigator —' Rogers grinned at his chief — 'I didn't go into that —'

'Very wise. Did she give a description of this — er — detective?'

'I wouldn't care to repeat it, sir.'

'For the purposes of elimination, sergeant?' Jones wanted to know.

'Ah, well, if you put it like that — rum cove, according to Mrs Gambol.'

Jones chuckled. 'I'll save that one up. What did you find out about Jemima?'

Dickens came in just in time to catch the name. 'Jemima Curd?'

'That's right,' Rogers replied. 'I found Mrs Fudge living in Hemlock Court an' she told me a bit about Miss Lambert. I remembered you'd been to Hemlock Court so I asked about Jemima Curd. Mrs Fudge directed me to one Nolly Turner at the coffin-maker's — turns out to be a relative an' he told me that the Curds are in the Holborn Union an' he knew that Jemima had gone for a post in Clerkenwell — to be a maid for some old friend.'

'Clerkenwell's a long way from Chelsea,' Dickens said. 'I might take a walk in the workhouse — research, of course, but, hold on, Stemp said you had something to show me — quite a mystery he made of it.'

'Do you recognise this portrait?' Jones asked.

Dickens took the paper. 'It's Flora Lambert — if that was her likeness I saw at the Anguish house. Where did you get it?'

'Mr Faithfull, the house agent, found it in an old chest —'

'Mr Poe, what did I tell you?'

'No letter, but these —' Jones pushed the jewels and coins in Dickens's direction — 'an old chest without a key, an old chest in an unused room. The sovereigns were neatly packed into the spine of an old book.'

'*The Mysteries of Udolpho*, was it?'

Jones gestured to the book, 'Sermons by some long-gone Wyatt.'

'That nobody's ever read, I'll bet. She —' said Rogers.

'Who?' asked Dickens.

'Rogers has a theory. Enlighten Mr Dickens, Alf.'

'Miss Lambert — I was thinkin' — did she hide them in preparation to run off with Mr Tony? She didn't know when Mrs Wyatt was goin' to die — it might have been ages. Mrs Fudge said she was desperate upset — afraid Mr Tony might leave her.'

'The jewels belong to Mrs Wyatt, according to Mr Faithfull,' Jones said.

Rogers warmed to his theme. 'Mrs Wyatt wouldn't know they'd gone — she'd be too ill, and Miss Lambert would know where they were kept, access to the keys an' if Mr Tony wanted money before —'

'He committed himself,' Dickens supplied, 'but why didn't she take them with her?'

Rogers's face fell a little. 'Intended to come back for 'em. They came back an' then…' He looked at the Superintendent, his face anguished now at the collapse of his theory.

'No, Alf, you're right. It won't wash, but I still think you're right about the hoarding of the loot.'

'It don' help much, though.'

'Not until we find out more about this Mr Tony.' Dickens studied the picture. 'Not signed. Pity … though something odd strikes me. The face seems unfinished — slapdash, really. I've seen a lot of pictures in my time, but the rest is very well executed. It flatters her, though, I'll say that, but then it would, wouldn't it.' He looked again. 'Sam, she's wearing the necklace — the Venetian glass beads —'

'And the cross?' Jones asked.

'I can't tell, the necklace is partly hidden by the bodice … it's not her dress — it's a costume. She's wearing some sort of robe in green, a sort of medieval style — not what Flora Lambert would wear, I'm sure, and the shape of the neckline.

Sam, he's copied this and put Flora Lambert's face in it. I saw all sorts of pictures like this in Italy.' It was familiar, but he couldn't recall where he had seen something similar. 'I wonder —'

There was a knock at the door. Constable Feak stood there. 'A body's been found, sir, up at Clerkenwell, St John's reservoir. Woman. Inspector Shackell sent —'

'Drowned?' Dickens blurted.

'Seems so,' said Feak.

'Rogers and I will come,' Jones replied. 'Charles?'

That curious sense of Time's curtain parted: unreal and spectral, a red sun hanging, making blood-stained streaks across the leaden sky; a sheet of water, just stirred by the wind, had a mournful look; a few trees on the margin and a group of figures looking down into the water. He had seen all this before.

Then the frozen picture cracked into pieces. Sam Jones, followed by Rogers and Feak, was striding ahead towards the figures, one of whom came forward. Dickens went on, shaking off that momentary chilling of the blood.

'I was up at the police office on Lower Road when the report came in,' Inspector Shackell was explaining to Jones. 'Knew you were lookin' for a girl so I sent word. Doctor's here.' He pointed to a kneeling figure.

They went to look at the body which had been pulled onto the water's edge — a young girl in a grey dress, the bodice of which had been pulled off the shoulders to expose the thin chest. Her little feet were bare. The hair was loose and wet, the face colourless. She looked very young. Not Violet Pout, then, thought Dickens. She looked like a servant girl. Jemima Curd's family were in Clerkenwell.

'Who found her?' asked Jones.

The inspector motioned. 'This young man — he was fishing.' The inspector's voice was stern.

The young man stepped forward. He looked white and frightened. Well he might, thought Jones. No fishing allowed, but he would ignore that. Poor devil, he looked like everyone else in these benighted parts — half-starved. Clerkenwell was no stranger to poverty — and crime, especially murder, unless this was suicide — for the usual reasons — a child on the way, and no other recourse but the workhouse. He could almost sense Dickens next to him, longing for him to ask about Jemima Curd, but he would take his time.

'Your name?'

'Ned Orrey, sir.'

'Do you know her, Mr Orrey?'

'Niver seen 'er, sir, I lives over by Sadler's Wells. I ain't seen 'er afore, though she ain't the first wot's gone in there.'

Why should he know her? Like most poor districts, Clerkenwell had a transient population. The place was packed with lodging houses for all kinds of workers — jewellery, ivory, watch-making, engraving, knife-grinding. And then there was the Sadler's Wells theatre where people came and went all the time: actors, musicians, producers, wardrobe ladies, wig makers — not to mention the audience. And there was Jemima Curd who might have been in Clerkenwell.

The doctor stood up, 'Superintendent Jones.'

Jones recognised him from the infirmary at the Middlesex House of Correction. 'Doctor Bennett.'

'I've sent for the mortuary van — I'll make a full examination in the mortuary, but I can tell you now that she did not drown. She was strangled. Look.'

Doctor Bennett pushed back the hair and they saw the sodden ribbon pulled tight around the neck. Dickens looked, remembering. Pulled from a canal because her rosary caught on something. Found in a water tank with her neck broken. *Something dark is coming* — so Madame Emerald had prophesied, looking at his palm. It had come. The red sun was sinking and the sullen water took on a black hue, deep and mysterious, and the wind rustled the grasses at the margin. He looked at the still white face of the dead girl. Her eyes were closed. Whose eyes had gazed into her trusting eyes and determined her end? What had she known that had brought her to this melancholy place and this death? It was Jemima Curd. He was sure of it.

'She is naked under the dress,' said Doctor Bennett. 'I'll examine her for any other signs of assault — it might be a rape as well as murder. The young man found her among the tree roots which go down into the water. That is why she didn't sink.'

'Why were you down there among the trees, Mr Orrey?' Jones asked.

'I ain't touched 'er —' Ned Orrey's face turned even whiter — 'Niver seen 'er — yer can't —'

'I am not accusing you, Mr Orrey; I just want to know how you came to find her.'

'Fishin' line caught — just went to free it an' then I sees 'er, all tangled up. Coulda just left 'er but knows it wasn't right —'

He could have, thought Jones; he was hardly likely to report the body if he had murdered her. 'Give your address to the sergeant. You'll be needed for the inquest.' Jones turned to the doctor. 'Doctor Bennett, I wonder if you would oblige me by sending the body to Doctor Symonds at King's College Hospital? I have another case which might be connected so I should like him to examine her.'

Doctor Bennett acceded and promised to send his report to Jones — he would be needed at the inquest and was quite content for Doctor Symonds to make a more detailed examination. Feak was to wait with the doctor then go to make the explanations to Doctor Symonds. Inspector Shackell's instructions were to get more men and make enquiries round and about the theatre and lodging houses, and he was to ask, in particular, if anyone knew of a servant girl named Jemima Curd.

'You think it is Jemima?' Dickens asked Jones as they moved away.

'She is missing. It makes sense to ask about and we do know where her parents are so we'll be off to the Holborn Union. We need to know when and where they last saw her, and to take the father to see this girl. Then we'll know — and then we can think about what we do know.'

Mr George Curd's dazed eyes wandered feebly and his breathing was shallow and weak. They had taken his clothes — burnt them most likely. He had been washed, but not thoroughly enough to rid him of the ingrained grime on his thin face and scrawny neck. His yellow hands like claws picked distractedly at the meagre coverlet. *He would never be picking oakum*, thought Dickens, as they looked at him. He would hardly be capable of answering questions.

'Pneumonia,' the infirmary nurse had said as they went into the ward where the sick who could not work for their keep were taken. He smelt the gin on her breath. Most of these workhouse nurses were illiterate and very often drunkards, but this one had a kindly face. The ward was a bleak sight with its rows of beds facing each other. It was cold, though there was an open fire. If you lay where Mr Curd was, you would freeze from the draughts from the cracked windows. Worse than anything was the smell: ammonia from a water closet nearby, the smell of sewerage, and of lives decaying. He hardly blamed the nurse for her gin.

'Mr Curd,' began Jones in a whisper.

The eyes, dark with pain, turned towards them, but there was no response.

Dickens took one of the restless hands in his own. 'I hope you are feeling better, sir, now that you are being looked after.'

The eyes looked at him, first in fear and then, as Dickens chafed the cold fingers, the expression changed to something more peaceful, and the other wandering hand stilled. Jones watched and waited, knowing it was no use asking about Jemima Curd. Mr Curd was following his daughter into the dark. He heard the breathing slow.

'God bless you,' Dickens murmured, and Jones sent up another prayer.

The eyes closed. There was only a slight change, and then, Mr George Curd, a wreck of a man who had endured only poverty and misery, died.

At least, thought Jones, he wasn't alone. He put his hand on Dickens's shoulder and they waited.

'A poor, bare fork'd animal,' murmured Dickens, 'that is what he was, come in this world to weep.'

'It was as well he did not know that Jemima is dead — the only hope that family had.'

'It is cruel,' said Dickens. 'I suppose we must see these poor orphans — which is what they are since the mother is missing.' The porter at the workhouse had told them that the mother had refused to come in with her children. She had been drunk and wouldn't go where there was no drink. He had seen her stumble off. She had not been back.

'We must, but what to tell them about Jemima?'

'They must be told that their father is dead — I wonder if something might be done for them. This is not the place for them.'

'Can I leave it to you?' Jones asked. 'I need to get down to Hemlock Court. Nolly Turner will have to identify her.'

'I will. I'll be careful about Jemima — I'll see what I can find out from them.'

'Don't feel you must press the matter for my sake — we don't know for sure.'

Dickens smiled at him. 'You are a good man, Sam. I'll meet you back at Bow Street.'

Dickens was taken to that part of the workhouse where the children were kept separated, told the wardswoman what had occurred, and asked if he might see the children.

She looked him up and down, appraisingly. 'Relative, are yer?'

'No, I was with Mr Curd when he died.'

The two children, Sarah and Daniel, were brought into a reception room. They looked uncomfortable in their workhouse clothes, made of rough material, but clean and neat. They were gaunt, however, old before their time, their yellow faces all bone, the childish roundedness worn away by hunger and cruelty. He thought of the drunken mother who had taken Jemima's money and promised, no doubt, that the children would be fed.

Their eyes were without hope. It was no wonder. Dragged from what wretched home they'd known, trailed about the streets, abandoned by their mother, separated from the only father they'd known, parted from each other, stripped, scrubbed, de-loused, disinfected and labelled. And now, their sister was dead, too, probably.

They looked at him without interest. He was just another stranger come to look at them as though they were animals in a zoo. The girl was the elder, about twelve, he thought, the boy, nine or ten. They stood apart from each other as if they were strangers.

'Sarah,' he began, 'I have just come from your pa.'

'Is 'e dead?'

'I am afraid he was very ill.'

'Allus woz.'

'You will be very sad, I know.'

She shrugged and looked away towards the window. *What did it matter*, he thought, to her? A father who had been able to do nothing for her.

'Where's Jemima?' the boy asked.

'I don't know, I'm afraid.'

'Pa sed she'd come fer us — telled a lie, a lie. A bloody liar, 'e is. Glad 'e's dead. Wasn't no good anyways. Liar, liar, liar...'

The boy howled; it was the cry of a stricken beast, but Sarah remained impassive. It was no good asking anything about Jemima. They had been here for several weeks and she had not been to see them. So where had she been? And where was she now? In Doctor Symonds' mortuary?

Sarah stayed staring at the window. Her brother's noisy cries had no effect. Dickens felt despair. There was nothing, not a thing he could do — no comfort in the world would pierce the carapace of that girl's suffering. It was enough to break the heart and hope of any man.

He went away, pausing to tell the wardswoman that they knew about their father, and to give her some money.

‘Look after them,’ he said. She looked at the coins. He knew she wouldn’t.

Dickens walked back down into Gray’s Inn Lane, past the gate through which he had gone into to Mr Blackmore’s chambers to do his work as a very junior clerk, but it had been a start, better than the blacking factory in those days when he had been a kind of vagabond child, roaming where he would when his father had been with the rest of the family in the Marshalsea. How easy it was to fall. Only luck had kept the Dickens family from the workhouse, he sometimes thought. Little Dan Curd would not be a clerk in anyone’s chambers. Only Jemima might have saved them.

‘It is Jemima Curd,’ said Jones as he went in, ‘Nolly Turner identified her.’

‘Then there is very little hope for those two children, if any at all.’

‘They didn’t know anything?’

‘I didn’t ask. Sam, if you could have seen them, they were hardly children at all, hardly human. The death of their father had no effect — the girl, Sarah, simply shrugged her shoulders, and the boy screeched that his father was a liar. How Jemima emerged from that swamp of poverty and despair, I know not.’

‘Nolly Turner told me something of that. A childless sister of Mrs Curd took Jemima when it was clear that Mrs Curd was never going to look after the child — of course no one could prevent the coming of more children — there are dead ones, too. The aunt, a respectable body, made sure that Jemima had some education to fit her for service, but that girl had a good heart and she did not forget those useless parents and the two surviving children. She did what she could.’

'And now someone has taken the little life of that loyal, generous girl — it wasn't an accident, I suppose.'

'It was not.' Jones's voice was grim. 'She was dead before she went into the water. It was murder and I should like to know why.'

'Someone wanted her out of the way.'

'Violet Pout? Rolando Sabatini?'

'Sir Neptune Fane?'

Jones looked at Dickens closely. 'Why him?'

'I heard something. I hadn't time to tell you about the reception. Mrs Carlyle heard a whisper — that Miss Mariana Fane is not in the country with relations, but is being cared for in a private asylum at Hammersmith. I thought of Doctor Forbes Winslow's.'

'Asylum — you think she might have suffered some mental collapse?'

'I think of Lady Fane's alarm and fear when I asked her about her daughter. I think of Mrs Carlyle's servant asserting that Miss Fane was sweet on Mr Sabatini, and I think of the disappearance of her lover and Miss Pout.'

'And Jemima Curd might have known of the daughter's madness.'

'What a scandal that would be — perhaps Jemima Curd knew something about Mr Sabatini's relationship with Miss Fane. Good Lord, Sam, suppose he had seduced her.'

'Sir Neptune would go after Sabatini, surely — that's maybe why he's vanished. Murdering Jemima Curd, though, I don't know. Still, I shall have to go to Wisteria Lodge. I must question Sir Neptune's servants about Jemima — in the absence of her mother or, indeed, any new person to give information.'

Dickens's eyes gleamed. 'We could —'

'No, we couldn't, Charles. Jemima Curd, their former servant is dead. I go there investigating murder. That has nothing to do with Charles Dickens who came to ask about Miss Pout and was told that Sir Neptune could not help. If I took you, think how it would look. You have no right to be there. Sir Neptune is a powerful man — he would be sure to complain to the Assistant Commissioner, who will ask me what business it is of Mr Dickens. I can hardly say that Charles Dickens heard gossip and believes Sir Neptune Fane to be suspect.'

'No, I see that, Sam.'

'I must tread very carefully — indeed, I quake to think how carefully, given what you have told me. We have no evidence — not even that Miss Fane is at Hammersmith.'

'I have thought of how I might possess myself of such evidence. Dr John Elliotson, my particular friend —'

'The mesmerist — is he to read Sir Neptune's mind?'

Dickens laughed, 'No, no — though he could. I daresay I could were I to get close enough to make my passes upon his noble brow.'

'Don't — I quake again. What have you in mind?'

'A piece for *Household Words* on Dr Winslow's excellent establishment, which advocates the gentle treatment of the insane. Dr Elliotson is also Doctor Winslow's particular friend.'

'I beg you, Charles, be discreet in the matter. No reference at all to Miss Fane.'

'My lips will be as tight as sealing wax, but I may discover something in general and there may be records.'

'Take care. I do not want the Assistant Commissioner ordering me to cease harassing Sir Neptune Fane about the matter of a former servant and prying into his private life in the process. Now, I must take Rogers and storm the citadel.'

'I am bound for supper with a lady — the aunt of Mr Sabatini.'

'A maiden aunt?'

'Not exactly — a rather beautiful lady. I shall press her — '

'Do not, I beg you,' said Jones, laughing.

'Metaphorically, of course — on the matter of Mr Sabatini and Miss Pout.'

'I doubt that Sir Neptune will wish to be pressed to my bosom.'

16: Superintendent Jones Asks Questions

Jones was early at Wisteria Lodge, hoping Sir Neptune would be at home. The tall footman said he would ask if his master would see the Superintendent after Jones had handed in his card. He and Rogers waited in the porch of Wisteria Lodge. Sir Neptune could hardly refuse — a public man with a public duty.

Rogers remained in the hall while Jones was shown into the library.

'I am much obliged to you, sir, for agreeing to see me.'

'It must be brief, Superintendent, I have an important dinner engagement with a member of the House. It is a matter of grave importance.' He did not ask Jones to sit.

So is this, thought Jones, but he merely said, 'I am making enquiries about a former servant of yours, a Miss Jemima Curd.'

Sir Neptune's hand rested on the mantelpiece. He picked up an ornament and put it down again, staring at it for a few moments. 'Oh, yes, I vaguely recall the name. The servants are Mrs Pick's business, and my wife's — when she is well enough.'

'Would it be possible to speak to your wife?'

'Certainly not, Superintendent. My wife's health is very delicate just now.'

'Miss Curd was your daughter's personal maid, I believe.'

'Yes, she was a nice kind of girl — so my wife said — Mariana seems to have liked her.'

'Why did she lose her post?'

'My daughter has gone to the country for an indefinite period — she is delicate like her mother so Miss Curd was not needed.' His words came slowly, rather more slowly, Jones thought, than was necessary to answer such straightforward questions. 'I believe she was paid and Mrs Pick would, no doubt, furnish her a character for another post.' He looked at Jones. 'Why do you want to know about her — not in trouble, is she?'

'No, sir, she is dead — she was found in the new reservoir in Clerkenwell.'

Sir Neptune paled. 'How very distressing — suicide, was it?' Seeing the surprise in Jones's face, he went on quickly, 'I thought perhaps, having lost her post, she might…'

Jones did not comment on that, but he stored it away. 'No, it was murder. Jemima Curd was strangled and her body put in the reservoir. Perhaps the murderer thought she might sink and not be found.'

Sir Neptune held Jones's gaze. 'I am afraid I cannot help you, Superintendent. Servants come and go. We cannot be responsible for what they do afterwards. We were as fair to her as was possible in difficult circumstances — I mean that my wife is ill and Mariana is not strong. It has been a great anxiety and I have many matters of parliamentary business, you understand.'

'You do not know where she went.'

'I imagine to her family.'

'Her father is dead; the mother has disappeared, and there are two younger children in the workhouse. Jemima's death is a tragedy for them.'

Jones waited, wondering whether Sir Neptune would show any interest in the two children.

Sir Neptune's face took on a look of concern. 'That is a pity. Perhaps something can be done for them.'

'They are at the Holborn Workhouse in Gray's Inn Street.'

'I will send someone to find out what can be done. Now, Superintendent, I must go. I am sorry I cannot help you further.'

Almost out-manoeuvred by the politician — thought Jones — almost letting him have the last word. Sir Neptune was ringing at the bell-pull by the mantelpiece.

'I should like to speak to Mrs Pick and the other female servants. I should like to know if they can provide information about where Miss Curd went when she left here and whether she ever talked about her family or friends.'

Sir Neptune looked as if he might dispute the point, but he thought better of it. 'Of course, I see that you must.'

'And my sergeant will question the male servants.'

'Very well. Mrs Pick will assist you.'

A tall footman took Jones downstairs to see Mrs Pick in the housekeeper's room and Rogers was shown to the butler's pantry.

Tears started in Mrs Pick's eyes and she sat down suddenly, groping in her pocket for a handkerchief. She had listened to Jones's account of Jemima Curd with horror. Jones gave her time to compose herself.

'Murdered, you say?'

'Yes, tell me about her.'

'She was a dear little thing. Brought up by an aunt who had taught her well. She was a humble girl and very meek and gentle. Miss Mariana —' Mrs Pick put her handkerchief to her eyes. Jones waited. 'Oh, dear, Mr Jones, who could have done such a wicked thing?'

'I don't know — yet, but I do want to you to tell me where she went after she left here.'

'Her aunt had died so I thought she might go to her parents — I don't know exactly. It was all so sudden and she was very upset. I gave her five shillings to tide her over.'

'Why was it so sudden?'

Mrs Pick's face was very red. She dabbed at her eyes again. 'Only that Miss Mariana was to go to the country — delicate, she is, like Lady Fane.'

'Miss Fane was taken ill suddenly?'

'Not exactly — just in need of good air, Sir Neptune said. She'd not been eating and was sick and faint… Sir Neptune was very worried and Lady Fane…'

Mrs Pick looked down, twisting the handkerchief in her hands. There was something, Jones concluded, but Mrs Pick was unwilling to say. Jemima Curd had been sent off — not with her pay, only with Mrs Pick's charity.

'Jemima didn't come back at all?'

'Oh, no, sir, that wouldn't have done. Sir Neptune ordered — said —' she wept again. When she looked up her eyes seemed to plead with him to ask no more — 'Jemima went home, sir, that's all I can tell you.'

Jones understood. Jemima Curd had been sacked. What had she done to be dismissed so summarily? And Mrs Pick was very afraid for her job. He did not want to entrap her, but he would have to speak to the others. 'Did Jemima have her own room, or did she share with another maid?'

'One of the under-housemaids, Jessie Sharp.'

'I shall have to speak to her.'

'I don't think, sir —'

'You need not worry, Mrs Pick; Sir Neptune has given his permission. Jessie Sharp may know something about Jemima's family or any friends she might have had. She had no follower?'

'Oh, no, sir, she was a very good girl.'

'Where will I find Jessie?'

'She will be in her room on the top floor. I can bring her down.'

'No, I will see her upstairs. She will be more comfortable in her own room.'

Mrs Pick took him up the back stairs to the attics where Jessie Sharp had shared the room under the eaves with Jemima Curd. He recalled the attic room at Mrs Wyatt's. Flora Lambert — he had almost forgotten about her and Dickens's Italian artist. Well, Flora Lambert was long dead. Jemima Curd was his priority now.

Jessie Sharp was about the same age as Jemima — not a pretty girl, but her round face and boot-button eyes suggested guilelessness. She looked frightened of the large policeman and glanced at Mrs Pick as if for permission to speak.

'You need not be frightened, Jessie,' said Mrs Pick, 'the Superintendent wants to know about Jemima.'

'What's 'appened to 'er?'

Mrs Pick sat next to her on the narrow bed. 'Poor Jemima is dead, Jessie. Someone killed her and the policeman wants to find out who did it.'

Jessie Sharp looked too stunned to cry. She gazed at Jones with uncomprehending eyes. 'Jemima's dead? Killed? 'Oo done it?'

'I don't know, Jessie, but with your help I might be able to find out.'

'Wot can I do? I don't know nothin' about killin' no one.'

'I know that, Jessie, but perhaps you can tell me about Jemima.'

Jessie looked at Mrs Pick again. Jones did not want Mrs Pick to be there and stifle Jessie Sharp by her presence. Jessie's eyes would ask that permission at every question. He would have to be firm.

'You may go now, Mrs Pick. I am sure that Jessie will be able to tell me a little bit about Jemima.'

'If you are sure, Superintendent.' Mrs Pick was reluctant.

'I am, and Jessie will be quite all right with me, won't you, Jessie?' He smiled at her.

'Yes, sir.'

Mrs Pick had no choice. Jones sat down on the ticking mattress of the other bed. 'You stay there, Jessie. Are you quite comfortable?'

'Yes, sir.'

'Now, tell me about Jemima. Did she like being maid to Miss Mariana?'

'Oh, yes, sir, and Miss Mariana gave 'er presents — some chocolates. Jemima shared 'em — that's wot she's like, always shared cos I dint get presents. Niver 'ad a present. We ate 'em up 'ere. No one knowed. Niver 'ad sich sweet things. An' she give Jemima ribbons an' Jemima give me one — a red one, an' she 'ad a blue one. Lovely hair, Jemima 'ad —'

Now, the little round-faced girl wept, remembering her friend's generosity and their secret simple joys. Just a child, Jones thought, so he waited and wished he could have given her a chocolate. She was as simple as six year old Tom, his adopted son, whose tears dried for a chocolate.

'She was your good friend, I know, Jessie, and that is why you must be a brave girl and help me.'

'Miss Violet gave Jemima presents, too. Jemima liked 'er. I dint much — she niver give me nothin', an' she laughed at me an' called me Sharp as if she woz the mistress, but Jemima thort she was beautiful. She give Jemima five shillin's wunce — don't know wot fer. Jemima sed she couldn't tell — it woz private, but Jemima give me a shillin' so I dint mind.'

'When did Miss Mariana become ill?'

'One time when they'd been out shoppin', Miss Pout brought Miss Mariana home, sed she'd fainted, an' she looked ever so pale, an' then after she dint seem the same. I dunno — like 'er mother. Some ladies is like that, sir — don't matter 'ow rich they is. In bed some days — breakfast in bed, they 'as, an' they sits by the fire, an' they 'as tea on a tray —' She looked wistful, Jessie Sharp, who had never had breakfast in bed or tea on a tray.

'Can you remember when this was?'

'Dunno, sir, mebbe a few months ago — I asked Jemima about it, but she sed it woz private to Miss Mariana.'

'And when did Miss Mariana go to the country?'

'A few weeks ago — for the fresh air. In the night, it woz. Her aunty came, Mrs Pick sed.'

In the night, thought Jones, how very odd a time to go innocently into the country. Perhaps Dickens was right about the asylum. He turned back to the subject of Jemima — Jessie Sharp had told him enough about Miss Mariana — and plenty about Miss Violet Pout.

'Did Jemima ever mention going to Clerkenwell to you?'

'Don't think so, sir. I niver saw 'er — she went that sudden, an' I'll niver see 'er no more.' The tears came again and she wept into her apron.

There was nothing more he could say except that she had been very helpful and he pressed two shillings into her little hand.

She looked at the money and up at Jones. 'A present, sir, fer me?'

'Yes, you have been a great help. Thank you.'

Jones went down the stairs to find Sergeant Rogers waiting. They made their way back to Bow Street.

'Nobody knows anything but that Miss Mariana Fane is in the country and poor Jemima lost her place — funny thing, sir, they all say the same.'

Jones heard Rogers's dry tone. 'Not all, Sergeant. I had a very interesting talk with a little maid called Jessie Sharp who didn't know what she knew.'

17: A Secret Told

Dickens walked from Devonshire terrace to St John's Wood. He had had scarcely time to change his dress, having taken a detour from Bow Street to Conduit Street in order to ask his friend Doctor Elliotson about a visit to the Hammersmith Asylum. Doctor Elliotson had been willing to take him the next morning.

He felt ill at ease: those children and the dead man, that poor drowned girl, and that queer scene at the reservoir, that memory of Ferrara which seemed to hang over him like a waking nightmare.

He hurried round Regent's Park and made his way up Grove Road to Florence Cottage, which turned out to be a modest house and a discreet one with a wrought iron gate almost grown over with bushes.

He stood uncertainly for a few moments, thinking about discretion and Sir Neptune's hand on Mrs Marchant's back and wondered what had passed between them in that conservatory into which Lady Fane would not trespass. He did not really know anything about her, except that she was beautiful — and that she had spied on him. And, of course, she was Rolando Sabatini's aunt and that was why he was there. He opened the gate.

The moon led his way along a path to a gravelled area at the front door. He saw that the path forked, the two arms leading to the back of the house. He walked along the path through the garden up to a smartly painted door with shining brass furniture. The door knocker was a coiled serpent — what an odd choice. Not as grand a house as Wisteria Lodge, but very well kept, a pretty house, a discreet house. A house for a single lady — was there a Mr Marchant? He felt a twinge of disappointment. But she had asked him to come to see her at "my house".

A pretty young maid answered his knock and he waited in the narrow hall as she went to inform her mistress, gazing at the pictures. Pictures from Italy. He wondered whether Rolando's father had painted them.

He was shown into the drawing room where Mrs Marchant waited. She gave him her hand upon which there was a beautiful emerald ring. He kissed it, feeling for a moment as if he were in a play or a novel of the silver-fork kind, though, as yet, he did not know his part.

'Mr Dickens, I am very glad to see you.'

'And I, you.' She was as beautiful as he remembered in her dark green velvet with her red hair coiled at her neck, which was encircled by a thin gold chain at the end of which an emerald rested on her bosom. Emeralds sparkled in her ears.

'But you look very cold and exhausted. You have had a busy day?'

'I have — much walking about, and —'

'Before you tell me, let me ask if you have dined.'

'No, I had not time.'

'Well then, let me ask cook to prepare something that we can eat here by the fire. I sometimes take a light supper here.'

There was a small round table by the fire upon which were glasses and a carafe of wine very similar to the one he had seen at St George Pierce's. It looked very inviting.

'Is there anything you would like — a little cold chicken? Some cheese? An omelette?'

'Anything at all.'

'Then do sit down while I speak to my housekeeper. Help yourself to some wine.'

Dickens sat down and poured some wine into a lovely red glass. Venetian, he supposed. He felt the warmth of the wine and the fire and closed his eyes.

When he opened them again, Mrs Marchant was sitting opposite him across the table, arranging some little dishes and silver cutlery. She put some chicken, a little cucumber and some potatoes on a plate for him. He experienced again that sense of unreality as if he were someone else entirely — yet it was very comforting and oddly familiar. The firelight and dim lamps gave a feeling of intimacy.

He thought of the early days of his marriage when Catherine would watch anxiously as he ate. When they were innocently happy — at Furnivall's Inn before the splendours of Devonshire Terrace. When had he and Catherine sat thus together by the fire? Well, that was his fault.

When he had finished, she rang the bell and the maid came to clear the plates. Dolly Marchant poured more wine and said, 'You look better. Now tell me what has made you so anxious?'

'A girl was found dead in the new reservoir at Clerkenwell.'

'Drowned? Not Violet Pout?'

'No, the girl was murdered, strangled. It was Jemima Curd.'

Dolly Marchant's hand flew to her breast. 'Miss Fane's maid?'

'Yes, I am afraid so.'

'Poor child. How dreadful. She seemed a nice little thing — I saw her once or twice at Wisteria Lodge. Did she live in Clerkenwell?'

'Her father was in the workhouse there and two younger children. Mr Curd has died of pneumonia. I was there when he died — he was a poor, wretched creature, half-starved. The two younger children have nothing now — not a hope in the world.'

'There is no mother?'

'A drunkard and no earthly use to her children. Their only hope was Jemima and she lost her place when Miss Mariana was sent to the country after Mr Sabatini and Miss Pout disappeared. It seems that Jemima had hopes of a position with an old friend — I wondered about Violet Pout.'

'I do not know, Mr Dickens. I cannot tell you anything about Jemima Curd.'

'You are willing to tell me about Mr Sabatini and Miss Pout.'

'My sister is in Ireland. I thought Rolando had gone with her, but he has not. I thought he might come to me.'

'Why?'

'Because he was in trouble.'

'About Miss Pout.'

'No, about Miss Fane.'

'Ah.' So, it was as he had surmised. Rolando had betrayed Miss Fane.

'He told me that he loved Mariana Fane and wanted to ask Sir Neptune for her hand. I told him to wait. Miss Fane is only seventeen, charming and pretty, but far too young and so is he. Besides, Sir Neptune would have been furious.'

'That is why she was sent away.'

'Not exactly — it is all rather complicated. I need to explain clearly. When Rolando told me, I said he must leave Wisteria Lodge immediately before Sir Neptune found out. I thought he should go to Ireland. If after six months he felt the same, he could return and I would speak to Sir Neptune.'

'You are sufficiently in his confidence.'

She looked straight at him. 'I am. Of course, Rolando did not take my advice. Then I found out that he and Miss Pout vanished on the same evening. Sir Neptune was as angry a man as I have ever seen him, but I could not believe it. It was impossible that Rolando should behave in that way.'

'Could not he have found solace with Miss Pout? She is a very attractive young lady — he might have been tempted.'

'No, Mr Dickens, I do not believe it. Miss Pout is a pretty girl, but there is something calculating and worldly about her. You would understand if you knew Rolando. He is charming and sensitive — unworldly, too — and he adores his mother.'

'And you have no idea where he might be?'

She was silent then and looked into the fire. He waited. Her face looked sad and the light showed him the lines about her eyes and mouth. Some secret sorrow, he divined.

'This is very difficult, Mr Dickens. I had thought only that I could defend Rolando, to assure you that he has no involvement with Miss Pout, that you might look elsewhere for her, but you have a way of asking a question which demands the truth, but the truth is very difficult to tell.'

'I will not press you, Mrs Marchant. I have no right.'

'I have a son, Mr Dickens.'

'You think Rolando may be with him.'

'I think it might be so, but I do not know where my son is. I have not seen him for several years, and it is a great sadness to me.'

'Your husband is dead?'

'Many years ago — I have forgotten him. I did not marry for love, Mr Dickens, nor indeed for money, though my husband was a wealthy man, and I found out my error very soon. He did not love me, either. My name is actually Doireanne —' she pronounced it "Doran" — 'My husband called me Dolly. He was English. My sister's name is Elvin after an Irish poetess who wrote a famous lament for her dead husband. Agosto Sabatini called her Elvina.'

She looked sad, then. She poured him another glass of wine and smiled again, a mischievous, glinting smile in her eyes, 'Doireanne came to woo the legendary hero, Finn, and gave him a magic potion.'

How her eyes showed her changing moods — like the sea, brooding one moment and shining at another as the clouds moved over.

'What did you write, Mr Dickens? "There is no disparity in marriage, like unsuitability of mind and purpose." You know much about the human heart, and its sorrows, I think.'

'David Copperfield's words — not mine.' Not wholly true, of course, but this woman, this stranger, saw too much. Bewitching, she was, and too frank, perhaps, yet he was drawn to her. She was unlike any woman he had met, but he could not tell her any truth about himself.

She made no comment, but went on with her tale. 'My husband was ambitious. He married me for my connections, my political connections. Sir Neptune was very much a rising man even in those days.'

'You have known Sir Neptune a long time?'

'My sister and I grew up in Ireland. Our father was a lawyer — Sir Neptune was the son of a clergyman connected to a powerful family … ours was a boy and girl love, but it was not approved by the Fane family. My father's family is Catholic — Mr Fane, the clergyman, Protestant. Sir Neptune's father was an ambitious man. He had great plans for his son. That is why Sir Neptune was much with the family at the great house, Rookwood. When Miss Mary French, daughter of Sir Julius French, came to stay at the Fane family seat, Sir Neptune was encouraged to…'

'He did not marry for love.'

'No. I came to London with my husband. He had no objection to my friendship with Sir Neptune.'

'You still loved Sir Neptune.'

She did not answer that question. 'My husband's tastes were not mine. He had his own life and a long liaison with a married lady. However, he died of a stroke and I inherited his wealth.'

'The other night when we met, I thought you seemed angry with Sir Neptune.'

'He is angry with me. I knew you had been to enquire about Miss Pout. Naturally, he did not want me to talk to you. I am not sure he believes that Rolando went off with Miss Pout, but it suits him to pretend so. It is a way of concealing Mariana's folly and he would not wish me to be defending Rolando.'

'But she is ill.'

'I believe so. She was hurried away to the relations very quickly. He would not discuss her with me. I told you he was furious about Rolando and he blames me, for it was I who persuaded him to engage Rolando. But, Mr Dickens, I feel certain that Rolando is not with Miss Pout.'

'Then with your son?'

'Possibly. I hope Rolando may contact me. His mother does not yet know he is missing.'

'Your son might?'

'I very much doubt it. I am afraid I cannot help you about Miss Pout.'

'Ah, well, perhaps the police may turn up something and find a connection between Miss Pout and Jemima Curd. And now I must leave you. It was good of you to talk to me.'

They rose and she gave him her hand. She took him out into the hall to get his hat and coat.

'One last thing, Mr Dickens, before you go.'

Something in her voice made Dickens pause in his preparations for leaving. He looked at her and saw that her eyes seemed to glint with unshed tears.

'My son is Sir Neptune's child.'

'Does your son know?'

'Some years ago, he found out his parentage. Convenience — Sir Neptune's and mine, I admit — meant that I lied to him. I am too ashamed to tell you those details, but suffice it to say that he felt humiliated and angry. He did not like Sir Neptune, who was cold to him. He left this house and I have not seen him since.'

'I am heartily sorry for that.'

'You have many sons, Mr Dickens, I hear. You are fortunate in your happy family. Daughters, too?'

'Yes, three, one a mere babe, Dora, whose little helplessness moves me every day. She is delicate and sometimes I fear...'

'I should have liked a daughter — to play with and to dress in pretty things, but to be a woman in this world is not without difficulty — it is very easy to make mistakes, especially those of the heart.'

'For men, too, I think. My heart was lost once upon a time, and not quite recovered.'

Dolly Marchant saw something in his eyes. In company they had seemed to blaze with life and humour, and they had looked upon her with deep sympathy when she had told her tale of Sir Neptune, and when she had talked of her son. But now, she thought there was something darker there, some unforgotten sorrow.

'There is more — you know of the stolen diamonds. They were never recovered. Lady Fane wears paste, but that is not known. I believe that my son stole them. I persuaded Sir Neptune to report that they had been found. I said I would get them back. My son would not use them for his own gain, I know that, but I cannot recover them until I recover my son. And that may never be. So much to regret.'

Dickens took her hand as he saw the tears spill down her cheeks. He felt her warmth and the scent of her perfume as he put his arm about her. She yielded to his embrace and laid her head upon his breast. How well she fitted to him and when after a few moments she lifted her lovely face to his, he kissed her, a long, deep kiss such as he had not given any woman, even his wife.

Charles Dickens did not go home. He walked swiftly away from Florence Cottage. He felt shaken to his very core. 'Now you know all my secrets,' Dolly Marchant had said when he was ready to go. And she had looked at him quizzically, but he dared not say what was in his heart, yet he felt the scar that he always imagined there pull as if it might open again. Heartache, that old unhappy want of something that resided within him.

18: A Midnight Visitor

It was midnight when Dickens finally arrived at Devonshire Terrace. Footsteps in the street were stilled now. Somewhere a dog howled, a lonely, lost, despairing sound. He thought of little Dan Curd howling his 'Liar, Liar, Liar', as if to the whole pitiless world. He heard the clocks strike the hour, at midnight a deeper sound than noon. It was bitterly cold. The stars were out — the cold stars that had winked at a murderer who pulled a poor girl's innocent ribbon tighter and tighter round her neck.

He walked on and coming up to his own gate saw a figure there, the tall shadow of a man, motionless, whose head was thrown back as he, too, gazed at the stars as if he might read there some answer to a profound question.

'No answer, eh?' Dickens observed loudly and cheerily — in case the man were mad, or bad, or dangerous. He grasped his stick more tightly.

'Mr Dickens?' came the reply, and as the man turned, Dickens saw that it was Pryor.

'Mr Pryor, is it not? What brings you here? Star-gazing?'

Pryor looked like a very ordinary man in his plain garb of greatcoat and hat. His splendour had departed.

'No, sir, but the vastness of that great black empyrean is mysterious to me. I look sometimes and wonder at myself and my part in the universe.'

Quite a philosopher, thought Dickens, and that word "empyrean" — he was wasted at Wisteria Lodge. 'The meaning is hidden from we mortals, I fear, Mr Pryor; we cannot read the alphabet of the stars.'

'No, sir, I —'

'You wish to speak to me of something. Come into the house before we both freeze.'

Dickens lit the lamps, stirred the slumbering fire, gave Pryor a glass of brandy and warm, and sat opposite him.

'This is to do with Miss Pout, perhaps?'

'In a way, sir, and to do with a little maid that was murdered — Miss Fane's maid, Jemima Curd.'

'I have heard of it.' Better not mention his connection with the police. It was obvious that Pryor had something to confide to him that he had not told Jones or Rogers, who must have questioned him earlier.

'I've thought about it since the police came. It is difficult, Mr Dickens — you've your duty to the family you serve. Sir Neptune's a good employer, provided he gets his way, but then he's an important man in Parliament. He has a temper — we know when to keep out of the way, which is more than —' he stopped. 'Lady Fane —'

'What about her?'

'I feel sorry for her — she is such a nervous woman and never well.'

'And if she does not keep out of the way of his temper?'

Pryor looked troubled. 'He can be cruel, sir — I've heard him be very sharp with her and sometimes I think she's frightened of him — you know like a little dog expecting a blow.'

Dickens did not comment, but it fitted with what he had seen for himself. 'But you feel compunction because of her and the children — you don't want to bring misfortune to them.'

'That's it, sir, and I can't complain of Sir Neptune. If you do your job efficiently and keep quiet, it's not a hard job, sir, not like some. My father kept a small farm. That was labour, sir — though I sometimes wonder if a man in powder and gilt is a man at all, or one of those automaton figures, trained up to do another's bidding, but there's loyalty in it, I suppose.'

Dickens understood. His own grandfather, William Dickens, had been butler to the great Crewe family in Cheshire and London. He'd stayed until his death. He must have been loyal to the Crewes — done his duty. His grandmother had served the Crewes for more than twenty-five years.

'You need not stay forever — you have been educating yourself, I can tell.'

Pryor looked surprised.

'That word "empyrean",' Dickens said.

Pryor grinned — he looked like a young man who knew himself and could laugh at himself. 'I'm trying, Mr Dickens. I should like to be — I beg pardon, I should be telling you about Jemima.'

'Go on.' Dickens poured him some more brandy.

'The police sergeant asked me what I knew about her, and I told him what we all knew we should say. No one told us what to say, but a servant knows what is due to the family. I could have told more and now it's on my conscience. What I saw and heard made me think that I had a duty to poor Jemima — she was a good girl. And you had come about Miss Pout —'

'Are the two girls connected?'

'I think so. Sir Neptune threatened Jemima with the police. She was that terrified she wet herself – poor kid. I saw her rush from the library. I heard him ask her about Miss Mariana and Mr Sabatini.'

'Those two were lovers?'

'Mrs Pick thinks that was what the row was about. Terrible screams and shouting from Miss Mariana's room. Mrs Pick blamed Miss Pout.'

'For running away with Mr Sabatini and breaking Miss Fane's heart?' Now, Dickens would see if Dolly Marchant's version of the story was true.

'No, Mr Dickens, I don't believe that Miss Pout is with Mr Sabatini. I know they went on the same day, but I never saw anything between them. In my position, I see a lot of coming and going and when you see two people together, you get a sense of what they are to each other. I could see it in Miss Mariana when Mr Sabatini spoke to her — the blushes, the secret smiles, and his tenderness to her — when he helped her on with her coat for example, but I never saw that between Miss Pout and Mr Sabatini.'

'Very observant, Mr Pryor.'

'There's more. I think Miss Pout had her sights a deal higher than the music man. I saw her with Sir Neptune — all shyness and blushes at first, but when I caught her looking at him there was something hard there, Mr Dickens, something calculating.'

Dickens wasn't surprised — he remembered her knowing look and Mrs Pout's "Sir Neptune". No wonder her daughter was ambitious. 'And, Sir Neptune?'

'He watched her, sir, and I saw them together, standing very close, and they spent a lot of time together in the library — supposed to be discussing the children, Master Alexander in particular. Now, he didn't like Miss Pout at all — telling tales, I'll bet she was. And, Master Alexander's a taking sort of boy, one of those that servants get fond of.'

'And what happened with Miss Mariana?'

'The family doctor came, and another opinion was sent for, and then we were told that the poor young lady was to go to the country, and one morning, not long after the second doctor came, she was gone.'

'In the night?'

'Yes.'

'And all this happened after Jemima's dismissal and the disappearance of Miss Pout and Mr Sabatini?'

'Yes, sir, and I did wonder if Jemima might have gone to Miss Pout. She was very much Miss Pout's pet. Jemima thought she was wonderful because Miss Pout gave her presents.'

'Why do you think she would do so? You have painted me a picture of a hard young woman, out for herself.'

'I think she was using Jemima. I think Miss Pout encouraged Miss Mariana and Mr Sabatini. There were secrets that Miss Pout wouldn't want told.'

'Nor Sir Neptune.'

'That's true, sir. I don't like to say it, but someone wanted rid of Jemima.'

'So they did — I shall have to tell the police what you have told me — I know Superintendent Jones very well. He will not use your name. He will have his own ways of using your information.'

'If you're sure, Mr Dickens.'

'I am — you need have no fear.'

Dickens took Pryor to the front door and bade him goodnight. 'As I said, you need not stay in your present situation forever — perhaps you might begin to look elsewhere if…'

He did not say more, but Pryor seemed to understand that he was thinking that ruin might come to Wisteria Lodge. A house in ruins like a house of painted cards.

19: Mariana in the Moated Grange

Dickens woke in his dressing room — Pryor had stayed very late. He had thought he would not disturb Catherine. Not that he had slept much — a night half-waking, half-dreaming, and the old familiar pain in his side which came on at times of anxiety.

He had dreamt of his dead sister-in-law, Mary Hogarth, for the first time in many years. In his dream she had materialised like a spectre — had risen, it seemed, from some subterranean place, a cell. She had hovered before him, faintly at the edges, but distinct in the features of the face, a face that dissolved into Jemima Curd's face and then the face of Flora Lambert, and, lastly, the face of Violet Pout wearing a necklace of red and gold beads.

He had sat up then — he had last dreamt of Mary in Italy on All Soul's Eve, and he had been thinking of that time in Ferrara and the cells in the castle there, and Venice, of course — that midnight scene by the canal. And the other three girls had come into his dream. They were connected, he felt sure; there was some quivering thread that linked them.

Just a dream — but he had read somewhere how in dreams questions which have puzzled and perplexed the mind when awake find their solution. Perhaps his dream had revealed a truth. Not that it helped a bit, since he had no idea of what the truth was.

He sat and thought — odd that he had not dreamed of Dolly Marchant, but then the whole of that experience seemed a dream in itself. He felt oppressed by a sense of guilt. Truth? Had Dolly Marchant told him the truth about Rolando and

Violet Pout? He thought so, and Pryor had confirmed her view, but what if Sir Neptune were guilty of murder? Would she protect the man she loved? Or did she? She had not answered his question, but Sir Neptune was the father of her child. What to say to Sam? Had he compromised himself in this case?

He sat on, unable to stir himself, aware of the sounds of the household — assorted footsteps coming up the stairs. Two pairs of skipping steps — Katey and Mamie going to their room on the next floor. Georgina's quick feet. He heard her talking to Frank and Sidney, then Catherine's heavier step which stopped at his door. *Don't come in.* A baby's cry and the footsteps went away. He waited until all was quiet and went downstairs for his breakfast.

Just as he was going in, there came a great clatter of boots — someone hurtling down the stairs. Walter, it would be, Walter due back to school this morning — he was a weekly boarder. And late. His coat would be on the wrong peg as always.

Walter saw his father's face and his usually cheerful face fell. Dickens felt unaccountably angry. 'Go to school like a gentleman.'

'Yes, Pa, sorry.' The boy hung his head and Dickens knew he had been unfair. Walter, aged nine, a steady, amenable boy, always good-natured. He saw Frank at the top of the stairs, ready to turn back. Little Frank, only six years, a handsome, fresh-faced boy, made nervous by his stammer. He thought of Dolly Marchant's lost son and felt ashamed. 'Oh, Wally, my boy, those boots. Think of your poor Pa's addled brains.'

Walter's face lit up like the sun coming out from behind a cloud. 'I will, Pa,' he said most earnestly.

'Very well — off you go then, and do well at your work this week.'

Frank had disappeared.

As Dickens left Devonshire Terrace, he felt guilty about Walter and Frank, as well as about that kiss, and to add to it, he felt guilty about John Elliotson, one of his oldest friends. He had not told him the truth about the visit to Doctor Forbes Winslow's asylum at Hammersmith. And what was he to say to Sam about Dolly Marchant?

That's what came of murder — it tainted everything. It was as if you opened a box to find another inside, and then another and another, and each contained something so foul that in touching it your hands became infected and you infected what you then touched. *Then give it up*, he told himself. *Leave it to Sam.* Did he think then that Sam was infected?

He stopped at a busy crossing. The sweeper was busy at his work. Dickens prepared to cross and gave him a coin. The man, a ragged and bent old specimen of his kind, touched his moth-eaten fur cap, and said, 'Bless yer, Mr Dickens, sir. I knows yer from afore when I swept on the New Road.'

Dickens looked closely. 'Charley Dodd, well, how are you, sir?'

Charley Dodd accompanied him to the other side. 'Pretty well, Mr Dickens, business is good enough these days; it's a better place, this is — not sermuch competition, though not everyone tips as good as you.'

Dickens laughed and gave him another coin. 'Let me make up for the meanness of my fellow men — and ladies, too, I shouldn't wonder.'

'Oh, the ladies is all right, mostly — it's the swells yer gotter watch.'

Dickens went on his way. Charley Dodd — a cheerful cove despite the privations of his calling. CD, eh? Be grateful, he chided himself. Do some good and be firm for Sam Jones, who will always be firm for you.

Doctor Elliotson was waiting and when Dickens saw his benevolent face and thought of his many kindnesses, he resolved to tell him the truth. It would ease some of his guilt.

As they went to find a cab, Dickens told him the real purpose of his visit.

Doctor Elliotson regarded him gravely. 'I do not know if I can sanction such a thing. Doctor Winslow is my close friend and colleague. He was my pupil once.'

'I would not ask, John, and I would rather tell you the truth as not, but this is a matter of murder.'

'Then why does not your friend, the Superintendent, visit the asylum officially?'

'Because Sir Neptune Fane might be a suspect. This is confidential, John, his daughter's illness might be a motive. In the interests of justice, John.'

'Very well, but you must not ask directly — you must not seem to know anything about a particular patient — and you will write a piece in *Household Words*.'

'I will. I will not compromise you, John.'

'Do not, Charles — despite our long friendship.'

The asylum, Sussex House, on Fulham Road was a fine residence, a Georgian mansion, built about 1726, standing in spacious grounds. It was built of warm red-brick. The entrance was handsome with fluted columns and curved pediment — a gentleman's house, the kind of house where you might take tea on the lawn, or dine in some splendour. Not the kind of house where you would be taken on a dark moonless night, tearing out your hair and weeping for your lost love; not the kind of house where you would be imprisoned as a lunatic — perhaps never to get out.

Doctor Winslow was not there to greet them, but his assistant, Doctor Jessop, a young man of a somewhat melancholy aspect, but with gentle eyes, explained that he would be honoured to conduct them; that Doctor Winslow was much gratified by Mr Dickens's interest and hoped that a favourable article on the treatment and care of the patients would be published.

'Doctor Winslow's treatment of our patients is based on kindness, gentleness and soothing tenderness. Those whom we call mad are not wild beasts to be restrained by prison bars, nor are they to be whipped into submission as beasts are. His belief is that they must not be punished in their fallen state; they are amenable to judicious kindness.'

Dickens thought he ought to make some comment in the interest of journalism. 'He is clearly a man who cares deeply for his charges.'

'That is so,' Jessop answered. 'The life of our asylum is a home life. Doctor Winslow lives here with his wife and children. Our patients are part of that family. We have concerts, dances sometimes, and games are encouraged for the sake of healthy exercise. There are nineteen patients at present — only two are ladies. The small numbers ensure the greatest attention.'

By now, they had seen the sitting rooms and dining room, all furnished most elegantly. Some patients, Doctor Jessop informed them, who were on the road to recovery, were allowed to go out of the gates. Others must be kept very quiet, and under surveillance — of a most unobtrusive kind, of course.

'Are their medicinal treatments, too?'

'Blood tonics, sometimes the application of leeches and cold water to soothe the heated mind, and the judicious use of opium to tranquilise the troubled spirit.'

They were upstairs to look at the bedrooms which were pleasantly furnished — they might have been the patients' own bedrooms at home, except for the bars at some of the windows. On others, Dickens noticed how stout nails had been hammered in. What must it be like to look out on the lawns and trees, and to know that you could only go out if permission were granted? How would it feel to hear the key in the lock at night? What loneliness, he thought, and in that dark solitude, what dreams may come? What did the mad dream of?

'Here is a poor old man —' Jessop was pointing through the glass window of one of the bedrooms — 'who was once a man at whose words of wisdom others listened with silent awe. He stood once before an assembly of the greatest men. His melancholia came upon him of a sudden. He had dined, felt faint and sick and was put to bed by his wife. Now he is lost in some dreadful nightmare, which only the tenderest care may alleviate.'

The old man crouched in the corner of the room with his face buried in his hands. What did he think of? Did he remember his fame or was it all vanished like a dream in the morning? Dickens felt an iciness at his neck. Oh, that it should come to this. It was terrifying — to raise the glass to your lips amongst your friends and in a sudden to be lost to the world.

They went up to another floor.

'See this poor girl. I cannot help but think of Tennyson when I look at her: "The night is dreary, he cometh not", but this girl almost never speaks — poor child, she has no notion of what has happened to her. Occasionally, there are a few broken sentences which are hard to make sense of. She weeps most of the time and sometimes tears at her hair. It is a most pitiable case, but with time and gentle treatment, she may recover her wits.'

Dickens knew then that he had found her — the doctor had quoted from Tennyson's poem: Mariana, who dwelt alone in her moated grange, waiting for her lover who did not come. He did not look at John Elliotson, but he did look through the glass of the door. His heart lurched, and he understood what Pryor had said about the dreadful screaming and the haste to conceal Mariana, and why that was done at night.

They continued their tour, the doctor expatiating on various other cases and the modes of treatment. He was an enthusiast. Dickens found he hardly needed to ask questions — to his relief. They looked about the grounds, the rose beds which would bloom in summer, the kitchen gardens which provided good eating for the patients, the greenhouses where fruit was cultivated, the cow houses — fresh milk was available for the sick — the summer houses where the patients might sit in the warmth and look at the sun — and every other thing which would make his article as long as one of his own novels.

At last, they returned to the front door. Dickens thanked Doctor Jessop and promised an approving piece. He would send Harry Wills, his secretary at *Household Words*, who also wrote articles. He would hardly dare come again. He wondered how much he would remember — his head was so full of what he had seen. And he wondered if Dolly Marchant really knew her nephew at all.

'You got what you came for, I think,' said John Elliotson as they made their way down the drive. 'Don't tell me.' He changed the subject, smiling, 'A good, and very long article for my friend and colleague, mind.'

Dickens knew he was forgiven. They shook hands at Hammersmith Bridge. Doctor Elliotson was going to see a patient and Dickens, of course, was bound for Bow Street.

20: A Divided Duty

'So, Mr Pryor believes in a relationship between Mr Sabatini and Miss Fane,' Jones recapped with Dickens, 'and thinks that Violet Pout used Jemima Curd in some way. Jessie Sharp said that Violet gave her presents.'

'Secrets, he said, that Miss Pout wouldn't want told,' Dickens added.

'Violet Pout knew all about Miss Fane and Sabatini.'

'According to Pryor, she encouraged it, and I think she knew more,' said Dickens, who had told of his midnight visitor after hearing Sam's account of his encounters at Wisteria Lodge. 'I went to Doctor Winslow's asylum this morning.'

'You didn't ask about Miss Fane!'

'No, no, the doctor — not Doctor Winslow, by the way — gave me her name inadvertently. He quoted from Tennyson's poem 'Mariana' — she who waits for a lover who does not come. I saw Miss Fane. She is certainly in a most pitiable state. She has virtually lost the power of speech — and no wonder — she is with child.'

Jones was silent for a few moments. 'Poor girl. I wondered about that. Jessie Sharp said Miss Fane had been unwell for some months. It would explain why she was spirited away in the night…'

'What are you thinking?'

'The unthinkable — that it gives Sir Neptune Fane a strong motive for murder. Mr Pryor told you how his fury terrified Jemima Curd. She was dismissed, but he must have thought, what if she told her story? He was very quick to suggest suicide, and he tried to give me the impression that he hardly knew her — servants are his wife's business, or the housekeeper's.'

'He might not have done it himself. He could have paid someone — will someone rid me of this turbulent servant and all that.'

'Maybe, but what can I do? How could I begin to accuse the Honourable Member? Servants' gossip — that is how Pryor's and Jessie's words would be interpreted.'

'There is something else — to do with Violet Pout. Mr Pryor seemed to think that there was something going on between her and Sir Neptune.'

'But she went off with Mr Sabatini.'

'Pryor did not believe that, and neither did —'

'Who?'

'Mrs Marchant with whom I supped last night, and there's another thing — she portrays her nephew, Rolando Sabatini, as a sensitive, romantic youth which hardly fits in with the idea of a cold-hearted seducer who runs away with another woman, leaving Miss Fane pregnant.'

'Did you believe her?'

'Well, given what I know now … and in the cold light of day…'

Jones watched the cold light of day play across his friend's features. Dickens's face was troubled and doubtful. He was usually so certain in his reading of character, and so often right. How had Mrs Marchant confounded him? 'Well?'

Dickens looked at him. 'I was … I confess it to you, Sam, and to you only … I was dazzled, I think. Mrs Marchant is a very beautiful woman, and she … told me things that I wished she had not. I forgot Jemima Curd and all the rest…'

All the rest, thought Jones, and wondered, but he kept to the point. 'Things which might be relevant to Jemima Curd's murder which you cannot tell me without betraying a trust?'

'I suppose so — a divided duty, but I feel I ought to — murder is so terrible a thing. My loyalty should be to you, but what I have done —'

'My advice to you is to sift what she has told you, and select what your conscience dictates that you must tell me in regard to the crime which has been committed. You are, in relation to my official capacity, a witness who must tell the truth. If what you keep back now becomes relevant, then you must tell me.'

'Or never more be officer of thine.'

'Never that — now, think it over.'

'Sir Neptune Fane is a man with secrets — a double life. I will not tell you the details unless they become relevant, but he has much to lose. His daughter in an asylum and pregnant, a servant murdered, an illicit liaison with a governess — and he has had a long love affair with another woman.'

Jones did not need to ask the lady's name. 'So, it is possible that he might be desperate enough to commit murder. He was uneasy yesterday, especially keen to distance himself from Jemima Curd, and he did not want me to question his servants.'

'I suppose he was afraid that Mariana's plight might be told.'

'Very likely,' Jones said. 'But Rolando Sabatini must be suspect, too — he has vanished, he had abandoned Miss Fane —'

'Mrs Marchant did not tell me that Miss Fane is with child.'

'She may not have known, or she may be protecting Sabatini from Sir Neptune Fane.'

'She says that she does not know where Rolando is.'

'But not with Miss Pout.'

'She thought Violet Pout worldly and calculating,' Dickens said, 'and Mr Pryor used the latter word. I didn't much like her, either, though I only met her the once — which is why I believed she had run off with Rolando Sabatini.'

'Jessie Sharp didn't like her — she had an unkind streak. Jessie said that she and Jemima had secrets.'

'Violet Pout must know about Mariana — that's why she left. She'd be frightened to death of Sir Neptune, even if they'd had some sort of liaison.'

'If she's not with Sabatini, then where is she?' Jones asked.

'Suppose Jemima Curd did go to her for the job she mentioned to Nolly Turner…'

'Clerkenwell? I've had the beat constables asking about her, and Stemp and Feak have combed the area round the reservoir, and they've not found anything so far.'

'No handy waistcoat button?' Dickens asked.

Jones gave him a twisted smile. 'And a fat lot of good that's been. Here's irony for you: one victim where there's probable evidence, but it happened five years ago. The murderer's long gone. In the other case, the murderer can't be far away, and there's nothing to go on, but a length of silk ribbon — Jessie sharp told me that Violet Pout had given Jemima ribbons so that's not much help.'

'Unless —'

'You're still thinking there's a connection — oh, your artist.'

'I know, I know — it's far-fetched, but I can't help wondering about Mariana Fane's portrait. Why would Rolando Sabatini tell St. George Pierce about it if there wasn't one? Violet Pout must have known about it.'

'We need to find her. I can't get at Sir Neptune — not without evidence, but Miss Pout seems to be at the heart of this — somehow. Your Anne Brown hasn't heard anything?' Jones asked.

'No, Mrs Pout has not heard from Violet,' Dickens replied. 'I'll go to Clerkenwell tomorrow — I'll take Scrap. A labouring man and his boy.'

'Disguise, is it? Oh, well, I can't think of anything better.'

'And, now I think of it, Violet Pout has very distinctive hair — so fair as to be almost silver at times. Someone may have seen her.'

'I hope so. In the meantime, I'll get on with my paperwork.'

Dickens went off. Jones remained at his desk, thinking about Jemima Curd and Flora Lambert. Drownings. He stood up, got his hat and coat and went out to see Sergeant Rogers.

21: A Wandering Minstrel

The sound of a concertina alerted Mollie Rogers to the presence of the stranger in the stationery shop in Crown Street. She managed the shop for Eleanor and Tom Brim, who had been adopted by Superintendent Jones and his wife, Elizabeth, and, of course, were too young to run it themselves. Their father had died of tuberculosis at the beginning of the year. Scrap was their messenger boy, general helper, and occasional detective when Dickens and Mr Jones needed sharp eyes and ears, 'an' a nose fer things', as Scrap put it.

The stranger, a ragged sort of individual in a long, shabby coat, an ancient top hat that looked like a crooked chimney, and green spectacles was playing the cracked strains of "Home Sweet Home". Madman, she thought, about to tell him to clear off. Scrap popped up from behind the counter, looked narrowly at the stranger and said casually, 'Arternoon, Mr D.'

The notes died wheezily away like air from a rubber cushion. The musician took off his green glasses and gazed on Scrap with a similarly deflated look. 'How d'you know?'

'Yer 'ands — the ring. Allus wears it. Seen it 'undreds o' times.'

It was true — Dickens always wore the little gold and diamond ring on his little finger. He had taken it from Mary Hogarth's finger when she died. He had sworn never to take it off.

He swept off his hat and bowed, 'Detective Scrap — Inspector, I suppose now — my compliments. I have need of you.'

Scrap vaulted over the counter. 'Murder, is it? Mrs Jones sed. I bin waitin' — fer ages.'

Dickens heard the reproof in his tone.

'Can you spare him, Mollie?'

'Never,' she answered, smiling, 'but I suppose I must. Where you off to?'

'Clerkenwell,' Dickens replied.

'Best dress the part then. Give us a minnit,' Scrap said.

While he waited, Dickens chatted to Mollie, who had married Sam Jones's Sergeant Rogers after saving his life in an old hayloft where there was a man with a gun — pointing at Charles Dickens.

'And your chopping boy?' Dickens asked. Charlie Rogers at two years old was a strapping boy with the red face and blue eyes of his father and with the same good nature.

'Into everything — he's at my ma's today — just as well, since you're takin' my assistant. He has been waitin' — he's been across to Mr Jones's house twenty times, hopin' that the call will come.'

Scrap came back, every inch the street urchin with his ragged trousers, dirty face and a cap that resembled a dead cat in his hand. He offered it to Mollie. 'Penny fer the music.'

'Call that music,' she laughed.

'Mollie Rogers, you wound me to the quick — if you had seen me at my last soiree. Mind, it's the only tune I can play on this.' Dickens fingered the keys again and out he went with Scrap, putting the instrument in its box.

'Clerkenwell, eh?' said Scrap. 'Yer'll need these —' he offered Dickens a pair of fingerless gloves — 'diamonds in Clerkenwell, Mr D — wot yer thinkin' of?'

Dickens put them on. 'And there was I thinking my green spectacles were the crowning touch.'

'I 'opes yer can see where you're goin'. 'Oo we lookin' fer?' Scrap asked.

'A lady — a nice looking lady with very fair hair. Name of Miss Violet Pout.'

'She done the murder o' that servant girl?'

'I don't think so, but she knew her and I think the girl, Jemima Curd, may have gone up to Clerkenwell to see her.'

'Where we startin'?'

'I have an idea about that. Here's a cab.'

The cab driver looked a bit doubtful about the ragged boy and the man in the green spectacles. They didn't look as if they had two farthings, never mind the fare to Clerkenwell.

'Two bob ter Clerkenwell.'

Dickens fumbled in his pocket for the coin, but he couldn't resist saying, 'A bob an' a tune, sir. I'm a poor man.'

'Two bob an' none o' yer tricks, you old rogue.'

The old rogue gave him the money and they climbed in.

Granted, Clerkenwell was notorious for its swarming alleys, its disreputable pubs, its crowded, dilapidated lodging houses, its population of prostitutes, thieves, fences, and its frequent murders, but there were still pockets of gentility. Dickens thought that Violet Pout — if, indeed, she were here — would be lodging in a better class of house, in Myddleton Square, perhaps, or Claremont Square which was built round a reservoir — the Carlyles had lived there once. Thomas had used to take a morning walk by the reservoir. Dickens had been round those squares when he had, some fifteen years ago, looked at a new house on the New River Estate — very pretty, he had thought, but too dear.

There were still professional men living up here: lawyers, architects, wine merchants, jewellers, watchmakers — and artists. And, Dickens had thought, while getting into his disguise, George Cruikshank, the artist had lived in Armwell Street for years — pity he had moved, but he had met George Hughes who also lived in Armwell Street with his wife Emily Nicholson, an artist in her own right. Just the kind of area an artist might live — Mr Tony, for instance. And some called Clerkenwell "Little Italy".

The cab dropped them in St John's Street by the reservoir where poor Jemima had met her death. She might, of course, have been in Clerkenwell looking for her drunken mother, but she had been strangled, and with a ribbon made of silk. Speculation, Dickens knew that, but what else could he do? He had promised Anne Brown that he would try to find Violet. Stick to that, he told himself.

A footpath known as Myddleton passage led from Sadler's Wells into Myddleton Square. It was a dark and very narrow passage with a kink in it where, even now, in the early afternoon, it was black as pitch — just the sort of place a man might use as a shortcut to the new reservoir — just the sort of place in which a man might strangle a girl before emerging into the raucous crowds milling about Sadler's Wells. Who would notice a man holding up a girl — drunk, they'd think, if they did notice. On one side of the passage ran the perimeter wall of the New River Head — it must have been seven feet high. On the other side was a wall broken at intervals by the doors to the gardens of the houses in Myddleton Square. They would be locked at night against intruders. Some looked as if they never were open. There was a gas lamp at the further end to which he and Scrap were walking. It wouldn't give much light at midnight, say, and he couldn't see any others. They waited, listening to the silence. No one came down the passage.

'Gives yer the creeps, don't it — feel as if I'm buried alive,' Scrap said.

'It does. Let's go on.'

Dickens and Scrap came out into the square where the church of St Mark's stood in the centre.

'Let's have a stroll round — get the lie of the land. See who's about.'

They walked along the south side of the square, looking at the houses and noting the passers-by: a young woman carrying a small child, who looked at them over the nurse's shoulder with wide eyes; a professional looking gentleman in a hurry; two ladies getting out of a cab and going up the steps to a house. Dickens looked up, hoping for a familiar face at a window. The east and South sides of the square were much the same. At the corner where the square opened into the street that led to Claremont Square, Dickens stopped.

'What now?' asked Scrap.

'A little light music, I think.'

He lounged against the railings of a house. Scrap took off his hat, laid it down on the pavement and squatted beside it. Dickens began his rendering of "Home Sweet Home".

It wasn't long before above them a window opened and a shower of coins descended, some bouncing off Dickens's top hat. 'Clear off, can't you? That's a dreadful din. Call yourself a musician.'

Dickens looked up to see a head disappearing and the window closed with a defiant thud. Scrap picked up the money and they went round the corner into Claremont Terrace. Here the passers-by were more numerous, making their way up to Claremont Square or down into Amwell Street. Some looked at the blind man and his ragged boy pityingly and gave a penny or two. A very tall clergyman loped by and dropped two farthings into the hat, murmuring, 'God bless you.' More often, people hurried past, grimacing at the sound of the concertina. Two ragged urchins, black as a couple of sweeps, stopped and stared as Dickens paused and took up his tune again.

'Play us another, old codger — we ain't got no sweet 'ome ter go ter.'

Dickens couldn't oblige. Scrap ignored them, too busy counting the money.

'Come on ol' buryin' face, give us a polka.'

The two of them danced about, enjoying themselves hugely, one of them holding up his one leg of his torn breeches as if it were the skirt of a genteel lady. The other bowed and said, 'Shockin' din, ain't it? Not much class about 'ere, miss.'

'Sling yer 'ooks then if yer don't like it,' Scrap growled, his patience wearing thin.

'Gran'pa deaf as well as blind, is 'e? Must be ter put up wiv that row —' Scrap stood up threateningly — 'Temper, temper, young 'un.'

'No need ter get the spike on. Ta ta, then, goin' ter the hopera we 'is.'

They ran off, screeching. Scrap turned to Dickens. 'This ain't no good, Mr D. We looks a pair o' fools.'

'You're right. How much did we make?'

'Ten pence that came from 'eaven, six pence and two farthin's, a bone button — cracked, an' a bit of ol' cake.'

'Not bad, considerin' —'

'The racket yer made.'

Dickens laughed. 'All right, let's go up to Claremont Square — I won't play anymore.'

They went up to the reservoir which formed the centre of the square and had a look at the water that looked placid enough in the winter sun. There was a raised footpath all the way round. A nursemaid passed them, pushing her three-wheeled perambulator in which a pair of infant twins looked out at the world gloomily like a pair of elderly senators going to the Forum in their chariot, and expecting disaster. A boy followed, bowling his hoop, his face rosy in the cold and his cap perched rakishly on the side of his head. Going home for tea by the nursery fire, Dickens thought, as they darted aside from the wobbling hoop.

They looked at the houses — but they were very like the houses in Myddleton Square and the ones beyond in Armwell Street, and, he knew, in Lloyd Square and River Street. They saw plenty of young women and various couples, but none resembled Violet Pout, and there was no artist carrying a handy palette and brushes to proclaim his calling.

'Call it a day?' Scrap looked disappointed. 'Nothin' doin'.'

Dickens took off his green spectacles, looped the strap of the concertina box over his shoulder, and they went back towards Sadler's Wells where the streets were rougher and more crowded. They passed a seedy looking pub. Scrap looked hungry — as always.

22: The Forlorn Hope

As its name suggested, The Forlorn Hope looked to be the last refuge of the gone to seed, never to bloom again. It looked like the lair of disbarred lawyers, unfrocked clergymen, out of work actors and down-at-heel ticket of leave men who drowned their sorrows in adulterated porter and played for pennies with greasy cards. There were labourers in leather aprons, hulking men who looked like coal-heavers, a few women who looked as though they might be touting for business, and a couple of toothless crones swigging gin.

The place was packed and reeked of tallow candles, tobacco fumes, stale beer and human degradation. Dickens went to the bar to buy a couple of glasses of pale ale and Scrap risked a worrying looking pie.

'Give us a tune, mister,' a woman shouted.

'Blimey, Mr D, you ain't —' But Dickens couldn't resist. He turned to the company and struck up "Home Sweet Home" to the yells of the crowd which rather too quickly turned to jeers.

Scrap hurried them to a rickety table near the door — they wouldn't be staying long.

'I 'opes one o' them ain't the cat's meat man,' said Scrap, stabbing the pastry with his fork. 'No, it looks awright —' he tried some meat — 'ain't half bad.'

Dickens looked about him as he drank his pale ale. Not the sort of place where Violet Pout might be found. It was no use — Sam's men would just have to keep making their enquiries.

A woman walked towards them — a woman in dark green velvet. When he saw her red hair, Dickens thought for a wild moment that it was Dolly Marchant and his heart turned over, but when she sat down, he saw that the velvet was worn and patched and the voice told its own story.

'Ain't seen yer about 'ere before — lookin' fer someone?' She had seen Dickens looking about him. 'Might be able ter 'elp. Name's Cassie — Cassie Hanlon.'

'Me and me lad, we're lookin' fer me daughter. She's left 'ome. Thort she might be workin' fer a Miss Pout. The boy, Dan'l, misses 'is sister.'

Scrap looked suitably downcast.

'Don't know 'er — what's yer girl's name?' Cassie asked.

'Jemima — Jemima Curd.'

She looked shocked. 'Bleedin' 'ell, mister, she drowned — Ned Orrey found 'er — murder, 'e sed. Perlice all over askin about 'er.'

Should have thought of that, thought Dickens. Too late now. Scrap burst into noisy sobs. Dickens ploughed on. 'Oh, gawd, not my girl, not my lovely girl, oh, gawd, gawd 'elp us.' He must have overdone it — suddenly a shower of beer was flung into Dickens's face. Tragedy was not really his forte on the stage — comedy was more in his line.

A raddled filthy hag screamed at him. 'Dirty bleeder, you ain't my Georgie an' 'e's no son o' mine.' A pewter pot followed the beer and caught Dickens on the cheekbone. He stood up, and so did Cassie Hanlon who screamed, too. The other hag screeched, 'Imposter,' and Mrs Curd — it must be she — shouted obscenities mingled with cries of 'Murderer.'

A man with hands as big as hams snatched up Scrap by the collar. 'Yer little bleeder,' he shouted, shaking him like a dog. Scrap had his tankard in his hand and bashed the hulk in the face, simultaneously kicking him in the groin. Someone hit the hulk with an iron trivet and he went down like a log. Scrap wriggled free — the iron might be meant for him so he made a quick retreat under the table.

By now, the motley company had surged forward, some out of curiosity, most from a desire to join in and lynch the murderer. Mrs Curd leapt forward, her filthy claws ready to tear at Dickens's face. She missed, but fastened her nails in his coat — he smelt the stink of fish — and worse. The table overturned and bottles and plates crashed down. Another woman yelled 'Murderer!'

Dickens snatched up his concertina in its box and swung it by the leather strap, causing a momentary parting of the crowd as some ducked. The box struck a man's face — Dickens heard the crack of bone.

Scrap darted from his refuge and through the temporary opening, shouting, 'Perlice' as he shot through the door, dodging a man who tried to stop him with a chair — the chair hit the wrong man, broke into pieces, and another brawl started.

'Perlice,' a voice shouted. ''E's a bleedin' rozzer.'

'Copper's nark,' shouted another.

Make up your mind, thought Dickens, as he made another attempt to swing his weapon. A hand grabbed it and he was dragged forward, hanging onto the strap, and feeling his arm half-pulled from its socket, his filthy incubus still clinging to him and screaming, 'Murderin' bastard.'

The gamblers had started their own row — someone had nicked the money. Someone shouted that ''E'd do fer Jecks!'

'Jecks,' the cry went up.

Not a popular man, Jecks. He was flung to the floor.

'Cheatin' bastard.' A wild-haired woman leapt on him, pummelling with her fists. Jecks roared and kicked out madly, catching another woman on the face. Blood spurted from her nose. Howling like a banshee, she joined her friend in the attack. Several men jumped in. Dickens's own assailant let go of the leather strap so that he could fall upon Jecks instead.

Dicken staggered back and Mrs Curd dropped from him at last and was lost in the fury of blows, flying chairs, screeches and curses. A fist aimed a punch, but just in time, Cassie dragged him away to the door, losing half the back of her dress in the process. Some enemy had taken the chance for revenge.

'Keep yer scabby 'ands off my Jemmy, Cassie 'Anlon, yer dirty tart.'

'Wouldn't touch 'im with a pig poke, Clem Trotters, get back ter yer stye.'

Clem Trotters lurched forward, but Cassie was too quick and they were out of the door in a trice just as Inspector Shackell was about to go in.

'We bin attacked,' Cassie shouted, 'me an' me friend — 'ere, where's 'is lad?'

Scrap appeared. 'Found a policeman. Lor, Mr Dickens, yer face is all over blood.'

Dickens looked a sorry sight, blood on his face, his coat torn, and his hat gone. Miraculously the concertina was still in his hand — the box had vanished.

Inspector Shackell took charge, sending in his burly constables with their rattles and truncheons. Some kind of order would be restored, no doubt.

'Mr Dickens?' he asked, astonished. 'Who started this?'

'Mrs Curd took me for a murderer — it influenced the company somewhat against me,' Dickens replied.

'You were asking about Jemima Curd?'

'I was actually looking for a woman called Violet Pout. Miss Curd's name came up — er — accidentally.'

Scrap hid his grin behind his hand and nodded. Cassie didn't comment. She wasn't a copper's nark.

'Want to press charges?' Inspector Shackell asked.

'No, no, but Mr Jones will be glad for you to take her to Bow Street.'

'So, he will, you've done me a favour, Mr Dickens, we've searched all over.'

The noise was beginning to die down. The door flew open and the hapless Jecks flew out to land at the Inspector's feet. He was a most pitiable object, but alive, if not kicking.

'Hook it, Jecks.' The Inspector was without pity.

Dickens helped Jecks to his feet — after all the beaten man had saved him from Lord knows what. It was his good fortune that everyone loathed Jecks. Jecks shambled away without a word. Inspector Shackell went in to arrange for Mrs Curd's detention.

Dickens turned to Cassie. 'Miss Hanlon, I think you may have saved my life. I am much obliged. You didn't think that I'm a murderer?'

'Nah, knew yer was a toff, though — yer cuffs, see. Clean — starched probably. I worked as a laundress once. An' yer boots is polished — I done that in me time.'

'Very observant, Miss Hanlon, my thanks.'

'Yer voice was good, but a few too many "gawds", I'd say. Overdid that bit. The lad was good — regular urchin, I'd say for a gent. Oughter be on the stage.'

'I am much obliged, Miss Hanlon.' Scrap bowed, and winked at Dickens, who kept a straight face.

'I owe you — the dress. My fault, I think,' Dickens said.

'Bloody Clem. I ain't touched the greasy little runt, Jemmy, nobody would, not even fer ready money. All the same, them

Trotters, swine at the piggin. It was Clem's doin'.' Cassie smoothed down her worn velvet, genteel as any lady.

'Nevertheless, you must have a new one.' Dickens took out all the coins from his pocket and dropped them into her hand. He thought about Cassie Hanlon's sharp eyes. 'Do you live about here?'

'Lodgin's at number four, Baker's Row, off Amwell Street.'

'If you could search about for a Miss Violet Pout, I should be very grateful. We were looking for her. She is tall and slender, with very pale hair — most distinctive, and rather pale blue eyes.'

'Lady?'

'Yes, she was a governess.' Dickens fished in his pocket under the long coat for a card. 'Wellington Street, over the Strand from Bow Street.'

Cassie Hanlon took the card. 'Obliged fer the money, sir. Let yer know.'

'She might be living with a man — an artist, possibly.'

'Lady, is it?' Cassie said satirically, and walked away, her head held high.

Dickens watched her. An independent girl, that one, and clever, too.

''Ow we getting' 'ome?' asked Scrap, having seen all their money vanish.

Inspector Shackell came out to report that Mrs Curd had been scooped up from the floor and was presently in handcuffs — just in case she thought to resist arrest for brawling.

'Lend us two bob, yer honour. I'm a poor man wot 'asn't 'is cab fare,' Dickens whined.

Inspector Shackell laughed out loud, 'You're a card, sir, and no mistake. I'll get a cab for you. Do you want that seeing to?' He pointed to Dickens's bloodied cheek.

'Thank you, no, we'll get on our way.'

'Mr Jones'll wanter know.'

'Good job you found me, young Scrap.'

They waited in the cab while Inspector Shackell spoke to the driver and handed over the fare. Scrap looked at Dickens's wet coat and sniffed. 'Coulda bin a piss-pot,' he observed philosophically.

'Very consoling, I'm sure,' Dickens answered, attempting to clean off some of the blood from his face with his handkerchief.

'Spit on it,' said his philosopher.

Dickens did so, wincing. Lord, it hurt.

Scrap looked at him pityingly. 'It woz the music wot did it.'

Dickens saw the glint in his eye and laughed. The concertina breathed out the last off-key note of its unmusical life.

The cab rolled away. Dickens gazed out into Amwell Street, holding his handkerchief to his throbbing cheek. A woman waiting to cross glanced at the cab — the way you sometimes looked without much interest at a stranger and held his eyes for a second or two — an unimportant moment, unless the seeming stranger was one you knew.

The woman was Violet Pout. She knew him, too, in a moment of startled recognition.

The cab was picking up speed. Dickens twisted round in his seat, but she was gone, vanished into the dark. There was only a faint mist wreathing the gas lamp.

23: Tales Told

The Superintendent was deep in the *Police Gazette*, peering at it through a magnifying glass when Sergeant Rogers ushered in the adventurers. Scrap's eyes were alive with excitement. When Jones saw the blood on Dickens's face and his swollen cheek, he wondered if he had enjoyed himself quite as much.

'Altercation?' he asked.

'With a pewter cup,' Dickens replied.

'Anyone interesting?'

'Mrs Curd — she threw her beer at me, too.'

'What on earth did you do to her?'

'What you might call a case of mistaken identity — she took me for a murderer in a pub called The Forlorn Hope.'

Dickens left it to Scrap to tell the tale. Jones would enjoy it more that way.

'Mr D ses 'e's lookin' fer Miss Pout — 'appens ter mention Jemima Curd an' we sort o' pretend ter be Mr Curd an' 'is boy. Mrs Curd — drunken ol' crone — takes offence and goes fer 'im an' — well — things go down'ill a bit. Folk gets a bit worked up, screamin' blue murder. Some great 'ulk collars me. Bashes 'im on the nose and kicks 'im in — well, yer knows where, an' Mr D goes at 'em all wiv 'is concertina —'

'Which I happened to have about me,' put in Dickens, seeing Jones's enquiring glance.

'Concertina box breaks a bloke's 'ead, an' I scarpers, shoutin' fer the perlice. Some feller tries ter stop me wiv a chair an' misses. Some other bloke cops it an' I gets out. Inspector Shackell's comin' along the street wiv 'is men an' some girl gets Mr D out of it. Concertina won't play again. Just as well — we dint make much from 'is playin' — got tol' ter move on a few times an' Mr D gives all the takin's away.'

'How much?' asked Jones mildly.

'One an' six an' two farthin's, a button, an' a bit o' cake — stale an' all so it ain't worth eatin'.'

'You said the pie was all right,' Dickens said, somewhat aggrieved.

'So it woz — not that I 'ad time ter finish it.'

'I do beg your pardon, Scrap — most disobligin' of me.'

'Wouldn't a' missed it, Mr D — not even the concertina.' Scrap winked at him.

'Inspector Shackell kindly paid for our cab. And, by the way, in case you were thinking we had achieved nothing —'

'Not at all, not at all — it is all — most interesting.' Jones was surreptitiously wiping his eyes.

'Inspector Shackell is bringing Mrs Curd along — soon, I should think, and there's more. The Forlorn Hope was not such a forlorn hope — I saw Violet Pout in Amwell Street, but I was in the cab and when I turned round, she'd vanished.'

'That is encouraging news. Now, I doubt very much if Mrs Curd will want to see your bloody visage again, so I suggest that you get away home to have your war wounds dressed. Scrap can go home with Alf. Heroic, you were, I know, but be careful what you say to Mollie.'

Scrap went out with Rogers.

Jones could not hold in his laughter. 'A concertina an offensive weapon — only you, Charles, only you. I didn't know you could play it.' He mopped his eyes again.

'One of my many accomplishments — the accordion is my preferred instrument — though Scrap wasn't impressed, and neither were two urchins who called me "ol' buryin' face". What a day — I shall feel it tomorrow.'

'Time you went home. I'll see you tomorrow — Mrs Curd might have something to tell us.'

At Devonshire Terrace, much exclamation greeted Dickens's injured face — he had deposited his coat and spectacles at the office in Wellington Street so there was no wonder at his torn garments and the smell of beer. Offers to bathe the swelling, to apply witch hazel, iodine, or a kiss from twelve-year-old Mamie were made — the last he accepted, and a cup of tea.

There was a gathering round the drawing room fire. Certain persons ought to have been in bed, but there was a general outcry at the injustice of such a suggestion. Bed was for babies like Dora, Henry and Sydney. Big boys like Alley and Frank, who had sneaked in behind Aunt Georgy, deemed themselves quite capable of hearing about Pa's encounter with an enemy.

'Pa, Pa, was it a fight? Did you win it? Did you punch him back?' This was Alfred, known as Alley, aged five, stocky already and putting up his little fists.

Frank, always more timid, nevertheless looked at Pa with shining eyes. Dickens remembered his fright at Pa's temper this morning. Forgiven, again.

'Sit by me, Frank. Not a fight exactly,' said Dickens, buying time to invent a story which would satisfy the sanguinary hopes of Alley whilst paying due to the delicacies of the ladies. He wasn't going to recount the events at The Forlorn Hope. A brush with a door post was now too late a tale — Alley and Frank were all eyes.

'If you'll sit down, Alley, my boy, I will tell all — about the mad dogs with their slavering chops, and the dark-haired gypsy man who had hands as big as hams. A villain of the deepest dye who deserved my vengeance…'

His audience was rapt. The tale was not a long one, but it was full of incident — not too gory, and the hero used guile and the utmost cunning to defeat his brutal enemy who had struck that one blow — only one, mind.

'What really happened?' asked Catherine later, as she bathed his cheek with witch hazel. 'Mad dogs, indeed.'

'An old hag threw a pewter pot at me.'

'Why?'

'I don't think she liked me.'

Catherine laughed. 'Were you with the Superintendent?'

'I was — research amongst the criminal classes for *Household Words*.' Dickens never told his wife much about their investigations. It would only alarm her, and she was nervous enough these days. Dora, the baby, was a fragile little thing.

She kissed him. 'Well, duck next time.'

'I will.' He kissed her round cheek and stroked the brown ringlets. 'Now, I have much to do — I won't disturb you, I'll sleep in the dressing room. It will be a long night's work.'

24: Two Letters

Dickens took an early breakfast. He wanted to be out of the house before there were any more questions. Alley was tenacious. He would want the story told over — again and again.

Two letters came. He recognised Mrs Carlyle's writing; the other hand he did not know. He took them with him to Wellington Street where, in his own office, he opened Mrs Carlyle's.

I must be brief. I have only just heard — just a rumour so far. Fanny picked it up last night. Lady Fane is very ill — a heart attack. Near death, it is said. I will write more when I find out…

Poor Lady Fane. He wasn't surprised. What she had endured. Her daughter's ruin. And had she known about Dolly Marchant? All those years — and the son? Had she known about him? Had she known about Violet Pout? He was certain there must have been something between her and Sir Neptune after what Pryor had told him. Sir Neptune had been kind enough to his wife. He had seen that, but she was frightened of him. He remembered her at the door of the library at Wisteria Lodge — how nervous she had been. She had not known then that he had come about Violet Pout.

If she died? What would that mean for Dolly Marchant? Did she still love him? She had not answered his question. But it would mean complete rupture from her son. She had wept about him. He could not believe that she would become the second Lady Fane.

He must go to tell Sam. Sam could hardly go back to Wisteria Lodge now — even if he had good reason. That was a thought — Lady Fane near death. If only he knew more. He supposed eminent doctors would be called — Sir Neptune could hardly … no, that was out of the question. Now, if she had died suddenly then his suspicions might have some weight.

He glanced at the other letter — a matter of business, perhaps. Probably a begging letter from some struggling literary man. He received dozens of them. Now, he looked closely, he thought the writing familiar. He would have a quick look — he could pass it on to Harry Wills if it were not important.

He opened it and glanced first at the signature: *Luigi Mariotti*

He felt that tremor go through him, that pricking of the thumbs as if an electric charge had passed through him.

Luigi Mariotti had taught Italian to him and Catherine before they had left for their year-long stay in Italy. Dickens had first met him on his voyage to America on the *SS Britannia* in 1842. Mariotti had been going to Canada to take up the Chair of Modern Languages at King's College, Windsor, but he had not stayed and had returned to London in 1843. Dickens had met him again and Mariotti had become their teacher — a good one, too. He was one of the many revolutionary Italians who had settled in London, and he knew a good many people: Robert Browning, an ardent supporter of Italian Unification; he was a friend of Lady Byron who was a sponsor of Giuseppe Mazzini's School for Italian boys in Hatton Garden — the school which Dickens supported, too.

Dickens had met him again at the Carlyles' house — Mariotti was a frequent visitor there, where he had met Thackeray and Bulwer-Lytton. He had made a great success of London as a writer and lecturer who had published a book on Italy and written many articles on Italian politics, as well as being a Professor of Italian at London University. He had reverted to his own name, Antonio Gallenga, in recent times. Mariotti had been an alias adopted in earlier revolutionary days in Italy.

The letter asked Dickens to dine at the Piazza that evening at six o'clock for he had someone he wanted Dickens to meet. If not then, could Dickens suggest another occasion?

Dickens was intrigued — who might this stranger be? Mariotti had many friends in London — perhaps the man was a writer of some sort, wanting to write for *Household Words*; perhaps Dickens had turned him down at some point and he wished to be presented in person. And, here was another point: Mariotti was a good friend of the artists Rossetti and Gambardella Spiridione, who had painted Mrs Carlyle's portrait. He would show Mariotti the portrait of Flora Lambert — he might know the original, or Spiridione might. He sent a reply immediately.

At Bow Street, Jones was busy with his magnifying glass. 'You have news,' he said, observing Dickens's face.

'I have, though it is not confirmed. Mrs Carlyle writes that Lady Fane is mortally ill — a heart attack. I thought you should know.'

Jones leant back in his chair. 'Well, that closes the doors of Wisteria Lodge to me. I can hardly intrude in a dying woman's house about a servant who no longer works for them and who was found dead in Clerkenwell — miles away from Chelsea.'

'It makes you think, though — convenient for Sir Neptune if she dies. She cannot talk about her daughter, or Jemima Curd. Suppose she knew about Violet Pout.'

'And you said he had a liaison with a married woman — I'll bet Lady Fane knew. It almost seems as if his house is falling away about him.'

'He might be desperate. What did Mrs Curd say?'

'You mean amid her drunken ramblings about the murderer 'oo oughter 'ave bin strung up? She was very firm on that point. She did remember seeing Jemima, but not when, and she did think that Jemima was working for some lady called Pott or Spot — too drunk to remember clearly.'

'Near enough Pout.'

'Inspector Shackell and his constables are combing the area round Armwell Street — concentrating on lodging houses of a respectable sort. He'll find her — eventually.'

'I asked that girl who got me out of The Forlorn Hope. Very sharp, she was. Knew I was a toff from my shirt cuffs and my polished boots. She complimented Scrap on his impersonation of a street urchin, given he was a toff, too.'

Jones laughed. 'What did Scrap say?'

'Convincing as you like: "I am much obliged, Miss Hanlon" — with the 'H'. I gave her my card and told her to come to Wellington Street if she finds Violet Pout. Now, as to our other matter, I am to dine this evening with Signor Luigi Mariotti —'

'Artist, is he?'

'Very droll, Samivel, but he knows a great many people. I thought I would take the picture of Flora Lambert. I feel sure I know it — not that I know how it helps.'

Violet Pout is listlessly shuffling her cards. She cheats, of course, tossing aside the Queen of Spades — Spades signify grief, sickness, worry — she is looking to turn up an Ace of Hearts which foretells good news, but the pack seems wholly made up of Spades. Violet throws them all across the floor. She has worries enough without the cards, not the least of which is that she is sure she saw Mr Dickens in a cab that passed her on the street. He had looked straight at her, and though he had a handkerchief pressed to his face, she knew it was he. It had been a matter of a few moments, but their eyes had met, and in that few moments, she had seen something.

He had looked — she thinks about it — not surprised, but as if he had known she would be there. She had turned back quickly into a passageway, and there she had waited, trembling. She had thought of that moment over and over. Was he looking for her?

She thinks again about Anne Brown and her mother — it would not be surprising if her mother had asked Anne Brown to ask Mr Dickens to make enquiries of Sir Neptune. Oh, yes, Mrs Pout would be proud to have her important connection, Mr Dickens, go to Wisteria Lodge. Mr Dickens would be concerned about Miss Pout — Sir Neptune would be impressed.

She burns with shame to think of what Sir Neptune might have said. He won't have told the truth about her, of course, nor will he have told the truth about Mariana, but he could say he had dismissed her because she had tried to seduce him, say she was immoral, tell Mr Dickens that she had gone away with Rolando Sabatini.

And, where is Jemima Curd? She had gone, she said, to look for her family — to ask her cousin in Hemlock Court, or some such place, and she hadn't come back. Jemima knows too much, and Jemima doesn't think so much of her as she used to. Perhaps, she has run away.

What a fool, she has been. She had been tempted by her other lover — she had thought that marriage would be better than being a mistress. Why had she not been satisfied with Sir Neptune's attentions? On the night when Mariana had been ill, she had gone to tell Sir Neptune. He had given her some wine. That had been the beginning. Sir Neptune had come to her room, and often. It had been exciting, and she had felt her power over him. But Mariana had continued to be ill, and then it was all too late. And she'd had no choice.

The rooms downstairs are empty. They are large and there are marble fireplaces. She thought at first that they were to inhabit those rooms; that they would be furnished with heavy silk ilk curtains, soft carpets, velvet sofas; there would be a dining room where candle light would gleam on silver, and on the mahogany table and chairs where they would eat with his distinguished friends — the house of her dreams.

But this — this is not what she expected — the house in St John's Wood where she had taken Mariana had only been lent. She had liked it and there had been a woman to bring tea when she visited. But, his friend was coming back from abroad and they had to move to these shabby top floor rooms of a narrow house, rented, so he said, from a another friend, a friend she'd never met — just as she had never met any of his artist friends, any of the rich friends she was sure he had. Two floors up, and she had been expected to carry up the coals from the yard and bring in food — until Jemima came. The light, he had said, he needed the light from the windows in the ceiling.

It is cold, but she has not dressed. Her hair is undone — it has lost its shine. Her petticoats are grubby; her velvet wrap is a shabby thing, its green faded, the golden thread loose. She picks at it sullenly. Green doesn't suit her. It makes her hair look tarnished and her skin yellow.

She looks round the frowsty room. The precious light from the windows just shows the meanness of everything, the worn chairs and chaise longue, the threadbare carpet. She thinks of Wisteria Lodge. She could weep.

She looks at the easel. There is no portrait. He never paints her face. There are her shoulders and her breast, and always the green robe and the jewels — trumpery glass things, and that stupid cross at the end. She doesn't understand that.

The hair is not hers. If anything, the hair is Mariana's, or Jemima's. Why does he not paint her angel's hair? Why does he not paint her blue eyes?

He is hardly here. She has no idea where he goes. He tells her nothing. She had been sure that he loved her. Now she thinks, he never said so. Sometimes he looks through her, his eyes blank as though he no longer sees her, as though he no longer knows her. She does not even know if he will come back.

And she has no idea what she will do. Mr Dickens must not find her. Perhaps she imagined him. What she cannot do is go home. There is no wedding ring, not even an engagement ring. There will never be. She imagines her mother's avid eyes and prying questions, her brother's pitying glance — James was so soft — she didn't want pity. She wanted the admiration he had always given her, and his fat wife's envy, not a future in the shop, or a grocer to marry, or a clerk in a shiny suit with inky fingers. She'd rather die.

She must not fail. She feels a rush of anger suddenly. She will write to Sir Neptune — or to Lady Fane. Lady Fane will pay for her silence… She owes them nothing.

She looks at the cards on the floor, too miserable to pick them up. She sees the Knave of Spades — a dark man, plotting some mischief.

25: A Death in Ferrara

Dickens presented himself at the Piazza at six o'clock where Luigi Mariotti greeted him with great enthusiasm, telling him that he had a tremendous surprise for him.

They approached a table where Mariotti's other guest stood. Dickens felt he was familiar; he stepped forward — a London restaurant disappeared, and he was standing by a bridge on a glittering Venetian morning. He held out his hand. 'You look better fed that when I saw you last, Signor Paladini.'

'You remember.' Aurelio Paladini gave him a broad smile.

'Very well, sir. I did not forget that ruined palace and that ghost story.'

They sat and talked of Italy and of exile.

'Mr Dickens is a true friend of our country, my dear Paladini.' Turning to Dickens, Mariotti said, 'I read the piece in *The Examiner*: "They seek a refuge here in England, the only free land where they may set foot, forlorn and penniless, bereft." Your words, I am told — as if I did not know the generous spirit —'

'Enough,' laughed Dickens, amused at Mariotti's dramatic rendering.

They spoke of their first meeting — the voyage to America, the storms, the drunken cook, the broken plates and the beer bottles rolling on the deck, and the dreadful sea-sickness.

'While I languished prostrate upon my sick-bed, I imagined our friend striding the deck, impervious to such weakness. I was recovered from the very instant I heard from the doctor that he had been obliged to put a mustard poultice on Signor Mariotti's stomach.'

The chops were good, and so was the wine. Dickens noticed how Aurelio Paladini ate heartily and felt glad.

'And this is the man who taught me your native tongue, though you, Signor Paladini, answered me in English.'

'And you, Mr Dickens, spoke to a beggar as if he were a gentleman, and gave me money. I did not gamble it away. I ate my hot dinner and took the train for my home town. It was time to begin a new life. You gave me that, sir. I did not know that my Signor Dickens was Charles Dickens until I came to London and read your *Pictures from Italy*. I knew it was you.'

'How so?'

'The wonder of so rare a dream … decayed apartments where furniture was mouldering away … Desdemona at her window — I knew.'

'What a memory you have.'

'It was a meeting that changed my life.'

Luigi Mariotti excused himself and went to speak to someone.

'Do you remember my story of the monk and the maiden?' asked Dickens.

'I do — your masquerade. Did you find your *bella signorina*?'

'No, I left Venice after that. I went to Verona, where I read the sequel to my story. The newspaper reported a girl dragged from the canal by the old Palazzo Mariano — thought to be strangled by her own rosary. Did you hear that?'

'I left Venice that night while my resolution was still strong in me — so, no, Mr Dickens, I did not know that, but I can tell you something else: I went home — to Ferrara.'

Dickens put down his glass. He almost expected to see sparks fly from his thumbs, and the hairs on the back of his neck prickled — that electric charge again. Aurelio Paladini looked at him with an expression of such disquiet that he hardly knew him.

'Go on.'

'Three days before I went home, a girl had been found drowned — on the evening of November the tenth.'

'Where?'

'Just before you enter the city, on the road from Bologna, there is a little bridge over some water —'

'I know it.' Dickens could hardly breathe.

'Some peasant girls standing on the bridge as they often did, in the evening sunshine, saw her. She was brought out — she had been strangled by her rosary. Some said it was suicide, but a verdict of accident was brought in — to save her from damnation.'

'But I was in Ferrara then — I did not hear of it.'

'It was hushed up at first so that enquiries could be made — there was talk of some lover, but she was the daughter of an eminent man who had the ears of others as powerful as he, so no more was published of that. She was a very beautiful girl, I heard tell, famed for her golden hair. A strange coincidence, I think, a horrible one.'

'What was her name?'

'Caterina da Vecelli.'

Dickens could not bear to tell what he had seen on his entry into Ferrara on November 10th, 1844 — he felt the shock of it too deeply, but he thought of something else — a picture from Italy. He felt in his pocket for the folded-up paper that Sam had given him. 'Do you recognise this?'

Paladini studied the portrait of Flora Lambert. 'It resembles a portrait from the Castello D'Este. There are some portraits still there, of the noble family, but the one I know is not signed — but this face is not the same – nothing like - though the robe is exactly copied, and the way the head is posed and the hair — the colour of gold and roses. Did you recognise the picture?'

'I knew it was a copy and thought it familiar. I must have seen it there — I saw many pictures. Do you know who is the subject of the original portrait?'

'No one knows — there are so many mysteries connected to the D'Este family.'

'Parisina Malatesta, for example.'

'Ah, yes, we spoke of her.'

'We did — I stood in that cell where Ugo D'Este, Parisina's illegitimate stepson was kept until his execution.'

'The old marquis, Niccolo D'Este, had another bastard son, Baldassare D'Este, a painter of many portraits of the family — all are lost, but some think the portrait I know may be by his hand. Some of his faces are seen in the frescoes in the Palazzo Schifanoia.'

'But, alas, no one knows who she is.'

'There is a story about Baldassare's daughter, Cassandra, who was ravished by three youths of Reggio — perhaps this is she? Parisina's own daughter, Ginevra, is said to have been murdered by her husband — a husband who was Parisina's brother, a husband who also poisoned his second wife. The grandson of the Marquis, Niccolo III, married Lucrezia Borgia — and we know what she did. A family stained in blood, Mr Dickens, and a portrait of a lost girl — a girl whose story we shall never know.'

'Tell me about the face in the portrait at the castle.'

Aurelio Paladini screwed up his eyes as if to recall the picture. 'One hand touches the cross at her breast and she looks out at you. Her eyes are full of light. It is not a sad face — *attento*, we say, but in English…'

‘Wistful?’

‘I think so — as if the woman in the picture longs for something that is not in this world. Did you see it?’

‘I think I do remember now you describe it.’

‘It is not known what happened to Baldassaro’s daughter — I wonder about a convent, or the portrait might be any young woman who leaves this world for a cloistered one.’

Dickens thought about all the faces he had seen in all the portraits — he thought he remembered the picture from Castello d’Este. He supposed he might have thought what Aurelio thought, but he could not be sure now.

Aurelio Paladini was still studying the picture. ‘I wonder why the artist here in this picture painted a different face. It is not well painted – how strange.’

‘I suppose to please her.’

‘Who is she?’

‘She is now dead — this was found among her effects. I was curious because I thought I had seen it before.’

‘Others think the picture might be by Francisco da Cossa — there are works of his in the Schifanoia. There is a face there, a face of great beauty. Her hair is red gold and her robe is deep green. She has a golden chain round her neck. She seems to look at a young man embracing a girl in a dress the colour of amber, but her expression is inward — she sees something else. Cossa was a friend of the great Lodovico Ariosto.’

‘The poet?’

‘Of Orlando Furioso.’

‘Yes, I saw his house in Ferrara.’

Just at that opportune moment, Luigi Mariotti returned to the table and expiated learnedly on Ariosto’s poem in which the lover, Orlando, whose long pursuit of Angelica ends in her betrayal and his madness. Dickens and Aurelio Paladini listened until Dickens felt it was the polite time to go — he did not want to talk again about the picture and drowned girls.

Aurelio Paladino took him to the door. 'Your girl — did she drown?'

'I don't know — perhaps —' Dickens thought for a moment and then said — 'I wonder, Signor Paladino, if you could find out any more about the death in Ferrara?'

'I will write to my mother. She will know — she takes an interest in her neighbours, especially the great ones.' He smiled at Dickens. 'Ferrara is a small town.'

'I would be much obliged.'

Bidding farewell to Aurelio, Dickens went out into the street to find a cab to take him to Norfolk Street, hoping that Sam would be there.

Jones answered the door and took him into the parlour where his wife, Elizabeth sat by the fire, near which a table had been drawn up and there were the remains of a meal — two had sat together, enjoying each other's company. A shared life.

'I am so sorry to intrude, Elizabeth, on your quiet evening.'

'You are always welcome, Charles. Let Sam and me clear the table — our little maid is in bed, and then I will leave you.'

'No, no, my dear Elizabeth, I should like you to hear this, if Sam doesn't mind. It is a curious story.'

'Not in the least. Elizabeth knows what we are doing — Scrap enlightened her — most decoratively. Now sit down and share some of this wine while we clear the table.'

When it was done, Sam and Elizabeth listened as Dickens told his tale of the drowned girl at Ferrara — famed for her rose-gold hair and that he had seen her death without knowing, and that he had thought of his own murder when he had seen that mournful sheet of water and a blood red sunset. He told of how it matched his story of the girl in Venice which he summarised for Elizabeth's benefit, and of the picture — copied from the one in Ferrara.

'And this artist put Flora Lambert's face in it, but it was not very good — why should he do that?' asked Jones.

'To please her, perhaps,' Dickens replied.

'I think so,' Elizabeth said, 'she would want a portrait painted by her lover — any woman would. I would.'

'For Flora Lambert, it would set the seal on their relationship — she hadn't much else,' Dickens added.

'And Mariana Fane was having her portrait done — you're convinced there is a link?' Jones asked.

Dickens thought about the girl he had seen in the asylum, and the portrait. 'I am, Sam. The hair — the girl at Ferrara had golden hair — a red-gold you often see in Renaissance pictures, and Flora Lambert has reddish hair in the picture — very striking, though she was otherwise unremarkable; Mariana's hair — I noticed because Doctor Jessop said she kept tearing it out — it was the same colour — very beautiful. Jemima Curd's hair was wet so I didn't think about it then…'

'Let me think this out — the details are important: in 1844, two girls are drowned in Italy, strangled by their rosaries; in 1850, Flora Lambert is found in a water tank, thought to have died, or been murdered five years ago, so possibly in 1845; bones in her neck are broken and a rosary is found; in 1850, Jemima Curd is found in water, strangled by a ribbon — a detail that may or may not be a link to the earlier ones, but where does Mariana Fane fit? She is mad not drowned, even if her hair is the same colour as Flora's and the girl's in the picture.'

'I don't know — but I think it's very odd. When we found Jemima in that reservoir, the scene reminded me of what I saw in Ferrara — I didn't mention it at the time. I just felt a kind of shudder of recognition, and then I found out from Aurelio Paladini that I had seen a group of girls looking down at a dead body, and murder had come into my mind then — my own I grant you. It's uncanny — fateful, inescapable.'

'It is,' Elizabeth said, 'most strange, and rather chilling as if you had foreseen, or somehow known of the murders in Italy.' She thought Dickens looked haunted.

'It is like dreams in a way. Dreams which foretell the future — I once dreamed of a woman in a red shawl. She turned and I saw that I did not know her — which is the way often in dreams — but she said her name was Miss Napier. And this is the uncanny part — at some event later I saw that red shawl and exclaimed "Miss Napier", and it was she — the very Miss Napier of my dream. She was a perfectly ordinary woman and still lives — I hope.'

'I sometimes dream of Edith and her child,' Elizabeth said slowly, recalling the painful vision of her own dead daughter and the child that had died, too, 'and in the dream, I see him as he might have been had he lived. I know him. How can that be?'

'There are more things in heaven and earth. What do you think, Horatio?' Dickens turned to Jones, who looked rather grave.

'I think that what you both say is true — you dreamed the past and the future, but I am thinking of the present.' Jones did not want to pursue the subject of Edith, their only daughter. He dreamed of her, too, always as the lovely child she had been and he always woke with his cheeks wet.

Elizabeth saw his face. She understood — it was painful ground. 'I suppose what we want to consider is if these experiences help us with your present conundrum. Are these murders connected? And, if so, will he do it again?'

'Admirably succinct, my love,' said Jones, 'and it doesn't matter just now if they are connected because whether the murderer is your artist with a passion for golden hair, Charles, or whether it is Sir Neptune Fane, there is a woman linked to both — who may be in danger —'

'Miss Pout,' Elizabeth finished for him, 'who is linked, too, to Mr Sabatini, though Sam told me, Charles, that his aunt speaks of him most affectionately.'

Dickens glanced at Jones, who shook his head very slightly. He had mentioned only an aunt, Dickens thought. He would not betray me — even to Elizabeth. 'She did, though I suppose no one knows what another, however close, might be capable of.'

'Especially if Violet Pout was, in part, responsible for Mariana Fane's ruin,' Jones pointed out.

'Then, I must go back to see Cassie Hanlon — she has lodgings in Baker's Row which leads into Amwell Street —'

'Where you saw Violet Pout. Would Miss Hanlon object to me?' Jones asked.

'She has sense.'

'Tomorrow morning then, at Bow Street, at nine.'

As Dickens walked home, he thought of Orlando, who in other works was Roland. Rolando enraged? Violet Pout, the betrayer. But Dolly Marchant had portrayed Rolando as a sensitive boy. She might be wrong. Love, betrayal, madness, murder. Those stories: Parisina and Ugo, Orlando and Angelica. That tale Aurelio Paladino had told him at the

Palazzo Mariano. People hadn't changed. Robes and furred gowns might hide all, but murder had been done for rage, for jealousy — for revenge — or, to rid the murderer of one who was dangerous to his peace, or his reputation. He thought of Sir Neptune Fane. Violet Pout knew too much about him — and his daughter.

26: Queen of Spades

Nine o'clock was too late. Jones met Dickens with the news. Violet Pout was dead — found at the Claremont Square Reservoir, that peaceful spot where Dickens had seen the afternoon sun glitter on the placid water and where he had seen that cheerful boy bowling his hoop.

'She was found early this morning. Shackell knew her by her hair — she didn't drown.'

'Strangled?'

'Yes, but not with a chain or a ribbon — bruises made by thumbs on her neck. She is with Doctor Symonds now. I would like a formal identification before I go to the family.'

'I'll come.'

Doctor Symonds was waiting in the hospital mortuary. Violet Pout lay with her silver hair pushed back from her forehead. Dickens looked down at the fine, straight brows, and the long silver lashes closed over the pale blue eyes.

He had not much liked her, but he thought now how fragile she looked now. She had been a self-centred, worldly girl, greedy for the good things, and hard because she could not get them, the daughter of a silly mother who had spoilt her and taught her nothing but ambition. But she was dead by a cruel pair of hands.

And below the lashes, her face was livid now and her tongue swollen and slightly protruded and the lips very dark. Her prettiness, however sharp and shallow, had been destroyed. Her mother should not see this.

Doctor Symonds drew back the sheet to expose the delicate neck. 'See here, over the left wing of the thyroid cartilage, there is a mark of a crescentric form, and another, though fainter on the opposite side. I shall need to examine what is beneath the skin here, but the marks suggest manual strangulation. Doctor Bennett, who was called by Inspector Shackell, gave that as his opinion, too. I can tell you more when I have made a full examination.'

'Would it be possible for us to look again at Jemima Curd?' asked Dickens. He wanted to look at her hair.

Jemima Curd still lay in the mortuary. Dickens and Jones saw as the sheet was lifted that her hair had dried out — to the colour of rose-gold.

'What now?' asked Dickens, as he and Jones walked back to Bow Street.

'I do not know that Lady Fane is very ill. I do not wish to distress Miss Pout's family about the identification so I am thinking that —'

'You might go to the house of her former employer to ask if someone might be willing to do it.'

'I should have to ask Sir Neptune Fane if he will allow it — perhaps he, or a servant — it would be very handy if he would. I should like to see his face when he sees Violet Pout's dead body, but he won't do it.'

'How do you know that Miss Pout was once in his employ?'

'Heard it on the wind — no, she was reported missing — not by Charles Dickens, of course, whom I know slightly — only slightly, for he is a great man, naturally, too high for my 'umble station.'

'A numble man, Mr Copperfield,' laughed Dickens, 'but, seriously, do you think Sir Neptune?'

'Strangled manually — that's a different thing from a necklace or a ribbon. I've thought about the picture and the rosaries and the ribbon — I think of murders which suggest something very different from two hands at the neck which speak of rage to me — impulse. A quarrel, a violent argument which ends with an angry man taking a woman by the throat and pressing very hard — not meaning to, perhaps.'

'And the jewels and the similarity of the hair in the picture to the girl in Ferrara, to Jemima Curd, and to Mariana Fane tell a different story — murder as a fine art.'

'Doctor Jobling — in your *Martin Chuzzlewit* — didn't he say something like that?'

'Yes, he did. It was almost a perfect murder — one drop of blood on the victim's waistcoat. The murderer was supposed to be a medical man who picked his spot so exactly at the victim's heart that there was just this pinprick of blood. Jobling maintains that if it wasn't the doctor then the murder was an extraordinary work of art.'

'Or he was lucky — murderers often are. The moment presents itself and like your man the murderer vanishes into the dark. No one saw a thing except two professional men in earnest conversation.'

'Or a man and a woman in a loving embrace — Sir Neptune and Violet Pout. That's a chilling thought.'

'I don't rule out your artist for her murder. Violet Pout's hair was fair —'

'But silvery — very different from the others.'

'If that's significant, it makes me think even more that I must consider Sir Neptune.'

'And Rolando Sabatini?'

'Anything is possible, and Miss Pout must have known about Miss Fane's condition — dangerous for her.'

'And for him.'

They walked on, each thinking of the possible suspects. When they arrived at the police station, Dickens turned to Jones. 'How about this? Mariana Fane's portrait — Violet Pout must have arranged that. Miss Fane could hardly have done it herself. The artist saw Miss Fane, saw her hair, and they went for sittings. Miss Fane is left alone with the artist. It is he who seduces her — Jessie Sharp told you that Miss Fane became ill after an outing with Miss Pout.'

'Why did he not kill Miss Fane?' Jones asked.

'Violet Pout was too close — she would have known. Perhaps she did know that the artist had seduced Miss Fane.'

'All very plausible, were it not for the fact that we don't even know that Miss Pout was living with an artist. We need to find that out. I suggest you make that trip to Baker's Row to see Miss Cassie Hanlon. She will have heard about Violet Pout's death. She may have found out something about where she lived and with whom. But I must go to Wisteria Lodge.'

'I need to tell Anne Brown that her god-daughter is dead. I shall have to take her to Mrs Pout before I do anything else.'

'Do you want to wait for me? I ought to do it — it should not be your burden.'

'It should be — Catherine and I owe a great deal to Anne Brown. That is why I took up the matter in the first place.'

'If you are sure?'

'No, I would value your presence above all, but I owe a duty to Anne Brown and her closest friend — more so in that I did not much like Mrs Pout or her daughter. Little did I know.'

27: Reading the Signs

Pryor answered the door. When Jones enquired for Sir Neptune, the footman did not think that Sir Neptune would see him. Lady Fane was very ill. There were doctors.

'Tell him, if you will, Mr Pryor, that the matter is urgent, but that I need only take a moment of his time.'

Pryor went to the library. He was back in a very short time to tell Jones that Sir Neptune would see the Superintendent for a few minutes.

Sir Neptune stood as he had before, one hand resting on the mantelpiece. He looked drawn and not at all pleased to see Superintendent Jones, who begged his pardon for intruding, an apology which Sir Neptune acknowledged with a curt nod.

'I have very little time, Superintendent, so I would be obliged if you will be brief. I think I have said all I can about Jemima Curd.'

'The matter concerns a Miss Pout, Miss Violet Pout, who, I believe, was recently in your employ.'

Sir Neptune's face did not change, but Jones noticed how his hand clenched involuntarily. He turned fully to Jones, putting both hands behind his back.

'She was, but she left us. I do not know what her subsequent fate has to do with us.'

'She is dead — she was found strangled at the Claremont Square Reservoir, not far from where your other former servant, Miss Curd, was found strangled.' It was blunt — the obvious link between the crimes could not but be suggestive. Jones did not quake — he merely waited in a silence that had become suddenly weighty.

Sir Neptune regarded him steadily, though his face paled. 'I am very sorry for it, but since both these deaths occurred in Clerkenwell, I fail to see what they are to do with this house.'

He did see, thought Jones, of course he did — only a fool, or a man with something to hide would not. Sir Neptune Fane was no fool, and the more he asserted his house's distance from these events, the more Jones must probe even though the man might just be protecting his daughter's reputation — and his own.

'I shall want to question your household again —' Jones chose his next words with blade-like exactness — 'your other servants may know something of her private life.'

Sir Neptune's voice was cold. 'My servants do not have private lives. I suppose you must ask your questions, but I beg you to be discreet. My wife is very ill — the doctor is with her now.'

'Of course, sir. I will not do it now, but I do have another request, which is to ask if you or anyone in your household would identify the body. I need to confirm her identity before I approach her mother.'

'But you said it was Vi — Miss Pout. Do you tell me now that you are not certain?' He was angry now — he could not conceal it. Jones noticed a muscle twitch in his cheek.

'I am certain, but I need an official identification.'

'And you expect me —'

'I thought that you might be willing — for her family's sake.'

Sir Neptune turned back to the fire. Jones saw by the movement of his shoulders how he made the effort to calm himself, but his voice was tight. 'My duty is to my wife, Superintendent — not to a former servant.'

A man capable of rage. Jones thought of Jemima Curd's dismissal. 'Perhaps one of your male servants would come with me to the mortuary now.'

'Very well, Pryor, the footman, may go with you.' He rang the bell.

'I am grateful, Sir Neptune.'

'I think you ought to know, Superintendent, Miss Pout left us with a young man, our music tutor, Rolando Sabatini. I believe that there was some kind of liaison between them. Jemima Curd knew of it. I tell you now because I think you might do well to search for him. He is connected to both these young women, and has turned out to be a thoroughly disreputable character.'

Connected to you, too, and you are not so reputable a character, either, thought Jones, but he merely said he would certainly enquire about Mr Sabatini.

Pryor appeared and Sir Neptune asked if he would go with the Superintendent. Pryor assented gravely and with admirable composure, and went away to change out of his uniform. There was another long silence. Sir Neptune still stood at the mantelpiece. Jones saw what strain he was under as he looked at the fire — contemplating the ruin of his life, Jones wondered. That tell-tale movement in his cheek continued to beat, and the hand that had grasped the bell-pull clenched and unclenched.

He turned to Jones suddenly, as if he could bear the silence no longer. 'I must ask you to excuse me, Superintendent. I must go to my wife. Perhaps you would care to wait in the hall for Pryor.'

'Certainly, sir, I am obliged to you. Good day, Sir Neptune.'

Jones went slowly down the stairs, breathing out as if he had held in his breath for ages. He hoped that the risks he had taken would not come back to haunt him. The library door remained closed. Pryor was waiting with Jones's hat, which he took his time to put on and buttoning his coat slowly. There was no sound from upstairs.

Pryor offered no word until they reached the steamboat. Jones led him to a quiet place by the rails and they watched as the steamer manoeuvred its way into the current. The river was leaden grey with a blank sky above, but Pryor breathed in the cold air and breathed out like a man released from confinement.

At last he spoke. 'You are sure it is Miss Pout.'

'Yes, she was murdered — strangled.'

'Like poor Jemima.'

'It is similar, but I don't want to go into detail at this stage. However, I must tell you so that you have no fear of any deception that Mr Dickens has told me of your conversation. You may trust him not to reveal it to anyone else.'

'I do — there is something about him that gives you confidence. He was kind to me. He listened.'

'He does. And you need not fear that your place at Wisteria Lodge will be jeopardised. I made no mention to Sir Neptune of your visit to Mr Dickens.'

'I shall not worry, Mr Jones; I doubt I'll stay there much longer — my fancy dress is beginning to feel too tight. I have savings — and ambitions.'

'I will confess to one deception. You do not need to identify Miss Pout. Mr Dickens has done that already.'

'I'm glad of that, sir, I shouldn't like to see her.'

'Sir Neptune pointed me in the direction of Mr Sabatini — for both murders.'

Pryor smiled ironically. 'I doubt that, Mr Jones, he was a nice young fellow — wouldn't hurt a fly. The romantic sort — very fond of Miss Mariana, he was. He shouldn't have left her, though — that was cowardly. To my mind, at any rate. I think Lady Fane must have found out. I suppose he was scared of Sir Neptune.'

'And you thought Sir Neptune and Miss Pout had an affair.'

'It was my impression — I can't say for certain, but you get a feeling about folk. Miss Pout was the sly sort. She'd get what she wanted, and Sir Neptune — well, Lady Fane is always ill. They have separate rooms — if you take my meaning. Sir Neptune has no time for his wife — I sometimes thought he wouldn't be sorry if she died. She is never well. And now — I don't know if she will recover.'

'It wasn't his habit to dally with the maids?'

'Oh, no, Mr Jones, nothing like that — beneath his dignity, I should think, but Miss Pout — who'd know?'

'Only someone with very sharp eyes.'

Pryor grinned. 'It was the way she looked at him — when he wasn't looking — greedy and calculating, and sometimes like the cat'd got the cream. He watched her, too.'

'Would she spill the beans about Sir Neptune — a spot of blackmail, perhaps after she left?'

'Sir Neptune had a letter two days ago. I handed him the letters before he went out — on the salver. It is his habit to skim through them and take the important ones with him. One seemed to disturb him. He usually handed Lady Fane's letters for Mrs Pick to take up — I'd noticed her name on one envelope. She didn't get many, but he didn't say anything, just dismissed me. He looked angry.'

'You didn't recognise the handwriting?'

'No, I only saw the word "Lady" and handed over the lot.'

'Pity — it might have helped. Still, the idea of a letter that angered him makes me wonder.'

Pryor looked out at the river. They were out of Lambeth Reach and had passed under Vauxhall Bridge and the huge fortress that was the Penitentiary House. Then they were approaching Westminster Bridge just by the Houses of Parliament. Pryor stared at the great palace. The wind got up, a brisk chill wind that pierced the very bones.

At last Pryor turned his raw face to the policeman. 'Sir Neptune's an important man in the Conservative party — he's at the centre of things. Lord Derby comes to Wisteria Lodge, Mr Disraeli, and others. You hear things. They seem to think that there'll be a Conservative government soon enough. Sir Neptune has a lot to lose.'

'About Miss Mariana?'

'You know, sir, don't you? You've pieced it together.'

'I have — and Miss Fane's illness adds to Sir Neptune's troubles.'

'Miss Pout knew all about Miss Mariana and Mr Sabatini — encouraged it, I reckon.'

'Why, do you think?'

'Gave her power — Miss Mariana was very dependent on Miss Pout — Lady Fane kept to her room. It was as if —' Pryor thought about it — 'as if Miss Pout wanted to worm her way into being the centre of things. She'd think she had power over Sir Neptune. She'd think what if Lady Fane was to die, she'd be the new one. But why she left I can't really tell. I mean Mr Sabatini would have been blamed for Miss Mariana losing her mind…' His honest face looked genuinely puzzled. Jones thought that he did not know about the pregnancy. He wasn't going to tell him — for the poor girl's sake. It might well come out — but not from him.

'Did you ever hear of Miss Mariana having her portrait done?' Jones asked.

'No, sir.'

'Where did Miss Pout and Miss Mariana go on their outings?'

'Shopping, the zoo, walks in the park — ordinary things.'

'Did Mr Sabatini go with them?'

'To the park or the zoo sometimes with the other children and the children's nurse. I suppose he could have met her at other times secretly. I doubt that Miss Mariana would want to something underhand, but Miss Pout might have arranged it. She could have persuaded her.'

The steamer arrived at Waterloo Bridge and they disembarked to stand on the pier.

'Was Sir Neptune at home last night?'

'I can't say, Mr Jones. He always came and went as he pleased, especially when the House was sitting. Sometimes he would be away all night, or for days. He had his own life. We were used to it. I wasn't expected to sit up.'

'Where did he stay?'

'He had rooms at the Albany. Mr Jones —'

'Yes?'

'Do you really think that Sir Neptune — I mean —'

'I know what you mean, and I don't know. I have to consider it. You said yourself, he has much to lose. He is an important man on the brink of great power, perhaps. Murder has been done for less.'

'What shall I do?'

'Carry on as normal.'

'And if I find out anything more?'

'You can come to me, or to Mr Dickens, wherever your conscience directs you. Now, you can go back to Chelsea whenever you feel the time is appropriate.' Jones smiled at him. 'I am obliged for your time and your thoughts.'

They parted. Jones went back to Bow Street to ponder on what he had discovered: whether one or two murders had been done by a powerful man upon whose face he had read signs of great disquiet, and whether Dickens's golden-haired girls had been murdered by quite another. Dickens had read signs in that red sky over the New Reservoir. Which were true?

No use, he thought, looking for portents in today's blank winter sky. He had a visit to make to the Albany in Piccadilly where wealthy men kept rooms.

28: Ace of Hearts

Anne Brown had gone to her room to rest. Catherine would look after her. On their way to Violet's home, Anne had told Dickens a good deal about Mrs Pout and her married life.

It had been a most painful interview with Mrs Pout, her son and daughter-in-law. Thank goodness they had been present, and Anne. Poor Mrs Pout had been stunned — all her dreams, her ambitions, her foolish plans for the daughter she had loved collapsed. The daughter who was to have the life she had been denied when she had stood at the counter of the grocer's shop in her neat apron after she had accepted the clumsy advances of the forty year old Herbert Pout who had hardly believed his good fortune. That pretty Abigail Carter had accepted him had seemed a kind of miracle. Not that Herbert Pout's mother thought so. 'Too young,' old Mrs Alice Pout had declared, 'too flighty', but he had persisted.

And he had sometimes repented his stubbornness — Abigail Pout could be sulky and sharp-tongued. He never knew what she wanted, but James, his son, was like him, a steady fellow, good-hearted and loyal. And his little daughter, come much later, had delighted him. Violet — Abigail Pout had dreamed of violets before the child was born, violets which foretold complete success in all undertakings. Herbert Pout did not believe in such stuff, but just like a flower the little girl was with her mother's fair hair, only more like silver. Angel's hair, he had told her. She could have anything she wanted, her little face and blue eyes lighting up at each new toy, each new ribbon, each new dress, or shawl, or scented gloves.

'She must go to a good school,' Abigail had argued, 'she is exceptional, she must do more than serve in a grocer's shop.' Herbert had felt wounded at her disdainful tone — the grocer's shops had bought her finery, but he had agreed. Violet wanted to be a lady — so it must be, but he feared that he would lose his pretty child. She would be too high for them. Not that Abigail saw that. She would rise with her daughter. It was fortunate that Herbert Pout was dead before he lost her entirely.

When Dickens and Anne Brown were shown in, Mrs Pout was seated in the parlour where she had dreamed her dreams and where she and Violet had devoured *The Ladies' Oracle* and consulted the cards which lay on the table now. Perhaps she had hoped for a sign. She had turned up the Ace of Hearts — portending good tidings — and the hope that had sprung up, died down when Dickens broke the news. In the parlour where her husband had dropped dead of a stroke — she hadn't seen that coming.

Abigail Pout wondered repeatedly: Did Sir Neptune know? What had he said?

Dickens said he did not know, but that he was sure that they would lament Violet's death. He did so, too, and Anne.

But, Sir Neptune — surely, he would want to see her, to condole with her, to mourn the death of the lovely governess. Surely, Sir Neptune had admired Violet; surely, Lady Fane had known that Violet was exceptional…

I hope not, thought Dickens uncharitably, but he murmured agreement.

James Pout had interrupted. He wanted to know what Violet was doing in Clerkenwell. Had his sister lived there with Rolando Sabatini? *No*, his mother had cried. She had never believed that Violet would run away with a music teacher. It was a mistake — Violet so foolish as to ruin herself — never! She hadn't seemed to take in the idea of murder.

Dickens told them that he had no idea — he knew only what the Superintendent had told him. He had made very discreet enquiries of the Superintendent whom he knew quite well. He had thought that he and Anne should break the news. He was profoundly sorry, but it was a matter for the police now.

The young Mrs Caroline Pout, a plump pretty woman, tried ineffectually to stop the tide of incoherence with some gentle patting and shushing murmurs, but Abigail Pout shook her off petulantly.

Sir Neptune and Lady Fane would bring their own carriage to the funeral, wouldn't they? They could hardly travel in the mourning coaches — there must be mutes and plumes. Caroline would have to see about the mourning dresses. Silk, they would be. She would like a lock of Violet's hair. Never was there such beautiful hair — almost silver. Angel's hair, her father had said. Here, Mrs Pout had burst into tears.

Caroline was quick with the smelling salts. She looked helplessly at Dickens and Anne.

Dickens thought of the silver hair pushed back from the dead face, and the swollen tongue. He felt deeply sorry for the foolish woman — the reality would crush her when she finally understood it.

James Pout had accompanied them to the shop door. 'Don't mind her,' he said, 'it's the shock. I'm shocked myself — I can hardly understand it.'

'I'll come back soon to sit with her,' Anne offered.

'When will the inquest be?' James Pout asked.

'There will be one this afternoon,' Dickens replied, 'but it will be adjourned. Inspector Shackell, who was at the scene, will tell the magistrate that he and Superintendent Jones are making further enquiries.'

'I can't understand it. Who would — I mean — this man you said she was living with — who —'

'I cannot say, Mr Pout. I can only say that the Superintendent is pursuing his enquiries. I am very sorry.'

'I should like to see her … she was a takin' little thing when she was an infant, seven years younger than me. Could get me to do anything…' His eyes filled at the memory of the little fairy thing he had loved. 'My father loved her. I must do it for him.'

Dickens offered to go with him to the mortuary at King's College Hospital, but James Pout declined.

'I am much obliged for what you have done already, Mr Dickens. It was good of you and Anne to come, but I'll go alone to do this. It is what's fitting.'

They left him, moved more by a good man's memory than by the mother's tears.

Anne Brown was very quiet in the cab. Dickens waited patiently. At length she spoke, 'She was a silly girl, I know, and vain of her prettiness. Her mother's doing, but she might have grown out of it. Except she hadn't time. It is cruel — for all of them.'She had wept then, and Dickens took her gloved hand in his and held onto it until they came along the New Road and near to Devonshire Terrace. She turned to him. 'You know more, sir, I think.'

'Not much, my dear Anne. I can only say that I do not believe that Violet went away with Mr Sabatini — I think she was involved with someone else, but I do not know who.'

'And that person killed her?'

'It could be, but Anne, be assured, Mr Jones will find him.'

29: Knave of Spades

Clerkenwell again. Dickens would take Scrap. He needed company — Scrap, whose trenchant observations always cheered him up. Scrap who had had nothing until Dickens had come across him in the stationery shop, and Sam Jones and Elizabeth had taken under their wing. Scrap, whose heart was as true as steel.

Scrap who was as an acute reader of the human face as the great writer saw that Mr Dickens looked somehow worn and depressed, agreed immediately, but he said, 'Ain't got that squeeze box, I 'opes.'

He was rewarded by a pair of eyes that lit suddenly with laughter. 'No, and come as you are. Toffs terday.'

Cassie Hanlon showed them the house in Amwell Street where she told them she thought she had seen Mr Dickens's "lady" go in. It looked deserted; the shutters were closed at the windows on the first two floors. Dickens stepped back to look up. Those windows were shuttered fast, too.

There was a narrow passage running between this house and the next down which they went to see what was at the back. There was lane with mews opposite the back doors of the houses. The door to number ten led them into a yard. The back door to the house was locked. They scouted round the yard for some sort of tool to force the door. Scrap's sharp eyes picked out a rusty trowel that he used to lever open the door, which gave eventually.

Scrap's boots clattered through the empty rooms where there was nothing to see in their shadowy spaces. They smelt of dust and the air was stale. No one had lived here for a long time. They went up the stairs. On the first landing a window gave them some light and Dickens noticed the chips on the wooden rails, and on the uncarpeted stairs he saw black smudges. He touched one with his finger — coal dust. Someone had carried coal up these stairs, and not so long ago. They looked around empty bedrooms, but there was no evidence of any recent fires. The grates were empty.

Another staircase, a narrow one, led up to the next floor. Servants' quarters, perhaps? By some unspoken instinct they stopped. They listened, but no sound came from above. Scrap took off his boots and signalled to Dickens that he would go up. Light and quiet as a cat, he crept. There was a long corridor with doors — all closed. He made his way on tip-toe, listening at the closed doors. At the end of the corridor was a little round window all furred with dust and cobwebs. He rubbed at one of the little panes and looked out into the yard and the mews opposite.

He turned back to look along the corridor. There was no one here. At the top of the stairs, he called down his opinion. Dickens and Cassie came up.

Dickens saw more coal dust and a few small lumps of coal. The first door opened onto a tiny room where there was a truckle bed upon which lay tumbled sheets and pillows as if a sleeper had risen after a night of troubled dreams. A blanket had slipped to the floor. This was a servant's room with a tiny fireplace in which the coals were cold; a cracked jug and basin on a marble-topped stand, and half out from under the bed a chamber pot. Dickens smelt the acrid smell of urine. He stepped forward and felt something crack under his foot and something rolled away as the other foot came down.

Over the floor were scattered some small beads — he looked at the wash stand and there dangling was a chain of beads. It was broken. It looked as though someone had made a grab for it and it had snagged on the finial of the mirror frame and the beads had scattered. He found the other part of the chain where it had fallen. He looked at the cross.

'Rosary, ain't it?' Cassie Hanlon whispered, 'my pa was Catholic — so Ma said. She kept 'is beads. Thought 'e might come back, I serpose. Didn't though.'

He had done it here, thought Dickens. He had meant to strangle Jemima Curd with the chain, but it had caught and broken so he had used her ribbon — the silk one given by Mariana Fane — or Violet Pout, perhaps. She had been asleep in her bed, her red gold hair loose on the pillow. Had he come to kill her, or for something else? And when she had resisted, he had killed her.

Her box was under the bed, the initials burnt into it with a hot poker: *J.C.*

'The girl wot woz murdered,' breathed Cassie.

The box contained a Bible, a little book of religious pictures of garishly coloured saints and oddly-proportioned angels with yellow wings and smirking faces. These lay on a folded petticoat, darned, but once good. Perhaps Mariana had given her that. There was a stale smell — an ammonia smell. He lifted the petticoat. Underneath was a crumpled-up pair of drawers which smelt of urine and a rolled-up pair of stockings which smelt the same.

Odd, he thought, looking round. On a bentwood chair were carefully folded another pair of drawers, some stays and a camisole. Underneath the chair, a pair of boots had been neatly placed. Of all the things, those boots wrung his heart — so small and tidy, and innocent — about the size of his daughter

Mamie's feet. He remembered Jemima's poor cold feet at the reservoir.

A crumpled white shift was flung on the bed. He had put the dress on her. That explained why she was naked under the dress when they had found her. He had done it here. He closed the lid.

Scrap who had gone exploring shouted out. 'In 'ere, Mr D.'

Dickens closed the door carefully. Jones would have to see this.

Scrap was at the open door of the room opposite. Light flooded this room and showed them a worn velvet chaise longue, a couple of chairs which had seen better days, an old three-legged table, and beneath the skylight someone had built a low platform on which stood a screen painted with a landscape seen through an arched window — the cypress trees told him that it was Italy. In front of the screen was placed a piano stool covered in worn velvet.

The streaks and circles of oil paint at a distance from the platform, beneath the skylight, showed where the artist had stood.

Dickens saw the playing cards spilled across the floor as if someone had tossed away a losing hand. He picked up the Knave of Spades.

'A dark enemy, that is,' said Cassie Hanlon. 'Spades is always bad news. See, 'ere's the nine — tidin's of death it means.'

Dickens thought of Madame Emerald looking at his palm and the dark gleam in her black eyes and he remembered the cards on Mrs Pout's table. 'You believe in this?'

'My ma was a gypsy — up Norland Hill. She woz allus right in 'er readin's, cept about Pa.'

'What does the Ace of Hearts mean?'

'On its own, a letter, good news, or a visit from a friend — with Spades it foretells quarrelling.'

Mrs Pout had turned up the Ace of Hearts and he had visited, but with bad news. You might as well read the entrails of a goose — or was it a chicken — as the Romans had done. But he had once made a test of taking a book at random to see what message it might convey about a new book. The random book had been *Tristram Shandy* and his thumb had rested on the words: *What a work it is likely to turn out. Let us begin it!* He had begun *Dombey and Son* — and what a work it was! Cassie's eyes were certain. Cassandra, he thought and felt that shudder of premonition.

He picked up another random card which he handed face down to Cassie who turned it over.

'Knave of 'Earts — don't mean much in itself. A man wot dreams only of pleasure, but two knaves, sir, that's evil intentions, fer sure.'

'You know the police office on Lower Road, near Percy Circus?'

'Yes.'

'Good. Scrap, you must go with Miss Hanlon to tell Inspector Shackell and then go on to Bow Street for Mr Jones or Sergeant Rogers. Quick as you can.'

When they were gone, Dickens explored the adjoining room where there was a double bed, made up this time. No one had left this room in a hurry. The pillows and the sheets were not fresh and the counterpane was dusty. Under one of the pillows was a white nightgown, not very clean, but with lace and ribbons. But two had slept here. The artist and Violet Pout? Of her there was no sign. Had she left with all her things? Had she gone to meet that other lover, hoping to rekindle their affair?

Or did the nightgown suggest that she had intended to return?

Violet Pout — she had fallen somehow. The grubby sheets, the stale nightgown were so at odds with what he had seen of her — so trim and neat in her grey costume and her pretty bonnet tied with blue ribbon.

He went back out into the corridor and looked through the little round window. He contemplated the mews on the opposite side of the lane and went downstairs.

The building belonging to number ten Amwell Street looked unused. The big doors were locked. He peered through the keyhole and then looked in through a dingy window, but there was nothing to see — just a couple of empty stalls where once horses had been kept. There was a staircase leading up — to a groom's or coachman's quarters, he supposed.

There were signs of life a bit further down the mews. He heard a horse whinny and the sound of hooves scraping cobbles. He went to see. A young man was brushing down a horse — a sturdy little cob. There was a cart with sacks on it — sacks of coal.

'Excuse me,' he said.

The young man turned and the horse shook its head. 'Sir?'

'Do you deliver coal?'

'I does.

'Did you deliver to the house across the lane?'

'A couple o' times.'

'Who lived there? It seems to be empty now.'

'Bin empty fer ages — since I rented 'ere. See, I gets the coal from the coal drop an' comes back 'ere — rented fer the 'orse, only family I got. Compact and comfortable, the pair of us. But, a bit ago, I sees that someone's moved in upstairs. The young lady asked me to bring some coal — Mrs Pout, she said 'er name was. Pretty girl, lovely 'air like silver — stuck up, though. Looked at me as though I woz the muck under 'er feet — wot she expect from the coal man?'

'Was there a Mister Pout?'

'Came down 'ere a couple o' times — they dint use the front door, I don't think. Dunno why. Saw 'im weighin' up the 'orse. Looked as if 'e was measurin' 'er — not that Polly minded it. Queer sort o' cove —'

'Why?'

'Went out ter see if they was wantin' more coal, but 'e just looked through me as if I want there. Dint speak an' I dint see 'im again.'

'What did he look like?'

'Why d-yer wanter know? Police are yer?'

'I'm making enquiries for a friend whose daughter has left home — with a man, they think.'

'Yer think she mighta — wait a minnit — them girls wot was found in the reservoirs — yer don't meantersay —'

'I'm afraid so. One of the girls who died was my friend's daughter. I think she was in that house so if you could tell me — the police are coming soon. It would help.'

'Tallish — taller than you — or me, fer that matter. Clean shaven — thin face, darkish complexion. Dint look English ter me — mebbe a foreigner. 'Ard ter say, sir, only saw 'is face the once.'

'Did they keep a servant?'

'Yer mean the little girl — oh, blimey, she dead, too?'

'Yes, I believe so — so if you do remember anything else, anything at all, please ask for Inspector Shackell at the police office near Percy Circle.'

'I know it, an' I will, sir.'

'What's that on your face?' Jones asked Dickens, after he,

Rogers and Inspector Shackell had been shown everything and they were standing in the yard. Shackell and his men were about questioning the neighbours, and Rogers was talking to the young coalman. There was no doubt, he thought, that Jemima Curd and Violet Pout had been here.

'What?'

'Dirty mark under your eye. Looking through keyholes does that.'

'So, it does, Samivel.' Dickens put his finger to his right eye and looked at the mark on the tip. 'That's oil, my lad, and I know exactly where it came from. Come with me.' He took Jones to the mews and put his finger on the lock of the door. More oil. 'This place has been used recently.'

Jones took some keys from his pocket. 'Allow me.'

'Skeleton key?'

'Fikey Chubb gave them to me —'

'Gave?' Dickens had met Fikey Chubb.

'Ah, well, he claimed they weren't his. Someone left them on his counter — couldn't tell who, of course. Naturally, I accepted the — er — gift. He'll have plenty more.'

They heard the key turn easily in the lock — lucky that it had been oiled recently — and pushed open one of the doors. The stalls were empty. Upstairs was a hayloft. Hay was piled into one corner, damp now, but a pitchfork showed that somebody had made that pile.

They found Violet Pout's box, and near the wall, an artist's easel and some canvases. There was picture of a girl with rose-gold hair in a green velvet robe — a portrait without a face.

30: Betrayal

'Shackell must find some trace of them,' Jones said. 'I told him to ask at the cookshops. They must have eaten something — bought it in, I should think.'

'I don't see Violet Pout slaving over the fireplace with a skillet,' Dickens observed, thinking of Violet Pout's ambition.

'No, there were a few pots and pans, but nothing out of the ordinary. He was quick. Violet Pout was found yesterday — died in the night and he's gone. Cleared the place out except for her box and the pictures and easel in the hay loft.'

'He was an artist — that's something we're sure of now, and it links him to Mariana Fane. Why should he leave his paintings behind?'

'Why should he leave Jemima's room untouched? That's a puzzle.'

'Why should he do any of it, Sam? I can't see what motive there is — not greed, not rage —'

'Violet Pout — why hide her box if he didn't kill her? If he did, why is it so different?'

'The rosary was broken. He might —'

'He could have used a ribbon as he did on Jemima Curd. Violet Pout's murder seems different to me. Why does her murder suggest rage?'

'One thing the coal man said struck me — when he saw the man looking at his horse, he went out to pass the time of day and the man didn't speak, just looked through him. "Queer sort o' cove", he said.'

'A lot on his mind, I daresay,' Jones observed drily.

'That picture without a face — he painted Flora Lambert's face, but the gown's the same — and the hair — not Violet Pout's hair. Did he mean to paint Mariana Fane's face, but the sittings stopped? And those pictures of a naked woman — again without a face.'

'Violet Pout, perhaps?'

'Could be, I suppose. Violet Pout's nightgown was left under the pillow as if she were going back. Jemima Curd was naked under her dress.'

'But no sign of sexual interference. She was a virgin. Doctor Symonds sent me his report. I'm waiting for more detail on Violet Pout.'

'So what now?'

'Rolando Sabatini — he's the only one who knows them all: Sir Neptune, his household, Violet Pout, Jemima Curd and Mariana Fane, and he is the nephew of Mrs Marchant. She is the only connection with that elusive young man.' Jones looked squarely at Dickens. 'You said that she doesn't know where he is.'

Jones's words hung in the air as if they were written in the blackest of ink for Dickens to read, and he did so, understanding fully that Jones was telling him that if he knew something more, now was the time to tell it — there were two young women dead, probably a third, Flora Lambert, and — he thought the unthinkable — there might be others.

'Mrs Marchant has a son by Sir Neptune Fane.'

'You should have told me. What difference would it have made to her? You said enough to tell me that she was the lady with whom Sir Neptune had a long affair. Sabatini could well be with this young man — we might have found him by now. He's the only one who knew about the portrait of Mariana Fane — who knew the artist, perhaps.'

Dickens felt like a razor the cutting of Sam's words — the implication that deaths might have been prevented if he had not been dazzled. 'I am profoundly sorry, Sam, but, in my defence…'

'Go on.'

'Mrs Marchant does not know where her son is. They are estranged. He left her when he found out the truth of his birth. She has not heard of him for several years. She did not tell me his name.'

'Well, I must see her. I cannot leave her alone for your sake.'

Dickens felt his face burn. 'I could go — you can trust me on this, Sam, I beg you.'

'Secrets, Charles, always come to the surface in the matter of murder. You know that. Murder is a filthy business.'

'Touch pitch —'

'Exactly — there is always betrayal, what you might call a necessary betrayal. A servant must betray a kind master, a wife her husband, a friend his boyhood companion. You know the rest.'

'I do — sometimes a mother her son. Oh, the damage the murderous act does — how the stone cast into the dirty water sends its ripples out to the very edge to muddy even the most innocent passer-by.'

'Or drown 'em.' Jones looked very sombre.

'You feel that?'

'Sometimes, and so do you, but we have a choice; for me retirement into shop-keeping; for you retreat to your books. Write about it, but keep your feet out of the mud, and we'll both wring our hands in despair at the state of the world.'

'We are all hurt in action — I've said that often enough.'

'You weren't entirely sure about Mrs Marchant — in the cold light of day.'

'I don't know now, but when she spoke of her son, it was with genuine regret, I think. I honestly don't believe she knew anything, but I will ask again. You'll let me go — if only to prove —'

'It's not a test, Charles, don't ever think that. I won't be wondering how far I can trust you. I can and do, but it worries me that if a time comes when you have to betray someone close to you, that the pain would be too great — even for you.'

'Necessary betrayal, you said — in the interests of justice for the dead. I have already betrayed her confidence and I must confess it to her. If I had told her how involved I was with you, she might not have told me her history.'

'She knew you were looking for Violet Pout. You told her about Jemima Curd and you will have to tell her about Miss Pout's murder. How if she be a true woman? You would not have been dazzled by beauty alone, I think.'

'There was something about her. She confessed her errors of the heart. Her honesty dazzled me.'

'Then be honest with her.'

'I will.' Dickens looked up at Jones and saw that he was smiling. He felt the tears start to his eyes, but he mastered himself and said, 'Old'un — uncommonly wise, that's wot you are.'

Jones laughed. 'Wisdom of age, is it? Now, get on and make your appointment.'

Dickens went to Wellington Street. Harry Wills gave him his letters which he determined to go through methodically. He needed to steady himself before he wrote his note to Dolly Marchant. In going to see her about Violet Pout and Rolando Sabatini, he had only been enacting his obligation to Anne Brown. However, once Jemima Curd had been murdered and he had willingly involved himself in that, he had been going to see a potential witness. A beautiful woman in a candle lit room had dazzled his eyes. Dick Swiveller, indeed.

The letters and the pressing business of *Household Words* completed, he began his note to Dolly Marchant. He did not want merely to ask if she would see him. That might — it would deceive her. He must prepare her, tell her that Violet Pout was dead, and that the police needed to find Rolando.

I know you will understand my concern in the matter

His pen made a blot. What an inky business this is, he thought, watching the blot soak into his words and spread. Here I am, temporising already, using my obligation to Anne to inveigle my way into her house. He wiped his pen and took another sheet of paper.

I am most sorry to tell you that Miss Pout is dead. The police need to find Rolando. Of course, I do not believe he killed her — she was living with an artist in Clerkenwell, but Rolando is an important witness. The artist must be found and Rolando may remember something. I am closely acquainted with Superintendent Jones of Bow Street, who is in charge of this case, and the case of Jemima Curd. He would come to see you, but I have offered in his stead and wonder if you can tell me about any friends of Rolando's, or

He stopped again. He was going to write "of your son's", but it seemed blundering and insensitive. He remembered her tears when she had told him that she did not know if she would ever recover him. He wrote "of yours", finished it with the usual politenesses, signed it, found an envelope and a boy to take the letter to the post, and sat down at his desk again.

31: Behind Bars

Dickens walked into Regent's Park from York Terrace. He had made no mention of a visit to the zoo at home. There would have been cries of delight — everyone would want to come. And then there would have been yells of disappointment. Going to the zoo and no one allowed to go with him. What a sell.

He went along the Broad Walk towards the South of the park where Mrs Marchant had asked him to meet her at the zoo. Her note had come in the morning, saying she would meet him at two o'clock. An odd choice, the zoo, he had thought, but he understood that a meeting in her house would be too intimate. The murder of Violet Pout and the reference to the police would have changed everything.

He waited by the entrance, looking towards the Albany Gate entrance through which she would come from Lodge Road. There was no sign of her. Perhaps she would not come. Perhaps she regretted her confidences. People often did. They would tell you something secret about themselves; something of which they were ashamed; something that ate at them, and which found relief in confession. But you were not a priest. You were an ordinary mortal whom they would surely meet again at a dinner or the theatre. And when you saw them again they avoided you, even though you had made that sacred promise.

That dangerous promise. Dickens thought of Jones's words about necessary betrayal. Not that he had promised not to tell about her son and his father. But he knew that that kiss had been the sign and seal of an unspoken promise. He had kissed her again and again, and they had sat together as close as lovers. He had betrayed her.

The temptation was to run from the place. But he must wait. And if she did not come then Sam must see her. He would write to warn her — he would give her another chance to tell him if she knew any more about Rolando Sabatini.

Perhaps she was here, watching him as he watched for her, wondering if she could trust him. He remembered how she had spied on him at Osnaburgh Terrace. For whom had she been waiting then — in secret, in the dark? She had not explained. Sir Neptune? It was Mrs Sabatini's house. Had she expected Rolando? But she had said she did not know where he was — she would not have lied to him — surely not. It was an uncomfortable thought.

Dickens looked across the park and saw her. She walked slowly as if she were reluctant. He went nearer so that she would see him. She came towards him. Her face was pale under her dark green bonnet, very pale against the black trimming and ribbons, but there was softening fur at the collar of her dark green cape. She looked weary and fragile, but to him she was still beautiful. He made to take her arm, but she moved away and walked stiffly as they went into the zoo.

They walked in silence until they reached an enclosure where Dolly Marchant stopped. Obaysch, the hippopotamus was one of Dickens's favourites. He had watched him often, writing about him in *Household Words* as an easy, basking, jolly fellow, guzzling his milk and dates with complaisant pleasure — all five hundred pounds of him. But today, even Obaysch had a despondent look about him. He looked at his pool gloomily. Dickens could have sworn that he shivered. He went back to his bed.

Dolly Marchant looked at Dickens. 'Do the police suspect Rolando of these murders?'

'No, truly, I do not believe it, but the Superintendent knows that Rolando is connected to all the people involved.' Dickens told her about what they had found at Amwell Street. 'Rolando is the one who mentioned an artist to St George Pierce. He said that Mariana was having her portrait painted. Superintendent Jones needs to know if Rolando can tell him the name of the artist.'

'I know about Mariana — that she is with child. Sir Neptune told me. He blames Rolando.'

'Is that why Rolando ran away, do you think? He found out about Mariana and was too afraid to confess?'

'It is so out of character — I cannot believe that he would be so heartless as to abandon her … but, Sir Neptune —'

'Is a formidable enemy.'

She didn't answer, but stood gazing through the bars. 'Poor prisoners. Bars to keep them in. Poor Mariana in her moated grange. Sir Neptune described her madness. I understood his rage. Rolando is very young — and foolish because he is young.'

'He must be very afraid. What will Sir Neptune do?'

'Flog him, he said. That is what he came to see me about. He thinks I know where Rolando is. I do not. I told him. He does not believe me — for all that is between us.'

He noticed how she rubbed at her wrist under her glove and how she winced. 'What did he do to you?'

'Nothing that he has not done before.' Her voice was hard. 'He has cruel streak and he will punish Rolando. He threatens to expose him as the vile seducer of an innocent child. The hypocrisy of it.'

Dickens wondered if she had an inkling about Sir Neptune and Violet Pout, but he did not ask. He said, 'Even if it exposes his own daughter?'

'If he thinks it is to his advantage. Mariana is lost — what further harm can be done to her? There would be sympathy for Sir Neptune and now Lady Fane is very ill. I doubt she will recover. Sir Neptune would be the tragic figure. His party would stand by him.'

'Then we must find this artist.'

'We?'

'The Superintendent — I have said I will help him. And you can help by telling me of Rolando's friends, of anyone who might know where he is.'

'You mean my son? Does the Superintendent know about him?'

'When Violet Pout was found, I had to tell him. Two murders have been committed.'

There was another silence and they walked on and stopped at the cage of the tawny lioness. Another prisoner. Dolly Marchant looked at her.

'I suppose murder leaves everyone connected to it exposed to the world's cold gaze. I don't care for myself, but my son — he does not deserve —'

'The Superintendent will not expose your secret. He just wants to find Rolando. He is a good man, Dolly.'

At the use of her name, she looked at him full in the face for the first time. 'I do not know where my son is — I would tell you if I did, and I would tell you if I knew where Rolando is. I have not lied to you, Mr Dickens — about anything.'

He felt his name as a blow. She believed he had lied to her, that he had deceived her. He had not meant to. He wanted to say that he had fallen for her, that he had been dazzled by her, that he was not like Sir Neptune Fane, but it was too late. She had turned away, closed to him.

They walked back towards the hippopotamus. She stopped and looked about her. 'I saw them — Rolando and Mariana — just about here. Last summer, in June, I think. The children were looking at the hippopotamus splashing about. They were with Miss Bedwin, the nurse. Rolando and Mariana were strolling on. Rolando saw me and came to meet me. I noticed a man go up to Mariana and Miss Pout who was tying the ribbons to Mariana's bonnet which had slipped off. Miss Pout seemed to know him. They stood for a few moments then Mariana came up to me and Rolando. They looked happy — I should have known then.'

'What about Miss Pout?'

'I left Mariana and Rolando with the children. I was going home to — I overtook them on the path, deep in conversation.'

'Can you remember anything about him?'

'Not much — I remembered thinking if she had a lover and what Sir Neptune would say about that, but it wasn't my business. His head was turned away from me —' Dolly Marchant looked along the path, thinking about what she had seen — 'I just had an impression of a tall, man in a light-coloured coat and straw hat and he — he was carrying a book —' she turned to look at him again — 'I see it now — a sketch book, the kind of book that my brother-in-law used. He is the artist.'

'I think he must be. Thank you.'

She gave him a half smile. 'I am sorry I did not find out his name.'

'Will you tell me of any of Rolando's friends?'

'I will think of any names and write to you. Your policeman should be able to find them. Now, I must go. It is too cold to stand about.'

'Shall I walk with you?'

'No. We should part here, I think.'

She gave him her hand and he held it. 'I am sorry.' It was all he could think of to say.

'So am I. I shall not forget our supper by the fire.' She drew away her hand and walked away. He let her go.

But the tender grace of a day that is dead/ Will never come back to me… Tennyson's lines came to Dickens as he watched her walk across the park, her figure diminishing to a shadow, and at last disappearing.

Dickens went home to eat a solitary lunch and to pick up any letters. He sat by the fire in his study. The house was quiet. Nothing had been gained from his meeting — just a vague description of a man in a straw hat. But so much had been lost, he thought. She had not lied to him. His was the sin of omission. Too many secrets.

Absently, he glanced at his letters. He recognised his brother, Fred's writing. It would be a plea for money, he supposed. Fred was like his father — a fool with money. *Neither a borrower nor a lender be*, so said Polonius. Fred was an inveterate borrower — usually from his brother. Dickens felt an urge to throw them all in the fire. Another lot of letters begging him to do something for each supplicant: to provide a greatcoat to go to India in; a pair of boots to take him to China; a hat to get him a situation in a government office; to give a pound to set him up for life; to save his wife's life, his children's lives — the penman blushes with shame at their destitution which seven and six, or better, a half-sovereign — dare he say a sovereign

— called for tonight, will instantly alleviate. A man had asked him for a donkey once — he had been entreated to leave it at the gate for the man to call for. He had not at the time had a donkey about him.

He set aside Fred's letter and opened the next and his heart skipped a beat. It was from Francis Pryor:

Mr Sabatini wanted to see Sir Neptune. He said he wanted to confess, that he had things to tell him about Miss Pout. He knows she is dead. I told him that it was impossible, that Lady Fane is very ill, and that Miss Mariana is away in the country. It was not my place to tell him anything else, but I told him of your interest in Miss Pout and that it was his duty to see you and reveal any information he might have. I told him that the police have been here.

I hope I did right, Mr Dickens. I did feel for him for he was very distressed. He looked quite wild and I was worried, but when I watched him go away, I saw another fellow who seemed to look after him. I did not tell Sir Neptune of his visit…

32: Old News

'There's a deal o' cases where the woman — or girl — was never identified,' Rogers told Jones. 'They'd been advertised for but no one came forward. Inspector Shackell remembered a girl pulled from the New River back in '47. She was never identified, but I went to see the man who found her. Shackell said I'd find him at The Three Kings. That's where the inquest was. Toby Jeddler, he's called, known as Jug. He remembered — after a bit o' promptin' in the form of a glass or two. He remembered because he found an umbrella nearby with the initials "A.M.". But no one claimed it, or the poor girl. Jug said there was gossip that she'd been an actress or dancer at Sadler's Wells, but that came to nothin'.'

'Any signs of violence?' asked Jones.

'Well, the surgeon — not Bennett, by the way — testified that there were marks on her neck which might have been made by her bonnet strings which were tied tight round her neck — because o' the water.'

'Now that is interesting —' Dickens came in, looking as though he had news.

'Been anywhere exciting?' asked Jones.

'The zoo to see the hippo in the company of a lady — both equally charming.'

'Good. Tell us about it in a bit. Alf and I have been delving into old cases.'

'Drownings?'

'Yes, it was something Ned Orrey said about a drowning before Jemima Curd's. It made me think. Alf's been up to Clerkenwell looking into a case which happened in 1847.'

'Who was she?'

'The victim was never identified, but the surgeon testified that marks round her neck could have been made by her bonnet strings —'

'Which were pulled tight round her neck,' put in Rogers. 'She'd been in the water too long for him to say more. The verdict was the usual one: *Found Drowned*.'

'Alf traced the man who found her, Toby Jeddler, known as Jug —'

'Ears?' asked Dickens.

Rogers grinned. 'Drink — as I found out.'

Jones continued, 'He said gossip went that she was an actress or dancer at Sadler's Wells.'

'Could this Jug describe her?' asked Dickens.

'No — too much damage.'

'Sadler's Wells — no one knew more?'

'No one came forward,' said Rogers.

'I wonder — artists, scene painters — makes you think.'

Jones agreed, 'It does, and there was an umbrella found with the initials "A.M." — might be a lead, but after all this time…'

'There's another one, sir, I was about to say,' Rogers added. 'It's a rum one, this is. Happened in '48. A woman called Emma Golightly who'd been in the Female Penitentiary, convicted of robbery. A Mr Williams who believed she'd reformed found her a new situation, but she disappeared with another lot o' stuff, and that was it until she was identified as drowned in the New River, but —'

'The drowned girl wasn't her, I take it?' Jones asked.

'Right, sir,' Rogers replied, 'she turned up a year later — someone recognised her and she went back to prison. O' course no one could tell anything about the girl that was buried under the name of Emma Golightly.'

'No one reported any missing girl?' asked Dickens.

'Not at the time — an' a year later it was too late,' Rogers replied. 'No way of knowing who she was.'

'It's a dreadful thing,' said Dickens, 'these poor girls — no one to care a straw for them.'

'Well, I did find some people who cared,' Jones replied, 'but not in Clerkenwell. An unidentified girl was found drowned up at the Barrow Hill Reservoir in 1846 — '

'Strangled?' Dickens asked.

'Same as the Sadlers Wells girl — bruising on the neck, possibly from the drag they used to pull her out, but the doctor at the inquest said that death was by drowning. And there are other things about this case which are very significant. It's all written here, Alf. You read it while I take Mr Dickens to meet a Reverend Harvest at Willesden. His believes that a girl pulled out of the reservoir on Barrow Hill was his daughter —' Jones counted on his fingers — '45, 46, 47, 48 —'

'1844 — Ferrara and Venice.'

33: A Lilac Gown

Dickens and Jones took the train from Euston. It would take them to Willesden, which was still a relatively quiet rural village. The Reverend Archer Harvest was Vicar of the Church of St. Mary's.

Dickens told Jones about his meeting with Dolly Marchant when they were in the train, and gave him Pryor's letter.

'I honestly don't believe that Mrs Marchant knows where Rolando is, even though he turned up at Sir Neptune's house.'

Jones looked at the letter. 'Pryor says the lad wanted to confess.'

'The relationship with Mariana, rather than murder, I think. If he loved her as much as Mrs Marchant told me, his desertion would weigh on him. No wonder he was wild and distressed.'

'And someone was with him who didn't go up to the house. Mrs Marchant's son?'

'I did think of that. Pryor didn't see who it was. I'll just have to hope that Rolando does come to me. He might since he obviously knows about Violet. It was in the papers.'

'Inquest adjourned — like Jemima's. The police seeking further evidence as to the family and friends of the deceased. Shackell knows the magistrate at Clerkenwell so it gives us some time. By the way, Pryor didn't know if Sir Neptune was at home on the night of Violet's murder — he comes and goes as he pleases — and he wasn't at his apartment in the Albany. I checked. I still have my doubts about him. Pryor told me that he had received a letter which angered him. He thinks it was addressed to Lady Fane, but he kept it.'

‘Violet Pout? Spot of blackmail, do you think?’

‘I did wonder — blackmail’s a dangerous game. Sir Neptune has a lot to lose.’

‘So he does.’ Dickens thought about Dolly Marchant’s arm. ‘I had the impression from Mrs Marchant that Sir Neptune … might be … capable of violence.’

Jones heard the hesitations — another betrayal? He did not ask for more, but he thought of violence against a woman. ‘I thought the same — that he was a man capable of rage. You said that you thought Lady Fane was frightened of him.’

‘I did — I thought it was about Violet Pout and Mariana, that she was frightened to speak of some possible scandal, but when I thought back, she seemed frightened when she came in — before she knew what I was at Wisteria Lodge for. Of course, they knew about Mariana’s pregnancy by then. I wonder if he had raged at his wife, blamed her for not keeping her eyes on her daughter.’

‘Plausible, but without any evidence against him…’

‘What about the Reverend Harvest?’

‘I’ll give you an outline — I hope to get more information from Harvest. In August 1846, he applied to the magistrate at Marylebone to have a body exhumed — the body of an unidentified girl found drowned in June in the reservoir on Barrow Hill —’

‘A stone’s throw from Regent’s Park where Violet Pout and Mariana Fane met a young man with a sketch book.’

‘Quite so. The verdict was the usual “found drowned”, and she was buried by the parish. The Reverend Harvest had reason to believe it was his daughter, Susan. Inspector Maxwell of Marylebone told me the story. The mention of the bruising on the neck and the other details were significant enough to lead me to write to the Reverend Harvest and make an appointment.'

'A clergyman's daughter.'

'There's more. She was companion to an old lady, Mrs Emmeline Danby, living in Charles Lane, St John's Wood.'

'Like Flora Lambert!'

'Just so — whose aunt and uncle live in Hamilton Terrace and who was killed we believe in 1845.'

'But not necessarily the first.'

Jones looked at him gravely, 'Nor the last. That's what frightens me.'

'1850 — he failed with Mariana. He killed Jemima.'

'Not Violet Pout then.'

'Her hair was a very different colour. I wonder about Susan Harvest's hair.'

'We'll ask. This artist, he must have lived in the vicinity of the park. The old lady, Mrs Danby, died and Susan Harvest disappeared. She was still writing home, supposedly from Charles Lane, after Mrs Danby's death when she was supposed to have gone home. Now, I am hoping that Reverend Harvest can tell us more about his daughter's life at Charles Lane and what was in those letters.'

The Reverend Archer Harvest was a widower whose sister lived with him to look after his children, the eldest of whom had been Susan. He was a tall, spare man with a pale, narrow face and the stooped shoulders and vague eyes of the scholar behind his spectacles. It was the face of a good man, but a man who had passed through a terrible strait, the record of which had never faded. Anguish might have been his name.

They went into his study and when the door closed sounds of voices became muted and then ceased. The Reverend

Harvest bade them sit down. Jones introduced himself and Mr Charles Dickens, whose interest in Susan's disappearance had to do with the disappearance of the daughter of a friend who was also found drowned. Mr Harvest expressed his pleasure at meeting Mr Dickens, whose works he had read, of course, and with great pleasure. *David Copperfield* was his favourite — his own childhood had been blighted by the loss of his mother and his adoption by a stern uncle.

'My wife and I wanted a loving home for our children, Mr Dickens — a home in which warmth and safety would be theirs, and from which they could go to fulfilling and worthy lives. Had my wife lived, she would not — that is — our dearest Susan would not have wanted —' His face was drawn and he looked away from them at a picture on his desk.

Dickens saw how the death of the cherished child was still a raw wound — and in such circumstances. Lost and found drowned. How would a father bear that?

Harvest recovered himself and turned to Jones. 'You wish to know more about Susan — it will help in your enquiries?'

'I hope so, sir. I am investigating several cases of girls who were drowned and unidentified — Mr Dickens's friend's daughter had some connection, I think, with St John's Wood, and so did another girl.'

'I do not know what happened to my daughter, Superintendent. But you seem to think that her death may be linked to the other girls?'

'I do. Is it possible for you to tell us about Susan?'

'I pray for her every day — I trust that whatever wrong she did, our blessed saviour will forgive her. Your Little Em'ly was forgiven by the good Daniel Peggotty, was she not, Mr Dickens? Foolish, girlish dreams led to Susan's ruin. I think she may have been involved with a young man. Your writing showed the feeling of your heart for that lost girl. How I thought of my dear Susan when I read of poor Martha and her desire for the forgetful waters of the river — but Susan did not kill herself, I feel certain, though that question was raised at the inquest.'

'She was led astray, you think, by a designing man?'

'I had better begin at the beginning so that you will understand her more thoroughly — if you will permit me, Superintendent. You need to know her innocence.'

'We will listen, Reverend Harvest, to whatever you wish to tell us. We are very sorry.'

'Susan was thirteen when her mother died, and for the next three years she became a mother to the younger ones — my boy, Cecil, was just one year old. I had five daughters, the youngest, Grace, was three. By the time Susan was sixteen, my widowed sister came to live with us. Susan was to go to school in London — my sister felt it was time she had some enjoyment from her responsibilities and was willing to pay her fees. She made a friend at the school, the daughter of a wealthy man living in Belgrave Square. He invited Susan to accompany the family to Italy at the end of their schooldays — in 1844 when they were eighteen. As you can imagine, it was an opportunity we had never thought — for any of our children.'

Italy, Dickens thought, but he did not look at Jones. They waited while a young girl brought in some tea. Reverend Harvest introduced her as Anna. She was a very pretty girl with a grave, silent face, dressed in grey with a neat lace collar. Her reddish-gold hair was gathered in a heavy knot at her neck.

When she had gone out, Reverend Harvest continued, 'Anna is sixteen — the same age as Susan when she went to school. She is content to stay with her aunt and me, and her younger sister. I am glad to say. Her older sisters are married. My son is at school.'

'She is like Susan?' Dickens ventured.

'She is — and I am glad. I see Susan as she was — not as she became. She wrote many letters from Italy — of her visits to all the famous places, Florence, Bologna, Venice, of course, and the interesting people she met. The letters were full of excitement — of visits to artists' studios, galleries, theatres, but…'

'There was some anxiety about her?'

'Only that I feared that the company of wealthy people and the luxury, and the dizzying pleasure, might be too much of a contrast to our quietness here. What was she to do when she returned? I had thought governess or teacher, but, Mr Dickens, your Ruth Pinch did not have an easy time with her manufacturing employer. I worried that she might find it lonely, but when Susan returned home, another opportunity presented itself. Susan was restless — she missed her friend, Miss Masters, and she wanted — she knew not what. An old parishioner of mine, Mr Octavius Nash, had an elderly cousin, Mrs Danby, who needed a companion. Susan was delighted. She would be in London — I think she thought to renew her friendship with the Masters family. My sister and I agreed. Mr Nash took her and all seemed well.'

'She wrote of her life in London?'

'She wrote regularly to me and to her sisters. She seemed content at first. Mrs Danby was a timid, gentle and undemanding lady. Susan pushed the wheeled chair into the park; the spring was fine and they visited the zoo and sometimes Susan was allowed to go shopping with Mr Nash's wife. Susan sent us her sketches of the animals in the zoo and the plants in the Botanic Garden. But when winter came, into her letters crept a note of dissatisfaction. She had written to Miss Masters in Belgrave Square and had hoped to meet her, but nothing came of it. There were fewer outings, more reading to Mrs Danby and long hours alone. Susan came home for Christmas. She seemed unhappy —'

'She did not say why?'

'Only that she wanted to stay at home — perhaps try to be a governess, perhaps in the future. However, she agreed to go back so that Mr Nash had time to find another companion. Oh, that I had kept her, Mr Dickens — her sisters wanted — but I was conscious of an obligation to Mr Nash. In the New Year — 1846 — her letters appeared more cheerful. She had found a friend — a lady with whom she spent some time — Isabella, she called her. They walked in the park, made some visits to friends.'

'No other name?' asked Jones.

'I am afraid not. Her letters became infrequent. Anna wrote to her asking for news, and so did I. She was very sorry, she wrote back, but she had been occupied — Mrs Danby had been unwell, but now the spring had come, she was much improved. Then the letter came from Mr Nash to announce Mrs Danby's death. He bade me to tell Susan that Mrs Danby had remembered her in her will —'

'He thought Susan had been at home?'

'Yes, she had gone back after Christmas, but after about two months — in March — Susan had expressed her wish to come home and told Mr Nash that I had sanctioned this. Susan left with a present of money and Mr Nash found a new companion. He was surprised and offended when I did not write to him, but thought that I was embarrassed by Susan's desertion. I went to London and told my story. He and I tried to trace Susan and the mysterious Isabella and then after months of searching, in August, Mr Nash received an anonymous letter — I have it —'

They waited. Reverend Harvest took it out of a drawer in his desk and handed it to Jones. It was an uneducated hand and the paper was the torn off sheet of a thick piece of paper. The printed words read: *look inter the inqwest on a pore girl taken from the barrer reserver in er lilac dress in june it wos*

Dickens felt the paper — it wasn't letter writing paper. It was the thick, ridged paper that an artist might use. Torn from a sketch book. He did not say anything.

The Reverend Harvest sat down again. 'Mr Nash went immediately to the police at Marylebone and found that a girl had been taken from the reservoir in June and no one had claimed her. He sent for me. My sister and I went to the police. A piece of cloth taken from the dress had been preserved. My sister knew it — she had made the lilac dress for Susan's trip to Italy. When Susan came back, the hem of the dress was torn. My sister repaired it, but the thread she used was a darker colour — she knew it, Superintendent Jones, and she knew that the white straw bonnet found with the girl with its pink and white ribbons was Susan's, too. She and Susan had trimmed that bonnet together.

'Mr Nash and I went to the magistrate to ask that the body be exhumed. He said I must apply to the coroner and the parish authorities — if they felt that the evidence was substantial, they could direct the body to be exhumed.'

'But you did not do that,' Jones said.

'There was so much horror attached to such practices at the time. There was that dreadful affair of the murderer, Jonathan Balls, who had poisoned so many of his family, his own children. The papers were full of the hideous details — it was unbearable, and to think of my poor girl — '

Of course they knew the case. Jonathan Balls, a grandfather of eighty-one, had committed suicide. His own daughter had reported him. Eleven exhumations had been carried out. The Home Secretary had reported to the House of Commons that Balls could have killed twenty members of his own family. All the grisly details of the exhumations had been in the papers. No wonder Reverend Harvest had shrunk from the idea.

'And then I thought what if it were not my daughter — some other's daughter, whose sleep I would disturb — those poor remains to be profaned by the hands of strangers. I found I could not —' Mr Harvest looked at the picture again. They waited for him to recover his composure — 'Mr Nash spoke against it, too, for the sake of my other children. He advised me to let it rest. Perhaps some other evidence would come to light, he said, and he would continue to make enquiries. There was nothing more — except…'

Reverend Harvest took off his spectacles and rubbed at his eyes.

'My curate spoke to me about Susan after he knew that I had enquired after her. He had walked with her at Christmas. He thought she was troubled, that she had something on her conscience. She asked whether love could ever be wrong — he told her that it was the purest thing a woman could aspire to, provided that the man was worthy of such love, and provided that he was honourable. He did not tell me at the time. He thought — and rightly so — that Susan was, perhaps, beginning to feel for someone and that she did not know the right of it. He advised her to tell me or her aunt. We would counsel her and he was sure that she would never be wrong in her choice. He believed that — naturally, he would — of one of my daughters. He married my eldest daughter, Lucy.'

'Susan did not give a name?' asked Jones.

'No, she never did, and she did not speak to me or my sister, or even to Lucy, who is nearest to her in age. Had it been an attachment formed with a man of whom we could approve, she would have told us, surely.'

'I think she would, from what you have said about your lives here. It does seem that she may have been led astray — she was lonely, it seems, and perhaps, this Isabella encouraged her in the relationship. Susan would be too innocent.'

'She was trusting, Mr Dickens — why should she not be? Here, in our village, there is no one she could not trust, but she went amongst strangers.'

Jones stood up. 'I will do all I can, Reverend Harvest, to find out about Susan, and I will write to you of what I find.'

'You are hopeful?'

'Given the similarity of the cases, I am. In each case there is a man whose identity we do not yet know, but we will find him.'

'If, Superintendent, you do find out what happened to my girl, if you come to believe, as I do, that she lies in an unmarked grave, then I beg you, help me bring her home this time.'

Reverend Harvest stared out of his study window to the graveyard beyond. They followed his gaze to look at the bleak winter scene where there were ancient yew trees which stood black against the ashen sky and gravestones so green and so old that they seemed to be growing from the very earth in which they stood.

'Susan must lie with her mother who loved her, and to whose arms she must return.'

'I will do all I can, sir.'

'And I, too, will see what my influence will do,' Dickens added.

With that pledge, they shook hands with Reverend Harvest who turned back to his Bible.

Dickens and Jones went back to the station to wait on the wooden platform by the little wooden office. It was quiet and they stood looking down the line towards London.

'Would it be possible?' asked Dickens.

'I am sure — if we can find enough evidence to say that the girl from Barrow Reservoir is Susan Harvest, and you know some powerful people — the Prime Minister himself.'

'I do — I shall ask his advice.'

On the train they had a carriage to themselves. For a while they watched the countryside unfold while they collected their thoughts.

'Italy, Regent's Park, sketching, a young man who might be an artist, a secret love affair, gone missing, found drowned — it is all very telling,' observed Dickens.

'It is.'

'Though we do not know how Susan met her death. It could have been suicide.'

'I don't think it matters at the moment. What matters is that we find out as much as we can about Susan's life in St John's Wood and before. There will be Mr Nash to see, and any servants of Mrs Danby's, the man who found the body — I'll ask Maxwell about that — and Miss Masters who lived in Belgrave Square — probably married now, but we should be able to find her.'

'And the mysterious Isabella?'

'Ah, that might be more difficult, but she must have lived somewhere near Regent's Park. I shall need Inspector Maxwell's help there. You and I will see Miss Masters and we'll see the finder of the body after I've talked to Maxwell. Rogers I will send to Mr Nash.'

'The anonymous letter.'

'Yes, I saw you feeling the paper.'

'From an artist's sketchbook, perhaps, Sam — torn off.'

'Written by a servant, I would guess — someone who worked for an artist.'

'Someone with a conscience, it seems.'

34: Daughters of the House

At Bow Street, Jones found Mr Octavius Nash in the Royal Blue Book and sent Rogers with Inspector Grove to ask questions about Mrs Danby and her servants, and to get any addresses. He found Mr Masters in Belgrave Square.

Miss Georgiana Masters was married and lived in Bedford Place, where two rows of identically cream-coloured houses gazed at each other across the broad street as if each row had withdrawn the hem of its garment and retreated into self-satisfied perfection and never a step further would they make. No question of meeting half-way here. It was quiet, too, away from the noise of Holborn and Great Russell Street — even the carriage horses seemed to go by on velvet hooves.

They were shown into a small, pretty parlour where Miss Masters, now Mrs Godolphin, very attractive with her dark curls and frothy lace, sat with a pretty little girl by a cheerful fire. The little girl looked at them solemnly and then hid her face in her mother's skirts.

'I will send for nurse,' Mrs Godolphin said after she had greeted them and expressed her delight at receiving Mr Dickens, and Jones had said that they wished to speak to her about a former schoolfriend. 'Clara has a cold, poor darling. Now, dearest, nurse will take you to the nursery for I must talk to these gentlemen. Take dolly with you.'

Clara stood up and gazed at them again. Quite liking what she saw, she held up the doll to Dickens. 'Katy.'

Dickens bent down and took the doll's hand. 'Why, Miss Katy, how extraordinary, that is my daughter's name. Now I have two friends named Katy.'

'I am Clara.'

'Well, Miss Clara, you are my only friend called Clara. That is a very special thing.'

'My papa is very busy. He works at a bank. What do you do?'

'I write stories.'

'About dolls?'

'Sometimes.'

Clara pointed at Jones. 'Is he your friend?'

'My very best friend.'

'What does he do?'

'He is — he keeps a shop. He sells pens and pencils and sealing wax, paper and inks in all colours of the rainbow.'

Clara looked at Jones consideringly. 'I shall come to your shop.'

The door opened and the nursemaid came in.

Mrs Godolphin said, 'You shall go shopping when you are grown-up. Now, go with nurse and I will come up soon.' Mrs Godolphin motioned them to sit. 'You are very kind, Mr Dickens. My little pet asks a thousand questions a day — but then you know children, do you not. Little Nell and Paul Dombey, and David Copperfield — but, forgive me, Superintendent Jones, you have come about a schoolfriend of mine.'

'It is about Susan Harvest.'

She paled then and her pretty, lively face looked sad. 'Oh, but she is thought to have drowned. My father told me that he had read in the newspaper that the Reverend Harvest believed that she had been taken from Barrow Hill Reservoir. It was very sad. I wrote to Susan's father.'

'Susan had been missing for a few months before the unknown girl was pulled from the water. I am trying to find out where she was on behalf of the Reverend Harvest.'

'I didn't see her after we came home from Italy. She went home and then became companion to an elderly lady. She wrote to me, but by then I was married. Clara was born in 1846, so I couldn't go to see Susan. I wrote to her, but then time passed and I lost a baby — a difficult time... I have two more children now — one just a baby — yet we had been such good friends.'

'I wonder if you might tell us about your time in Italy.'

'We were eighteen, and it was a quite wonderful experience. I read your *Pictures from Italy*, Mr Dickens. It brought it all back so vividly — your dream of Venice.'

'Thank you. Reverend Harvest said that you visited the galleries and churches and artists' studios.'

'I met my husband, Percival, in Florence — he was travelling with his uncle who knew many people. Our heads were quite turned. So many receptions — there were English families and Italian counts and countesses. And they took us to look at pictures everywhere.'

'You did not meet anyone whom you remember taking particular notice of Susan.'

'There were lots of young men. Susan was so pretty — and quiet, though. She was shy — she had led such a retired life at home. She never — oh, I do remember. It was something we giggled about. It seemed so romantic to such girls as we were. On one Sunday morning, Susan went to church. I was busy — choosing a dress to wear for an outing with Percival. When she came back, she looked so excited. She had met a young man who was copying a painting. He spoke to her and told her she had beautiful hair and that he would like to paint her. She did have beautiful hair — thick and golden, almost red in some lights.'

'Did she meet him again?'

'I don't know. She might have done. I confess that Percival and I contrived to be alone.'

'You don't know his name?'

'I'm afraid I can't remember. He was Italian, I'm sure, although he must have spoken to Susan in English. She could not speak Italian. Perhaps he was English — I really don't know. We left Florence soon after and Susan didn't talk of it again. It was just an adventure.' She turned to Jones. 'Could it be important, Superintendent?'

'I don't know, Mrs Godolphin, I promised Reverend Harvest that I would investigate. It is a great sadness to him that Susan may be buried in an unmarked grave. He would like to prove her death and take his daughter home.'

Mrs Godolphin was silent then. 'To have lost his daughter — oh, how very sad. When I think of how Percival dotes on little Clara. Do you think that Susan could have met this young man again — in London?'

'It is possible.'

'I am sorry that I cannot help you more — except that he was an artist. I am more than sorry that I did not keep up with Susan. I think of her now — so pretty in her lilac dress, and all her life before her as mine was.'

They left her to her regrets. They would pass, Dickens thought. It was the way of things. She had her little pet and her baby. But for the Reverend Harvest and that grave sister, their lives were blighted. And Sarah and Dan Curd, Mrs Pout, James Pout — all their lives changed, bruised, scarred, choked off by the murderer's hands.

'When you think, Sam, what Susan might have had — that little Clara — it is heart-breaking, and the others, all their futures destroyed.'

35: Watcher

Dickens and Jones went up to Albany Street, the headquarters of S Division, where Inspector Maxwell told them that the finder of the body was one Walter Child, known as Watcher, who had been the watchman at the Pump House at the reservoir. He was still about and could probably be found at a pub in Wellington Terrace. Maxwell had his constables enquiring at the houses nearest the reservoir — certain streets that Jones had thought worthwhile. They were to ask about Susan Harvest and a possible friend named Isabella.

They walked across Regent's Park, making for the entrance gate, which led into Avenue Road. On the Broad Walk, Jones remarked to Dickens, 'A pretty golden-haired girl with a sketch book might well attract an artist. And Violet Pout walked beside a man with a sketch book. This is where he picked them up.'

'And he had probably been in Clerkenwell near Sadler's Wells, perhaps, and to there he returned. That house in Amwell Street, did you find out who owns it?'

'A Mr Mitchell, who let it to a lady who is abroad for her health, but still pays the rent. Her furniture is in storage. Miss Pout and her paramour seem to have been cuckoos in that nest.'

They passed the zoo.

'Mrs Marchant,' Jones began, 'did she understand?'

Dickens did not look at him. 'She understood how murder taints everything. Not that she forgave me. She thought I was looking for Violet Pout. She did not know I was looking for a murderer — in league with Superintendent Jones of Bow Street.'

'I'm sorry.'

'My own fault.'

They reached the gate. Ahead lay Avenue Road, at the top of which were quite a number of scattered houses in their own grounds. To the right lay Barrow Hill Place and a path leading to the reservoir. Barrow Hill was not a hill, not in the way that its neighbour, Primrose Hill, was. It had been a hill, but its aspirations had been crushed by the engineers who had built the reservoir.

Inspector Maxwell had told them that occasionally it had been an attraction for those who desired a watery grave, but the preference was for the canal or the lake in Regent's Park. As far as he knew no murder had been done at the reservoir — not recently at any rate — there'd been two men killed over a lady years' back, and an Italian poet had fought a duel with a man who had criticised his poems. Maxwell laughed. 'Foscolo — the name was — Ugo — that's it — sensitive, I suppose — about his work.' Maxwell had addressed his historical remarks to Dickens. Sam Jones had heard these tales already. Dickens had laughed in agreement, but he had shivered inwardly. Ugo Foscolo — the Italian poet who had been Agosto Sabatini's patron. Fate weaving its net.

By some unspoken agreement, Jones and Dickens took the path to the reservoir, the path along which Susan had gone in her lilac gown and innocently pretty white bonnet. Whatever she had done, however she had fallen, her ruin had been brought about, Dickens thought, by the artist in murder. He looked at Sam's face, worn by the cold and read there his own sorrow about all those drowned girls.

Looking to the west, away over the horizon, the heavy indigo clouds were touched on their undersides with gold. A splash of molten gold showed where the sun was setting. They watched the cloud masses lower and weigh down the brightness which shrank to a thin roll of gold. The dark grey water before them was still as lead. Somewhere a bird called its goodnight. The air was bitter and the water looked horribly cold and depthless. It might have been a million fathoms deep. Dickens thought of the poor girl sucked down into the dreadful silence and a dark man slipping into the shadows.

'Let's go and find Watcher,' said Jones. 'I've seen enough.'

There were lights coming on in the windows as Dickens and Jones walked along Avenue Road: a maid was closing the shutters; piano music came from an upstairs window; a nursemaid turned into a gate manoeuvring a perambulator; a woman holding a little child stared out at them; in another firelit window, in a comfortable room which looked like a study, Dickens saw a man with his head in his hands, his elbows on a desk, an open letter before him.

'Samivel — there's a story, I daresay… I think that with employment for the mind, exercise for the body, a domestic hearth, and a cheerful spirit — a man may still be many things wanting to complete his happiness — and he may be confoundedly miserable.'

'So he may, but what have you told me, many a time —'

'And oft — not necessarily on the Rialto —' Dickens smiled a crooked smile — 'what pearl of wisdom have I cast before you?'

But Jones's face was grave and his eyes looked at Dickens with sympathy. He felt sad, too, remembering his friend's words about David Copperfield: that old, unhappy want of something. 'Courage, persevere — that's what you say.'

'I do — and I will. We will.'

They found their way to Wellington Terrace where, tucked behind The Asylum for Orphaned Children of the Clergy, they discovered the pub where Inspector Maxwell had told them they would likely find Walter Child: The Friend in Need. The landlord pointed him out.

Watcher sat alone at a small table by the fire. There was a look of a wild bird about him, a bird of prey for which his curved beak of a nose was exactly right. There was a manner about him of one lying in wait. Well, that was his occupation — on the watch for trespassers, waifs and strays, midnight swimmers, would be robbers, would be suicides — murderers, perhaps.

Dickens procured them some drinks. Watcher took the proffered brandy and warm with scarcely a flicker of his hooded lids. Jones was always patient — he waited until the first drink had been enjoyed and put his hand over the second. At this, Watcher's eyes flew open. Dickens saw how sharp they were — the brown-yellow colour of a falcon's or a hawk's with two black pinpoints of pupils.

'June, 1846, the girl in the lilac gown — what do you remember?'

'Pretty girl, white straw bonnet, golden hair.'

'How do you think she went in?' Jones removed his hand.

Watcher drank again then looked at them, his sharp eyes glinting. 'Rare to get a suicide up there. Folk goes where they knows. Suicide's an odd game. They goes to a place they bin afore, usually, most often, I thinks. Young girl wouldn't go ter the reservoir. She'd go ter the lake in the park or the canal. A girl wouldn't go up there — at night.'

'Why should she care?' asked Dickens. 'If she planned to kill herself? What could be more frightening than the prospect of death itself?'

'See, sir, that's 'aporth —' Watcher took another gulp. They waited — ''aportheticle, see, logic yer speakin'. But logic ain't no use in suicide. If yer woz thinkin' logic, yer wouldn't do it at all. A woman, or a man, fer that matter, 'as their mind on their own death — it seems the only way. T'ain't nothin' — wun minit yer 'ere sufferin', next yer can be gone where no wun can foller. But afore yer go, yer might see ter things. Yer might be frightened o' the dark so yer takes a lantern; yer might be worried about the weather so yer takes an umbrella; yer don't wanter get lost so yer treads the familiar path. Wun part of yer mind works along the way it's allus worked — automatic like…'

Another philosopher, thought Dickens. 'You seem to know a good deal about it.'

'Waterman wunce — down Lime'ouse. Knowed a deal o' folk wot took that way. My wife — fished 'er out meself. She'd gone but she left me a chop — plate on the 'ob — see she couldn't go without settin' things right — an' she went in at Lime'ouse Cut — knowed it, see.'

'So if the girl didn't take her own life, did someone push her?' asked Jones.

''Ard ter say. Want no sign o' sich. Eyes open — yer gets a feelin' about the last thing they sees.'

'What?' Dickens asked. He'd thought that about Jemima Curd.

'See, a suicide closes 'er eyes — nat'ral, ain't it? Yer don't wanter see. An' very of'en there's somethin' peaceful — they've gone an' they ain't sorry. But other times — not many

— I seen somethin' different. That girl in the lilac dress — frightened. She saw an enemy last of all — that's wot I thinks.'

Watcher's eyes were hooded again as though he looked into himself, remembering the murdered eyes he had seen.

Could it be true? Could the victim's eyes retain the terror of the last moments when she realised that the hands at the throat were not those of a lover who only meant to caress?

'At the inquest, the doctor reported that there were marks on her neck. Did you see those?' asked the practical Jones.

The eyes opened, 'Nah, jest saw the bonnet floatin' be'hind 'er. 'Ooked 'er out —'

'How?'

'Use an iron 'ook on a pole.'

'No, how did you hook her?'

Watcher understood. 'Caught 'er by the neck — pulled 'er in ter the shore gentle-like. Mighta left a mark, I serpose. No one asked abaht that.'

'Did anyone ask about her?'

'No wun — that's why I thort she wouldn'ta gone ter Barrer. 'Ow'd she know 'er way up there? But a bit arter, arter the inquest, somewun did come ter see me 'ere.'

'Who?'

Watcher lifted his empty glass. It was time to pay the philospher a bit more. Dickens obliged.

Watcher drank. 'Young woman — servant, I thort. Wanted ter know about the dead girl. Did I see anywun with 'er? Did I think she'd committed suicide? Sed I dint see anywun — jest saw 'er dead in the water an' inquest jus' sed found drowned. When the reverend gentleman an' 'is friend came, told 'em, but I don't think they ever found 'er.'

'Did she give a name?'

'No, but there woz another girl waitin' at the bar. Went out together an' I 'eard the name Lilian, but I can't tell yer which woz Lilian. Both servants, I'd say.'

Dickens and Jones left Watcher to his last drink and went out into Wellington Road and walked down Park Road towards York Gate and Devonshire Terrace.

'A servant girl called Lilian — it's something, I suppose,' Dickens said.

'Not much — she might be anywhere. And, remember, we don't have any evidence that Susan Harvest was murdered by anyone, let alone an artist. There were some marks on her neck — maybe the bonnet strings, maybe Watcher's pole, we don't know. I'd have to ask for an exhumation — to be able to tell if her neck was broken. It might not have been. Flora Lambert was particularly fragile. And if there were no evidence the Reverend Harvest would be put through that horror for nothing.'

'True enough, but what about old eagle eye there — his notion that he saw something in her eyes. What do you think?'

'No idea — he puts away enough drink. I don't know, Charles, I just want some facts — not visions.'

'Lilian is not that common a name — Maxwell might trace her and Isabella.'

'I'll go and tell him. You go home. There's nothing more to be done tonight.'

'You won't come in?'

'No, thank you. I shall go home after I've seen Maxwell.'

'Courage, persevere — if you will, I will, as the boys say.'

Jones laughed. 'Something will turn up, I daresay.'

'Bless you, Samivel.'

With that, Dickens turned away into York Gate.

There were the usual letters which Dickens put to one side. And there was a piece of folded paper sealed with wax and addressed to him. He opened it. There were just two words: *Rarx. Midnight.* And a little drawing, the clever outline of a black and white bird. A magpie.

That was a facer. It had to be from Magpie. Midnight near Hemlock Court. Rarx and his blunderbuss, not to mention that it was a crooked place of labyrinthine alleys. Dangerous. When you went away from the streets where gas light made darkness visible, there was always a sense that the darkness in those alleys, many no wider than tunnels, was thicker, deeper, suffocating and more terrifying — if murder were on your mind. Somewhere at a distance clocks would chime midnight, but time in those places meant nothing to the houseless ears of the vagabond, to the street sleeper bundled in his doorway, to the robber slinking from his lurk — or to the ghost rising from his grave. Once, he had met a boy in the most threadbare rags who had looked at him as if he had been the ghost and when he had put his hand out, the creature had twisted out of its garments and vanished, naked and houseless into the dark.

Magpie? What could he want? He had liked him, but he knew nothing about him. Except that he had told Magpie that he was looking for Jemima Curd. Perhaps he had found out something about her. It must be secret. Else why midnight? Unless that was simply Magpie's flair for the dramatic — Dickens understood that. Or might it be something to do with Rarx and the stolen jewellery from the water tank? Unlikely, but a temptation nonetheless. Whatever it was, Magpie lived on the edge. His conduct, however quixotic, was criminal. That brought him to Sam. Ought he to tell him? Tell him what? That he was meeting a thief.

He thought about the young man who had whirled him through those alleys and whose good humour and shabby theatricality had appealed to him. And that beautiful, silent girl in her old-fashioned velvet dress. There was a mystery there.

He looked again at the note. A thought struck him. He looked at the wax seal which had cracked in two as he had opened it hastily. He joined the two pieces together and, taking a magnifying glass from his desk, examined it closely. One letter came into focus: *J*. The other twisted round the *J* might have been an *N* — it was too broken to tell. Magpie had a name then — though, of course, it might not have been his seal — the snapper-up of trifles. Green wax. Men usually used red. Ladies used colours. From whom had he received a note sealed with green wax? Dolly Marchant. He had burnt the note, of course.

He would go. Of course he would. A night walk in his long coat and a low-crowned hat.

36: On an Amateur Beat

Sam Jones was anxious, too. He had gone home to play with his children, and to talk to his wife at supper by the fire.

'What's worrying you?' asked Elizabeth as they sat in the parlour.

The children were in bed and Scrap had gone back to the stationery shop in Crown Street, disappointed that there was nothing in the detecting line required of him. Jones had promised to send for him if he were needed.

Jones told Elizabeth about Susan Harvest and the Reverend who grieved so hard for her, and about Watcher and the Barrrow Reservoir.

'So you don't know if she was murdered?'

'No, it's just those suggestive bits of evidence — nothing in themselves, but tantalising pieces of a jigsaw with big pieces missing. I'll have to be patient and see what Maxwell and his men turn up. I hope I'm not wasting time on Susan Harvest.'

'It won't be wasted if you can take her home — even if her death is not connected to the others. It will be a good thing for the Reverend Harvest.'

'Of course, you are right, my love. There's little good I can think of doing just now. Who is he? And what's his motive?'

'Do you know, I thought about the girls you told me about and Dickens's experiences in Italy and I thought about Browning's *Porphyria.*'

'Who? You'll have to explain.'

'It's a poem about a man who strangles his lover with her own hair.'

'His motive?'

Elizabeth laughed. 'Well, Mr Superintendent, that's what made me think. He waits for her in a deserted cottage. He thinks that she is held back by fear of her reputation. He wonders if she loves him at all. She comes and tells him that she does, and in that moment when she leans against him, in that perfect moment, he kills her. The point is that he is mad — I wondered about your artist. Is he mad?'

'Possesses them and kills them to keep them?'

'Well, from what you told me, he gains nothing by their deaths — not money, at any rate. Not greed, surely. He can't be jealous — they can't all have had lovers who supplanted him. He can hardly be killing all of them out of rage.'

'My lady detective — I'll try that theory on Charles Dickens. It will appeal to him, I'm sure, and it's the only explanation that makes any sense to me — mad though it is. But looking for a madman, Elizabeth…'

Jones sipped his brandy and stared into the fire. Dickens's words came back to him: *a domestic hearth … things wanting … confoundedly miserable.* What sadness in those words. He sighed.

Elizabeth watched him. 'What about Charles — you sounded anxious when I asked if he was coming.'

'Only that he found himself in a dilemma. He went to see Sabatini's aunt, but didn't tell her about working with me. She told him some confidential information and eventually he had to tell me.'

'But that's bound to happen. He knows that.'

'Oh, he does — he was —'

'A young and charming aunt was she?'

Jones chuckled. 'I am not at liberty to say. I don't want to betray his confidence.'

'You just did in that word "confidence".'

'Too sharp for me, you are. Thought of joining the force?'

'That'll be the day. A lady policeman — that would be a thing. However, I am guessing that the lady was somewhat smitten, magnetised by a pair of shining eyes.'

'Something like that but I was concerned. I thought about what might happen if he were faced with a painful choice involving someone really close to him. And, I think about Scrap, too — putting them in danger.'

'Try keeping them away.'

At the shop in Crown Street, Scrap could not sleep. Little Charley Rogers, Charles Samuel after his godfathers, had cried — for hours, it seemed. Teething, Mollie had said, letting the little boy suck on her finger, dipped in sugar and wine. Eventually, he had slept and Mollie had gone exhausted to her bed.

But Scrap was wide awake now. Mollie's words had sparked a memory. A baby crying, a baby with red cheeks all crumpled up and his own finger dipped in gin — they had no sugar — and his mother in her bed, unable to get up. He remembered her cough — a terrible noise which had frightened him. She seemed unable to breathe and he had given her gin, too. And then she and that baby were gone. Silly, he had called her, not understanding it was really Cecilia. In his boyish way, he had thought it apt. His mother had called him Scrap. He had been very small. Silly had been a big baby. He remembered lugging her about the single room they had lived in. To keep her quiet when his ma was at work.

He hadn't known that he had forgotten it all until Charley Rogers had screamed his head off. He didn't know where his mother and Silly had gone. No one had told him.

His pa had come back. He had called him "Son". Not that he wanted a son. He had wanted a slave, someone to bring in money, by working for it or thieving. Pa didn't care. Son? Scrap? He didn't know what his name was. He must have one. Charley Rogers, Charles Dickens, Sam Jones, Eleanor Brim — they all had names. How would you find out such a thing? Charley Rogers had been christened. He'd cried when the water poured on him. Scrap had watched it all intently, but he didn't know if he had been through the same thing. One thing he did know: he wouldn't have cried.

He hadn't cried when his pa's woman had slapped him — more than once. He hadn't cried when his pa had clouted him for coming home empty-handed. He had run and he had stayed away. They didn't care. He'd gone back from time to time, slept, and helped himself to what little food they had — when he was desperate — and listened to their drunken rages. 'Opeless, they woz. Dead loss.

And when he had found the little dog, Poll, property of Eleanor and Tom Brim, he had returned again and again to the shop to look after them. Their pa was dying of consumption. He was needed.

But that memory, so long forgotten, of his mother's cough and poor little Silly, brought tears to his eyes. He had a sense, sometimes, of not belonging anywhere — not quite at Crown Street, especially when Charley Rogers had come. He felt most at home at Mr Jones's house where Eleanor and Tom were, Eleanor, especially, and Mrs Jones, of course. He loved her. But did he belong?

No sense in squawking, he told himself, dashing away the tears. *Yer lucky. Mr Jones needs yer still, and Mr D — 'e'd be the man ter ask 'oo 'e woz. Mr D would know 'ow yer could find out on the quiet.*

He looked out into the street. It was quiet now. No one much about. Scrap liked watching, wondering about the folk he saw. That queer old woman in the white dress wot rambled about talkin' ter 'erself. Looked like some ancient bride wot 'ad lost 'er way ter the church. Should tell Mr D about 'er. There was the man wiv the wooden leg, stumpin' about usually, pickin' up rubbish from the street. Yer'd think 'e'd found treasure the way 'e grinned an' gibbered at 'imself. Madman, he supposed.

An 'oo's this cove comin' down the street? Lookin' like a sneak wiv 'is collar up an' is 'at low down over 'is face. Scrap pressed his nose to the window. The gas light caught two moony discs of glass. *Blimey, I knows 'oo that is.*

Scrap snatched up his jacket and cap, opened his door, listened up the stairs, crept down one flight, tip-toed into the shop, took the key from the drawer under the counter, put his hand on the bell so that it wouldn't ring, unlocked the door and slipped out into the street just in time to see his quarry disappearing into Goodge Street.

37: The Night Bird

It was easy enough. Scrap kept his distance. He followed Dickens across Oxford Street into Soho Square. There were enough late-night folk about so that he could dodge behind someone when Dickens crossed Long Acre. *Woz 'e going to Bow Street?*

But Mr Jones wasn't there. If Mr D 'ad somethin' urgent to tell him 'e'd a' gone ter Norfolk Street. In 'is disguise, too. Some secret meetin', must be. Ter do with the murder? It might not be safe. Mr D took risks — want afraid o' the streets. Knowed 'em all like 'e 'ad a map in 'is 'ead, but Mr Jones told 'im ter be careful — yer not immortal, 'e'd sed. Scrap had looked up the word in Eleanor's dictionary — and the other word — that was a hard one, but Eleanor had guessed it and had shown it to Scrap: in-im-it-ab-le, she'd said.

Inimitable — good word that. Meant that there woz no one like yer, so Eleanor sed. Scrap had wondered if he was inimitable. Now he thought he was — no one else called Scrap. Mr D had stopped. Scrap dodged into a doorway, nearly stepping on some houseless sleeper who did not stir from his dreams of a cottage garden where a woman waited for news.

Scrap watched Mr Dickens look down Bow Street. Thinkin' about Mr Jones, p'raps, but then he passed on into Drury Lane.

'E 'ad a friend livin' in Lincoln's Inn Fields — that Mr Forster. Bit late fer that. Then they were in Carey Street. It was quieter now. And darker. Mr Dickens turned into an alley. Scrap stood still. He could hear Mr Dickens's footsteps. He peered round the corner into the darkness. Best get a move on.

Someone tapped him on the shoulder — a young woman — more a girl, really, hollow-eyed and stinking, clothed in a threadbare frock and barefoot. 'Gotta penny?'

Scrap shook his head. He was anxious now — the footsteps had faded. But the girl grasped his jacket with hands that looked like claws. 'Giv' us a penny — I'm starvin'. Do yer fer a penny.'

He tried to shake her off, but she held him tighter. He didn't want to create a row and fumbled in his pocket. Sixpence. He gave it to her and darted into the alley, running as fast as he could on tiptoe. The alley turned into another. Only one way to go and then there was a corner and two dark tunnels. Which one?

Then he heard it. A sudden cry. He didn't wait, but flung himself into the darkness. At the end of the first tunnel, under a miserable gaslight two men were grappling. The bigger man with his hands at the smaller man's neck and the smaller man's head pulled back.

'Perlice!' shouted Scrap, running with his arms whirling, looking in the shadows, bigger and threatening. The taller man dropped his victim and ran off.

'Mr Dickens — yer awright?' Scrap was there in an instant, picking up the hat which had fallen to reveal the victim's identity.

'Scrap! What the devil?'

'Follered yer — tell yer later. What 'appened?'

'He jumped me and tried to strangle me with this.' He showed Scrap the dirty bandage which had been thrown round his neck.

'Garotter — yer woz lucky.'

'I got my hands under it. Good job I remembered to wear the gloves this time. Glad you turned up, though — he was bigger than me.'

'Yer not 'urt?'

'No — gave me a shock. I didn't see him or hear him.'

'That's 'ow they does it. Where yer goin'?'

'Ah — to a midnight meeting.'

''Opes that wozn't 'im, Mr D.'

'I don't think so. He's a man who goes by the name of Magpie. I told him I was looking for Jemima Curd.'

'Wot was murdered. Are yer sure this Magpie cove ain't the man wot attacked yer?'

'No — he didn't know Jemima, but he wanted to meet me at Rarx, the pawnbroker's. He didn't say why, but I wondered if he knows anything about Jemima now. Her murder was in the papers. I'm sure he wasn't my attacker — too big, too rough and he stank like the very devil. No, Scrap, I'm sure.'

Scrap wondered about the girl who'd accosted him. Accomplice, p'raps. 'I'll come wiv yer then. Jest ter be sure. Where?'

'Near Hemlock Court.'

Scrap gave him a look. 'Poison ain't it — 'emlock?'

They walked on into Little Shire Street and to Rarx's shop on the corner. They waited in the shadows, hats tipped over their eyes, for the man who walked in the darkness, for the man who called himself Magpie.

They heard the clocks striking the hour, the spreading circles of vibration echoing out into eternal space. Then Dickens felt the silence profounder. Not a footstep. No light in Rarx's shop window or in the window above from where he had shot at the thief and his night time accomplice. Perhaps Magpie would not come.

Then they heard it. In that stillest of silences, the sound of a footfall, of someone who came by stealth. Then a low whistle.

They waited — to be sure that it was not the midnight garrotter. A figure appeared from the shadows beside Rarx's shop. He was wrapped in a long cloak with a hood. For a moment, Dickens thought of the monk by the Palazzo Mariano. Or Count Dellombra walking the night? Just a legend. But he hesitated and they watched. The muffled figure looked this way and that. He was waiting for someone.

'I'll go across,' whispered Dickens.

Scrap stayed in the shadows.

Dickens stepped out of the shadows and called quietly, 'Magpie?'

'Mr Dickens.' Magpie held out his hand. Dickens grasped it. Magpie's handshake was firm, the clasp of a friend.

'What is this all about?'

'I must take you to see someone — someone who very much wants to see you.'

'There is someone with me — a boy only.'

'You didn't trust me?'

'Jemima Curd has been murdered — I expect you know that. And Violet Pout, the governess at Sir Neptune Fane's house —' he looked hard at Magpie — 'you know that, too.' I know him now, thought Dickens. I have seen that face since our first meeting, or one very like it in the mouth and eyes. A handsome face.

'I do.'

'You are taking me to Rolando Sabatini — you are the man about whom Pryor, the footman, told me.'

'I am. Rolando did not kill them, Mr Dickens. You will believe me when you see him. He is in hiding — at the theatre in Drury Lane. Will you come — and your boy?'

Dickens whistled and Scrap came across the street to be introduced to the cove Magpie. Scrap looked at him closely and took the proffered hand.

'Where we goin'?' he asked Dickens.

'To the theatre in Drury Lane.'

Scrap nodded, satisfied. A stone's throw from Bow Street.

Magpie led them through a black tangle of alleys which took them across Clements Lane into Clare Market where the smell of charcoal from the braziers and the smell of offal and meat from the slaughterhouses still lingered. There were a few urchins scrabbling about under the stalls, grubbing for food, and a few loungers in doorways. A young man in a black coat and carrying a black bag passed them, looking about him confusedly. There was a story about a young man, supposedly the ghostly presence of a poor fellow from the country who had lost his way to the Strand and was doomed to circle these lanes and alleys for eternity. Perhaps he was that young man — or a doctor going to an emergency case.

From Stanhope Street they came into White Horse Yard and crossed Drury Lane into where a little alley led to a back door. Dickens knew it well. He had been at this very door with William Macready, his great friend who had acted Henry VIII just a couple of years ago. Magpie had a key — a skeleton, no doubt. Handy thing to have.

The familiar smell that always set his heart aflame. The smell of sawdust, solvent, greasepaint, of smoke and of gaslights. The smell of a world set apart — a world in which you could become someone else — as Magpie had.

They went down some stairs to where Dickens knew there were cellars. Magpie pushed open a door and they were in a property room lit by Magpie's dark lantern — a resourceful fellow, he — Dickens felt at home amongst the robes and cloaks, even the masks gazing with their blind eyes. They threaded their way past the weaponry, the pikes and halberds, a dagger — Macbeth's, no doubt. Surely those were the gouts of blood. The armour clinked, a helmet with its visor up, out of which he expected to see the ghostly face of Hamlet's father. There was a wreath of flowers, dried and crumbling — Ophelia's, perhaps. Poor drowned girl. Magpie pushed aside a long black gown which reminded him of Macready as Hamlet, and there was the arras behind which Polonius had hidden and through which he had been fatally stabbed. Dickens looked back at Scrap who was gazing about him in wonder.

There was a little low door behind this arras. Magpie knocked and whispered his name. 'Only Jack.' So, it was he, as he had thought. Not J. N. — the initials on the green wax, the green his mother used — J. M. Jack Marchant.

They bent to go through into a little room full of old bits of scenery and broken gas footlights. It smelt of dust and age, and there, sitting miserably on a basket, was the man for whom they had been seeking: Rolando Sabatini.

'Mr Dickens — I am so glad you came. Jack persuaded me that you would listen and help.' Rolando Sabatini looked at him with red-rimmed eyes. He looked dusty and ill-kempt, and he looked like a boy who needed comfort. Not yet, though.

They all perched on various baskets — the room was far too low to stand in with any comfort. Jack Marchant fetched a collection of tin and wooden goblets and poured some wine.

'This is about Miss Pout?'

'Yes, Jack read that she was dead — murdered. He brought me here. I thought — I was terrified that —'

'You would be suspect.'

'Yes, I left with her…'

'Why — why did you desert Miss Fane?'

'How do you know about Mariana?'

'I spoke to your aunt, Mrs Marchant.' He did not look at Magpie — that enquiry would do for later. 'I had been asked to enquire after Miss Pout by her mother. Mrs Marchant told me that you were in love with Miss Fane and wanted to marry her. She told you to leave the household and if you felt the same after six months you could ask Sir Neptune, but then you disappeared with Miss Pout. Why?'

'Violet said that Lady Fane knew.'

'Knew what?' asked Dickens sharply.

'About Mariana and me. Violet said we must leave, or we would be sacked.'

'Why Miss Pout?'

'Because she had known about us and had not reported it to Lady Fane. She blamed me — it was my fault — I should not have — we met in secret. Miss Pout felt sorry for us. I felt I owed her something. And she was so upset — it wasn't her fault. Aunt Dolly warned me —'

'You told St George Pierce that Mariana was having her portrait painted. Tell me about that.'

'Miss Pout told me that a friend of hers wanted to paint Mariana. He had seen her at the zoo one day. It was to be a birthday surprise for Lady Fane. That's why it was a secret.'

'How many sittings did she have?'

'I don't know. It could not be many. Sir Neptune did not approve of too many outings, but a few months ago, Violet and Mariana went out together on a number of occasions. Mariana went with Violet to the dentist — Violet was afraid to go alone and Lady Fane relented. She is very kind. I don't suppose she told Sir Neptune. There were some trips to the shops when Sir Neptune was away.'

'You didn't see any portrait?'

'No, Violet told me that Mariana did not like to deceive her mother and she was afraid Sir Neptune would not like it. And one time, Mariana told me she had fainted. She seemed frightened and then…'

'What?'

'She never seemed well after that. She was very quiet. I wondered if she still cared for me.'

'And did she?'

'She said so. I begged her to allow me to speak to Sir Neptune, but she was too afraid.'

'And it was how long after the fainting that you left?'

'It was in September that Mariana seemed not herself. I left in November — nearly three months, I think — when I saw Mr Pryor he said that Mariana had been sent to the country. They must have known about us and it is Mariana who has been punished. My fault — my cowardice. I betrayed her.' He wept then. Magpie sat next to him and gave him his handkerchief.

He is innocent, thought Dickens. *He knows nothing of Mariana's condition.* He would have to tell him.

'I am afraid it is worse than that. Miss Fane is in an asylum at Hammersmith.'

'She is ill?'

'She is with child.'

Rolando and Magpie stared at him. Their astonishment and horror was genuine. Rolando put his hands over his face, which had turned so white that Dickens thought he would faint. Magpie made him drink some more of the wine.

'You have to tell us everything, Rolando. Tell the truth if you know anything of this.'

Rolando looked up. He wiped his eyes. 'No, no — it is impossible. I would not have — could not have. She so innocent, so pure. I wanted to marry her. I loved her.'

'I believe you did, and I believe that you did not seduce her.' Dickens felt certain.

'Then who — she would not have betrayed me — there was no other —'

Magpie understood. 'This artist — it was after she fainted that Mariana became ill. And —' he looked at Dickens, his thin face hardening — 'Violet Pout knew. That is what she was afraid of — it was her friend. Who is he?'

'I do not know — the police are trying to find him. It is possible that he killed Violet Pout and Jemima Curd — you knew about her.'

'I read of it. I remembered the name and I remembered you, Mr Dickens, which was why I sent you the message. I was afraid for Rolando.'

'Who is your cousin.'

'You know who I am.' Magpie's face looked haggard in the dim light — that impudent, carefree young man was gone.

'I do, Mr Marchant. Your mother suggested that Rolando might be with you. Did you know Jemima's name when I first mentioned her?'

'No, I did not know Miss Pout's, either. I know nothing of Sir Neptune Fane's household. It is not a house to which I was ever invited. I have not seen my mother for over two years — we have our differences. But this man who may be a murderer?'

'I hoped that Rolando might be able to give me some information.'

Magpie turned to Rolando who sat as one stunned. 'Rolando, try to remember something, anything that Miss Pout might have said.'

'St John's Wood — she said that's where she was going when we parted.'

'That may be helpful,' Dickens said. 'Your aunt told me that you and Mariana met her at the zoo last summer and that a stranger spoke to her and Violet Pout. Do you remember?'

'I remember meeting Aunt Dolly, but I don't remember a stranger.'

'You didn't see a man talking to Miss Pout.'

'I am afraid not. Was this man the artist? Did my — my aunt remember him?'

'Only vaguely. Now, Mr Sabatini and you, Mr Marchant, must come to Bow Street tomorrow morning to see Superintendent Jones. You need not fear, Mr Sabatini, he will listen and he will think as I do, but he must be told if you are not to be suspect in this. Do I have your word?'

'We will come, Mr Dickens, you have my word.' There was a trace of the smile that had first attracted Dickens to the insouciant thief.

'Then take him away from here, take him to your mother's house. She is worried about him —' Dickens saw the refusal in his face — 'or take him to your room. Perhaps Miss Jianna can take care of him.'

'Jianna is not with me anymore.'

'Wherever you think fit — he needs to rest.'

Magpie took Dickens and Scrap to the stage door. As they were about to go out, Magpie said, 'But Violet Pout and Jemima Curd were found in Clerkenwell. Can it be the same man?'

'We don't know that, either. We do know that Violet Pout was living in a house in Amwell Street with an artist. There are two other cases of suspicious drownings there — one a girl thought to have been an actress or dancer at Sadler's Wells. It made me think of an artist who —'

Magpie looked stricken. 'Oh, God, Mr Dickens, you are thinking of an artist who paints scenery.'

'I am — why, what is it you are thinking?'

'There was a man — an Italian — here some weeks ago — an artist. Jianna did sewing for the costumes. He talked to her. She said she had known him before when she was an artist's model. He wanted to paint her — he admired her hair. Oh, God — Mariana Fane's hair, it is the same colour as Jianna's. Is that why —'

'It may be significant, but tell me about them.'

'I sensed that she liked him — we were not bound to each other. She came to live with me because she had nowhere else. He disappeared — it happens. People come and go all the time — and then Jianna was gone.'

'He wanted to paint her?' Dickens wanted to be sure.

'She said so — she liked the idea of being an artist's model again. She believed he would pay her well. I didn't think —'

'Why should you? But I need to know about him.'

'Jianna — could be in danger. I must find him — I must — Oh, God, poor Jianna.'

Looking at Magpie's agonised face, and fully understanding his need to act immediately, Dickens, for whom delay was agony, found himself cool as ice. His counsel must be restraint. 'You cannot do it alone. What you can do is come to Bow Street tomorrow. Superintendent Jones has policemen searching Clerkenwell and St John's Wood. He has information about other girls —'

'But I must —'

'What was his name?'

'Antonio Polidori.'

'Think hard about the man, every detail, and tell Superintendent Jones all you know. Then come back here. Talk to everyone who knew this man. Search every corner of the scenery store. See if you can find any trace of him.'

'I can 'elp yer,' Scrap piped up.

Magpie looked at Scrap.

'It is too late to do anything now, except to get Rolando from here — and do what you can for him. Come to Bow Street at nine in the morning. Then my friend, Scrap, will come and help you search. He'll not miss anything.'

Magpie still looked doubtful, but he agreed.

Dickens took his hand. 'Use your wits, Magpie — they're more use than tearing about the streets with no idea where he is.'

'I will. I am much obliged that you came. Thank you.'

'Home, then,' said Dickens as he and Scrap walked along Bow Street to Great Earl Street. 'I'll walk you back to the shop. Got the key?'

'I'll slip in. Mollie'll never know I was out. What've we ter say ter Mr Jones termorrer?'

'Everything — before Magpie and Mr Sabatini arrive. He might not be too pleased with us, but we'd best tell the truth — make sure he knows you saved me from the garrotter.'

'I wouldn't lie ter Mr Jones, Mr D. Even if 'e ain't too pleased. An' yer've got some more evidence. Might make up fer it — a bit —' he grinned — ''E knows I got sense in the streets — I bin out an' about long enough.'

'He might not be too sure about me, but I felt I could trust Magpie when I first met him.'

''Ow d'yer meet 'im?'

'He had just robbed the pawnbroker's — Rarx — he shot at us.'

Scrap laughed. 'Goin' ter tell Mr Jones that?'

'Ah, I'll have to see whether it's necessary.'

They walked on to Seven Dials. *Another necessary betrayal*, Dickens thought, but it might not be necessary. There would be enough to do when Jianna's story was told.

'Magpie's girl,' said Scrap, reading his suddenly anxious face, 'd'yer think…'

'I don't know, Scrap. Let's hope Magpie remembers something about him so that we can find him. Now, here we are at the shop. Get you in — I'll see you tomorrow — at Norfolk Street before Mr Jones goes to Bow Street.'

Dickens went up to Oxford Street and crossed into the quiet of Newman Street. Somewhere a clock struck two, followed by others, the strokes echoing in the stillness. Then the silence again and the loneliness profounder. The dead time of the night. Yet he sensed that the city was not asleep as Wordsworth had it. In the tumble of barely lit courts and alleys behind the respectable streets, there were the houseless and the sleepless, shapeless drifting spectres on their endless walks through the night. The dead and the undead — the shadows of shadows.

And somewhere, not far away, perhaps a woman asleep, undisturbed by any dream of what was to come, her red-gold hair spread upon a pillow, and beside her a man with a jewelled chain watching her by the light of a corpse candle.

He watches the girl on the couch. She does not stir. Her eyes are closed and her beautiful hair is loose upon her shoulders and the green velvet gown is unfastened. Her white breast gleams. The jewelled chain is clasped in her hands which lie still as fallen birds on her breast.

The jewels on the chain catch the light of the branched candles on the small table by her head. He moves it so that a shadow falls and her neck is hidden from his view. The jewels wink at him. Once, he preferred rubies. That was a long time ago — it doesn't matter now. He has painted all kinds of jewels: pearls for tears; moonstones to wear by moonlight; sapphires for midnight, golden flecked beads from Venice. Ah, once — the jewels at her breast are mere glass, but the candlelight lends enchantment even to these on their brass chain which looks like gold. Rubies for blood. For death.

She is perfect now. He looks at his work on the easel. It is nothing to him, though he knows that the green robe is painted so finely that you might touch its velvet smoothness; the jewels are alive with light, and the hair is the hair of a living woman. But there is no face.

He had found her at last. She for whom he had sought so long had been sitting in her green velvet dress, quietly at her sewing, her hair copper gold in the gas light. Gaslight which drew sickly shadows on most faces, draining them of life. She might have been sitting in sunshine. She sat in front of a bit of discarded scenery — a painted scene of Italy with an arched window and cypress trees beyond, then hills. Ferrara, he had thought, and such an anguish possessed him that he almost cried out.

She came with him. She trusted him — as she should, she who had known his heart. But he could not catch her on his canvas. Her face was warm and living as he looked at her, the faint rose blush on her cheeks, the red of her lips, the wistful look in her eyes, all these he knew of old.

She had been disappointed. 'My face?'

'Soon,' he had told her, 'but I must study you, I must look at you so that I may read your heart. Then I shall know you and your face will be my most perfect work.'

She had been patient. She had sat so still, her eyes gazing beyond him to some far-off place. There was always a remoteness about her. Sometimes he watched her at her sewing and she would look up, sensing his gaze. She would smile and he would go back to his easel. She never said much. He liked that quiet about her.

He sits and watches her. Still she does not stir. Caterina, his lost love found. They will not be parted again.

She is the painting. The most beautiful thing he has ever created.

38: Cold Water

What are they up to? Sam Jones asked himself as he came out of his house the next morning, but making a business of locking his door, he ignored the two on the opposite side of the road and went away swiftly.

He heard the hurrying footsteps and paused. 'Ambush, is it?' he said as Dickens and Scrap appeared on either side of him.

'Yer'd seen us,' Scrap said, indignantly, 'yer woz pretendin'.'

'Cunning's what they pay me for. It's a bit early, isn't it?'

Scrap looked very pleased with himself. 'Somethin' ter tell yer — evidence an' witnesses.'

Dickens thought it was time he said something. 'I had a message from Mrs Marchant's son.'

'About Mr Sabatini?'

'Yes, he took us to him at the Drury Lane Theatre — they are both coming to see you at nine o'clock. But there's more —'

They were crossing Oxford Street. Jones stopped at an early morning coffee stall. 'You'd better tell me over a cup of coffee — I don't suppose you had time. Some bread and dripping, Scrap?' he asked, handing over some money.

While Scrap placed the order, Jones spoke to Dickens. 'Something serious?'

'Yes. Mr Marchant was living with a young Italian woman, Jianna — I don't know her other name — but she left him. She'd met an artist at the theatre where she sewed costumes. He was painting scenery —'

'You thought of that when Sadler's Wells came up. Mr Marchant doesn't know where she is?'

'Exactly. This artist said he wanted to paint her portrait.'

'Name?'

'Antonio Polidori — Antonio, Sam — I instructed Mr Marchant to take Sabatini home and to think of everything he could about the artist.'

Scrap came back with the coffee and his bread and dripping. Before he tucked in, he asked, 'Told Mr Jones about Magpie?'

'Magpie?' Jones sounded startled.

'Mr Marchant leads something of an unconventional life — an actor at the theatre, tumbler, acrobat — goes by that name.'

'Ah, and this lady, Jianna, she is Italian?'

'Yes, and she has red-gold hair.'

'You met her? When?'

'Very briefly, right at the beginning when I was looking for Jemima Curd. I did not see her hair then — it was dark and I didn't connect her with any artist — she was with Mr Marchant, but I didn't know that Magpie was Jack Marchant — I'd never heard of Jack Marchant then.'

'When did she go off with this Antonio Polidori?'

'That's the puzzling part — nearly three weeks ago, just after I met him.'

'She couldn't have been at Amwell Street.'

'That's what I thought. Jack Marchant was wild to search for her last night, but I told him that he should go to Drury Lane this morning after he has seen you and ask everyone he knows if they remember him. I know James Anderson, the manager — I thought Scrap and I could go with him.'

'I'd better come as well, and Rogers — there must be hundreds of people who work at the theatre in one role or another.'

'Jianna worked in the seamstresses' room and he must have worked in the painting shop. That would narrow it down. The stage manager would have taken him on or the chief scene painter.'

'Good — we'll go across to the theatre after Mr Marchant has given us some names.'

'And I told Rolando Sabatini about Miss Fane. I don't believe he seduced her — he was devastated. He did remember that Violet Pout mentioned that she was going to St John's Wood when she left.'

'Did he now? Let's hope that Inspector Maxwell finds this Lilian. We'll be off then.'

Jack Marchant was brought into in Jones's office by Rogers at exactly nine o'clock. Jack Marchant was respectably dressed — without his cloak and in his black frock coat, he looked like any other young man, though his face showed his anxiety. Dickens wondered if there was a touch of defiance in the black and white waistcoat. He would not shed his Magpie identity entirely.

'Mr Sabatini is not with you?' asked Jones after the introductions were made.

'No, Mr Jones, he is in a dreadful state. I fear for him so — I — took him in a cab first thing to — my mother's. Mr Dickens knows her — she will look after him. If you need to question him — he will be there. You have my word.'

'Very well. Now Mr Dickens has told me about Miss Jianna. You know her full name?'

'Jianna Rizzo.'

'You must tell me everything you can remember about this artist whom you believe she is with.'

'I do believe it — she has nowhere else to go. I have thought about him — he is tall, about my height, slender, a short beard at his chin, very dark hair. I saw him with Jianna — he seemed fascinated, but then she is beautiful. I wasn't surprised when — she left me — we were not bound —' he looked at Jones half defiantly like a boy who feared a schoolmaster, or a disapproving father. Dickens thought how young he was for all his careless adventuring — 'but I did — do care — that she may be —'

'But you did speak to him?'

'No, I never did. I passed them in a passage way a few times.'

'How did you know he was Italian if you did not speak to him?'

'The name — I just assumed — he looked Italian. Jianna is Italian and she'd known him before when she was an artist's model. She seemed to like him. He hardly seemed to see me at all — his eyes were only for Jianna. I hoped that she — his being Italian, I thought they might be suited — I should have — what must you think of me? Just to let her go —'

Jones gave him a hard look. 'This is not a time to think of yourself, Mr Marchant. You can help me by coming to Drury Lane with Mr Dickens and me. Ask everyone you know about Antonio Polidori. Mr Dickens and I will talk to the manager. You know that Miss Pout and Miss Curd were both connected to an artist and both are dead, and Miss Fane is in an asylum. I need to find him urgently. Someone might know where he lives.'

'Mr Dickens said that there might be other girls.'

'I have other leads to follow, but I do not wish to waste time in explanation. I will tell you that my enquiries centre on St John's Wood, and I have Inspector Shackell in Clerkenwell, and I have one of my men watching at Rarx, the pawnbroker's shop — some stolen jewels connected to this case were found there. Now, I suggest that we go over to the theatre.'

Jones's tone was firm. Dickens saw Jack Marchant blink at Rarx's name, but he said nothing. Jack Marchant was a young man used to his own way and doing as he pleased — he had a certain arrogance where the police were concerned. Clearly, he knew better now. Sam Jones could be very formidable.

Constable Feak came in as Rogers took Jack Marchant out. 'Message from Inspector Maxwell, sir, says he's found a Lilian Judd.'

'Send Sergeant Rogers back in and wait with Mr Marchant.'

'Alf, I've to go to Marylebone. You go with Mr Dickens and Scrap to the theatre and keep that young man under your eye. Charles, you talk to the manager and whoever else is in charge. Scrap, use your eyes and ears.'

'You don't think Jack Marchant…'

'A young man whose been missing from home for several years, who seems to have more than one identity, and who is connected to Miss Fane and knew about Jemima Curd and Violet Pout — it does make me think.'

Dickens felt as if he had been struck in the face with ice cold water. Not Jack Marchant, not Dolly Marchant's son.

39: Vanishing Act

James Anderson, manager of the Drury Lane theatre and fine actor in his own right, was a man with much on his mind. He looked at Charles Dickens as a man might look at a famous man suddenly gone mad, one eye expressing a kind of humouring deference — the other on the door.

'Polidori,' he repeated nervously, 'the vampire man?' Doctor John Polidori had been dead for nearly thirty years. In any case what would that author of *The Vampyr* be doing at Drury Lane? There were tales of ghosts, of course, but nothing about vampires.

'No, no, Mr Anderson, though I must say I hadn't thought of Doctor Polidori. The man I am seeking is an Italian, a Mr Antonio Polidori who, I was told, worked here some weeks ago, painting scenery.'

'I'm sure I would have remembered the name. Vampires were quite the thing a few years ago — not that we go in for them.'

'No, indeed. Shakespeare, I see, for your opening season.'

'*The Winter's Tale*, and of course it's the pantomime season: Harlequin and Humpty Dumpty to follow Leontes and Hermione. You should go along to the painting shop — you know Mr Cuthbert.'

'I do — he did the scenes for Mr Macready's *Hamlet*.'

'We've a lot on for the new season. They'll have taken on a number of assistants — some don't stay, of course, but he'd remember the name. You'll have to excuse me, Mr Dickens, I've the whole company on stage in a while — if they all turn up.'

Dickens went down some stairs which led to the stage behind and then up again to the huge painting shop where the enormous painting frames were fixed to the walls. On these, the scenery was mounted for painting. They could be raised or lowered through slots in the floor so that the artist could reach all parts of the work. The smell was of size, paint, turpentine, glue and sawn wood.

He stepped gingerly across the floor strewn with glue pots, brushes and scale drawings to find himself gazing at London Bridge. Moonlight cast a mysterious glow on the river where the water, touched by light, seemed to ripple. In the background the dark shape of the Tower loomed menacingly. He might have been standing in that very darkness, feeling the chill of the east wind.

Mr Cuthbert, who was gazing, too, with some satisfaction, turned round. 'Mr Dickens. What brings you here? Not that you are unwelcome. Always a pleasure.' Mr Cuthbert put his brush and mahl stick in his pocket and wiped his hands on his apron.

Dickens shook his hand. 'That's quite marvellous. I feel the cold just looking.'

'Much obliged, sir. Euston Station over yonder —' Dickens saw the familiar Doric Archway which led into the station and the great hall — 'and the Crystal Palace. Mr Anderson wants a spectacle. They've a Boulogne steamer at The Prince's Theatre — seems to sail across the stage. The Haymarket have the Crystal Palace as well —'

'Not as fine as that, I'll wager,' Dickens said, looking at the representation of the shining plate glass, an uncanny replica of that which he had seen in Hyde Park.

'We'll see what the critics say. We've a fairy bower, too. Lot of new work this season and a lot of assistants I've had to take on. Some worse than useless.'

'That's what I came about. Did you take on a Mr Polidori a few weeks back?'

Cuthbert looked surprised. 'I don't think so — I'd have remembered the name.'

'That's what Mr Anderson said. He is an Italian — tall, thin fellow, short beard and dark eyes. Not much to go on, I know.'

'Sorry, Mr Dickens, I don't remember him. Artist, is he?'

'Yes.'

'Well, as you know, we might take on a good painter as an accessory principal — he'd be paid on a piece-work basis. I'd remember that. We have colour grinders, apprentices, labourers, but no one of that name. What about the property shop? He might have been taken on in there — all sorts of things to be painted. Mr Perkins will know.'

Dickens left him at London Bridge and made his way by Euston Station, through the fairy bower, up another staircase to a long corridor which ran above the stage where were situated the property shops and carpenters' shops. Mr Perkins seemed to stand in an Aladdin's cave, surrounded by an extraordinary variety of articles: a cow, full size, a calf, a slightly wonky church steeple, a balloon and its basket, Britannia's trident, an assortment of chimney sweep's brushes, a chimney to go with them, and a comically grotesque, monstrous head to which he was attaching an equally monstrous nose.

Dickens stood still while this delicate operation was performed. How the lights, the music, the scenes and the actors would transform all this by the magic of the theatre into something rich and strange — *art to enchant*, he thought.

But Mr Perkins had no magic to conjure up Antonio Polidori. He had no recollection of the name or the man. Dickens asked about Jianna Rizzo and was directed to the mantua makers' along the corridor — Miss Mantalini might know the lady. If not, then he should go to the seamstresses' shop.

The mantua makers knew Jianna in passing, but knew of no Mr Polidori. The seamstresses were more forthcoming. Jianna had left a few weeks ago. She lived with a man they knew as Magpie — they all knew him. He'd left before her. The last play had finished — then there were Mr Julian's concerts. They thought she might have gone with him to another theatre, Astley's Circus, perhaps. Magpie was an acrobat as well as an actor — magician, too.

'Vanished in a puff o' smoke, p'raps,' put in a pert, pretty girl who winked at Dickens. Black eyes like two shining beads and unruly curls lent her an appealing prettiness.

'You've never heard the name "Polidori"?'

'Vampire, ain't 'e?' The pert girl was enjoying herself.

'That's enough from you,' the older woman was sharp. The pert girl gave Dickens another wink.

'No, he was a scenery painter, I'm told.'

'Tried Mr Cuthbert?' the older woman asked.

'I have, and Mr Perkins.'

'Well, I'm sorry we can't help — so many folk come and go, sir. If he'd been an actor we might have known. We might have fitted him. You're sure, Maisie Bolton? I've seen you hanging about the painting shop.'

Pert Maisie was sure. She had seen Jianna with Mr Magpie, but not with any other man. Her black bead eyes were suddenly serious. 'Beautiful, she is, sir, Jianna, but she never said much to any of us. Quiet, she was — mysterious.'

Dickens left them. He felt uneasy, remembering Jones's words about Jack Marchant. It was odd that no one seemed to know anything about this artist. He ought to find Jack and Rogers — perhaps one of Jack's fellow performers had seen Polidori. And where was Scrap?

Scrap was having the time of his life, his ears alert and his eyes on stalks, especially now. He was at the side of the stage. Quite how he had arrived there, he wasn't sure. The place was vast. Dawdling along, stopping to peer into rooms and boxes and alcoves, he had soon lost Sergeant Rogers and Mr Marchant. But Mr Dickens's name had opened all sorts of real and metaphorical doors.

'Catching up with Mr Charles Dickens,' he had said to anyone who asked, 'a matter of business.' He surprised himself with the voice he had used — the voice of a toff. A boy, younger than himself, racing along a corridor, carrying a wig, had called him "Sir". It was like that sayin' in Ali Baba — Mrs Jones had read that to them — "Open sesame", they said and the cave had opened to reveal the treasure of the forty thieves.

But now, he was just a boy gazing in awe at another boy on the stage, a boy performing wonders, balancing on a globe which rolled beneath him — the whole world at his feet. And what was more remarkable was the fact that the boy held aloft two sticks with plates spinning on them — plates! The globe stopped rolling, the boy jumped lightly off, dropped the sticks, and caught a plate neatly in each hand. Scrap applauded and the boy turned to look at him and bowed.

''Ow d'yer do that?' Scrap said as the boy came towards him. In his wonder he forgot to be a toff.

'Practice. Ain't seen you before.'

'About some business fer Mr Charles Dickens — lookin' fer someone.'

'Who?'

'Antonio Polidori — scene painter, or was, until a few weeks ago.'

'Italian cove?'

'Yes, know 'im?' Scrap's heart leapt.

'No — just the name sounds Italian. Hundreds of people work here, though, and lots of painters, carpenters, property men.'

'He is a painter — an artist.'

The boy looked at Scrap with a hint of condescension in his eyes. 'Oh, well, I might not know him. I'm an actor — performer, as you saw — Frederick Clarke's the name. I wouldn't necessarily know a scene painter — unless he was one of the principals like Mr Cuthbert or Mr Grieve. What you want this Polidori for?'

Scrap didn't give his name, feeling again the lack of a second one in the presence of this superior being. 'We, that is me and Mr Dickens —' asserting his own impressive credentials — 'think he's gone away with a lady — friend of Mr Dickens.'

Frederick Clarke's eyes gleamed, 'A lady, eh? Think they're in hiding? Lots of places to lay low here — tunnels, cellars — you can get down to a pit, right under, if you know your way about. Want to see? You ain't afraid of ghosts, I suppose.'

Scrap was torn. He did want to see, but — a murderer down there in the dark. He ought to get Mr Dickens, but then he thought that they couldn't have been hiding for weeks, unless there was a body down there. He looked at Frederick Clarke's waiting eyes — there was a challenge there. Ghosts — not likely. Scrap felt superior then. Mr Clarke knew nothin' about murderers.

'Might as well,' he said, not wanting to seem too eager. He wasn't a kid. He followed Frederick Clarke.

Dickens caught sight of Scrap with someone else going off the stage. Who was he with? His glimpse of the leading figure showed only that it was a man. He crossed and saw them descending a narrow staircase which he knew led to the cellars, various storerooms and tunnels, and to the room where Jack Marchant had hidden Rolando Sabatini. Had Scrap met someone who knew that they'd been down there?

He went down and saw them disappearing into the tunnel. It was dark down here — no wonder there was talk of ghosts. Legend had it that there had been a tunnel leading to the river in the old days. The theatre was an enormous place — he thought of the labyrinth of staircases, the boxes, the odd rooms for actors changing between scenes, the refreshment rooms, the water closets and the secret places down here. Anyone could come and go, pretend to be someone else, follow a girl in a green velvet dress. He remembered Jianna in Magpie's fusty lodgings in her dark velvet dress — a silent, unspeaking face. Like a girl in a painting, he had thought then.

He hurried into the tunnel and saw the shapes of Scrap and his companion ahead, in earnest conversation. The taller figure did not seem threatening. Nevertheless, he called out for Scrap and saw that the man with him was very young, not much more than a boy.

'What brings you down here?' he asked.

'Mr Clarke knows all the secret places — thought it woz worth a look.'

'I've seen you before, Mr Dickens. The name's Clarke, Frederick Clarke. I do the spinning globe.'

'Of course you do. I've seen you — most remarkable, Mr Clarke. Do you know the man they call Magpie?'

'Course, I do — went to Astley's I heard.'

'You've not seen him since?'

'No.'

'And Miss Jianna who did needlework?'

'His lady friend — went with him, I suppose.'

'He doesn't know Mr Polidori, either,' Scrap put in.

'Places down here a man could hide,' said Frederick Clarke. 'Thought I'd show your friend.'

They went further down the tunnel. Frederick Clarke opened various doors, but there was nothing to see but lumber, old props, costumes, bits of old gas lights and pipes — just the same sort of thing they'd seen in the room to which Jack Marchant had taken them. There was no one to be seen until they reached the end of the tunnel where a door led into a back yard. Here was the engine which worked the pumps providing the water from the underground reservoir constructed to deal with fire. Dickens thought of all the entrances and exits a man might use to slip in and out — just as Magpie had done. Polidori, or whoever he was, would not be found here.

Scrap and Dickens went back up to Mr Anderson's room outside of which they had arranged to meet Rogers and Jack Marchant.

'What?' asked Dickens as Rogers appeared, his usually cheerful face looking grim.

'Gave me the slip, your Mr Marchant. Crowd of people on the stage — some kind of meetin' with the manager was to take place and he was asking people he knew then he was gone and I've no idea where. Of course no one saw him. I tell you, Mr Dickens, I felt a fool standin' gapin' an' a lot o' folks laughin'. "Vanishin' act", some wag said. Course I looked in the wings and at the back o' the stage. But it's no use — he could have gone anywhere. Labyrinth this place.'

'No one knew of Mr Polidori, I take it.'

'No, an' that's what worried him. I could tell he was getting' more and more upset. Suppose he thinks Mr Jones won't believe him.'

'Did you?'

'Damned good actor, if he's lyin' — why go through all that pantomime of askin' if he made it all up? He didn't have to tell you about his lady friend bein' missin'.'

'No, I suppose not, and he was very distressed when I mentioned the possibility of a scenery painter as a murderer. I believed him — then. But no one we've spoken to has heard of Polidori.'

'What's Mr Jones goin' to say — that's what I'm distressed about.' Rogers looked very glum.

They went out into Little Russell Street to make their way back to Bow Street. *Vanished in a puff o' smoke*, thought Dickens. *So he had, Magpie. The bird had flown.*

40: A Woman in Black

'The young fool,' was what Mr Jones said, but he sympathised with Rogers's anger and humiliation. 'I know Alf — in a crowd like that, it would be impossible to find him. No doubt, they'd be on his side, too. He's a clever devil, that's certain. Charles, have you no idea where he lives?'

'No, only that it was somewhere near Drury Lane.'

'We'll not find him — he's an actor. All you can do, Alf, is to tell the beat constables to keep an eye out.' Rogers left them and Jones turned to Dickens. 'Well, does this Polidori exist, do you think, or has Marchant made him up?'

'Not a name you'd choose if you had any wit. Doctor John Polidori, Byron's doctor, wrote a story called *The Vampyr* back in 1818. Theatre folk know it — vampires were very popular a few years ago — dramatizations and so forth. Surely, he'd choose something —' Dickens remembered as he spoke, a long black shape hanging from a window and thinking of a vampire then. But then he remembered two laughing eyes — surely not — 'something more ordinary — even the name of someone who did work once at the theatre — to send us on a wild goose chase — if he's guilty, that is.'

'You don't believe it?'

'No, I don't think I do — he was genuinely upset about Jianna. Rogers said he must be a damned good actor to make it all up. And, wait, I can't imagine that he seduced Mariana Fane. He knows she is Sir Neptune's daughter, his own half-sister —'

'Byron did,' Jones said. Dickens looked startled. 'Elizabeth has told me about Byron — and she told me about Robert Browning.'

'Browning? How does he — oh, *Porphyria's Lover.* Strangling and madness.'

'It sounded mad to me, but the lover killed just the one woman. I suppose that made some sort of sense.'

Dickens shook his head, banishing the image of Ferrara and Parisina's cell that the name "Byron" called up. 'I don't think Marchant's mad — odd, perhaps, but who isn't? I do know that he hated Sir Neptune. That was the cause of the estrangement from his mother — when he found out that Sir Neptune is his father, but incest — it would be monstrous. He's had his revenge, anyway.'

'By leaving his mother?'

'No, according to Mrs Marchant, he stole Lady Fane's diamonds. She wears paste. Sir Neptune knows.'

'He told the police they'd been returned.'

'She persuaded him that she would get them back — perhaps Sir Neptune lied about the diamonds for her sake.'

'Not wanting a scandal more likely. A thief — not for his own gain —' Jones gave him a knowing look — 'Magpie, eh?'

'You are a cunning old cove. You know all about Magpie, don't you?'

'I'd heard the name. Stemp knew all about him. Rarx has complained about theft — ironic, ain't it? How did you meet him? You never said.'

'I rescued him just as he had relieved Rarx of a gold watch belonging to a friend — I didn't know that at the time. Rarx blew my hat off with his blunderbuss.'

Jones laughed. 'Serves you right — consorting with criminals. "Relieved", indeed. Robbery I'd call it, but being a thief does not make him a murderer. This friend, now — he must have pawned the gold watch so Rarx must know who he is. That's a lead. I'll send Stemp. I'll tell you something else now. Polidori is not the name Lilian Judd gave me. She told me what she knew about Susan Harvest. Lilian Judd was a kitchen maid at a house in William Street next door to one belonging to an artist where a Mr Antonio Ferrara was staying.'

'Ferrara!'

'My thought, too. The owner of the house is a James Everard, who has gone to America — the house belongs to someone else now, but Inspector Maxwell is trying to trace any relatives of Mr Everard who might know something of Antonio Ferrara.'

'What did Lilian Judd tell you?'

'That Susan lived there with the artist. That she was unhappy, that she'd felt sorry for her. They talked sometimes. Susan seemed lonely, but said she couldn't go home. Her father was a vicar — she couldn't tell her family that she was living with a man. Then they were gone. Lilian read about the drowned girl — she read about the lilac gown and the white bonnet and thought about Susan which is why she asked Watcher.'

'Why didn't she come forward?'

'Too frightened of her mistress — a tartar, she said, frightened she'd lose her place. She felt guilty so when she read about the Reverend Harvest asking for the exhumation, she wrote to him. The paper belonged to her mistress — not the artist. Lilian's married now to a butcher whom she told. His advice was to leave it alone, but he did mention it to a cousin, a constable of Maxwell's. He thought it too late to do anything — it was two or three years later. No way of telling who the dead girl was by then, but when he heard Maxwell was looking for a Lilian in connection with a girl drowned in 1846, he told Maxwell who went to find her.'

'What about the mysterious Isabella?'

'She didn't know the name, but a woman did call occasionally —'

Dickens looked at him eagerly. 'Description?'

'You'll hardly believe this.'

'Samivel, I can believe anything about this case.'

'A woman in black, always wearing a veil. Lilian never knew her name. What say you to that?'

'Bah, humbug — veiled forsooth. Ghost, was she?'

'Not much use is it?'

'None whatsoever — what could she tell about Antonio Ferrara?'

'The usual — never saw much of him. Just tall, dark and silent.'

'Jack Marchant is tall and dark, but not the silent type. Remember what the Armwell mews coalman said about the man he met — queer cove, looked right through you.'

'Mrs Fudge said the so-called Mr Tony was odd, too, and I've remembered something else —' Jones paused as if thinking something out. He closed his eyes, the better to keep Dickens waiting.

'What? What?'

Jones opened his eyes. 'Ah, I have it, Mrs Fudge's laundress, a Mrs — erm — yes, Gambol — she'd received a visit from someone asking a lot o' question — rum cove, she said — very rum.'

'Very droll, Samivel, rum cove, forsooth — she was a hideous creature. I thought she was going to strike me with a very large piece of soap like a bit of mantelpiece.'

'But none of the descriptions sound like Jack Marchant to you?'

Dickens fell silent for a few moments. 'No, and William Street is not far from his mother's house in Grove Road.

Surely he wouldn't masquerade as someone else on her door step, so to speak. She said he'd left home several years ago — no, she didn't — she said she had not seen him for several years, but still, we're talking about a man living in William Street way back in 1846 — Jack Marchant would have moved well away, surely.'

'How old is Jack Marchant?'

'I don't know — older than Rolando Sabatini, who is twenty-one or two — twenty-five, perhaps. Mrs Marchant said that her relationship with Sir Neptune was a boy and girl romance. Perhaps she had a child then. I assumed her son was born after her marriage and Sir Neptune's, but perhaps not. Say she was eighteen. She would be about forty-three now and Sir Neptune — I don't know —'

'I'll have a look in the baronetage.' Jones went to a shelf where he kept all sorts of handy volumes: the *Royal Blue Book*, the *Post Office Directories*, mapbooks of London, *Taylor's Medical Jurisprudence* — all the things that might be useful to a policeman in search of information.

'Faith, Marmaduke; Fakenham, Earl of; Falmouth, Marquis of; Fane, Sir Neptune, born 1807 — forty-three.'

'Jack Marchant could have been in Italy in 1843. He'd have been eighteen then. Susan Harvest was eighteen… He'd have been twenty when Flora Lambert died. No, I can't believe it. Oh, and Mrs Marchant, what a tragedy for her if…'

'Let's not rush at it. I need to find out about him — where he was in those years. That will clear it all up. I shall have to go to his mother — supposing she knows where he was.'

'And you can find out if he was in Italy — in Ferrara. Anyway, he's not —'

'What? You've gone quite pale.'

'I was going to say that he is not an artist — but on that note he sent me, he'd drawn the outline of a bird. A magpie. It was very clever.'

'Just a sketch?'

'Yes, but I've remembered something else. When I was at Mrs Marchant's I looked at some paintings in the hall. Just landscapes of Italy — not portraits. Rolando's father was a portrait artist. I am not saying they are Jack Marchant's, but —'

'I'll find out.'

'This is very dreadful, Sam. I have betrayed her now.'

'But he would have come to you because of Rolando, anyway. Pryor told Rolando about you. Nothing to do with his mother. Now Jack Marchant is missing and I have no choice but to question her and Rolando. I will be very careful — I will make no accusation, you can be sure of that.'

'I know you will — it's surely in Jack's favour that he took me to Rolando, and, remember, Jack told me about Jianna. Why should he tell me if he has killed her?'

'That's reasonable... I'll bet he's gone chasing around in the hope of finding her. He'll think he can do better than the police can — he's lived so long outside the law. And he might have more chance of finding her in that warren of alleys. He might have remembered something about her, someone she knew — she can't have materialised out of thin air to go and live with him.'

'Artist's model — I thought when I met her that she was like a girl in a painting. Jack Marchant said she worked as an artist's model before. He is a young fool — why didn't he stop to think?'

'That sort never do.'

'Give me that painting we found in the mews at Amwell Street — that reminds me. What about Violet Pout in St John's Wood? Not the same house, surely?'

'No, it was sold in 1847. Ferrara — or whoever he was, must have moved on. What do you want with the painting?'

'To take it to an artist I know — where I should have taken it after we found it.'

'Who?'

Dickens was at the door already. 'Mr Stanfield at The Greenhill.'

41: The Mourning Girl

'Hampstead, Hob, and hasty.'

Hob, the cabman in his thick-caped coat was lounging against his cab in deep conversation with the waterman while Bob, his horse, was munching stolidly away in his nose-bag. A pail of water stood ready. Job Grime, the waterman, greeted Dickens with a wave. A little, wiry man — he might be any age from thirty to sixty — wearing, as was his custom, an assortment of torn coats cleverly contrived to make up a whole. The bottom layer made the main body, other layers providing successively: two unmatched sleeves, a green cape, a worn velvet collar, the last topped by two mufflers, skilfully arranged so that the top one covered the holes beneath. A leather cap and a pair of fairly decent wellington boots completed this picture of sartorial ingenuity.

'New boots, Job?' asked Dickens, remembering Job's ancient leather ones which he swore fitted his old feet like a pair of old gloves.

'Tapper Jack's gone,' Job said, removing his hat. Tapper was another of the watermen whom Dickens knew from a cab stand at the top of Bow Street.

Dickens removed his top hat. 'Legacy?'

'That's it, sir, an' the two pails. Jack's water's turned off fer good. The widder brought 'em. Nice little body. Needn't 'ave…' Job Grime stared into a distance. He was a single gentleman, Dickens knew.

Hob touched his hat — he never took it off as far as Dickens knew. He wondered if Hob's head might come off with it.

'Get a move on,' Hob said to Bob, 'let's not keep Mr Dickens waiting.'

The sagacious Bob merely scraped his hoof on the road and continued his dinner. Dickens waited for the magic moment when Bob, having munched his way to the bottom of the bag, would, with a flick of his nose, invert the bag and catch the scattered oats as they came down. He was prepared to wait. Hob was a driver who always contrived, by some supernatural means, to get out of any Gordian knot of the drays, carts, wagons, cabs, coaches and omnibuses which clogged the streets — could turn his cab on a tanner was his boast. He could have made a fortune in the circus. Bob, too — the nose-bag juggler. They'd get to Hampstead quick enough.

''Ampstead, yer sed?' Bob was ready and Hob swung himself up into his seat. Job opened the door for Dickens who passed him a florin.

'Have a drink on me for Tapper.'

'Bless yer, sir, I will.'

'And Mrs Tapper, perhaps?'

Job grinned. *Mind*, thought Dickens, Tapper had not possessed any teeth. Perhaps Mrs Tapper would quite like the few that Job had, despite their likeness to Bob's similarly brown ones.

'The Green Hill, Mr Stansfield's house, Hob,' Dickens instructed as he got in.

Clarkson Stanfield, Dickens's old friend, was a marine painter, but he had been once chief scene painter at Drury Lane. Admittedly, it was way back in 1834, but he had designed and painted the scenery for Macready's Drury Lane *Macbeth* a few years ago. More than that he was a member of the Royal Academy and had been President of the British Institute of

Art. He knew people. He might know something — anything, thought Dickens, like the name Ferrara for example, or Polidori. Not that he believed in that name. Suppose all the names were false.

Suppose, suppose, suppose, the wheels seemed to say, unhelpfully, as the cab rolled away up Tottenham Court Road, across the New Road and into Hampstead Road.

And as he was supposing about false names, he remembered something which turned him suddenly sick. Jack Marchant had told him that he knew nothing of Sir Neptune's household, but he had stolen the diamonds. How? From where? Had he been in Wisteria Lodge and lied about it? Perhaps it was a half-truth — Jack did not know the members of Sir Neptune's household, but he had got in — the acrobat that he was — and stolen the jewels. It did not mean he had seduced his half-sister, or that he was a murderer. Dickens could not believe that of him. But that was a detail that he would have to pass on to Sam. Where was the foolish young man? He was making things more complicated.

They passed Euston Station — Jack could be on a train, gone to the South, the South, East or West — come to that so could Ferrara. It was no use thinking that — concentrate on the practical thing like asking Stanny. The cab was moving faster now that they were further South, going past Granby Street where he had gone to school at Wellington House Academy, and then they were into High Street behind which lay Bayham Street where his life in London had begun. There had been fewer streets then and fields beyond them, and he and his sister, Fanny, had run outdoors to see a cab go by — a marvel in those days. And creditors came to demand money for unpaid bills — his father couldn't keep out of debt even then, but he was there, and he loved his children in his cheerful, improvident way.

Unlike Sir Neptune Fane, whose coldness to his first son had been the wound that had sent him about his vagabond days — but not about murder, he thought. Sir Neptune Fane who might use his daughter's madness and ruin to garner sympathy. He could more imagine Sir Neptune as the murderer of Violet Pout than Jack Marchant.

Bob was going at a smart trot now, back on Hampstead Road and up Haverstock Hill. The houses and buildings were thinner and they were soon enough bowling into Rosslyn Street where the road forked and led to the Green Hill. Dickens asked Hob to wait. Bob would appreciate the break. There was an inn in Pilgrim's Lane. Dickens would find him.

But Stanny wasn't there. So his son, George, told Dickens, but his mother was upstairs with the children — Stanny had twelve children in all, ten by his second wife, Rebecca, who was upstairs. But Dickens hadn't time for one child, never mind twelve, not even one wife, charming as Rebecca Stanfield was.

'I can't, George, I'm pressed for time, but you can do something for me and look at this.'

George Stanfield, at twenty-two, had already exhibited at the Royal Academy and had drawn the plates from his father's designs for the illustrations of Dickens's *Pictures from Italy*. He might know who had painted this.

'No face,' George said as he scrutinised the picture, 'how odd, and yet the rest is well painted. It is peculiar. It's the wrong way round — the portraitist sketches in the head and the features of the face first. Here there is just a blank —' George looked more closely — 'Not a pencil mark. You wouldn't finish the dress in all this detail and the background and then paint the face — there has to be softening so that the sitter emerges from the background. It has a Renaissance look. Copy, is it?'

'I think so. You don't know who might have painted it?'

'I'd say someone copying an Italian portrait. Rosetti might know. That hair, it has a look — that red-gold colour. Have you seen Rossetti's *Girlhood of Mary Virgin*? It is quite remarkable.'

'No, I haven't —' Dickens was thinking furiously. Obviously not Rossetti — he was far too young — George's age, but his father was professor of Italian at London University. Mariotti knew him. Oh, Lord, the time he had wasted — he should have — time, time — a thought occurred to him — 'Your Rossetti, does he use a model called Jianni Rizzo?'

George looked startled, 'No, I don't think so, but I know someone who did.'

'Who?'

'The sculptor, Cipriani Lloyd, Academician — he did that figure "Grief" in St John's Wood Church, and a mourning girl in St Marylebone Church — he used Jianna Rizzo.'

St Marylebone Church — opposite York Gate where his own house was. He passed it nearly every day. He had been in dozens of time. And there she had been — waiting for him to see her and recognise her: a mourning girl.

'Where can I find him?'

'Avenue Road — it's the first house you come to where the Finchley Road forks after the Swiss Cottage Tavern. Remote place, really, but a big garden and studio.'

Dickens bade a bemused George Stanfield a hasty farewell, promising to come back soon to see his father. He strode away to meet Hob. Pray genteel Bob wasn't taking afternoon tea. Dickens was in a hurry now.

Cipriani Lloyd told him about Jianna. Yes, she had modelled for him, four years ago, perhaps, but she had moved on. This part of the world was inconvenient for her — she'd used to come to his former house in Gloucester Place. No, he didn't know what had become of her. Beautiful girl, he said, quiet — remote somehow — ideal for the work he had been doing. Mourning figures, he'd done for St John's Church and the Marylebone Church. Had Dickens seen them? Wanted to know who she was? Something for *Household Words*? Given the Pre-Raphaelites a pasting, hadn't he, in June — sorry for that. Cipriani Lloyd liked them — Rossetti's *Girlhood of Mary Virgin* — now, that was worth seeing —

Dickens almost blushed. He had written a stinging denunciation of Millais's painting: *Christ in the House of His Parents* — but the last thing he wanted was a disquisition on the merits or otherwise of the so-called brotherhood, but Cipriani Lloyd was a talker — a portly, curly-headed, smiling, immediately likeable, but garrulous man of thirty or so.

'Colour, Mr Dickens, and precision of form — that's the new —'

'I don't doubt I may be wrong, Mr Lloyd, but I can assure you I do not want to write about Jianna Rizzo. I just need to find her.'

'Why, though?'

'It's a long story. I think she may have known a girl who is missing — the god-daughter of my wife's personal maid. I said I would try to trace her.'

'Then I am sorry, indeed, that I cannot help you. Artist, was she?' he asked, pointing to the picture which Dickens had set down on a table.

'Oh, no — this is — well, perhaps you will look at it for me. I don't know the artist.'

Cipriani Lloyd uncovered the picture and stared at it. 'Where did you come by this?' He sounded puzzled and angry.

'Do you know the artist?'

'I am certain I do — it is by a man called Anthony Ferrars.'

Dickens stared back. 'Not Ferrara?'

'No — Mr Dickens are you quite well? You've turned quite pale. Will you not sit down and take some wine?'

Dickens sat. 'A sudden faintness — I do beg your pardon.' He took a gulp of the wine and steadied himself, 'What can you tell me about Mr Ferrars?'

The smiling face frowned, 'I should like to know why, Mr Dickens, and how you came by that painting.'

'It is another long story — I will be frank with you. It involves more than one missing young woman. The police are involved, so I cannot tell you more, but I beg you to tell me about Mr Ferrars. The picture was found at an address in Clerkenwell where the young woman I was seeking was last seen — she was thought to be living with an artist who is connected to Jianna Rizzo.'

'And you think this artist is Anthony Ferrars?'

'Well, now that you have identified the picture.'

'He did meet Jianna — he met her here back in 1845. I'd just moved here and Jianna was sitting for a last commission — it was a little statue of Philomel — grace and charm, the critics said … sorry, you don't want to know about the critics, but she had that, Jianna, I mean, and that look of remoteness about her as if her eyes were on another world. That's why I used her for *The Mourning Girl.* But it was only a brief meeting — he asked me about her afterwards, said he'd like to paint her, but I didn't know where she had gone.'

It fitted with what Jack Marchant had told them — she knew the man who called himself Antonio Polidori — but she had known him earlier as Ferrars. Why had she lied to Jack? He felt like a man caught in a net. He struggled to free himself. It was time to be a lot more blunt with Cipriani Lloyd.

'Tell me about him, Mr Lloyd. Jianna Rizzo is missing, believed to be with a man who calls himself Antonio Polidori, and the young lady I was seeking is dead — found strangled in a reservoir in Clerkenwell.'

Cipriani Lloyd's merry brown eyes blinked and his face now paled. 'Polidori?'

'Yes — I don't know why, but I need to know about him.'

The sculptor poured more wine for both of them and drank his at one gulp. Then he poured another, filling Dickens's glass, too. Dickens thought he would go mad as he watched him. *For God's sake, tell me.*

'Mr Dickens, I honestly don't know where to start.'

'I suggest you begin with Mr Ferrars — tell me how you know him and what you know of his history.'

Cipriani Lloyd ran his fingers through his curls — he looked like a good-natured cherub, except that his eyes were anxious. 'Anthony Ferrars was brought up in Venice. His father was a banker — an agent of Coutts Bank — he made his money from the commission charged to English travellers and from foreigners who lived in Venice, either permanently or for a longish stay.'

Dickens nodded — he had used the same system when he was in Italy. You presented your letters of credit from your London bank — his was Coutts, too — and were charged for the issuing of the money.

'His mother died young — that's where Polidori comes in. Mr Ferrars knew Byron and Polidori. Polidori was some family connection, so Tony told me. He was proud of it. Anyway, Byron and Polidori were in Venice in 1816 —'

'How old is Anthony Ferrars?'

'Thirty-six. Same age as I am. His mother was a sleep-walker. Tony told me that Doctor Polidori was something of an expert in somnambulism — he'd written a paper on it and Mr Ferrars called him in to treat his wife. I don't know what treatment he gave but it didn't cure her. When Tony was eight she drowned — in the night. Someone had left open the door down to the water steps and she was found in the water. His father sent him to England to school when he was twelve and that's where I met him. He didn't fit in — neither did I, for that matter — too fat — no good at cricket or anything. Sipsy, they called me, and they thought Tony was mad as well as foreign. We were chums.

'He was a sleepwalker, too. He'd go missing at night and sometimes he'd be found on the stairs. Sometimes he'd get as far as the lake. He could never remember anything about it. He'd go off into these trance-like states. He missed Italy — well, you would. The light, Mr Dickens, the sunlight — that's why I went for six months. I was —'

Dickens interrupted, 'Mr Ferrars?'

Cipriani grinned. He really was an engaging fellow. 'Sorry, it's a passion of mine. Well, he stuck it at school until he was sixteen, then he went back to Italy. The next I heard was that he went up to Oxford and hated that, and went back to Italy again. Then he turned to art — went to Henry Sass's Drawing Academy. That would be about 1840. That's how we met again. I thought he'd go to the Academy Schools afterwards — plenty did. Rossetti, for example — '

'Did he know him?'

'Rossetti is much younger, but there is another connection. Doctor John Polidori was Rossetti's uncle — died before he was born. Suicide, people said. Though, the verdict was "Visitation by the Hand of God" — quaint notion, don't you think? Tony was quite struck with that.'

'He didn't attend the Academy Schools?'

'He went back to Italy — always going back and forth. In one sense he couldn't stick to anything — always flitting off, but then he'd take up an idea which would possess him for a while. At school, it was swimming. He was drawn to water — always in the lake or the river. And in his sleep, as I said. Because of his mother, I suppose. That's what the alienists would say. And it was always Italy — Venice, of course, but he went everywhere, Rome, Parma, Bologna, Ferrara. And Byron — he said he remembered him though he was only a little child, I don't know, but he became obsessed by the poems — he used to quote from one called 'Sleep'. All about sleep being another world, or something like that. Same with Polidori, he was fascinated by the man — not just the vampire stuff. It was what Polidori had told Tony's father about sleep. I may not have it right, but he had a theory that there are two minds — one working during sleep and one working during wakefulness, each unaware of the other. I suppose his mother's death haunted Tony — he sought an explanation.'

'Did he continue to sleepwalk?'

'Sometimes. He came back in 1845 and stayed with me here for a few months. It happened then — he seemed troubled, but then took a house in William Street and I didn't see much of him — we were both busy, and he could be —' Cipriani looked at Dickens ruefully — 'difficult at times. You never knew where you were with him — he could be charming and affectionate then cold and silent, but, well, school and all that. You remain loyal.'

You did, thought Dickens. The merry brown eyes were clouded with memory — two lonely boys thrown together in a place they hated, one a good-hearted, steadfast friend over all the years; the other — well, certainly troubled and unpredictable, and haunted, deeply disturbed, perhaps.

Cipriani continued, 'He was painting, I do know that.'

'Were there any women in his life — any love affairs?'

'There was someone — in Italy, he said, a girl who died. That's when he became possessed by the colour green. This green — that's how I knew the painting was his. It became another obsession — finding the perfect green — this deep, rich green. Renaissance artists used Verdigris, the most vibrant green, and Malachite. You find it in Botticelli, Ghirlandaio, Bronzini —'

And in a portrait in a castle at Ferrara, thought Dickens, but he just nodded.

'Modern painters use Viridian and Emerald Green — highly poisonous, the latter. And, of course you can get your paints in tubes now, but Tony mixed his own pigments — it had to be perfect. His brush work is very distinctive. See —' Dickens went to look and Cipriano handed him a magnifying glass — 'he uses very small watercolour brushes to produce layer upon layer of colour on a white ground. It's on a wooden panel — Tony preferred that — very smooth. Expensive, though. And I've a picture just like it. That's why I was so surprised that you had it. I couldn't have lost it — Tony left it here — like yours, it is not finished — the face, I mean. Tony never —'

'When?'

'A few weeks ago.'

'You've seen him recently? Here?'

'No, no — he moved away from William Street. I called, probably in 1846, but he wasn't there. I assumed he'd gone back to Italy — it would be just like him. I didn't hear anything of him until April 1850. He wrote to me — said he was back. He was looking for somewhere to live, he said. I was leaving for a six month tour of Italy so I wrote and offered him this house —' he saw Dickens's surprise — 'I counted him as a friend — I had known him for so many years. In any case, I didn't want to leave it empty. He said he didn't need the servants — just a woman to come in and cook and take the laundry. I came back a few weeks ago and he was gone. Not a word, but that was characteristic, I'm afraid. Not a notion about where he is.'

'What about family? Friends, the Rossettis — anyone?'

'You could try them. Oh, there was a cousin or something — but that was years ago. Isabella — a widow, I think, older than Tony, but I've no idea where she lives.'

The mysterious Isabella, thought Dickens. Not that it helped at all. Was she a Ferrars before she married? That might help in tracking her down. 'You don't know her other name?'

'I don't know, Mr Dickens — I'm baffled by all this. The murdered girl you mentioned. Are you saying that Tony … I mean Jianna, is she in danger?'

'I do not know, Mr Lloyd — I am saying only that he must be found.'

'I see that and I am sorry I cannot be of more help.'

'There is one more thing you can do. May I look at the other picture?'

'Yes, of course. I'll get it. You will see that it is just the same. It is Tony's work — there is no doubt.'

It was exactly the same and on a wooden panel. Cipriani placed the pictures side by side. Dickens looked. Two portraits without a face — sinister, somehow, and haunting, as if the sitters had vanished, leaving a blank behind. And that distinctive red-gold hair. Cipriani gave Dickens the magnifying glass again. He knew what to look for now.

'Look at the hair — that colour. You see it in so many Renaissance paintings, Mr Dickens, and the brushstrokes are so fine that you can see every hair.'

Dickens moved the magnifying glass from one picture to the other. The same artist had painted these. There was one difference.

'This inscription,' he said, 'can you make it out?'

Cipriani took the glass and read the tiny words: *The love where death has set his seal.*

'Byron,' said Dickens.

Cipriani Lloyd looked at him, his cherub's face as gaunt as if he had fallen from heaven.

42: A Pauper's Grave

It was the case of Eliza Williams that had distracted Sam Jones. In 1849, Eliza Williams had cut her own throat, 'beguiled,' as the *Police Gazette* had reported, 'by the arts of a policeman'. Jones had remembered the case — the policeman had vanished, his uniform abandoned at his lodgings — Police Constable Bentley Griss of K Division. Jones hadn't known him, but it was the reference to the old case, the policeman and the suicide that had diverted him from his earlier search for cases in 1849.

Eliza Williams had been delivered of a bastard child and the beguiling constable had abandoned the 'hitherto virtuous young female' and she had killed herself.

And three wooden legs had also led him astray for beneath the long piece on Eliza Williams's misfortune, there had been an account of a suicide in the Regent's canal. The inquest on John Davis, an unemployed clockmaker, returned a verdict of 'found drowned'. His two wooden legs had been left on the bank. More distracting still, had been the second inquest on the same day on a beggar 'found drowned' with his one wooden leg still attached. Jones had relished the thought of telling that story to Dickens and had then turned to the other accidents, suicides and unexplained deaths by water in the year 1849, none of which served his purpose.

Yet, since that occasion when he and Dickens had thought of that sequence of numbers: 44, 45, 46, 47, 48, Jones had brooded on the number 49. It was worth another look.

He had missed the few lines given to the drowning of an unknown female person in the Regent's Canal where it flowed through St. John's Wood — a young woman so disfigured that she had been unrecognisable. Now, in another newspaper, he found the inquest report which included the testimony of John Bate, a bargeman:

who was proceeding along Regent's canal, and arriving at that part which flows by the gardens of the houses on the South Bank, nearing the tunnel under Grove End Road, his attention was attracted by a bundle floating in the water. Using his boat hook, he retrieved the bundle in which he found a shawl and a pair of nearly new women's boots. He summoned a policeman. Inspector Day of D Division had attended…

D Division, thought Jones, at Marylebone Lane Police Station. Perhaps that was why Inspector Maxwell of S Division had not mentioned the case. There were so many drownings. So many suicides of those driven into all the waters of London by poverty, debt, shame, loneliness — and murder, he thought. Fathers, mothers, husbands, wives, lovers shoved into the Thames, out of the way ponds, canals, wells even; or doing the shoving, either from the motives he had listed in his mind, or from hatred, cruelty, jealousy, revenge, or greed. He thought of those cases of mothers who had drowned their children so that they could collect the money from the burial club. Murder. And madness. Were they all mad or maddened by their circumstances to do that act from which there was no return — neither for the victim or themselves? He thought of Elizabeth's story of Browning's poem of the madman who had strangled his lover. Had this unknown girl been strangled? He turned back to the inquest report.

The drags were procured and the body got out and taken to the St Marylebone Workhouse. The surgeon's opinion was that the disfigurement of the face had been caused by its striking an old anchor which had been brought up by the drag. The injuries to the neck were consistent with the anchor chain having wrapped itself round the woman's neck and torso. The body was much decomposed — it was the surgeon's view that the young woman had been in the water for several weeks. Despite the description of her clothes: a black silk bonnet and brown merino dress, and of her beautifully plaited golden hair, no one had come forward to identify her

"Beautifully plaited golden hair" — she had not known she was to die. She had gone to meet her lover by the canal, all unknowing. Or had she known? Watcher had talked of logic. Would a young woman dress herself up to die? Perhaps she would — pride, vanity? Did those things matter if you were planning your own death? He supposed they did — for a beautiful woman. To remind her false lover of what he had lost when he saw her lovely hair as he had known it in life.

This case didn't make much difference. It might be a waste of time. That's what he had said about Susan Harvest, and Elizabeth had put him right. Justice. This poor girl and Susan Harvest, buried by the parish in the cheapest of pauper coffins with a number scrawled on the lid. Just a number.

It would be a New Year soon — 1851 in a few weeks. Jemima Curd was murdered in 1850 — perhaps Violet Pout. Had the murderer had his fill? Would Jianna Rizzo live until 1851? Was there time to save her? Perhaps Dickens had found some discovery at Mr Stanfield's.

Could there be some clue in that pauper's grave in the St Marylebone Burial ground? Jones knew Inspector Elijah Day at Marylebone Lane. It would be worth making an enquiry. He would take Rogers. Mr Edward Tait had presided at the inquest. Jones knew him, too. He was the man he would have to see if he wanted an exhumation. If he wanted to know if Susan Harvest had been strangled.

43: A Most Dreadful Face

Dickens walked down Avenue Road, thinking on Byron's words: *the love where Death had set his seal.* Did that mean that whoever had sat for that unfinished portrait was dead? Two faceless portraits simply left behind. Perhaps there were others. Anthony Ferrars was a man possessed of a single idea — to find a face, the face of a girl who had died in Ferrara — Caterina Vecelli, surely. He had lost her — killed her, or she had killed herself. Either way, he had lost her and sought her in the years that followed. But when he could not paint the faces of the red-haired girls he found, he killed them. Flora Lambert's face had not been the right one.

Perhaps Caterina had looked like the girl in the painting Aurelio Paladini had seen at Ferrara. Anthony Ferrars had seen that painting, fallen in love with the face, had found its living counterpart, had been denied the fulfilment of his love, but he could not forget. Dickens had not remembered it except in a vague way, but he supposed it could happen to some young, impressionable, lonely man — a young man who could become possessed of a single idea.

The picture he had remembered most vividly was one he had seen at Rome — the portrait of Beatrice Cenci. It had been her expression of sorrow and desolate helplessness that had remained as clear as the paper on which he had described it. It was supposed that the painter had seen her just before her execution. He remembered it now, but it was a memory of beauty like the memory of a poem or a rose. He had not fallen in love with a face.

Was Ferrars mad? Or — what had Cipriani Lloyd said about Polidori's theory of sleep? Two minds in two states of being, neither knowing the other's working. He had a book entitled *The Philosophy of Sleep* by Robert MacNish — he would have to look it all up, but he did remember the writer's ideas about reverie. MacNish had written something along the lines of too much reverie disturbing the balance of the mind, affecting the understanding. Did Anthony Ferrars not know what he did in those trance-like states? There were cases of murder done by those possessed by some nightmare. Were even the sane mad in their dreams? Somnambulism was, according to MacNish, allied to madness.

Theories were all very well, though. The urgent thing was to find Jianna Rizzo. Find her and find Anthony Ferrars? It seemed likely. He ought to go to see Sam, though, first, to tell him about Ferrars. He was nearly at the path leading to Barrow Hill reservoir. He looked along the path and saw a figure coming slowly down the incline. He stopped to watch. It was a woman, dressed in black, a woman who looked like a walking shadow — it was an unearthly sight. He could hear the wind sighing in the hedges and there was the eerie call of an owl. He thought of Susan Harvest risen from her pauper's grave, going back to the scene of her death, gazing down into that black water, and returning to her grave at cock-crow. Except it was not dawn. It was nearly dark and she should be going the other way to the water.

He shut his eyes and opened them wide. The figure was gone. A waking dream — *I am haunted by these deaths and by Italy. Even by Byron*, he thought, whose old house he had passed every day when he had lived at Albaro near Genoa. A dreadful weariness came over him — too much of Cipriani Lloyd's wine. How many glasses had he drunk? He made to walk on, but she was there again. She walked haltingly and he noticed that she used a stick. She was real then. Watcher had doubted that a young woman would go up to the reservoir at night. It was odd that any woman would, Dickens thought, watching her slow progress. What could she have wanted up there in the dark? Perhaps a meeting, perhaps in remembrance of someone who had perished there in the water. She might be a widow in her weeds.

As she came closer, he shrank back into a gateway. He heard the scrape of her stick on the gravelled path, then the two footfalls. It sounded strangely as if a one-legged person were being followed by one who paused before continuing his relentless pursuit. He saw her come from the path into the road. She was heavily veiled. Sam's veiled woman? He watched her cross towards Henry Street, a shadow shrinking as she went.

Go home, he told himself — you need hot tea and food, but as if he were sleepwalking he followed. She turned into Charles Street and he followed her into Barrow Hill Road. He found that he was not at all surprised to see her turn into William Street — the street where Anthony Ferrars had lived with Susan Harvest. She stopped by a gate, looked at the house, but she did not go in.

She went on down into Portland Town Road. Gas lights came on and he saw her in patches of light which gave a horrible intensity to her blackness. Then she dissolved into shadow and each time he thought she had vanished as a spectre, but she came again, always walking at that same slow pace, her stick making that third eerie footfall. She turned into Park Road. He saw her again in gaslight then she was gone.

He looked down Park Road. There was no entrance to Regent's Park until you got to Hanover Gate. He started down the road, but there was no sign of her. She would need to have hurried to get that far. There were two possible turnings off Park Road: one into Lodge Road and one into North Bank where the gardens of the houses led down to the banks of the Regent's Canal. He retraced his steps and turned down North Bank.

Nothing. She might have been swallowed into the earth. He walked along the road, looking at the houses where sometimes curtains were closed against the night, shutters were fastened, or where he could see lights and fires blazing cheerfully. He went on to the end to where he knew the canal flowed through a tunnel under Grove End Road. There was a bridge over the canal and beyond that some gardens, very dark now where there was no gaslight. And there was a house there in those gardens, a solitary house. He crossed the bridge and there at a gate leading into a gravelled path there was a sign: *To Let.*

Ivy Cottage had the desolate look of a house abandoned. Only Time had thrived here, judging by the ivy which grew over the windows and onto the roof to wind itself round a broken chimney. Time had devoured the rank and overgrown garden and the gravel path where weeds sprouted. Laurel bushes grew too tall, rhododendron crowded over the path and willow trees trailed their branches over his head. Silence had moved in here, too, heavy as a shroud. The smell was of the grave, earthy and bitter.

But she was there on the steps up to the front door. He stepped forward and his foot scraped the gravel. It sounded very loud in the silence. She turned. He hesitated. What right had he to follow? She was a woman alone and a stranger had pursued her to an empty house.

However, she stood quite still as if she were made of black marble. 'Who are you?' she asked. 'What do you want?'

'Anthony Ferrars,' he said, not that he had intended to.

She did not move. He advanced slowly as a man might approach a wild creature. She remained motionless. He stood at the bottom of the steps looking up. Her face was a faint smudge beneath the veil.

'Who are you?' she repeated, stepping back. Her voice was low and hoarse as if from disuse.

'I am looking for a missing girl. I am told she might be known to Mr Ferrars.'

'What girl?'

'An Italian girl, Jianna Rizzo — she has red-gold hair.'

'Why do you tell me that?' There was a note of alarm now.

'Susan Harvest had red-gold hair — Susan who drowned at Barrow Hill. I saw you there.' Dickens had no idea where this exchange might lead, but he was certain that this woman knew all about Anthony Ferrars and that he must shock her into telling. 'You met Susan in the park — dear little Susan, so young and so innocent. Did she love Anthony?'

'I should not have taken her there. I wanted to please him. He was so unhappy.'

'Because of Caterina?'

'You know it all. How do you know?'

'I saw him in Venice.'

Now she was very frightened. He saw how she grasped her stick more tightly and how she shrank from him, a stranger in the dark. Madam Emerald. He was the darkness come. Cassie Hanlon's Knave of Spades — the dark enemy.

'You need not be frightened. I mean no harm to you. Jianna Rizzo must be found. She is in danger, I believe.'

'Who are you?'

'Let me come into the house and I will tell you. I won't harm you.'

She turned to unlock the door and he went up the steps to follow her inside. It was too dark to see anything but shadows in the hall. There was only emptiness in this house, he thought. No one else was there. He heard her open a door and went after her. Her feet sounded on the bare floorboards. If only there were some light. He heard her cross the room and the sound of a catch lifted and the creak of a shutter opening. The she stood in silver moonlight, just a black silhouette. But the moonlight showed a stub of candle in a holder on the marble mantelpiece and some Lucifer matches. He lit a match on the candlestick striker and put the flame to the candle.

He looked about him, the candle flame creating moving shadows on the walls. The woman remained still as stone. There was an oil lamp with just a glass chimney — the broken shade lay on a table, one of the very few bits of furniture left. He lit the lamp which smoked at first and then a flame flickered and sprang into life. She looked more human now. He could see the folds of her dress, the fur trim on her cape and the silver collar on her stick, but her black veil was still unnerving.

'I must see your face.'

She lifted the veil. Dickens remained absolutely still and kept his mouth firmly closed before any gasp could escape. There was nothing to be horrified about. It was just that in this dim light half her face looked black. Her mouth was crooked and she looked at him, with dark, frightened eyes as if he were some necromancer who exerted a dreadful power over her. He took a step towards her, but still she stared, and in the better light he saw that half her face was horribly puckered and dark red. He felt his power over her; he was certain that she knew all about Anthony Ferrars. She might even know where he was.

'You have come from Venice for him?'

'No, but I did see him there, and I saw the girl and his hands around her neck.'

Something between a sob and a choking sound came from her and her black-gloved hands covered her face, and she seemed to shrink before him as if she were her own shadow dwindling before the light. But he caught her before she fell and helped her to a chair beside the table with its broken lampshade. She sat and wept, a hard, dry, wretching sobbing, her shoulders heaving, her hands still covering her wounded face.

Now, he pitied her, for the sound was that of one who had stored up years of grief and anguish which poured out now before a stranger whom she thought was a messenger from the past: nemesis. He felt in his pocket for his flask. There was brandy in it. He poured some into the silver cup which formed the top and placed it on the table. The he knelt in the dust beside her and gently took her hands from her eyes. There were no tears. Half the face was a mask of grief, the other maimed half unchanged. It was the most dreadful face he had ever seen. He took the silver cup and placed it at her lips.

'Please, drink, it will help.'

She sipped at the brandy and gradually became still again. She looked at him as if he, too, had been transformed from something unearthly to someone human with a human heart.

'I thought you were a ghost. Tell me who you are, I beg you.'

'I am sorry I frightened you. I came from Cipriani Lloyd. You know the name.' She nodded. 'He showed me a portrait without a face, the work of Anthony, and I showed him another. The picture is of a woman in a green robe with a jewelled cross round her neck. The woman has red-gold hair.

The second painting was found in a mews in Clerkenwell where I had gone to find a missing girl who was a servant —'

'Your servant?'

'No, but I was tasked to find her by a friend. The girl is dead. She was pulled from the reservoir in Clerkenwell. She had been strangled.'

In the silence that followed, Dickens heard the faint creak of a floorboard in the hall. He strained to listen. He felt his own heart beating so hard that he thought it must be heard in the thick silence. The woman heard the noise. She looked at him in terror. Then it came again, the slight creak as if someone had put down a foot. Someone was there. He had left the front door open.

44: A Signal

A fool's errand, I'll bet, Jones thought as he and Rogers made their way along Park Road.

Inspector Day had told him about the case. No one had come forward to claim the girl with the plaited hair. Plenty of people had been questioned and there had been the usual notice in the paper. Someone had thought she might have been in service at Ivy Cottage, a large secluded house at the end of North Bank near the canal tunnel where she had been found. Inspector Day had doubted that — the victim's clothes were too good and the hair so elaborately dressed, but he'd sent his sergeant to the house. There had only been a widow lady there and she knew nothing.

'What is the widow's name?' Jones had asked.

'Mrs Isabella Ferrars, but she isn't there now. The house is to let. It's empty.'

'Isabella,' said Rogers, 'the name Reverend Harvest gave you, and a widow lady.'

'Quite — and a veiled woman in black who called at William Street sometimes according to Lilian Judd.'

'Worth a look?'

'We might as well. We can find out who the letting agent is — he might be able to tell us something about Mrs Ferrars, though she could be dead for all we know. I feel as if we're wasting time, Alf, but —'

'Nothing else we can do until Jack Marchant turns up — you didn't find out anythin' useful from his ma?'

'No — well, he hasn't been to Italy so that rules him out, I think. I don't believe he is the murderer, nor Sabatini. He's just a lad and heartbroken about poor Miss Fane and Marchant's a hothead. Clever, though, clever enough to find Miss Rizzo, maybe, and impetuous enough to get himself into trouble — that worries me.'

'What's Mr Dickens doin'?'

Jones grinned at him. 'The word "impetuous" make you think of Mr Dickens?'

Rogers grinned back. 'Course not, sir, he'll be all right, Mr Dickens, he knows what he's about. Scrap tells me he's — in — inimitable — that's the word. Your Eleanor told Scrap it meant no one like him an' that's true enough.'

Jones laughed, 'So, it is. We'll call at Devonshire Terrace on our way back. He's been to see one of his artist friends with that painting we found at Amwell Street. He might have found out something.'

They turned into South Bank. Inspector Day had told them about the little bridge which crossed the canal and led to Ivy Cottage on North Bank. The path was parallel to the canal and the bridge just before the tunnel where the girl had been pulled out. It was very quiet, almost like the country, thought Jones, looking at the gardens which reached down through the path. It would be lovely in the summer to watch the barges go by. The tunnel led into a basin surrounded by streets. The Maida Hill Canal began on the other side of Edgeware Road and then there were fields. There was no reason that Mrs Ferrars should be connected to the drowned girl — if she had been murdered, the perpetrator could have fled along the footpath which went under Grove Road. He could have vanished into those crowded streets or those empty fields. It was only the name "Isabella" that —

'Good God! Ferrars — Ferrara.'

Rogers understood. They hurried on to find the bridge which led to Ivy Cottage. The notice board advertised the letting agents: *Lewis and Holmes, The New Road, Marylebone.* They might need that.

The gravel path brought them through the neglected garden. The house was not empty for there was flickering light in one of the downstairs windows and the front door was open. Jones motioned Rogers to stop.

'Let's go quietly. I should like to know who's lurking about a house that's supposed to be empty.'

They moved into the shelter of some overgrown laurel bushes. Rogers removed his truncheon from his belt and handed his bull's eye lamp to Jones who lit it and swivelled the cowl so that the light was concealed. They went forward on the grass of the circular lawn. Rogers crept up the steps and waited and Jones saw him slide into through the door. After a few moments the door opened a little wider and Jones slipped in. His foot made a slight creaking on the floorboards. Wavering light was coming through a door that was ajar. Rogers moved forward but the floorboards creaked again. He stopped. They held their breath in the silence.

'Someone is there — someone. Oh, God, Anthony! Don't come in!' It was a woman's voice.

A familiar voice shushed her. 'No, no, be calm. There is nothing now. Listen.'

Dickens waited. The woman put her hands to her face. There was nothing. Just the old house creaking, perhaps. But he couldn't help thinking of Anthony Ferrars. Then there was a brief flame of light. Darkness again. Light again. Darkness. Light. Darkness. It was a signal. A dark lantern? A signal for the veiled woman.

He surreptitiously picked up his stick and crossed the room as quietly as he could. Surely, someone intending harm would have come in. He did not want to meet Ferrars face to face. What might he do? But he couldn't turn back. He had to know. He could fight it out, he supposed, take the person by surprise with a sudden blow. He gripped the stick tightly.

He showed himself at the door. The lamp was raised and he saw to his great relief the face of Sam Jones gazing at him. He didn't look surprised. The other was Rogers — he did not need to see his face. He pointed to the front door. Jones just nodded went to close it. Dickens returned to the room.

'There is no one. I have closed the front door. You are safe.'

'You said a girl was strangled. Not Anthony, no, no!'

'Please, do not distress yourself. Tell me about Anthony.'

'He is my brother. He is the younger by ten years. I looked after him from the day he was born. Our mother was too fragile — she was never well after his birth. She took no interest in him. She took to her bed in the day time, but she was well enough when guests came to the palazzo. She liked to be the centre of things — she was beautiful. But she walked in her sleep. She did things — I saw her by Anthony's bed. She was holding a pillow over his face. I screamed and screamed and she stopped. Anthony was terrified. My father said that she did not know what she was doing. She would go out at night and the servants would bring her back. Nothing was said about what she did at those times. Mr Byron came with Mr Polidori. My father knew them. Mr Polidori had written a paper on sleep and advised my father that she should be locked in and given laudanum.

'One of the servants failed to lock the room. She came to my bedroom and held the candle to my face and her hand over my mouth — she was so strong. She burnt me. A servant heard my screams. Afterwards, my father said she had drowned when she was sleepwalking but there was no funeral. Later, I heard the servants talking. They said she was mad. She was locked away forever, they said… I told Anthony that she was dead, but he found out. We never speak of it. I cared for him — he walked in his sleep, but I locked him in and stayed with him and gave him laudanum. I did not tell my father — Anthony would have been taken away like my mother. I had no one else.

'But I lost him when he was sent to school — I lost him…' She wept again.

Dickens was conscious of the time passing and Jones waiting. There would be time after they had found him and Jianna — time then to piece it all together.

'Where is he?'

'He said he would come here — that he had found — that he needed me to — to —he said I must not go to his house — what has he done — what has he done?' She struck her gloved hand on her knee and rocked back and forth. There was no time.

'I must find him — I will bring him to you. Only tell me where he is.'

Just at that moment there was the dreadful thump of the knocker on the door, followed by two more. Jones nearly dropped the lamp, Rogers jumped, and inside the room the woman dropped the brandy cup as she started up. Dickens caught hold of her. Thank God Jones and Rogers were in the hall. It had sounded like the knocking of a madman — who the devil?

The door was opening, a voice shouting urgently, 'Miss Ferrars! Miss Ferrars! I know you're there.' The door banged shut and the indignant voice said, ''Oo the dickens are you two?'

Dickens felt weak at the knees, but he held onto the woman. He heard Jones's voice calmly addressing the irate female — for it was another woman's voice he had heard.

'I am Superintendent Jones of Bow Street —'

He was cut off by the woman's cry, 'Oh, gawd, 'e ain't 'ere, is 'e?'

'Who?'

'Mr Ant'ny — she's bin waitin' fer 'im — I knew she'd come 'ere. Let me through.'

The door burst open and Dickens saw a stout woman wearing an immensely large bonnet and wielding an umbrella. She barrelled into the room with a cry of, 'Miss Ferrars! Come away. 'E ain't comin 'ere. It's best ter wait at 'ome — come away.' The she seemed to realise Dickens and asked belligerently, ''Oo are you?'

Dickens couldn't stop himself, 'Mr Dickens, madam.' Then he felt a fool.

'Very clever, I'm sure. Don't tell me then. I don't care — just leave my poor lady alone.'

'I'm not —' no point in explaining — 'do you know where Mr Ferrars is?'

'Wot's it ter you, Mr — whatever yer name is?'

Jones came in. 'I need to know, madam. Come into the hall. Miss Ferrars is quite safe.'

Hearing the command in the policeman's voice, the stout woman obeyed and went out.

'Who is that man?' Miss Ferrars asked.

'He is a friend — a policeman. He needs to find Anthony and Miss Rizzo.'

Isabella Ferrars turned her ravaged face to Dickens. 'Susan committed suicide. Anthony told me. It wasn't his fault. He needs me. He is ill. The girl in Venice — it was an accident — he didn't mean it. He wouldn't harm —' she sat down and wept again.

She knew enough, thought Dickens, enough to be terrified at the word "strangled" and she thought he had come as an avenger from Venice. She was too distraught to answer anything more.

Jones came back in with the now subdued stout woman — not so subdued that she did not elbow Dickens out of the way to put her arms around Isabella Ferrars and whisper, 'There, there, miss, come away now. Let's go home. There, there.'

Jones moved Dickens away to the door. 'She is Mrs Slack, Miss Ferrars's housekeeper. They used to live here. Miss Ferrars is not a widow, obviously. Rogers has gone to get a cab — he will take them home and stay with them until he hears from me.'

'Do you know where he is?'

'I have an address.'

He hears an owl hooting in the woods. He thinks of the ghostly shape he has seen floating in the trees. There are only the birds and he saw a fox once, its ears pricked and its coat a flash of russet. It had gazed at him for a few seconds. Then it had turned and trotted away on silent feet. No one comes here. There is only Caterina and himself.

He looks down at her unmoving face and strokes the red-gold hair. 'Caterina,' he whispers, 'Caterina.' But she does not answer. She does not wake. She will. She will come back to him. The jewelled cross has slipped from her hands. He crosses the room to look at his work. She does not seem to be perfect now. Her eyes are closed but her mouth is open — she looks almost ugly. Her lips have lost their fullness and her skin, that rosy flush on her face seems to have turned to wax and she is so cold and so still. She is his masterpiece — why is it changed so? But he can put it right. She can be restored.

He tries to rearrange her hands, but they are stiff and hard. He pulls the rosary tighter so that the cross rests on her breast — a memory comes to him, a memory of a girl who had worn a mask, whose eyes had gazed into his and laughed at his costume. 'You are Death,' she had said, 'come to take me.' And she had laughed again, a silvery peal of laughter. She had taken his hand and they had gone down the stairs away from the palazzo, away from the party, into the silent streets.

She had run ahead of him, her laughter trailing behind her like notes of music. He saw her pause under a lamp. Her dress looked green and her red-gold hair flew out, catching the light. Then she was gone into darkness, but he heard her feet running. He followed and she was waiting for him under another lamp by a canal — the one where the bridge was topped with iron. He caught up with her. She was breathless after her dash, but her smile was beautiful. She caught his hands in his. 'Ah, Death,' she said, 'let me see your face,' and she reached up a hand to take away the mask of the skull which he had worn for the festivity.

'You first,' he had said, releasing her hand so that she could take off her mask. She took it off and shook out her shining hair. Then she looked up at him, her dark eyes glittering in delight and her round face dimpled with laughter. There was a jewelled cross at her neck. 'Death meet the Countess — that is who I am tonight — a noble lady — just for one night.' She curtseyed.

She was not beautiful — he remembers that. She had a coarse skin and he had seen that her white teeth had been an illusion — only a few of her teeth remained. She had put up her arms to kiss him. Her breath was foul. He had reached out for the rosary. A single gondola had glided by, just a shadow on the water. The lamp had gone out.

He shakes his head — the memory vanishes. He looks at his love. Why is she so changed? He had achieved the perfection of his art. Why can it not remain? He lights fresh candles. He weeps to see how altered she is — so cold, so pale. He takes his palette and puts his brush in the carmine red and mixes it with white. The colour becomes a rosy blush. He begins to paint the waxen face. His final work.

45: Ordeal by Touch

It wasn't far. Dickens and Jones could have walked from South Terrace in half an hour or so. But Jones was cautious. They would go to the Police Station at Marylebone Lane. They'd find a cab on Park Road which would take them there in ten minutes. Time to collect a couple of constables and take the police van to Keeper's Cottage. They would need to lock him in one of the cells in the van. The cottage, according to Mrs Slack, was located in the woods surrounding Westbourne House just off the Harrow Road — just South of the Regent's Canal. Inspector Day knew exactly where it was. They could be there in the same time.

It was more remote than Ivy Cottage. They left the van and the driver on the rutted road that led up to the woods and then took a path. The woods were dark, but there was an overgrown path to the house. An owl hooted — the fatal bellman which gave the stern'st goodnight. *A portent*, Dickens thought, as if they needed one. He saw the white shape drift through the trees, but there was no other sign of life. Only the moon, glimpsed occasionally through the canopy of trees, looking down at them like an anguished face.

Jones had told the constables to be as quiet as possible. He did not even know if Anthony Ferrars would be there, but if he was, Jones judged that he must be taken by surprise. If he were warned of their approach he might escape, or he might kill the girl. If he had not done so already. He had not much hope from what he had heard in Ivy Cottage — the man was possibly mad and that perhaps made him dangerous. Jones fingered the flintlock pistol which he had borrowed from Inspector Day — just a precaution.

The gate was open and they looked up at the hidden house. There was faint light coming from one of the rooms at the top of the house. Someone was there. He directed the slighter of the two constables to go up to the front door. It was locked. He signalled to the man to stay where he was. He and Dickens and the other policeman with his bull's eye lamp went round the back. Here the trees grew right up to the house. There was no back garden and they pushed through the trees to see if they could find a back door. Jones lit the lamp that Rogers had given him.

In the light of the lamps they could see that this was the door that had been used to go in and out of the house. There were footprints on the damp ground — a man's footprints. Very slowly and very carefully, Jones turned the handle and pushed at the door. The lamplight showed that there was a pantry and beyond that another room in darkness. They waited, but there was no sound but the occasional drip of water. *The time seemed interminable between each drip which marked each long … minute*, thought Dickens, like a clock run slow, but still Jones waited.

Jones moved to the entrance to the other room. Dickens followed and he and the constable stood in the pantry and then they followed Jones into the farther room from which a staircase led upstairs. Jones indicated to the constable that he should wait by the door into the pantry. Then he and Dickens crept up the stairs, holding on to the banister rail and testing each step as they went. On the landing they waited again, but there was no sound. There only the faint edge of light seen under a door — the door of the room they had seen from outside.

They listened outside the door. The silence was profound. They hardly dared breathe. Dickens felt a sense of dread. This was the end of it, he was sure. He knew in his heart that Jianna Rizzo was dead. The silence told that. Perhaps she lay even now in the Regent's Canal, taken through those woods in the dead of night, her slender neck circled by a jewelled chain which had killed her. But the light told, surely, that someone was inside that room. Perhaps Anthony Ferrars was dead by his own hand.

As if he could bear it no longer, Jones seized the door handle and pushed, taking the pistol from his pocket.

The painter did not turn. He stood with his palette in his hand, looking at the figure on the bed. They stepped into the room. Dickens looked, too. He could not work out what it was. A waxwork figure? A life-sized doll? He saw the red-gold hair and the green velvet, but the face was a horror — a painted face, unreal and grotesque. He and Jones stood frozen to the spot and watched the painter take his brush and bend over the figure.

'Mr Ferrars!' Jones's voice was loud and commanding.

The painter turned round and looked at them, his eyes blank. He simply stared. Then he turned away and made to paint again. The red paint dripped from the brush.

Jones was about to move, but Dickens stepped forward and took the brush from him. 'Your work is finished, Mr Ferrars.'

Ferrars looked at him and smiled. 'You are right, sir. It is beautiful, is it not?'

Dickens looked down. He understood then. Underneath the paint was the dead face of Jianna Rizzo. 'Yes, it is, but you should come with us now, sir. Your sister, Isabella, sent us. She would like to see you. She said you promised to go to her.'

'Isabella? Did I? I don't remember, but I cannot leave Caterina here alone. I have waited so long for her.'

'I will take care of her until you can come back. She will be safe with me.'

Dickens took the palette from him. He guided him towards Jones who had pocketed the pistol. Anthony Ferrars did not resist.

Jones led him away. Dickens heard them go down the stairs. Anthony Ferrars said nothing, but he heard Jones address the constable and then he heard the front door open and more hurried words. Then Jones came back upstairs.

'I've had to handcuff him. I'm afraid that he will come to and realise what's happening. I need to get him to Bow Street and I need to get a doctor.'

Dickens nodded. 'I'll stay with her.'

'An hour or so. You'll be all right?'

'She should not be left alone.'

'I'll leave one of the constables outside.'

Dickens sat waiting with the dead girl in the candlelit room. He could hardly bear to look at her. He remembered her in Magpie's lodgings in her velvet dress. She had looked like a girl in a painting. How odd that he had thought that without knowing anything of the painting he had carried about with him. He had left it at Ivy Cottage — the portrait without a face.

He looked at her then. There was something grotesque about what Anthony Ferrars had done to her face. The pink painted on the cheeks was crude and clumsy, barely covering the waxen pallor. Red paint had dripped onto her eyes as if she were weeping blood. He thought of his friend, Daniel Maclise's painting, *Ordeal by Touch* — the old belief that if the murderer touched the body of the victim it would bleed. He saw the red circle round her neck and the cross on her breast — full circle.

And the lips were more horrible still — he had painted a pair of lips over the dead ones. It looked like a clown's face. He had made her ugly. Where was his fine brushwork now?

He looked round the room. There was water in a jug on the table and some rags beside it. He found the cleanest and dipped it into the water. Then he set about gently cleaning the dead face.

PART III: THE PLEA OF INSANITY

46: The Inquest and Trial

The Morning Chronicle, Monday December 10th

Yesterday afternoon a very respectable jury was summoned to attend before Mr Box, the coroner for Marylebone.

Mr Box explained that the purpose of the inquest was to establish the cause of death and the circumstances that surrounded the event. This court was not the proper tribunal in which to establish any person's guilt or innocence. If the evidence were sufficient to direct suspicion on any party then he the coroner would send the accused before another tribunal where ample opportunity would be afforded the accused to establish his moral innocence. That would be the proper tribunal to institute the inquiry as to the sanity or insanity of the accused. The question at present would be whether or not after hearing the evidence, there should appear to the jury a prima facie *case made out sufficiently strong against any party to induce the said jury to send the party before another tribunal.*

At the mention of the question of insanity, much interest was felt in the young man brought before the court. According to the evidence put forward by Superintendent Samuel Jones of Bow Street, this young man, Anthony Ferrars, an artist, had been found with the body of the deceased young woman, Miss Rizzo. He had made no confession nor, indeed, had he spoken of her death. He had only asked where was Caterina? The name, according to Superintendent Jones, referred to a young woman he believed had died in Ferrara, Italy. Enquiries were being made in Italy about this young woman. Superintendent Jones had called in two doctors and on their recommendation the young man had been transferred to the Bethlehem Asylum.

Constable Pickering (D Division) offered his evidence as to the discovery of Mr Ferrars at a cottage in the woods by Westbourne Manor House.

There was no evidence of any other person's presence in the cottage. He had guarded the back door. No other person had entered or left during his watch. Constable Weeks (D Division) had been detailed by Superintendent Jones to keep watch at the front of the cottage. No other person had entered or left.

Inspector Day gave evidence that he and various other men of D Division had searched the premises and the woods nearby. There was no evidence of any other person residing at the cottage other than Mr Ferrars and the deceased.

Much sensation was caused by the appearance, as a witness, the celebrated author, Mr Charles Dickens, who, our readers will no doubt recall, was an important witness at the inquest on the death of a doctor last year. Mr Dickens's interest in this case was explained. He had been tasked to discover the whereabouts of a young woman, Miss Violet Pout, formerly a governess in the household of Sir Neptune Fane, Member of Parliament for the Chelsea District. This young woman was god-daughter to Mrs Dickens's personal maid. Mr Dickens's enquiries led him to Mr Ferrars. Superintendent Jones had accompanied him to the cottage in the woods.

Further evidence was put forward by Superintendent Jones, who told the coroner of the death by strangling of Miss Pout and her servant, Jemima Curd, who had also once been in the employ of Sir Neptune Fane. There was evidence that both these young women had resided in a house occupied by Mr Ferrars in Clerkenwell. The bones of another young woman, Miss Flora Lambert, had been found in the water tank of a house in South Crescent. She was believed to be known to the accused. The inquests on those deaths had been adjourned pending further enquiries by the police.

Doctor Alfred Symonds of King's College Hospital gave the medical evidence which showed that the young woman, Miss Rizzo had died by strangulation. Doctor Symonds described the livid circle round the lower part of the neck, created, he said, by the use of a chain of brass which had been found looped through the victim's hands. There were glass beads on the chain and a cross. The marks on the circle corresponded to links in the chain. The internal appearances of the body were those of asphyxia. The lungs and right cavities of the heart were distended with thick black blood. Death had occurred between eight and twenty-four hours previous to his examination. Rigor Mortis was passing from the body.

After a short time of deliberation, the jury returned a unanimous verdict of wilful murder against Anthony Ferrars. The Coroner issued his warrant for the committal of Anthony Ferrars to Newgate to await his trial. However, the Coroner said he would consider an application from Doctor Matthew Mellor for further medical examination of the prisoner at the Bethlehem Hospital.

The Morning Chronicle, Thursday, December 13th

CENTRAL CRIMINAL COURT — THIS DAY

Before Mr Justice Rightman:
Mr Edmund Needle for the Crown, assisted by Mr Penn and Mr Jameson; Mr Cornelius Craft for the defence, assisted by Mr Simple and Mr Wiggott.

At the sitting of the court this morning, Anthony Louis Ferrars, aged thirty-five, was placed in the dock charged with the murder of Jianna Rizzo, a seamstress.

On being called upon to plead, he replied, "Not Guilty" in a most feeble and hoarse voice.

Mr Needle, QC, for the prosecution stated the facts of the case which, though but recently set before the public, we may notice briefly. The prisoner at the bar was discovered in a remote cottage in woodland near Westbourne Manor House where the body of the deceased seamstress, Miss Rizzo, was also found. She had been strangled by a chain of brass. The prisoner had been found in the act of painting her face. Mr Needle averred that evidence would show that the prisoner had committed the dreadful deed.

Mr Craft, QC, addressed the jury on behalf of the prisoner and said that upon the facts he felt the jury could come to no other conclusion than that of returning a verdict of guilty against the prisoner. But he had to urge upon their attention the state of mind of the prisoner which he would be able to prove was from his childhood upward unsettled, and was, at the time of the commission of the offence, unquestionably in a state of insanity.

Superintendent Samuel Jones of Bow Street was the first witness called by the learned counsel…

47: Mr Needle and Mr Craft

Day two of the trial

Dickens shifted uncomfortably in his seat as the court waited for Mr Justice Rightman to close the day's proceedings. Mr Needle and Mr Craft were about their business with their assistants. He looked contemplatively at Cornelius Craft, a beetle-browed, coarse-haired little man with a pugnacious set to his shoulders and big hands. He looked like a boxer ready to throw a punch — at Mr Needle in the present circumstances. He looked at Needle from under his heavy brows with an expression very like a sneer. Cunning, he looked. Crafty, of course.

Edmund Needle was tall and as thin as his name promised. Born to stab, thought Dickens, or rather to prick — secret weapon, he was. A dangerous expression of blandness was his forte. Sometimes he seemed to smile at some joke that only he knew. When a man laughs inwardly, it bodes no good to other people.

Should you be in the dock, he asked himself, glancing at Anthony Ferrars, who would you fear most? Craft's cunning or Needle's sharp point? Neither seemed to have much pity for the prisoner — or the victims, come to that. Words, words, words — he might be inclined to bet on Needle's rhetoric if it came to a toss-up.

He had felt the sting of Mr Needle's pointed questions, having given his evidence about Violet Pout, Jemima Curd, and the discovery of the body of Jianna Rizzo. Mr Needle had eyed him as the cat might a trembling mouse. Not that Dickens trembled, but he had felt a certain foolishness when Needle had pressed him as to why he had tampered with the evidence by wiping off some of the paint from the face of the deceased young woman. The judge had looked down his long nose. He had merely nodded when Dickens explained the horror and pity the sight had evoked. That had been a distinctively uncomfortable moment. Mr Needle had looked at him with his blandly menacing smile. He had suggested that Mr Dickens, however eminent in his own sphere, had overstepped the mark. It was not the business of the novelist to meddle in criminal matters. Some members of the jury had given him a sympathetic look when he returned to his seat. Nevertheless, the law had had its revenge for all those foolish or deceitful lawyers he had created. He thought of Sampson Brass, whose bland forbidding smile had by some foretelling anticipated Needle's. Perhaps the lawyer had read *The Old Curiosity Shop* — and hadn't liked it.

Superintendent Jones had given his evidence on the first day, as had the other officers from Marylebone Lane. Jones had explained how the investigations into the deaths of Miss Flora Lambert, Miss Violet Pout and Miss Jemima Curd had led to the discovery of the body of Miss Jianna Rizzo in the cottage. The only other person present had been the prisoner, Mr Ferrars. Doctor Symonds had repeated his medical evidence regarding the death of Miss Rizzo by strangulation.

Mr Needle had been remorseless in in his pursuit of the facts. The evidence of Miss Ferrars had been the most painful part of the business. The prisoner's early life had been laid bare — his mother's madness and incarceration, the prisoner's sleepwalking habits, his attempt on the life of a servant, his strange disappearances, his grief at the death of his first love in

Ferrara, Italy, and the suggestion of his involvement in the death of a girl found drowned in a Venetian canal.

Jack Marchant had given his evidence, too. He had turned up, sleepless, unshaven and haggard, to confess that he had been searching for Jianna. Then he had read the news of her murder. The young man was shaken to the core. Dickens sympathised — not so Mr Needle who had interrogated him in exquisite detail about his relationship with the murdered girl. Poor Miss Rizzo, he had observed to the jury, to have fallen into the hands of two unscrupulous men. Mr Marchant seemed to have been quite content to let her go with a man who called himself — "Polidori". He had a way with pauses, did Mr Needle. That was the way, he supposed regretfully, in artistic and theatrical circles. Jack Marchant could not answer.

Poor Jack — he had looked crushed. Magpie's wings had been well and truly clipped.

A collective gasp from the courtroom had been heard when Miss Ferrars had been asked by Mr Craft, to remove her veil so that the jury might see her injured face — she had looked shattered at the end of her ordeal. Dickens hoped that her tragic bearing would influence the jury — she and her brother had suffered dreadfully at the hands of their mother, as Mr Craft had been at pains to point out.

The paintings had been brought in for the jury to examine. Cipriani Lloyd identified them at the work of the prisoner. He spoke of the prisoner's interest in Miss Rizzo who had been the model for some of his own sculptures. Mr Craft pointed out the absence of faces — surely evidence that prisoner was not in his right mind.

It would be for the doctors, Dickens knew, to convince the jury that the prisoner was insane. Doctor Winslow looked benevolently confident — or was that complacency? Doctor

Jessop wore his usual melancholy air. Sam had told him that Doctor Mellor of the Bethlehem Hospital had been called by Mr Needle. Mellor looked irascible — not the kind of man to suffer fools gladly, even to save them from the gallows.

He looked at Anthony Ferrars again. He might as well have been absent — when asked his plea he had spoken in a voice scarcely more than a whisper: "not guilty", but Dickens felt that he had no idea what the words meant. He would not be called to give evidence — how could he?

48: The Evidence of Doctor Forbes Benignus Winslow

Day three of the trial

Anthony Ferrars looked yet more haggard and confused. He rested his manacled hands on the ledge — long, sensitive, painter's hands, hands that had looped a chain round a girl's neck and more than once. Had he known what he was doing?

There was a whispering in the court, the shuffle of feet, and a sudden sense of expectancy. Dickens looked away from the white face. Doctor Forbes Winslow was being called.

Mr Craft was ready with his question: 'Do you consider the prisoner at the bar to be of sound mind, and a responsible agent?'

The jurymen shifted in their seats. People in the public gallery craned forward to see the famous alienist. Doctor Winslow looked perfectly composed. He was an impressive figure, broad-shouldered with a high domed forehead from which his greying hair receded. A thick moustache and far-seeing eyes gave him a grave dignity. The reporters had their pencils poised. Dickens stole a look at Mr Justice Rightman. His long face was sombre, but perfectly neutral. He was not known, as some judges were, to be very much opposed to the insanity plea. Ferrars was fortunate enough not to have come before Baron Rolfe, whose view was that the insanity plea was a defence too often upheld. Still, neutrality was no guarantee.

Doctor Winslow cleared his throat: 'I do not.'

'The court would be obliged if you would explain your views of the prisoner.'

'The principle with regard to a diagnosis of insanity is to look at the personal character of the individual, to his grade of mental power, to the whole course of his life, as well as to the nature of the act with which he is charged. Miss Ferrars, the prisoner's elder sister, has testified to his childhood sleepwalking and propensity to abstraction and reverie. These manifestations began after his own mother, in a somnambulist trance, had attempted to suffocate the boy. He was three years old at the time. And, as the jury has seen, the burns to Miss Ferrars's face were inflicted by the mother who held a burning candle to her daughter's face. Later, the children were told that their mother had drowned when sleepwalking. They discovered that she had actually been confined to the lunatic asylum in Venice.

'Miss Ferrars protected her brother by locking him in his bedroom and giving him laudanum. Miss Ferrars has told how her brother evaded her supervision and in his sleep trance pushed a servant into a canal. The servant survived and was compensated by Mr Ferrars senior. The boy had no recollection of the incident.

'The misguided father sent the boy to school in England, believing that a complete change of scene, a cooler climate, and a healthy, vigorous regime such as our public schools operate, would improve him. Mr Cipriani Lloyd has recounted the loneliness and melancholy of the boy at school. The other boys thought him a mad foreigner and shunned him. Mr Lloyd was his only friend and has testified to his sleep-walking habits, his fascination for water, and his tendency to become fixed on one subject — the poems of Byron, for example and the works of Doctor Polidori, or the colour green. These aspects of the prisoner's early life and character are sufficient to indicate latent insanity.

'Doctor Polidori was a visitor at the prisoner's Venetian home. Doctor Polidori had written on sleep disorders and was invited to treat Mrs Ferrars. The treatment — laudanum, cupping, and locking her in her room, did not work. It is significant to me that the prisoner assumed the name of Polidori — a harking back to his childhood terrors.

'The prisoner adopted the name Antonio Ferrara — again a retreat into the past. This was the place where his tragic love affair took place — the death of Caterina Vecelli, an account of which has been heard in the letter from Mr Aurelio Paladini, a native of Ferrara. This young woman who had returned his love found that her father opposed it — Mr Ferrars, he thought a mere artist, unworthy of his daughter of aristocratic lineage. Moreover, he disliked the English — I remind you that the prisoner took an Italian name. Miss Vecelli committed suicide although a verdict of accident was brought in because she was found with her rosary coiled round her neck. Mr Ferrars does not believe that Caterina Vecelli is dead.

'The law states that the plea of insanity can only be upheld when the accused is suffering from delusions. A delusion is a belief of things as realities which exist only in the diseased imagination of the patient, a belief of facts in which no reason could believe.

'The prisoner came to believe that Miss Vecelli was alive somewhere and that he must find her. When he saw a woman with distinctive red-gold hair, he pursued her. He wanted to paint her. His diseased imagination told him that he must preserve his beloved forever. But he could not paint the face of the woman he had found nor any of the others. He does not know why. His melancholia is such as to contribute to acute degeneration of his mind.

'I should mention here the traces of paint found on the cheeks and lips of the deceased woman. When I questioned the prisoner on this point he told me that Caterina was changed. He wanted to give her back her beauty. This is a delusion out of which he cannot be reasoned.

'He cannot remember the other young women who died. My colleague, Doctor Jessop, and I have tried him with the names, but he remains mute about them. He does not know who Miss Rizzo is. The only subject which elicits any spoken word from the prisoner is Caterina.

'As to the question of whether the prisoner knew at the time that his act was wrong, I do not believe we can apply that question. We cannot know for he cannot tell us, but we can take into consideration his childhood history of sleepwalking and reverie and the incident with the servant.'

Mr Craft: 'Are you able to say whether walking in the sleep is indicative of a disordered mind?'

'Yes, of a disordered state of the brain. I refer to Mr Robert MacNish on the point of sleepwalking states and of trance. There is a waking-dreamlike state which may afflict the habitual somnambulist. Mr MacNish calls it "Reverie" which fallen into continually can damage the whole fabric of understanding.'

Mr Craft: 'I should be obliged, Doctor Winslow if you would now state your conclusions as to the state of mind of the prisoner.'

'From my detailed examination of the prisoner and those of my colleague, Doctor Jessop, I am prepared to say that the prisoner demonstrates symptoms of hereditary insanity, erotomania — that is obsessive love for a particular object — monomania, a state of insanity aroused by one subject. From these latter two, his delusions originate. I do not believe he is of sound mind.'

Doctor Winslow made his bow to the judge. Mr Justice Rightman nodded, but his face was as still as a mask. Dickens looked at the jury. Were they as convinced as he was? Winslow's account was lucid and so true, he thought. The man was mad. He had not a grain of a doubt. Mr Edmund Needle, however, was deep in discussion with his colleagues. Planning his rebuttal. He seemed to be laughing inwardly.

49: The Needle's Point

Day four of the trial

Mr Needle adjusted his gown, put down his papers and stepped with a certain confident indolence into the limelight. He turned his inquisitor's cold gaze upon the twelve true men. Dickens fancied that they shrank a little. He knew how they felt.

He began rhetorically: 'What is the law respecting alleged crimes committed by persons with insane delusions in respect of one or more particular subjects?

'In this case we are to consider the prisoner's belief that the murdered woman is still alive and is not Jianna Rizzo but his first love, Caterina Vecelli? That this is a delusion has been convincingly demonstrated by Doctor Winslow and Doctor Jessop. I do not doubt that the prisoner now believes that his beloved is still alive. Medical evidence tells us that a profound shock may induce madness. We can imagine the shock the prisoner experienced when Superintendent Jones came into that darkened house to find him with the dead girl.

'Doctor Winslow tells us that in this case the test of whether the accused knew what he had done cannot apply, but the law demands it. The law demands that the question to be answered by the wisdom of the jury is: at the time of the crime did the accused know that he was acting contrary to law?

'The prisoner's guilt is beyond reasonable doubt — he was found with the deceased young woman. No one else was at the house. There was no evidence of any other person having lived in that house. He killed Jianna Rizzo, but the onus is his — he must, through the medium of his defence counsel, prove that he did not know that his act was wrong.

'Mr Craft and his witnesses, Doctor Winslow and Doctor Jessop, have contended that the prisoner has suffered from delusions for a length of time. He pursued young women in the mistaken belief that they were his lost Caterina Vecelli. However, we must consider that when he discovered, by his reason — by his reason, I say — that these young women were not the woman he wanted, he set out to rid himself of them. He knew that they were not Caterina Vecelli — he was not deluded then.

'Doctor Winslow's view is that the prisoner's belief that Jianna Rizzo was Miss Vecelli amounts to insanity. He talks of erotomania and monomania — his fine words may be true. But, as you have heard, the prisoner is a man who has been cunning enough to remove himself from the scene of his alleged crimes. He has lived in at least three places, and under false names. It is a sane man who knows that he is in danger and takes steps to escape that danger by changing his place of residence and assuming false identities.

'Mr Jack Marchant tells us that Miss Rizzo disappeared from the lodgings where he kept her as his mistress. Mr Marchant understood that the man she went with was named "Polidori" — Polidori, you will remember, was the name of the celebrated author of *The Vampyr* — a most gruesome tale. A man with predation on his mind might well choose such a soubriquet. Miss Rizzo was never seen alive again.

'She was found by Superintendent Jones and Mr Dickens in a remote, abandoned cottage deep in the woods. This is his habit and his craft — his craft, I say — the house in Amwell Street was abandoned by the tenants. The prisoner moved secretly into the top floor and inveigled Miss Pout and Miss Curd there. These two young women were found strangled. Mr Gilpin, the coalman, saw him only once. No other tradesmen ever saw him. Because, because, I say, he was in hiding. You have heard of Miss Susan Harvest, the clergyman's innocent daughter whom the prisoner seduced. After the drowning of Miss Harvest, the prisoner fled to Italy. He was sane enough, no doubt, to buy a ticket, take a boat and several trains, and to return by the same means.

'Why should he make his camp in a lonely cottage in the woods — and camp it was — if he were not fearful of discovery — if he did not know what he had done? You have heard the testimony of Doctor Mellor for the prosecution. He has told us that actions alleged to be symptomatic of mental derangement are motiveless in their origin — a man who is mad can have no motive. But the motives of the prisoner before you are as clear as daylight. He is an artist who promised to paint their portraits and when he found that they were not the women he wanted, he killed them. Doctor Winslow gives evidence of the painting of the dead girl's face to show that the prisoner was deluded, but he knew she was dead. Else why would he attempt to bring her back to life? And if he knew she was dead, then he knew he had done it.

'Doctor Winslow testifies that the prisoner is unable to comprehend what he has done. He answers no questions now; he has nothing to say about any of the young women whose names have been heard in this case; he merely asks: "Where is Caterina?"

'Yet Superintendent Jones has testified that the prisoner heard him call out and turned in response to his name. Mr Dickens tells us that the prisoner understood him when he spoke to him about his painting.

'Thus we can say that the prisoner can hear, understand and speak, but he will not speak now. He could speak to Mr Dickens then; he listened to him when Mr Dickens told him that his sister, Miss Ferrars, wished to see him, and he went willingly with Superintendent Jones. Mr Dickens's attitude to the law may be somewhat cavalier, but he is known to be a most persuasive speaker. Doctor Winslow, alas, is not always so persuasive. We asked him how he could know that the prisoner was not feigning. Doctor Winslow tells us that it his by his long experience that he can distinguish shamming from genuine insanity. Doctor Mellor tells us by his long experience that the prisoner's conduct reveals a man of most acute intelligence and cunning. The prisoner pretended to his victims that he wanted to paint their portraits — perhaps he is pretending again.

'Whether the prisoner is now feigning madness, however, is not the pertinent question: the point to be decided is whether, according to the rules laid down by precedent, the prisoner was conscious that he was committing a crime against the laws of God and nature.

'If so he is to be considered amenable to justice and must expiate his crime on the gallows. There is no doubting the prisoner's guilty act — and, there is no doubting the prisoners' guilty intentions, nor, indeed, his guilty knowledge. *Mens rea*, my Lord.'

Mr Justice Rightman addresses the jury: 'You are not duty-bound to accept the experts' opinions if they do not accord with your own common sense and experience. It is the defendant's responsibility to demonstrate madness and if you should be satisfied there is proof that he was not able to distinguish a right from a wrong then you must acquit him.

The question is one of fact. The question is, whether the prisoner, at the time he committed the fatal act, was not responsible for it, by reason of a deranged state of mind. I remind you that it is for the unlawful killing of Jianna Rizzo that the prisoner has been tried.

'However, if you believe that the prisoner was not so afflicted then you must find him guilty of the charge. And you must bear in mind the deaths of all the other young women to which the police have adverted. If the prisoner knew that the killing of Miss Rizzo was against the laws of God and nature, then he will be arraigned for the murders of Miss Flora Lambert, Miss Violet Pout and Miss Jemima Curd.

'In summary, if you believe that the prisoner was suffering from delusions and was not of sound mind when the act was committed, you must set him free. It is my duty as judge to decide his fate thenceforth…'

In a quiet corner of The Magpie and Stump, near The Old Bailey, Dickens gulped his brandy and warm, Rogers supped his pale ale and Superintendent Jones gazed into his drink as if the verdict might be read there.

'Dadd was acquitted on the grounds of insanity.' Dickens was thinking of Richard Dadd, also an artist, who had stabbed his father to death in 1844. He was in the Bethlehem Asylum and would be, he supposed, for the rest of his life.

'One murder and plenty of witnesses to his irrational conduct. He attacked a man in France and they locked him up — he was so obviously deranged. The jury at the inquest could see that. He never came to trial.' Jones remembered the case.

'Three other girls dead, though,' said Rogers, 'that'll be the stumbling block — and that girl in Venice. He'd been seen with her.'

'And Susan Harvest — that did him no favours. The seduction of a clergyman's innocent daughter — Mr Needle got that out of Miss Ferrars and Lilian Judd. The respectable jury will think of their innocent daughters.'

'Or sons,' suggested Rogers, 'they might have sons.'

'True, Alf. And I do wonder if Needle went too far with that bit about the gallows — over-dramatic, maybe. Juries of reasonable men — with sons, perhaps — are not so keen to send a man to the gallows.'

'If they can spare his life and send him to Bedlam,' Dickens said.

'I know, yet, on the other hand, given the controversy surrounding the plea of insanity — you've seen the letters in the papers. There was one from someone calling himself "The Ropemaker", fulminating about cheating the gallows.'

'But his whole demeanour and his history — Winslow convinced me. And the fact that he doesn't speak and he looks so —'

'Mad,' Rogers put in.

'He may look mad, but I'm not so sure that Winslow was so convincing on the subject of feigning — that was a bad moment. I mean, how can you tell?' Jones asked.

'Any murder is a kind of madness, I suppose — all murderers are a horrible wonder apart.'

'On that theory, all murderers should be acquitted. No, the main point is whether he knew what he was doing at the time.'

'What about Winslow's stuff on sleepwalking and trances?' asked Rogers. 'He could have been in some sort o' trance, I daresay.'

'As Mellor pointed out somnambulism is very common — it does not generally pose a threat to others —'

'Not "generally" therefore it might,' Dickens said. 'I read that book Winslow spoke of, MacNish's book on sleep. There are examples of murder done in sleep. If he was in a state of unconsciousness — unaware of the deed, he can't be responsible.'

'If the jury believes that.'

'Knife-edge, then?'

They returned to the Central Criminal Court to hear the verdict.

The clerk to the court asked, 'Members of the Jury, have you reached a verdict?'

The foreman of the jury responded, 'We have, my Lord. We find that from the derangement of his mind at the time he committed the act that the prisoner was not responsible for his actions.'

Mr Justice Rightman replied, 'That is, in fact, a verdict of "Not Guilty" on the ground of insanity. Let it be so entered. The Court orders that the prisoner shall be detained until Her Majesty's pleasure be known.'

Dickens went back to his office in Wellington Street. He stood looking out of the window. "Until Her Majesty's pleasure be known" — that would be forever. Like Richard Dadd, for the rest of his life, sealed up in Bedlam. Then what dreams and visions might come? Would his beloved come in his dreams or would Caterina come to him transformed into that waxwork figure with the hideous lips? Would he then know what he had done? Would it have been better that Anthony Ferrars be hanged? He would be out of it then … out of his madness … safe in his grave. Nothing could touch him there, neither fear nor censure.

But what a grave — to be buried under the stones of Deadman's Passage, that grim passage from the condemned cell to the scaffold. To have been displayed on that before the jeering, hissing crowd, the scaffold on which the last embrace would be of Calcraft, the hangman, upon whose stony breast his head would slump as he was cut down. That was monstrous to think of, too. What a mystery it all was. What madness it all was.

He felt profoundly sorry for the man, but equally for his victims. Now that Anthony Ferrars was declared mad, he could not plead in any of the other cases, but the postponed inquests on Flora Lambert, Violet Pout and Jemima Curd would come on and the Coroner would have to accept that the accused person was insane. They would have justice of a kind. And Susan Harvest's poor corpse would be exhumed and she would be sent home to lie with her mother. They would never know if Anthony Ferrars had killed her — perhaps it was better so for the Reverend Harvest.

And what of those other girls? It was too late. There was nothing to be done. God must look after them in his mercy. He prayed it would be so.

All lovers young, all lovers must
Consign to thee, and come to dust.

50: Dying Breath

A week later

Dickens put down his pen and looked at the words he had written: *That old unhappy want of something.* He had not signed his name. There was no need.

He parcelled up the two volumes of *David Copperfield* and wrote the name and address on a label: *Mrs Doireanne Marchant, Florence Cottage, Grove Road, St. John's Wood.*

The messenger boy came in with the letters. Dickens gave him the parcel before he could change his mind. The boy made to go.

'Just a minute, Tommy —' he fished in his pocket for some coins — 'deliver it by hand — er — just leave it on the doorstep —' It could take its chance, he thought.

'But wot if the lady —'

'She'll know.'

Dickens looked at the rest of the letters. He recognised Mrs Carlyle's hand and opened her letter. It was short. He skimmed the few lines. Then he picked up his hat and went out.

'You've heard the news, I take it,' said Jones, indicating the letter Dickens was holding out to him.

'From Mrs Carlyle. Not unexpected, I suppose, after her heart attack.'

Jones looked at him thoughtfully. 'I had a visitor.'

'Someone came to tell you?'

'Mr Pryor, who, incidentally, has resigned his post.'

'What did he want?'

‘He has suspicions — something the nurse told him — the nurse engaged to look after Lady Fane.’

‘Phew!’ Dickens sat down. ‘Tell me.’

‘A mirror. There was a mirror on the Lady Fane’s bed — a silver hand mirror. The nurse had not held the mirror for Lady Fane. Lady Fane had no interest in what she looked like, but there was a mark on the glass as though someone had breathed on it —’

‘Her dying breath?’

‘The mirror was at the bottom of the bed. She would have to have tossed it there. If she had held it, she was so weak she would have just dropped where her hand lay.’

Dickens gaped at him. ‘Someone else put it there … someone who held it to her mouth to be sure that she was dead.’

‘The pillows were rumpled as well.’

‘Doctor?’

‘Sir William Gresty.’

‘Ah — brother of James Gresty, Conservative M.P. for Vauxhall.’

‘Just so — Sir William signed the death certificate. The nurse didn’t dare say anything. How could she? William Gresty appointed her. Mrs Pick was in and out of the room. She took the children in sometimes to see their mother. Sir Neptune visited each day, but never at the same time so she can’t be sure if he had been in the room, but he was in the house at the time.

‘The nurse went for a cup of tea and Mrs Pick took over. But when the nurse returned to the bedroom, there was no one there. She realised that Lady Fane was dead and went to call for Mrs Pick. While she was waiting she automatically picked up the mirror and returned it to the dressing table. She noticed the mark, but it wasn't until afterwards that she thought about the strangeness of the mirror on the bed. She hadn't left it there. Mrs Pick would hardly have put it there. Of course, she couldn't say that room was empty — she would have been accused of neglect. She could hardly accuse Mrs Pick — or Sir Neptune. She told all this to Pryor. They got quite friendly, it seems.'

'He did it,' said Dickens flatly. 'And he killed Violet Pout.'

'I think so, but there is no evidence. He'll have burnt Violet's letter to Lady Fane — if there was one as Pryor thought. And there's not a damned thing I can do about it. But there was never anything I could do about him. The Home Secretary made it perfectly clear to the Assistant Commissioner that Miss Fane was not to be mentioned at the trial. Sir Neptune insisted that a man called Sabatini is responsible for his daughter's illness. I had to agree — how could I drag that poor girl into it? What she has suffered already. But it meant leaving Sir Neptune out of it — apart from the brief reference in connection with Jemima and Violet Pout.'

'Wisdom of Solomon, eh?'

'No choice, in reality. Imagine what the Home Secretary would have said if I had voiced my suspicions about Sir Neptune and Violet Pout.'

'You'd have been in Bedlam, too. Will the nurse talk?'

'Pryor says not. He's a sharp fellow — he knew it would do no good. Challenging the verdict of Sir William Gresty, casting suspicion on the household, on Sir Neptune Fane, M.P.? Hardly — the poor woman would have been arrested — another case for Bedlam.'

'He's right, of course, but it's no comfort.'

'None at all.'

'Well, Sam, as the Stratford man says: the whirligig of time brings in his revenges.'

'Perhaps he'll lose his seat.'

'Or be shot by a disgruntled constituent — and that wouldn't be your business.'

'I'd be grateful for that … I wonder what his motive was — against his poor wife?'

'Perhaps she knew about Violet Pout — he couldn't risk her recovery.'

'I wouldn't put it past him.'

'He's probably got someone lined up to be the next Lady Fane.'

'Not —'

'Mrs Marchant? No, that's all over, I imagine. I heard from Jack Marchant, they are all off to Ireland — for good. Mrs Sabatini is already there.'

'Mr Rarx will be pleased — not that I care about him, either. Perhaps he'll shoot himself with that blunderbuss. Anyway, I've got other matters to deal with. A young fellow, name of Horder, cut his wife's throat while they were in bed. No known motive.'

'Mad?'

'Don't.' Jones shook his head wearily. 'Are you off home?'

'I'm going to the shop. I've something to tell Scrap.'

'About his name? Elizabeth told me. She thought he'd been looking a bit down in the mouth. Mollie told her that she thought the baby was keeping him awake —'

'Not sleuthing by midnight?'

'I didn't mention that. Anyway he came to us and stayed the night. Elizabeth got it all out of him. Charley Rogers was teething, Mollie told Scrap, and that sparked a memory — this happened on the night you went to meet Jack Marchant. It was a good thing he saw you because what he remembered upset him.'

'What was it?'

'He remembered his mother and a baby sister whom he called "Silly". He told me about his mother once — when Mr Brim died and I didn't want him at the funeral. He put me right about that. He never knew where his mother was buried and he wanted to be able to tell Eleanor about her father's funeral — if she ever asked.'

'And the sister?'

'He had forgotten all about her and that upset him. He thought about little Tom Brim forgetting about Eleanor or anybody forgetting about anybody — himself for instance.'

'He feels a bit lost, I think, not sure of his place in the world. "That Magpie fellow, he's really Jack Marchant, and you're Charles Dickens", he said. "You know who you are." I didn't disabuse him of that notion. Who is it that can tell me who I am — so said King Lear, and he was mad at the time. Makes you think.'

'I've had quite enough of madness,' Jones said. 'Tell me something I can get hold of. Did you find the father?'

'I did. Scrap remembered where they lived — a one pair back in Finger Alley, off Compton Street. Needless to say he wasn't there. Neither was his fancy woman. They both used to beat him which is why Scrap ran away. But I did find a neighbour who knew them. The father was known as "Knuckle".'

'Not very enlightening.'

'Well, he'd done a bit of bare knuckle fighting — quite successful until the drink did for him. The neighbour dredged into the muddy shallows of her mind and came up with Kevin. Knuckle was Irish. I thought therefore Catholic and took myself to St Patrick's in Soho Square. I thought Scrap must have been baptised, working on the assumption that Scrap's mother had been a good Catholic girl. Scrap once quoted her as telling him "Waste not, want not, my lad, and don't forget your prayers." I saw her fully just for a moment in all her common sense and goodness.'

'You found her?'

'I think so — the dates fit. I found a boy born to Kevin and Mary Donnelly in 1837, baptised on June 20th, the day of the Queen's accession and I found a little girl, baptised in 1842 as Cecilia Donnelly.'

'Silly.'

'Must be. And we think Scrap is about thirteen so —'

'And the name?'

'Hugh Donnelly.'

'The mother's death?'

'Not in the register at St Patrick's so I don't know, and there's no trace of the baby. Scrap couldn't remember where they lived — only that his father turned up to take him from somewhere to the place he remembered. His mother and the child would have been buried by the parish — but what parish? I don't know what to tell him about that...'

'Tell him everything. He'll confide in Elizabeth — she'll comfort him and perhaps he'll tell her more about his mother.'

'Good of yer,' Scrap said.

'Well, I had the squeeze box to make up for.'

Scrap grinned briefly and went back behind the counter to count the quill pens. Dickens left him alone while he browsed the inks and sealing wax. Green — a colour to which he had always been partial, now the colour that had haunted the case of Anthony Ferrars.

He took a sidelong look at Scrap. He didn't look like Hugh Donnelly. He was still Scrap — it suited him. Small and wiry and quick, he could get in and out of all sorts of places. Scrap, of whom he was so fond, the boy he might have been had John Dickens remained in the Marshalsea, all his debts unpaid, and his eldest son in the factory pasting labels on blacking bottles.

Sam Jones — he could not imagine another name. It was a comforting name — solid and dependable as the man himself. Alf Rogers was an Alf — no question. Dolly Marchant, however, was not a "Dolly". Her husband had meant something by that change from Doireanne — he had not loved his Irish wife.

He picked up a bottle of the green ink that his daughter, Katey, wanted. He put it down again and looked at the goose feather quills — the kind he liked.

'Mr D.'

'Scrap?'

'I jest wanted ter know who I am.'

They walked together to Norfolk Street, Dickens and Scrap, in silent companionship.

As they neared Jones's front door, Dickens spoke: 'Going to tell Eleanor and Tom?'

'Nah, I'm Scrap ter them … an' it's wot my ma called me. I shan't forget 'er. Yer shouldn't forget people.'

'No, indeed — I'll remember that.'

'I'll keep that name fer when I need it — yer might need a toff another day.'

Scrap, himself again, gave Dickens a wink and knocked at the door.

Finale: What's in a Name?

Dickens signed his name to the letter he had just finished: *Charles Dickens.*

He thought about names: Ferrara, Ferrars, Polidori — poor, mad Anthony Ferrars who no longer knew who he was, nor did Mariana Fane. What would become of her child? Doctor Winslow had talked of hereditary insanity — dreadful thought. The sins of the father.

He looked at his own name. He saw it everywhere: on the spines of books, on the covers of *Household Words*, in the newspapers, on theatrical posters. Yet sometimes he did not know who he was.

There was Scrap; there had been Magpie, Jug and Watcher, Nolly Turner and Peely Peel, all names to fit the face and the man — or the boy.

Mr Dickens, Charles Dickens, Charley, the Inimitable, the Sparkler of Albion, Planet Dick, Young Gas — not so young now. Which of these was he really?

He looked at the portrait above the mantelpiece — a portrait with a face. The face of a handsome, young, curly-haired man, whose eyes looked upwards in dreamy contemplation — a poetical young blade.

Portrait of Charles Dickens, painted by Daniel Maclise in 1839. "Here we have the real identical Dickens", so Thackeray had written.

There were only two styles of portrait painting, he had written once, the serious and the smirk. Mac had made him serious, that young man of twenty-seven. That young man who wouldn't look him in the eye. Was that a smirk in the mouth or just the firelight? That young man knew something and he wasn't telling. Laughing inwardly, he supposed.

He turned down the lamp. The young man's face vanished. Portrait without a face. He went out into the hall. There was another face there — in the looking glass. An older man who looked careworn and troubled. He caught a glimpse of another figure behind him, but he was walking away — without a word. There would be one waiting to meet him at the top of the stairs — frowning at the chips in the paintwork made by so many boys' boots. And another in the drawing room, smiling perhaps, at his wife.

And tomorrow morning there would be another, putting on his hat, making ready to go out of the door, to begin another day — to take on the world.

''Oo the dickens, indeed?'

HISTORICAL NOTE

In 1844, Dickens was living in Italy where he wrote his Christmas story 'The Chimes' and began *Dombey and Son.* He rented a house in Genoa but visited Ferrara and Venice in November. Accounts of his travels can be found in his book *Pictures from Italy* and in his letters to friends, including John Forster to whom the first letters in this novel are addressed.

The essay on Venice in Dickens's book is entitled 'An Italian Dream', in which Dickens evokes a ghostly sense of unreality as his gondola takes him along the canal: 'Before I knew by what or how, I found that we were gliding up a street — a phantom street; the houses rising on both sides, from the water, and the black boat gliding on beneath their windows. Lights were shining from some of these casements, plumbing the depth of the black stream with their reflected rays, but all was profoundly silent.'

The first letter which concerns the scenes he saw on approaching Ferrara is taken exactly from his letter as are his thoughts about Byron's poem 'Parisina'. The description of the peasant girls looking down into the water made me wonder what it was the girls had seen. Naturally, I thought it could have been a body! And Dickens's words about being murdered there and his phrase 'a more emphatic chilling of the blood' set in motion the plot.

In Ferrara Dickens visited the house of the poet, Ariosto, whose poem, 'Orlando Furioso', links to the themes of madness and love in this novel and gave me the name of Rolando. From Venice he wrote to Forster about imagining the monk in the cell beneath the Doge's palace and this was another inspiration for this story. He did not think that he saw a murder. I invented the second and third letters from Dickens to John Forster, but I have used some of Dickens's own words about Italy and Venice.

In Dickens's collection of ghost stories, *To Be Read at Dusk*, there is a story set in an old palace not far from Genoa, not unlike the Palazzo Mariano. The story concerns the haunting of a bride by a mysterious dark stranger, Signor Dellombra, whose name I borrowed and promoted to Count.

Dickens wanted to rent Byron's old house in Albaro near Genoa, but the house was nearly a ruin and was let to a wine shop. Byron's friend Doctor John Polidori wrote a treatise on sleep and trance-like states and the two did meet in Venice, so that allowed me to invent the visit to the fictional English family, the Ferrars. Polidori wrote *The Vampyr*, which was based on a fragment of a story written by Byron at the Villa Diodati in Geneva in 1816. Percy Shelley and his wife, Mary Shelley, were staying at the villa at the same time. Mary Shelley worked on a story which became her novel *Frankenstein*.

Polidori was uncle to Dante Gabriel Rossetti who does not appear in the novel, but is referred to by Cipriani Lloyd, my fictional sculptor. Polidori was thought to have committed suicide by prussic acid in 1821 — he had many debts. The verdict at the inquest was natural causes, or as Cipriani Lloyd quotes from the newspaper: 'visitation by the hand of God'.

Luigi Mariotti or Antonio Gallenga (1810-1895) met Dickens on the boat to America in 1842 and he taught Italian to Dickens and his wife before they departed to Italy in 1844. He is mentioned in several of Dickens's letters. In a letter to John Forster, Dickens writes, 'A blessing on Mr Mariotti my Italian master.' Mariotti was a frequent visitor to the home of Thomas and Jane Carlyle, though if he met Dickens again there I do not know. I invented his letter asking Dickens to meet him and the fictional Aurelio Paladino, but Mariotti's reference to Dickens's words in *The Examiner* is real. Mariotti wrote of Dickens 'who dwelt with so much zest and humour on the horrors of our first voyage to Yankeeland.'

Mariotti became a distinguished scholar and writer under his real name Antonio Gallenga. He wrote a critical study of Ugo Foscolo, the Italian poet in exile, who fought a duel on Barrow Hill. Antonio Gallenga adopted the name Luigi Mariotti as he had fought in uprisings against Marie Louise, the Duchess of Parma, Napoleon's widow, and in the revolution of 1831, which resulted in a provisional government put down by the Austrians who reinstated Marie Louise.

Antonio Gallenga was regarded as a dangerous agitator and he fled to France under the name of Mariotti which he kept until 1847. There is a biography, *Antonio Gallenga: An Italian Writer in Victorian England* by Toni Cerutti (Oxford University Press, 1974). Dickens knew Mazzini and supported the cause of Italian unification which is why he wrote so sympathetically about the Italian exiles in his letter to *The Examiner*.

Clarkson Stanfield (1793-1867), 'Stanny', was a great friend of Dickens and painted the scenery for some of the plays put on at Tavistock House, the home to which Dickens moved from Devonshire Terrace in 1851. Stanfield was a renowned marine painter as well as set designer at Drury Lane Theatre. A biography of Stanfield revealed the details of the painting room at Drury Lane.

I researched the Italian Renaissance artists of Ferrara and found Baldassare D'Este (1443-after 1504) who was believed to be the illegitimate son of the Marquis and painted portraits of the family, though most are lost, except the one I found which is possibly by Baldassaro and which I used as the model for Caterina Vecelli. Francisco da Cossa (1430-1477?) is thought to have worked on the frescoes at the Palazzo Schifanoia in Ferrara which depict the faces described by the fictional Aurelio Paladino.

James Anderson was actor-manager at Drury Lane in 1850 and Dickens knew him, as well as Mr Cuthbert who was one of the principal set designers and painters. Frederick Clarke was famed for his spinning globe act as I found out in the newspapers of the time where I found the details of the programme at Drury Lane for the winter season of 1850.

Anne Brown was Catherine Dickens's maid and she did go to America and to Italy with the family. I invented her close friend, Amelia Pout, and, of course, Violet Pout, the governess.

Doctor Forbes Benignus Winslow (1810-1874) established two private asylums in Hammersmith, one of which was Sussex House, and his writings reveal his ideas about the humane treatment of the mentally ill. He is mentioned in the footnote to a letter by Dickens written in February, 1847, the year Winslow's asylum opened. His books *The Plea of Insanity in Criminal Cases* and *On the Preservation of the Health of Body and Mind* gave me the material for the trial of Anthony Ferrars. Byron's poem 'Sleep', Polidori's paper on sleepwalking, and Dickens's own comments on Robert MacNish's book *The Philosophy of Sleep* gave me the material for the ideas about the mental state of Anthony Ferrars. Doctor John Elliotson was Dickens's close friend. He advocated the use of hypnosis in therapy and the use of mesmerism by which Dickens was fascinated. Dickens successfully mesmerised his friend, the artist, John Leech when he was seriously ill. Dickens sent Elliotson to treat William Thackeray who recovered from a life-threatening illness under Elliotson's care.

Dickens's children in this novel:

Mary, known always as Mamie (1838-96) was called 'Mild Glo'ster', a nickname that reflected her gentle nature. Her sister, Katey, (1839-1925) was a much fierier character, nicknamed, 'Lucifer Box', after the matches.

Walter (Wally, born 1841) was a weekly boarder at Mr Joseph King's School. Dickens describes him as 'a tougher subject than Charley (Dickens's eldest son) … a hard-working, patient, capable child.'

Francis (Frank, born 1844) was the son who looked most like his father. He seems to have been a very sensitive child who had a stammer and suffered from sleepwalking.

Alfred (Alley, born 1845) was 'a good steady fellow', according to his father.

Dora, born August 1850, died at eight months in April, 1851. Dickens's great friend, Mark Lemon, sat up all night with Dickens who did not break down until an evening or two after her death when some flowers were delivered, and, according to his daughter, Katey, it was then that Dickens 'gave way completely.'

A NOTE TO THE READER

Dear Reader,

The inspiration for this story came from Dickens's letters about his time in Venice and Ferrara where he saw the girls looking down into the water. Of course, I had to research drowning and I turned to my old friend, Alfred Swaine Taylor, the 'father' of forensic medicine and his *Manual of Jurisprudence* (1844) where I found the grisly forensic detail: 'the eyelids livid, and the pupils dilated; the mouth closed or half-open, the tongue swollen and congested, frequently pushed forwards to the internal edges of the lips, sometimes indented or even lacerated by the teeth.' The details about hanging and broken necks came from the same source.

I also turned to the British Newspaper Archives to find reports of drownings in the late 1840s and early 1850s — there was an astonishing number of cases of which I'll give just a few to demonstrate how I arrived at the cases which Superintendent Jones discovers in the *Police Gazette*. The story of the men with the wooden legs is true — the inquests were held on April 8th, 1849 and a verdict of suicide recorded in both cases. Dickens told the story of the woman who jumped into a water tank in a letter to a friend.

The story of Emma Golightly who was presumed drowned and turned up again was a true one. It was never discovered who was in the grave thought to be hers.

I needed an unknown drowned girl, unclaimed, buried at the expense of the parish, and forgotten. The *Morning Post* in February 1842 explains: 'In London the bodies are taken to any obscure vault, public house, or police office. The Coroner directs the parish to advertise the body, often in vain.'

I found several cases of unidentified females in the newspaper archive. In July 1841, according to *The Morning Advertiser*, a young woman was pulled from the London Dock. She was never identified. I was intrigued by the report's dark observation that 'No one could walk into that water by accident.' Unknown, too, was the identity of the 'fine-made' young woman taken from the Serpentine in October 1845 and deposited at St George's Workhouse. Yet she had a distinctive mole on her left cheek, dark hair and hazel eyes. And for which moustachioed seducer had she worn her white straw bonnet trimmed with pink and white ribbons and the lilac-coloured gown? Surely somebody noticed her. Seduced and abandoned, perhaps, like poor Eliza Luke found in the New River in April 1844.

However, this is a crime story, so, naturally, I needed a drowned, unknown, murdered girl. This was more difficult. Such was the damage done by the water, or the bridge, or the rocks of some lonely reach that it was often impossible to find enough evidence of murder. However, there was the case of Eliza Rayment — there's a name for my notebook — found in the River Thames in October 1847. There was a deep cut under her chin. 'Four inches in length, an inch in depth', so reported Mr Bain, the surgeon, at the inquest, and there were 'two arteries divided'. The wound might have been inflicted by the deceased, but 'a person using the right hand would naturally make an incision on the left hand side.' Eliza Rayment was right-handed. The incision was deeper on the right side suggesting a left-handed person. Mr Bain attributed death to the loss of blood from the wound.

Poor Emma Ashburnham who was formerly Emma Meyer had once lived 'in some splendour' in York Road under the protection of 'a gentleman of fortune', but it was not discovered how she came to be in the river at Waterloo Bridge with a deep and ugly stab wound in her side.

I found some very intriguing clues in some of the reports, for example the 1847 case of the unknown drowned young woman wearing a false plait at the back of her hair; the one in 1842 in which an umbrella is found nearby, bearing on its ivory handle the initials 'F.H.'

Yes, I found unknown and murdered girls, but I still needed a strangled one. I dug deep into the newspaper archives and I found it — just the one, and the indefatigable Mr Bain was on hand to assist. The body was found in October 1848 near Battersea Bridge, much decomposed, appearing to have been in the water some time. Nevertheless, Mr Bain's post-mortem revealed evidence of a ligature encircling the neck, though what this might have been he could not say.

It was quite enough for me. Possible death by strangulation. Just what I wanted.

Oh, all right, I admit it: the body was that of a sailor. But it did happen. Evidence of a ligature was found. I put an 's' before the 'he' — I didn't think you'd mind.

Reviews are really important to authors, and if you enjoyed the novel, it would be great if you could spare a little time to post a review on **Amazon** and **Goodreads.** Readers can connect with me online, on **Facebook (JCBriggsBooks)**, **Twitter (@JeanCBriggs)**, and you can find out more about the books and Charles Dickens via my website: **jcbriggsbooks.com,** where you will also find Mr Dickens's A-Z of murder — all cases of murder to which I found a Dickens connection.

Thank you!

Jean Briggs

Sapere Books is an exciting new publisher of brilliant fiction and popular history.

To find out more about our latest releases and our monthly bargain books visit our website: **saperebooks.com**

Printed in Great Britain
by Amazon

36486805R00234